"At turns charming, funny, and inspiring, *The Secret War of Julia Child* is a vividly written and deeply imaginative new take on World War II. By letting us see this historic moment through the eyes of a beloved American icon, Chambers beautifully captures the spirit of the women of the greatest generation."

—Dr. Lena Andrews, bestselling author of
Valiant Women: The Extraordinary American
Servicewomen Who Helped Win World War II

"An exciting, little-known reveal of the story behind Julia Child's WWII service, showing her resilience and bravery in the spy world as well as giving fascinating insights into the war being raged in Asia. A must-read."

—Rhys Bowen, *New York Times* bestselling author

"A compelling story with an unexpected (and thoroughly delightful) heroine—Julia Child, who served with the Office of Strategic Services (OSS, the precursor to the CIA) during World War II. Chambers paints a vivid portrait of the tall, awkward Julia, who volunteers for a post in India, becomes involved in secret intelligence cases across Southeast Asia and China and meets her future husband, Paul Child. With riveting twists and turns, the novel's not only a vivid exploration of a lesser-known chapter in the life of one of America's most beloved personalities, it's also an impeccably researched roller-coaster ride with spies, danger, deception, heroics, and romance."

—Susan Elia MacNeal,
New York Times bestselling author

"Chambers's gripping novel unveils another dimension to Julia. In this fictionalized account of Child's real-life work with OSS during World War II, Chambers humanizes Julia and manages to make her even more remarkable. You'll fall in love with Julia all over again and with this tantalizing novel."

—Nina Schuyler, award-winning author
of *The Translator* and *Afterword*

"In these pages, I was thrilled to discover a Julia who claimed her own strength and conviction before the world defined who she was…Set in the smoldering days of WWII, this novel has everything I love— romance, intrigue, mouthwatering food, and a woman who makes no apologies for her voracious appetite for life!"

—Kim Fay, bestselling author of *Love & Saffron*

"Full of intrigue and romance, *The Secret War of Julia Child* is a fascinating glimpse into the early life of one of America's most beloved celebrities. Perfect for fans of this complex, compelling woman."

—Julia Bryan Thomas, author of *The
Kennedy Girl*, *The Radcliffe Ladies' Reading
Club*, and *For Those Who Are Lost*

"Before there was a Julia Child, there was a Miss McWilliams…Julia McWilliams called herself a simple file clerk, but in truth, she lived and worked in situations steamy not just with heat but with deceit, teeming with international spies and lies, wartime intrigue in which many lives were at stake…Chambers's impressive research informs this engaging novel—and yes, the food is spectacular!"

—Laura Kalpakian, author of *American
Cookery* and *The Great Pretenders*

"In this gripping novel, a young and intrepid Julia Child tumbles headlong into espionage and romance in World War II Asia. Author Diana R. Chambers merges little-known details from Child's personal history with true wartime events to build a dynamic tale. More, please!"

—Sujata Massey, award-winning author
of *The Mistress of Bhatia House*

THE SECRET
WAR
OF
JULIA
CHILD

A NOVEL

DIANA R. CHAMBERS

To Everett
and
To Lili,
My companions of the road.

Published by Sourcebooks Landmark, an imprint of Sourcebooks
P.O. Box 4410, Naperville, Illinois 60567-4410
(630) 961-3900
sourcebooks.com

Cataloging-in-Publication Data is on file with the Library of Congress.

Printed and bound in the United States of America.
LB 10 9 8 7 6 5 4 3 2 1

The Secret War of Julia Child is a work of fiction inspired by my admiration for Julia McWilliams Child. It is a product of my imagination, based on ten years of extensive research across a myriad of disciplines and historical resources. From this material, I extracted various hints, allusions, and suggestions that fed my personal interpretation of Julia's little known but formative OSS service in World War II Asia. However grounded in the reality of this period, my novel is only a story.

"I did want to be a spy, and I thought I'd be a very good one because no one would think that someone as tall as I would possibly be a spy."
                        —Julia Child on *Fresh Air* with Terry Gross,
                                    1989 broadcast, WHYY and NPR

———

"[The employee] agrees 'to keep forever secret this employment and all information which she may obtain… [and to] assume absolutely, all risks incident to this employment.'"
                        —OSS Special Operations contract

———

"…A major from Washington…told us…we were going to London and that we would be engaged in secret intelligence work [for OSS]—but that should anyone ask we were merely to say we did clerical work."
—Katherine Keene, *Memoir of Service in WAC or WAAC*,
                        Papers of Katherine Mildred Keene

SOUTH ASIA THEATER OF WWII BY FANITA LANIER

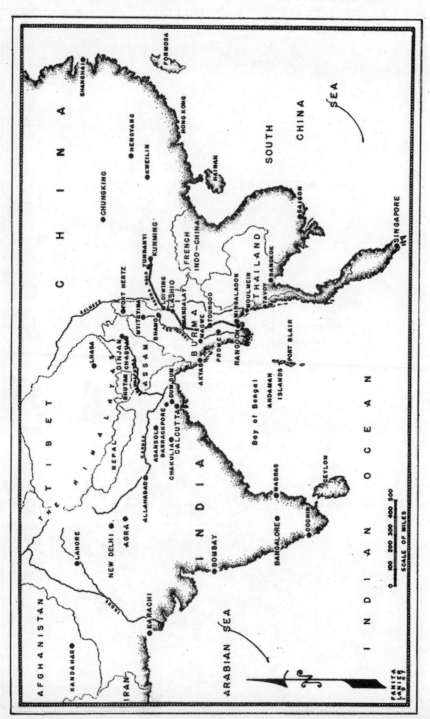

CHINA-BURMA-INDIA THEATER OF WWII

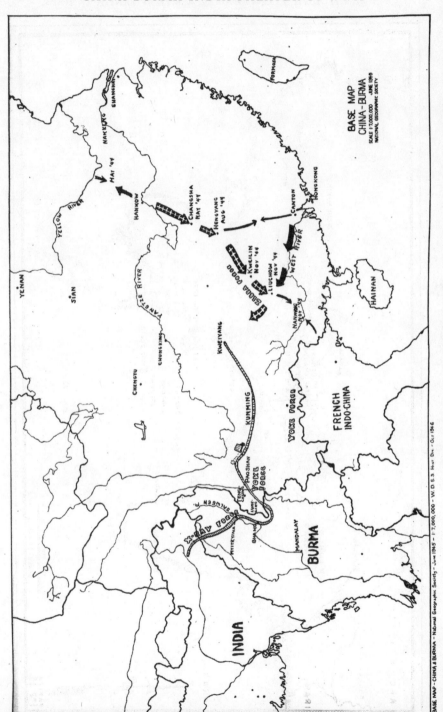

BASE MAP
CHINA-BURMA
SCALE 1:7,000,000   JUNE 1945
NATIONAL GEOGRAPHIC SOCIETY

WWII ACRONYMS AND ABBREVIATIONS

CBI: China-Burma-India Command; Allied theater of war under US, British, Chinese leadership

FANY: British First Aid Nursing Yeomanry

FDR: US President Franklin D. Roosevelt

KMT: Kuomintang, Nationalist Party of China, led by Generalissimo Chiang Kai-shek

MO: Morale Operations, OSS department

OSS: US Office of Strategic Services (influenced by Britain's Secret Intelligence Service—and Pearl Harbor—President Roosevelt charged General William Donovan with creating America's first espionage agency)

OWI: US Office of War Information

R&A: Research and Analysis, OSS department

SACO: Sino-American Cooperative Organization; Chinese–US Navy intelligence and sabotage service

SEAC: South East Asia Command; Allied theater of war under British-American leadership

SI: Secret Intelligence, OSS department

SIS: Secret Intelligence Service, British espionage service

SOE: Special Operations Executive group, British intelligence and sabotage service

SOS: US Services of Supply

WACS: US Women's Army Corp

WAVES: US Women Accepted for Volunteer Emergency Services

WRENS: British Women's Royal Naval Service

Santa Barbara, California
September 2002

Julia turned her face into the hot Santa Ana wind, which had swept in as if it owned the place, whipping the linen curtains, aerating the small room like a cook whisking cream. Beyond were masses of white peaks...rising from the blue Pacific, a fearsome force that could turn bleak and threatening in a moment, or mournful, or sparkling with promise. She'd seen every one of those moods during her ship's March 1944 passage into the unknown. On those far shores, her life had really begun, which was to say she began to live. Even amid the darkness that was World War II.

It was in Asia that her taste buds came alive—all her senses, to be frank. Every day was a discovery. Here, from her desk, where a characterless computer had replaced her trusty old Royal, she filled her lungs with the tangy scents of sage, eucalyptus, jasmine, and sweet peas... which transported her to the Kunming Flower Circle—and the outdoor market where she'd bought the garter belt and stockings. Shocking, wasn't it? Not what you'd expect from Julia Child.

How *ever* had she become an icon? That had surprised even her. To her audiences, she was a dear friend, a favorite teacher, or an aunt. They invited her into their homes and watched her television show, tried her recipes. It was her great pleasure to have been part of their lives, shared her passion for good French food, and wished them, "*Bon appétit.*" They told her they felt as if they knew her. But they knew Julia Child, *The French Chef.* That was her creation.

Julia McWilliams was a born performer—and writer and director, producing costume dramas in her family's Pasadena attic. The lanky leader of the neighborhood pack, Julia was well cast as a buccaneer, less so the delicate romantic lead. Then, too, there was "the Voice," inherited, like her height, from Mother Caro. The way it swooped and fluttered, entirely out of her control…well, it used to pain her no end, until Paul advised her to relax and simply be. *To know you is to love you*, he'd told her eons ago in China, when he finally came to see her charms.

Her husband had been her rock and inspiration, until a long illness carried him away. With him went half her heart. The other half, surprisingly, continued to beat, and she continued to be Julia Child. People depended on her and loved her; it wasn't the same as Paul's love, but it sustained her. That, and a good roast chicken, a hearty Burgundy, and fresh crusty bread. Yet she often doubted she could carry on or that it was worth it. Then she would hear her mother's firm counsel: *You must keep your chin up and move forward.* So she had to.

She'd always known she was meant for something, a belief she had confided to her girlhood diary but not dared proclaim aloud. Now she had crossed into the twenty-first century, where it was normal for a young woman to be ambitious. Few could imagine the shame she'd felt at wanting to achieve. Paul helped her break through that nonsense, too. When they moved to Paris, he encouraged her to stand up to those pompous (male) chefs and keep at it.

How hard she'd worked. But she did it. Imagine, mastering the art of French cuisine—and bringing it to the world. Yet she would not have become that woman without her experiences in the cauldron of WWII, where she'd learned what she could really do. Memories of those days still had the power to shake her. The war demanded everything of them, and so they gave everything. Some of them survived, but none were ever the same. Simply put, the war made her.

It was a path that still astonished her. The dreams and stubborn will that put her there, the chances she took…If she hadn't dared reach for that frontline post in Asia and stepped into the unknown, she would have never met the man of her life, Paul Child. She would have become someone else, not Julia Child.

PART ONE

Keeper of the Secrets

ONE

—— *//* ——

Washington, DC
September 1943

Cowboys, General "Wild Bill" Donovan's foes called the intrepid OSS operatives who served their nation around the globe. *Adventurers*. Even *daredevils*. Yet how could that be a bad thing when you had the world to save? Julia was proud to be doing her bit at the Office of Strategic Services—America's first intelligence agency, created by Donovan under President Roosevelt's mandate. A World War I Medal of Honor winner, he often proclaimed, "You can't succeed without taking chances."

But as she darted out of headquarters into the moist September evening, she understood the difference between Donovan and herself: she was not a wounded colonel, charging enemy fire. She was Julia McWilliams, supervisor of the OSS Registry of secret documents and files. Yet her boss wasn't there, and she was—with the lives of "thousands of good souls" in her hands.

Pausing at the top of the steps, she surveyed the circular entrance drive—a few parked vehicles, not a taxi among them. Set on an isolated knoll above the Potomac River, the old stone complex was dark and quiet, wispy clouds obscuring the crescent moon. A perfect setting for a spy novel. This was not fiction, though. She was taking an enormous risk now, following her conscience into an unauthorized mission. There would be consequences.

The shadows parted. She jumped.

"Leaving before midnight?" the armed sergeant asked.

His Massachusetts accent, reminiscent of her late mother's, had brought forth a sense of tenderness toward the earnest young man, who chafed at his rear echelon duty. Julia understood the feeling: she, too, yearned to get out into the world. "Dinner date," she replied, her voice rising as she tried to conceal her nerves. "Haven't eaten all day!"

"Have a martini for me, doll. With two olives."

"You can count on it." Julia waggled her fingers, uncomfortable with the subterfuge while also imagining herself inside the character of a real operative. She felt on the verge of a larger life, challenging and dangerous.

Preparing to hotfoot it to E Street for a taxi, she was halfway down to the entry drive when, out of the darkness, a dazzling yellow cab came rolling up. Adrenaline surged through her body. As a suit-clad leg emerged, she raised an arm and dashed for the door. The civilian caught her eye and held it. Then, emerging from a clump of shrubby dogwoods, two army officers hopped in. One flicked a cigarette butt out the window. Was she invisible? Or merely outranked?

Before they could make their getaway, she leaned in. "Excuse me, sir. I've an emergency at Georgetown Hospital. My little brother…" she improvised, hand over beating heart. She only hoped Mother Caro wasn't viewing her duplicity from above. "He's army, too—a training accident. I'd be grateful if you could give me a lift."

"Sorry, sister. We've a train to catch." The jug-eared lieutenant frowned. "But for an army man…least we can do is drop you partway. Get in."

Sliding into the front seat, she made a private apology to her not-so-little brother, John McWilliams III, serving somewhere in occupied France. Her fears for him fueled her anxiety over the phone call she'd just taken from an agent who identified himself as Dan O'Connell of the SI Division—Secret Intelligence. His raw whisper reverberated through her brain: *I have actionable intel.*

The last one in the office, she'd been clearing her inbox when a pimpled Messages fellow handed her a decrypted cable from the OSS station in Berne, Switzerland—*ALARMING REPORT RE FINAL SOLUTION*. Noting the time, Julia logged it in, then scanned the text…Her stomach turned. She lurched to her feet, crossing the anteroom to Donovan's inner sanctum, where she propped the message against his red telephone. He would not miss it when he returned from the Marlene Dietrich war-bond rally.

Then the red telephone rang. Startled, she stepped back. Julia could almost see the instrument throbbing with urgency. Its private number was known only to a few, including the boss's Secret Project agents. It was not her place to answer it. But there could be an emergency, life or death…She took a deep breath and answered the call.

Now here she was, gesturing frantically on a Georgetown street corner, where the yellow cab had dropped her en route to Union Station—but still some distance from the O'Connell meeting farther uptown. As the taxis shot by, she kept hearing the secret agent's final words: *If I don't see you before one hour, you'll be responsible for the deaths of thousands of good souls.*

"To heck with you!" Ignored by another cab, Julia hurried north toward the hospital.

This was not the first time she'd been tested since snagging a clerical job last December at the new Office of Strategic Services, which Donovan had staffed with some of the nation's most brilliant, unconventional minds, including Ivy Leaguers, movie directors, and safecrackers. Women, too. Her boss lived life full tilt. He had a photographic memory, a voracious work ethic, and the Irish gift of gab, ready to chat up everyone from the shoeshine man to President Franklin D. Roosevelt—to her. Challenged by the creative ferment, she gave it her all.

Under clotted clouds that had swallowed the moon, she checked her Hamilton wristwatch again—only thirteen minutes left! Suddenly the cobblestones were coming up at her as she caught the tip of one of her loafers—men's, worn in lieu of the rare 12A women's. Angrily righting herself, she hurried past a thriving Victory Garden, its cornstalks towering over even her. Her throat tightened. It came upon her sometimes, being so tall and ungainly, so different. Never the girly girl, always the pal.

So what? Mother Caro used to declare throughout her high school years, insisting that Julia's time would come. Soon, she'd be back east at Caro's alma mater, Smith College…making lifelong friends, writing and staging plays, skiing, maybe also captaining the basketball team. Then on to achieve her dream: becoming a great woman writer. Julia McWilliams was free; that was more important than any boyfriend. First, *live.*

She powered on, propelled by the long legs her mother had passed down, along with her copper curls, strong opinions, and free spirit, her name itself. A Mayflower blueblood, Julia Carolyn Weston McWilliams—Caro to everyone—had bequeathed "Julia" to her firstborn.

As Georgetown Hospital drew into view, her sky-blue dress stuck to her back and her hair was a frizzy mess. After smoothing herself out, she flung open the door and made a beeline to the front desk. "I'm here to see Dan O'Connell." She reined in the emotions that often sent her voice fluttering.

Her white cap bobby-pinned to salt-and-silver hair, the nurse checked the register. "Down the hall, up the stairs, then the last corridor. Visiting hours are almost over."

One patient was asleep; the other regarded her with fevered impatience—O'Connell, his bandaged right leg hanging from an overhead device. His left foot was propped on a black briefcase.

"Julia McWilliams," she said, flashing her blue and white OSS ID. His face stubbled with dark beard, he looked disreputable. *Perhaps his cover?* "What's this about?"

"The chief borrowed me from SI Scandinavia for a special op." He squinted at her as if to make sure she understood the gravity of his words. "A few hours ago, I'm heading to meet my contact when some jerk backs into me, smashes me against a parked truck."

Given the situation, she had to consider the worst. "Was he trying to stop you?"

"I thought I was clean, but…" O'Connell shrugged angrily. "Next thing I know, I'm in an ambulance, fighting the medics for *this*." He tapped his heel on the scuffed briefcase.

Whatever *this* contained was driving the man. Julia nudged her chair closer. "I sympathize, Mr. O'Connell. The general will get on it first thing tomorrow."

"Tomorrow's too late! My contact is leaving the country. *Tonight*. Even if I could break out, I'd never make it in time." He scowled at his bum leg. "Union Station is our final fallback. I need someone there." His burning black eyes met hers. "You're it."

"Oh my." She stared back, electrified. After Pearl Harbor—the intelligence failure that led to the birth of OSS—a Japanese sub had surfaced off the Santa Barbara coast, practically next door! Galvanized, she'd joined the Aircraft Warning Service in downtown Los Angeles. Commuting in her 1929 Model A jalopy, Eulalie, over the new Pasadena freeway, she spent long hours surveilling air and sea. Proud to finally have serious work, she made her way to Washington—and before long, an OSS clerical job that shook her into new life. Eighteen months later, she was gatekeeper for America's spy-chief, his Keeper of the Secrets, with the highest security clearance. Every incoming cable, diplomatic pouch, and crumpled, mud-stained agent's report landed on her Registry desk, to be logged, cross-referenced, and channeled to the relevant unit, a locked file, or the boss's desk. She was hungry, though, to get out of the files and into the field—to write her own reports.

Her heart sped up, then stopped. "I want to help you, but I could lose my job—"

"Or get promoted," O'Connell interrupted in a barely audible tone. "German telegraph traffic to occupied Oslo goes through Swedish-leased cables. The Swedes, although officially neutral, broke their code and have been passing us intel."

Julia nodded, having seen many of these dispatches.

"This time there's a price tag: fifty thousand dollars. But not for anyone's greed. The Nazis have issued a deportation order for Denmark's entire Jewish population, to be interned—at best."

She stared, still appalled by the *Final Solution* cable from their Berne station chief, whose German informant had been "invited" to supply prussic acid for a prison in Auschwitz, Poland. "And…?"

"A giant rescue operation is underway to smuggle them across Oresund Strait to Sweden, where the king will grant asylum. Almost every boat in the land is being mobilized; some are charging passage. Stockholm will transfer the funds to the Danish Resistance." He shot a meaningful look at the briefcase.

While fearing the wrath of Donovan, she shared O'Connell's resolve. This was her opportunity to make a difference. She raised her chin in assent.

"My contact will board the midnight train for New York—before flying on to Stockholm," he explained brusquely. "The meet is at 23:45. There's vital intel in it for us."

"What?"

"I was told only that there's a thank-you from Swedish friends." He shifted his leg off the case. "Open it."

Lifting the briefcase onto her lap, she undid its brass clasp and removed a large novel, *Gone with the Wind*. Her bookworm mother had owned the same edition—Rhett Butler carrying Scarlett in his arms, her heaving bosom a reminder of Julia's own feminine deficiencies. Fortunately her gams—

"Now open it."

Inside, a rectangular cutout held a stack of hundred-dollar bills about two inches high. The book felt hot in her hands; she swiftly closed and returned it to its case. Hearing the clasp's loud click, she glanced at the immobile patient in the other bed. Was he dead? Or playing dead?

"My contact is unknown to me. He'll be at the end of the platform holding *Assignment in Brittany* by Helen MacInnes. You'll hand him *Gone with the Wind* and say, 'Here is the novel I promised. I wish you safe travels.' He'll give you his book, saying, 'Thank you. The same to you.' Then he boards, and you leave." O'Connell looked at the wall clock. "Union Station is always jammed. You're in no danger—but need to move fast. You have fifty minutes."

Outside the hospital, she nabbed a taxi vacated by a harried doctor. "I know everyone tells you they're in a rush," Julia told the graying driver, "but I really am. It's a matter of national security." She felt as if she'd stepped from the wings onto the stage. He eyed her through the rearview mirror. She returned a steady look. He hit the gas.

A year ago, she had arrived at Union Station with two trunks, her portable Royal typewriter, and a passion to serve. Then, the crowds had energized her. Now they were a hindrance to her urgent lifesaving mission. The whole world, it seemed, was on the move, but she had to give priority to the desperate Danish Jews. Patting her mother's pearls for luck, she hastened through the great domed concourse, gripping the precious briefcase. The tiled hall echoed with the clatter of feet and voices as masses of people milled about, their faces grim or impatient, shiny from the humidity that had followed them all inside.

Elbowing through their midst, she passed a curly-haired Travelers Aid volunteer showing a map to one of the uniformed men waiting three-deep across her oval counter. They sat, slept, and smoked on packed wooden benches, coats and duffel bags at their feet. Everyone going off to war—or already there.

Americans will always fight for liberty. 1778–1943. The large poster depicting three GIs backed by three Revolutionary soldiers had been designed at the Office of War Information. Thanks to her Smith history degree and a family connection, Julia had obtained her first Washington job at the OWI Research Department, where she'd typed file cards on every government official at record speed. After two months and ten thousand cards, she moved on to OSS.

Wondering if the two army officers who'd commandeered her taxi would spot her, she headed for the Departures board, which indicated the Manhattan-bound train was on time. The big clock read *11:39.* *Six* minutes till the rendezvous. Six minutes to save thousands of innocent lives—children, their mothers and fathers, grandparents and cousins—from Nazi poison gas. Her sweaty hand clutched the leaden briefcase.

The gate was swarming with military and civilian passengers rushing to board. Halfway up the platform, the person in front of her came to a dead stop, searching for his carriage. She almost crashed into him. Cutting off his profuse apologies, she pushed on.

But there was no man waiting with a book. Only a couple embracing, saying their farewells. And a tall voluptuous blond in a deep-purple dress and mink cape. *She* was holding a book, *Assignment in Brittany*. Their eyes connected.

Julia approached the fashionable woman. Seeing the expected title, she fumbled open the briefcase and, with a shaky hand, reached for *Gone with the Wind*. "Here is the novel I promised," she said, her voice waffling with nerves. "I wish you safe travels."

They exchanged books. "Thanks. The same to you." The agent offered an easy smile, which she then focused on a tall captain carrying an overnight bag. "Hey, good looking."

As Julia lowered *Assignment in Brittany* into the briefcase, the man with whom she'd nearly collided was staring. The embracing couple parted. One boarded; the other turned her way. Sweat trickled down her spine.

Keep your chin up and move forward, Caro urged. She strode down the platform, through the gate, and into the crowd. Then threw herself into the next cab.

Back at the Brighton Residence Hotel, she raced upstairs to her studio and jammed a chair against the door. Collapsing on the bed, she kicked off her penny loafers. Inside the MacInnes novel was a similar cutout—containing a miniature Minox. A spy camera, carrying who knew what secrets. She placed it under her pillow, then flopped back, remembering her girlhood heroine, Nancy Drew. Overcome, she giggled…pretty soon she was shaking with laughter. Hugging herself to keep silent.

A matter of national security. Of all the plays she'd written, parts she'd enacted—this one took the cake. By the time her giddiness faded, she was drained but utterly exhilarated. Stars shot through the blackness behind her eyelids. Julia had never felt like this before and couldn't wait to tell her boss.

Her actions might end up in Donovan's morning briefing for the president.

Now she'd never sleep.

TWO

———— // ————

"You what?"

General William Donovan rarely raised his voice, and as he did now, Julia flinched, feeling the force of his anger. Jaw tight, he regarded the tiny Minox camera on his desk. Lined up between them were his telephones, including his direct line to the president—and the red one, which she'd had the temerity to answer last night.

"I had to, sir. The lives of thousands of Danish Jews were at stake."

He tapped the red handset. "You are not authorized to answer that phone."

Julia steadied herself, digging her fingernails into her palms. "I'm sorry. We'd just received the Swiss cable—about a Nazi *Final Solution* to the Jewish problem! I was putting it on your desk when the phone rang. I was pretty emotional and guess I had a feeling it was important."

"You *guess*?" he demanded in a withering tone. "In this business, feelings and emotions can be dangerous. Guesses can cost lives."

Julia cast her gaze to the floor, wanting to sink through it. "Of course, you're right. I overstepped. But…" She *needed* to make him understand. "O'Connell said I had to pass operational funds to his contact at Union Station—before midnight. That it was actionable intel. You were at the Dietrich bond rally, not expected till later. There was no one else."

"The man is reliable," Donovan conceded; then his look hardened again. "But you didn't know that! So don't try to justify yourself."

This could be it: the consequences she'd feared. Would he demote her back to the clerical pool? Or *fire* her? The end of everything she valued. Barely breathing, Julia waited to hear her fate.

He frowned at the world globe on his desk. "We suspect a leak somewhere between Stockholm and here, so I had O'Connell report directly to me. The German cable traffic is too critical to mess with."

Her heart raced. "I knew I was taking a risk. But—"

He directed his focus back at her. "Reckless behavior, McWilliams." Under a thatch of silver hair, his bright-blue eyes were dark and weary. Bill Donovan had little time for sleep, communicating with every time zone from HQ—or hopping around the globe on a Pan Am Clipper seaplane, overseeing operations.

He'd always seemed invincible, but Julia now glimpsed the man beneath the myth, human after all. While hating to cause him additional grief, she had to persist. Her actions had been necessary. "In exchange, the Swedes would pass us a valuable thank-you." She glanced at the Minox.

He pushed it toward her with the curt order, "Get this into processing."

"Yes, sir." She closed her fingers around the little device.

As they shared a sharp glance, she watched his weathered face. *But all those lives, aren't they worth fighting for?* "You've often said you'd prefer a young lieutenant with the guts to disobey an order to a hidebound old colonel."

"But you're not a young lieutenant," he shot back. "And despite your high-security clearance, it's not high enough to answer that telephone."

Julia felt diminished, utterly hollowed. Then she planted her feet. "Sir. Working here is the greatest privilege in my life. Your leadership has inspired me, your life. " Hearing her voice rise, she tried to force it back down. "In the last war, you refused a French *Croix de Guerre* until your Jewish comrade was equally honored. I want to stand against injustice, too. O'Connell's mission seemed a just one." She pushed on before it was too late. "It was also in our interest."

He made no comment, revisiting his globe—so many blue seas…so many coastlines, bordering so many bloody battlefields.

Feeling his dismissal, she cleared her throat. "I hoped I might prove myself—out in the world. I'm resourceful and can think on my feet." Now she was really overstepping.

"On your way, McWilliams," General Donovan said coolly. "That's an order. Which you would understand by now had you been accepted by the WACS—or even the WAVES."

It had been a bitter blow, and she still burned with humiliation. Both the Army WACS (Women's Army Corp) and Navy WAVES (Women Accepted for Volunteer Emergency Services) had judged her *too tall* to serve her country. That was injustice, too.

"Frankly, you'd probably be little more than a drudge in the military." His glance warmed a degree. "Here, we're creative. We play a central role in the war effort, and you're part of that. Witness your escapade last night."

Creative. Julia stood taller. This was where she belonged, "escapade" or not. "I prefer to see it as my duty." She held his look. "I am sorry about answering the phone, but once I did—I couldn't say no."

He lifted a shoulder. "It's what we do in this service: improvise. Sometimes you need to act first and worry later. I won't second-guess you."

Her heart swelled with pride.

"But don't expect any gratitude. At OSS, we are content to work in the shadows."

Donovan made a shooing motion. "Well? Don't you want to see if your insubordination was justified?" He reached for his green scrambler phone.

"Sir." She hustled out the door. Maybe she still had a chance for an overseas post.

———

But maybe not, she thought, walking back upstairs from the dark, pungent basement lab where the microfilm would be developed and printed by late today or tomorrow. Maybe the Minox would contain nothing noteworthy. And maybe Donovan would no longer consider her worthy of her high-security position. His reprimand had left her anxious.

A distinguished colonel marched past her, then a woman in a fashionable suit. A professorial type who seemed to be spinning maps in his head. This place meant so much to her. Too much. Think of it: Julia McWilliams, lifelong reader of mysteries and spy novels, landing a job in espionage—for the legendary Wild Bill Donovan. Other than Mother Caro, there was no one to whom she owed more or whose approval was more dear.

If she didn't make it here, Julia feared she'd be drawn into marriage with her longtime suitor, *Los Angeles Times* heir Harrison Chandler. Last month, on turning thirty-one, she'd received Pop's card—a cheery housewife rolling out pie dough.
Hundreds of BIRTHDAY WISHES,
All rolled into one.

Another reminder that she might yet avoid spinsterhood. But she wanted more than a suitable husband whose kisses were dry and adequate. She was holding out for one who made her head spin and knees weak. She'd known such a man and, despite the painful outcome, still believed love was possible. Her creative dreams also remained unfulfilled. This job might be her last chance.

At the end of the faded pea-green corridor, the door rattled shut behind her, and she beheld all she'd helped build—this large cluttered Registry of secret files stored in locked cabinets stacked to the high ceiling. Amid the clackety-clack of Remington keyboards, the rustle of papers, and whirling fans, her clerks were immersed in their duties. Many she had hired personally, looking for go-getters like herself.

One of them, a petite Chinese girl from Seattle in a faded but starched dress, was descending a tall oak ladder, arms laden with folders. A solitary worker, Sally Lu put in the longest hours; sometimes Julia wondered if she had nowhere else to go, or something to prove. She felt a sudden kinship with the girl, for Julia McWilliams did have something to prove: she mattered. She, too, had put her heart in this place.

With a nod at Sally, Julia continued toward her desk outside

Donovan's office—OSS command central. After taking her seat, she attacked her teetering inbox.

At some point, the scrape of chairs and rising voices announced lunchtime. But after last night's "escapade," she wanted to be at the boss's beck and call. From her bottom drawer, she produced an American cheese sandwich—the cheese, she'd learned, actually lasted longer than the bread. She unwrapped the wax paper and sniffed, just in case, then put it down and yanked what appeared to be a diplomatic pouch from her pile. She cut through the seals on the scratched leather portfolio and gasped. Inside were detailed sketches of the Normandy coast, photographed by Britain's Special Operations Executive group—SOE, the espionage-and-sabotage counterpart of OSS. Julia leaped to her feet.

With a quick wave at Millicent, the loyal secretary who'd followed Donovan from Wall Street, she tapped on his door and entered—only then understanding her warning look. The boss, in his sitting area, was taking tea with Lord Louis Mountbatten, dashing in sharp navy whites.

Mortified, she tried to keep her voice in a professional register. "I'm terribly sorry to interrupt, sir. But we've received some vital documents." She handed him the envelope of images, critical for next year's top secret landing in France.

As Donovan glanced through them, his chest seemed to broaden— things were looking up! "Julia McWilliams," he said. "Admiral Lord Mountbatten, chief of South East Asia Command—SEAC. This woman is my third hand, couldn't run things without her."

"Lovely to meet you, Miss McWilliams." The British leader rose on long legs, looked her in the eye, and offered a firm handshake. "Might you happen to be a Scot?"

"My father's side, sir." Julia barely heard Donovan's praise, so dazzled was she. A war hero, debonair, and gracious, too. "It's an honor."

"We are engaged in the common defense," said Mountbatten. "On that pressing note, I must excuse myself." He paused at Donovan's globe, where they conferred over the Normandy documents. Then a British navy officer escorted the leader out the private rear exit. A sticky Potomic breeze blew in.

"Have a seat, McWilliams." Donovan gestured at the armchair recently occupied by Mountbatten. With no sign of his earlier pique, he poured her a cup of tea. "Through some serious horse-trading—including a rare pair of tickets to the Broadway musical *Oklahoma!*—I've exacted Mountbatten's authorization for an OSS station in Delhi."

India. An electric jolt surged through her.

"The Brits have not been keen on us mucking about 'their' territory. However, as they are willing to take our men and money, we want a seat at the table—Empire or not."

She glanced at his map wall, pushpins marking networks and ops, military positions and battles around the world. Since yesterday, he'd moved his Asia map front and center. "Imagine all the paperwork, all the secret files. I know the perfect person to organize a new Registry there."

"Who?" he said.

"Me." She put down her teacup with a click.

Donovan laughed. "I like a person with confidence. And I agree with your assessment. However, you're too valuable *here*. I want you to train someone for Delhi. Now, on your way."

The electricity drained through her feet. "Sir." But she was not about to give up.

———

Over the next few days, tidbits of intel from the Mediterranean, liberated Sicily, and OSS agents inside Italy began trickling in. Julia's personal concerns took a back seat to the momentous news: Allied landing craft were massing along the Sicilian coast. The invasion of mainland Europe was imminent.

THREE

So far, America had been spared the worst of it. Her protective oceans
were getting bloodier, though. German U-boats had sunk hundreds
of supply ships, and rationing had been instituted across the land.
But while there was a black market for everything, Julia had come to
Washington to support the war effort, not go around it.

As yesterday's coffee grounds bubbled in the percolator, she popped
two slices of bread in her old Toastmaster, purchased at the hardware
store down the street from Smith—where, they used to joke, Caro had
enrolled her daughter at birth. They'd taken the train together across
the country, laughing all the way, and now, in the toaster's reflection, she
could almost see her mother's joyful face. Embraced in Caro's threadbare
blue chenille robe, Julia buried her nose in the collar…finding the scent
that lived perhaps only in her memory.

With an angry swipe of her eyes, she bent over the little Frigidaire
to remove some jam and a can of sweetened condensed milk—a handy
substitute for sugar and waiting in line for fresh milk. Sadly, margarine
was no stand-in for butter. At least she had bread, though—sliced, even,
now that the government had bowed to America's protesting housewives
and rescinded its ban.

It was already hot in the tiny Brighton Hotel studio she'd been lucky
to find in overcrowded Washington. When she leaned over the sink
to push up the window, a blast of humid air bounced off the dawn-
streaked alley wall almost near enough to touch. A long diagonal crack
down the bricks reminded her of the Italian coastline, those valiant

fellows preparing to wade out of their landing craft into the Salerno surf—and the unknown. Last night, she'd learned of Italy's imminent surrender, but also of German forces massing outside Rome.

She sniffed. *Coffee boiled is coffee spoiled*, their cook often declared. Turning to the hot plate, she sniffed again. *Burnt toast.* "Oh my."

Mother Caro used to say she could burn water, but she'd said it with such tenderness that Julia felt embraced rather than criticized. Feeling the warmth of her smile, she closed her eyes. *With your bright future, Jukie, you need never step into a kitchen. You'll be too busy to cook.*

Tucking away her pain, she dropped the toast in the trash. Fortunately, the OSS cafeteria produced delicious deep-fried doughnuts.

But first, that Minox.

———

Gasoline was on the ration, too. With the buses packed even at 7:00 a.m., Julia usually hoofed it to work. Today the local Victory Garden's red-studded tomato vines seemed especially hopeful. It was great to think of Mussolini getting the boot—*ha!* But Italy was only a fingertip on the map of Europe. The Germans were entrenched everywhere else. And the Japanese controlled most of the Far East. War was certainly a geography lesson, a horrid one. Pushing through the clammy heat, Julia picked up her pace.

"*Extra! Extra!*"

Surprised to be downtown already, she looked about. People's faces bloomed with smiles. Strangers hugged one another, sharing the news, the astonishing headline.

"*Secret armistice. Italy surrenders,*" called the freckled newsboy, brandishing the latest *Washington Post.* "Hot off the press! Read all about it."

Although Julia had known "all about it" since last night, she dug into her pocketbook, then handed him three cents. There would be more news to come as the Allies prepared to invade the mainland from Sicily.

"Hope it's not over before I get there," the boy said, offering the paper. Wearing faded overalls, he was a foot shorter than her—barely the height of the streetlight's cut-off switch box, which would cast Washington into blackness in case of air attack.

Why isn't he in school? she wondered, until realizing his pop might be a soldier posted far from a home in need of the boy's income. Then her thoughts returned to the spy camera.

As she brooded over Donovan's rebuke yesterday, a yeasty smell wafting up from the old riverside brewery announced her destination—the quadrangle of stone and brick buildings that housed the Office of Strategic Services. In the fifteen months since its launch, the OSS had grown like Topsy, a maze of rough temporary structures sprawling down to the Potomac.

On pins and needles, she hustled to the basement film lab. Nothing.

The Registry was empty when she entered and switched on the ceiling fans. The stale air stirred to life, lifting the damp hair from her scalp. There, off in the corner, was her first desk, the only one open at the time—*her* desk, her opportunity. How excited she had been that morning, how bubbly; then she'd gathered herself together and gotten down to work. That hard work had brought her here, to this pillared alcove outside the boss's office.

As she was settling in, the quiet clerk from Seattle, Sally Lu, arrived and went straight to it, as usual. By 8:00 a.m., there was the click of high heels and swell of voices sharing the Italy news. "Lipstick girls," some called them, the thousands of young women who had flooded Washington to become typists and stenographers, cryptographers, propagandists, and spies. The men had always had a chance to serve, but now the women did, too.

Punctuated by the first ring of a carriage return, she skimmed a typed, double-spaced New-York-to-Buenos-Aires letter that had been intercepted in Bermuda:

Dear José, It is almost a year since I have seen you last. Too bad we had to get into this war… Now visible in pink, a secret message scrawled between the lines revealed the latest merchant marine shipping schedules out of Brooklyn Navy Yard—intelligence meant for Nazi subs. The spy signed off, *Heil Hitler!*

Julia's disgust turned to fury, then pride in their work. She gazed around the girls' altars of photos—fervent or proud or shy faces of absent husbands, fiancés, and brothers. They were bound by their tears, one of the few things in America not in short supply.

She was adding the intercept to Donovan's briefing folder when Millicent peeked out from his office suite. "He wants to see you, Julia."

"Shut the door, McWilliams," the boss ordered as she entered Room 109—hence his code name, 109. Humid river air passed through his private rear entrance, as had Mountbatten yesterday.

She braced herself, seeing the prints face down on his desk.

"The brilliant Danish physicist, Dr. Niels Bohr, is Jewish on his mother's side. Without the funds you transported, many of the boats would not have departed, including his. The Germans, who wanted his services, were left high and dry. 'The elbow is near, but try and bite it,' as our Russian friends say." His smile was cold. "Bohr's research should be invaluable to our defense."

Sensing there was more, she waited, abashed that he'd beaten her to the photo lab.

"As to that Minox with the Swedish thank-you…" He flipped one of the prints to reveal a handwritten message. "The microfilm reveals a Nazi plot to assassinate FDR, Churchill, and Stalin in Tehran."

What if she'd left early? *Or hadn't dared answer Donovan's red phone?* Julia was shocked to realize the power of her position, a position that put her in the center of history. "Now what?"

"I would imagine a venue change," he said dryly. "Perhaps the Soviet embassy. Although certainly bugged, it's locked down tighter than a drum. But that is up to wiser minds than mine. After I briefed the president, he commended my sources. Well done."

Staggered by the honor, Julia tried not to blush. "Thank you, sir."

"Now, get me someone for Delhi," he barked.

That's it? Surely she deserved more than a patronizing pat on the back for saving FDR's life. And Churchill's. "I know I could be useful there, sir."

"Without a doubt. But I told you. I need you here." His eyes drifted to the prints on his desk, then back to the globe. He spun it.

Like any general, Donovan had his grand strategy and moved a great many pieces—she was only one of them. Yet Julia had her own vision. She stood there, clinging to it so hard that she couldn't move.

"You may be on your way, McWilliams. I've got a Clipper to catch."

She knew he wouldn't miss it for the world—the amphibious invasion of Salerno. "Safe travels to you, sir. And all the boys." She held up Churchill's V for Victory sign, then strode out. *Victory*. The more he denied her the Delhi post, the more she wanted it. While Julia might never fulfill society's expectations, she had her own. She believed she was meant to achieve…something. She wanted Donovan to believe in her, too.

———

When she joined her chums Betty and Jane at the cafeteria, Betty immediately asked, "What's wrong?"

"Do you ever feel underappreciated?" Julia scowled.

"We all feel that way at times, dear." She passed her a sandwich. "This will perk you up." With the same high forehead and dark waves as Hepburn, Betty MacDonald was a whip-smart Japan expert at Morale Operations, which created "black" propaganda to undermine the enemy, such as the garish flyers of Japanese atrocities against civilians she'd had air-dropped over China. MO's counterpart, the Office of War Information, where Julia had typed all those index cards, produced positive "white" propaganda to benefit their side.

She bit into minced Spam. "Pickle relish. Tasty."

"Goes well with scrambled eggs, too," suggested Betty, a former Honolulu reporter whose Pearl Harbor reports had caught the OSS's attention. "And stir-fry."

"Girls. It's *Spam*." Jane grimaced. "As they say, 'A hog in a silk waistcoat is still a hog.'" Jane Foster was Morale Operations' specialist on the East Indies, where she'd lived with her ex-husband, a Dutch diplomat. A bohemian artist from San Francisco, she detested fascism and was dedicated to its defeat. They called her their "Cadillac Communist."

Julia smiled. "We could always cut off the crusts and make tea sandwiches."

"Sure. Put the recipe in the Junior League cookbook." Jane tossed her ash-blond curls.

"Or," Julia suggested, "the next edition of *Keeping on the Ration.*" The book had been a gift from Jane's Nob Hill mother. But really? Slaving over a hot stove…Who'd ever want to?

"I doubt any of us has much time to cook these days," Betty observed.

"Thankfully," Jane said. "Last night, while you were burning the midnight oil, Betty and I discovered an absolutely divine Georgetown bar. You could have been in Manhattan. Lots of interesting fellows."

Was Jane alluding to Julia's unmarried status, or was she just being sensitive? Or was it her monthly? "I'll be happy to accompany you this evening," she said aloofly. "Drinks on me."

"You're on." Jane pushed away her sandwich. "I wouldn't mind running into Husband Number Two one of these days."

"I'll be matron of honor." Betty smiled.

What did that leave Julia—*bridesmaid*? "I thought lefties consider marriage bourgeois," she blurted, a tightness in her throat.

Jane's eyes twinkled roguishly. "Not if you recruit a bougie to your cause." Then her tone turned lofty. "Besides, wasn't everyone a leftist back in the day?"

With some effort, Julia regained her composure. "Not everyone. I didn't vote for FDR until 1936. His second term." But she and Caro had done so secretly, so as not to rile Pop, who scorned East Coast intellectuals as pinkos, the French as snooty. And Roosevelt—as a Democrat.

"I meant, every progressive, every *artist.*"

That stung. Julia had begun life as an artist. *Gifted*, everyone had called her, admiring her leadership and creative drive. After college, she'd taken an advertising job at New York's posh W. & J. Sloane Furniture Store. Although the work had left her cold, she was in love with the city, in love with love—until a failed romance sent her back to Pasadena and half a decade of drifting. Still feeling the pain of self-doubt, she regarded Jane evenly. "You've no monopoly on progressive ideas. FDR was born into the 'ruling class,' yet he's a revolutionary in his own way."

"Well said, Julie." Betty nodded. "We're modern girls. With careers. One day, I hope to be a foreign correspondent. My Alex wants to write novels."

Feeling less alone, Julia regarded her through sisterly eyes. "Any newspaper would be lucky to have you, Betty. I've always planned to be a writer, too, but thought I'd find my subjects out in the world…"

"*Voila.*" Jane fluttered her jazzy red fingernails. "The biggest story of our lifetimes."

"Not that we willed this war," Betty stated with calm firmness.

"Surely not," Julia added emphatically. "I want to help win it. I know I'm capable of more than filing papers."

"*Carpe diem.*" Jane opened her palms and squeezed them shut.

"*Seize the day*. As my mother always said." Julia touched her pearls, that warm spot above her heart.

"Maybe you'll write spy novels, Julie," Betty said. "International intrigue."

Jane snorted.

What does that mean? Did she doubt Julia's abilities? Jane couldn't possibly be jealous, petite and adorable as she was. If Betty was the sensitive sister, Jane was the self-seeking one.

"Speaking of foreign shores…" Jane leaned closer, twisting a curl around her finger. "I hear that dishy Lord Mountbatten is recruiting for his new South East Asia Command in Delhi. Some of our people are already on their way—Visual Display."

Julia perked up. "My pal Jack Moore is one of their mapmakers."

"Supposed to have quite a perfectionist chief," Jane added. "The notorious Paul Child."

"Jack's a talented artist. I'm sure he'll do fine."

"Nothing official," Betty said. "But we hope to conduct propaganda ops in India."

"After all, I know the region *quite* well," Jane added with her superior look.

If Jack could get posted to the field, so could she. Julia smiled sweetly. "I *met* Admiral Lord Mountbatten."

Jane raised a pale eyebrow. "You've been holding out, darling."

"Security, *darling*. Let's catch up later." Julia headed for the door. Her college roommate used to tease her about reading spy thrillers instead of textbooks. Since then, she'd learned a thing or two about twists and turns. She would find her own way to make a difference.

FOUR

— // —

Even from her paper-laden desk, Julia could see the scene: Wild Bill Donovan hopping from his Clipper seaplane onto a rocky bit of Sicilian coast and then into one of the boats lurching for Salerno—Operation Avalanche. Fearful, she read intel of fierce German resistance on the beach. Nonetheless, fascism was dealt a mighty blow, and they popped champagne at headquarters that night. Julia wanted to believe their rowdy cheers could be heard all the way to the Italian shores.

With a sense of euphoria, she finally fell into bed, then dreamt of the moon over Delhi, the Taj Mahal and turbans, elephants.

Yet with the gimlet eye of dawn, Julia understood India would present a much less glamorous reality. This was a theater of war she knew little about. What she did know was that the subcontinent's east coast—across the Bay of Bengal from occupied Burma—had been bombed, the Japanese were pushing up toward India's northeast, and there was widespread famine. Delhi, though, was in the middle of this vast country, far from the front lines. Still, the war would likely heat up in the region. Julia had to determine whom among her clerks was best suited to establish a Registry there—or, if fate permitted, take over for her in Washington. Sally had a strong work ethic and seemed likely to adapt culturally, but did she have the leadership skills required for either post?

By late morning, Julia received word that Donovan would continue on from Italy to India and then China. His travels gave her some breathing space to observe her staff and also prepare herself. By the time the boss returned two weeks later, Julia was immersed in material from their Research and Analysis department, so she gladly waved goodbye when he set off again for consultations on Operation Overlord—the Normandy invasion—in London.

In mid-October, she invited Sally for a drink. Not overly impressed by Jane's "divine" new Georgetown bar, Julia opted for tried and true. A venerable Washington institution, Harvey's Restaurant was packed, but she spotted two empty stools at the end of the bar and moved quickly. As the crowd grew hushed over Glenn Miller's rendition of "The White Cliffs of Dover," she ordered martinis and bean soup—it was Meatless Tuesday.

Little by little, Sally opened up about her life. How good America had been to her immigrant family. How hard it was for her China relations, tenant farmers obliged to give most of their rice to the landlord. "Unless the Japanese Army shows up first. Now America is helping the Chinese people. My folks were against me leaving Seattle, but I wanted to do my small bit."

"You're doing more than that." The martini wasn't cold, but Sally's relatives barely had rice to eat—how could Julia complain? Sally moved her spoon in circles. "What's wrong?"

"This fellow I was dating, works for *Collier's* magazine. He was polite and attentive, never asked me out on the weekend." Sally finally tasted her martini and blinked. "I learned he has a family on Long Island." Turning into the corner, she began to sob.

Julia glowered. "How rotten. One of those dollar-a-year men, I bet."

"What's that?" Sally mumbled through her tears.

"Business executives who volunteer for government service in DC. Some are fine fellows, I'm sure…Well…it can be convenient." With a sigh, she put an arm around Sally's heaving shoulders. "You know how people say they understand? They don't! But I do."

As she sniffled, Dooley Wilson launched into "As Time Goes By" from *Casablanca*. Julia's chin quivered. Her mission, though, was to shore up Sally, not burden her with more grief.

"After college I landed a swell job in Manhattan. Found a funny, beguiling guy, Tom Johnston. A freethinker—even taller than me, a rarity. A writer, too, full of Melville, mad for literature. One day, I got a letter: he was marrying his high school sweetheart from Milwaukee. *Bye-bye, see you around.*" Julia stabbed the other half of her olive. "I didn't know she even existed. Probably five foot two, demure, everything I'm not. After I dragged myself home, my mother reminded me that she hadn't married until *thirty-three*. I had to be patient. The same for you."

While Sally dabbed her eyes with an embroidered hankie, Julia ordered two more martinis—*cold*, this time. "It happens to every woman. You might call it a rite of passage. So screw him and the train that brought him."

Sally returned a crooked smile. "I've never heard you swear."

"You've never seen me mad. And you don't want to."

When the bartender served their drinks, Julia tipped her glass against Sally's. "Here's to survival. And being the best person you can—married or single."

"I am a decorated major in the Indian Army, sir," came a clipped British voice from the door. They turned to see a dark-skinned man standing straight as an arrow in starched khaki.

"We have restrictions." Arms crossed, a balding manager type wearing a shiny navy suit confronted the dignified officer. "You'll have to find another place to eat."

Julia saw red. About to leap to her feet, she felt a gentle hand on her arm.

"You can't fight these people," Sally said in a whisper. "They might come after me."

She stared at her colleague. "Why?"

"They might think I'm Japanese—you know…" She winced. "We all look alike."

Outraged, Julia watched the Indian major stride out the door—an Allied soldier. *One of us.* And so was Sally, an essential worker for the US government who'd been made to feel like an outsider. She knew that feeling, rejected by the WACS and the WAVES for her height. She saw some mid-level officer in a shiny navy uniform stamping her application: *Not Fit.*

With a defiant stare at the manager, she raised a hand. "Check."

The air outside was cleaner, but still Julia felt soiled. "I always thought we were all in this together." Suddenly she wanted to get far away from that place.

Staggering after her, Sally stumbled. "Sorry. I'm not used to drinking. I don't think I've ever had two martinis at one time."

Julia took her arm. "One day, I was shopping for shoes and the salesman asked if I was one of those 'lipstick girls.'"

Sally made a face. "Last month, I used up my last lipstick. Never had time to replace it."

"Yeah. When I wear makeup, I feel like I'm in wardrobe."

"You mean, in a *play*?"

"Never the love interest, though," Julia said matter-of-factly. "I always play the character parts, the comical ones. That's why they call it *acting*. Did you know I'm really a drudge?"

"I know you're the last one to leave every night. You're my inspiration, Julia."

She shrugged. "An advantage of being one of the boys is you learn to hold your own. I can throw a softball, hunt, fish—and drink most of them under the table. I made up my Registry job as I went along." Julia stared, making her final decision. "Now I have my sights set on a new post in South East Asia Command. Think I can train you to take over *here*? When I go to Delhi?"

"My parents urged me to keep my head down. One thing I admire about you is your directness, your strength." She returned Julia's testing gaze with new resolve.

"All you need is to raise up your head and look 'em in the eye. Think you can do that?"

Sally squared her shoulders. "That's what I came to Washington to learn."

"Then let's give them hell."

———

That could be their motto: *Let's give the bad guys hell.*

With Operation Avalanche advancing up the Italian peninsula, everyone's hearts and souls were fixed on the coming Normandy invasion. At the same time, Donovan was laying the groundwork for their Asian operations. The OSS was critical to the national defense; Julia was proud of what she'd built and trusted Sally to take over. She yearned to do the creative building again.

Butterflies took up residence in her stomach. She worked harder than ever, training Sally while spending most evenings studying Indochina research. So only grudgingly did she agree to meet with her old beau Harrison Chandler, who'd landed in town with "big news." She suggested a midday walk in Rock Creek Park.

After scrambling about for a lift uptown, Julia was a bit late reaching their meeting place, the old Peirce Barn at the park's southern entrance. It was her first time out of the office in weeks, and she was invigorated by the brisk breeze and dazzling fall colors. Harry was crunching through a pile of gold and scarlet leaves, boyish and happy. A Stanford alum with little time for books, he preferred the California ski slopes, beaches, and golf courses. He glided through life.

As she approached, his placid features opened into a happy smile. "Grand, isn't it? A real autumn." He moved as if to hug her.

She stepped away. "You look well. What brings you to DC?" She feared he'd found a government job and would continue to woo her despite her efforts to break free from the past.

"I took a navy commission, hope to serve in the Pacific. I wanted to see you…before."

Surprised—even impressed—Julia knew he could have found an easier, safer path. "What about the newspaper?"

"My brother will run it."

"And your father—what did he say?"

"He felt volunteering as a dollar-a-year man here would have been sacrifice enough."

"Tell him we've got plenty." Thinking of Sally's no-good beau, she inhaled the fresh air, relieved to have found her own life. "Our fathers are much alike. *Down with Roosevelt. Up with making money. Let others do the war work.*" She looked him in the eye. "I'm aiming for Delhi."

Frowning, Harry draped his plaid muffler around her neck. "India is a dirty place—a hardship post, in my estimation. I could pull some strings, help you get a job in London."

"I can pull my own strings, thank you very much."

"No offense, Julie, but you don't want to wear yourself out. Think of dear Caro."

That was a stab. Her mother's high blood pressure and weak heart. He was implying she might have inherited one condition or the other. "Exactly why I have to live...for us both."

"You haven't changed, Julie. A firebrand and freethinker." Harry regarded her fondly. "Even if you turned Democrat, I wouldn't mind."

Julia raised an eyebrow. Two years earlier, Pop had insisted she marry before her thirtieth birthday. He doubted she could do better than Harrison Chandler—tall, handsome, devoted, impeccable pedigree. But Pearl Harbor had changed everything. She turned thirty here.

"You're a creator," he continued earnestly. "I'm a businessman. I am hoping when it's all over...you might reconsider."

She took a breath. They wouldn't always be at war; she wouldn't always be at the OSS. She'd have to find other ways to fulfill her aspirations. At least Harry respected her. Softening, she gazed at a little boy and girl playing hide-and-seek among the trees as their parents watched proudly, arm in arm. The husband was in uniform, the wife pregnant. Harry was a good man, who'd toss the ball with their son and take their daughter on pony rides. Who'd make Pop proud.

It was an appealing scenario, but there was no part for her. *I know you will choose your husband wisely*, her mother had once said at the beach. *I always wanted to go to Cairo.*

Caro's wistful remark still pained Julia. Harry didn't seem like the traveling sort, either. "I'm sorry," she said with true regret. "I can't go back."

His eager, hopeful look faded. Years of memories passed between their eyes.

"I'm grateful. You suggested I take the civil service exam for Washington."

"Maybe I should be kicking myself."

"You never know where life will carry you." Gently, she returned his soft plaid muffler.

Harry hesitated before accepting it. "Take care of yourself, Julie."

"You, too, dear friend."

"We didn't have our walk, did we?" he said slowly. "Think I'll stay awhile."

She glanced up the path. Amber and marigold and maroon leaves stretched around the bend...into infinity, maybe. "I don't blame you." She turned away, wishing for what might have been. But she had work to do. *You never know where life will carry you.* Fate, some called it.

As far back as Julia could remember, she'd been taller than the other girls. She was different, which gave her a certain freedom. Julia McWilliams was *of* society, while not quite fitting into its plan. She was everyone's friend, no one's girlfriend. She attended the best schools, where she excelled mainly as Organizer of Fun, staging musicals, tossing jump shots, and later, exploring speakeasies. But academic enthusiasm wasn't expected from a woman because marriage was waiting at the other end...homemaking and child-raising, supervising the cook. She didn't fit into that plan, either. Over the years, watching her well-bred friends pair up, making homes and babies, she longed to be one of them. Yet she couldn't settle. She wanted to follow *her* plan—achieve something of note. And hold out for the right man.

Before any of that came to be, the war swept her off into its own plan.

FIVE

—— // ——

The next morning, the crackling autumn leaves were gone, seemingly forever. Under blustery winds and gunmetal skies, Julia walked to work, moving briskly to keep blood pumping through her bare legs. She had been able to avoid covering her best feature for most of the year in Southern California, but Washington winters called for trousers. As women's trousers were cut too short, she'd been stuck wearing men's too often—and too often mistaken for a man from behind. Despite plans to locate a tailor that fall, she'd never taken the time.

The large open Registry felt equally cold. Weak, wintry light streamed down from the high windows. Sally was already at work, wearing her thin brown coat. They exchanged conspiratorial smiles, but Julia remained apprehensive. The boss was due back any moment and would soon demand her candidate for Delhi.

A little past noon, General Donovan marched in, his uniform rumpled, tie askew, yet looking so alive. Unzipping his flight jacket, he dispatched his two subordinates elsewhere in his empire. He paused at Julia's desk, then nodded toward his office. "109," he said, his voice curt.

She shot to her feet. Clutching his briefing folder, she followed, rehearsing her sales pitch: After careful scrutiny, she'd found Sally Lu to be her hardest-working, most resourceful clerk. But Sally's parents refused to let her go to India—so she suggested that Julia go while she took over in Washington.

Donovan lowered himself into his chair. He did not invite her to sit. She shifted to the other foot, looking down at him, yet, for once, not feeling tall.

He spun his globe slowly, then abruptly brought up his broad palm to brake it. "I can read you, McWilliams. I know you're getting ready to finesse me. Don't bother."

She tried to keep her face expressionless.

"They call India a subcontinent. It's a grand, albeit chaotic, place—ruled from Delhi by our British allies, the last great Imperial capital not in enemy hands. As such, it is a city of administrators and military brass—ours, too, now—everyone tripping over each other, with China and Burma under one command and Southeast Asia under another. After much consideration, I realize how much I need you—*there*. I'll accept Sally as your replacement."

"How did…?"

"I know you're an upright young woman," he pressed on. "Presbyterian, as I recall. But what we do around here is spy—even on our friends. Do you have any qualms about this work?"

"No, sir. This is war, sir."

"Correct." The boss gestured toward a chair. "I want you to turn your sharp eyes on SEAC communications—official and unofficial. You've heard of the Great Game?"

"The Great Powers vying over Afghanistan, India, Central Asia." Julia perched on the edge of her seat. "I was an A student in International Relations." Her only A, she didn't admit. "I understand the importance of South East Asia Command from a strategic point of view."

He nodded briefly. "After France, the Game moves to China—our springboard to Japan. The Brits are playing chess all over the region, with the aim of regaining their colonies. As we favor democracy and free markets, we need to monitor their actions." Donovan gave her a pointed look.

A private intelligence mission. He wanted her to *spy* on Admiral Lord Louis Mountbatten. Her heart was thumping a mile a minute. "Are you recruiting me, sir?"

"You have proved your initiative. You are organized, dogged, and ambitious."

She *was* ambitious, a trait many thought unbefitting a woman. "I—"

"I mean that in a positive way. However, no one must know of your secret efforts. As an intelligence officer, you may not keep a diary nor disclose the nature of your job. Should anyone inquire about your new posting—"

"I'm just a file clerk." Julia stared him straight in the eye as her heart did a flip-flop. *Intelligence officer.*

He grinned. "You'll be signing a contract to that effect. Clear your weekends. You begin field training after Thanksgiving. I managed to get you in the class with Foster and MacDonald."

"Whatever the trainers throw at me, I can handle."

"I'm depending on that," Donovan said forcefully. "Mountbatten recruits his people from the highest society. Wartime or not, there will be dinners and balls. As a clever and attractive young woman, you might begin shopping for gowns. Remember, everyone has an agenda—as you know." He cocked his head. "Have fun. Work hard. Trust no one."

Julia wanted to leap up and cheer but was too dizzy. The boss saw something in her even Caro could not have envisioned. He'd seen her hunger before she acknowledged it herself. At that moment, she would have killed for Wild Bill Donovan. "I won't disappoint you, sir."

"I'm certain of that. Once training is complete, you will ship out around March."

"Sally's a quick study. I could push up that timeline."

"You probably could, having been showing her the ropes already." Donovan raised a shaggy eyebrow. "However, the OSS is part of the government. We have procedures."

"And bureaucrats."

"I've no doubt you could take them on, *too*." His blue eyes twinkled. "But, that might delay you further, McWilliams."

She smiled. "February, it is."

"Then you can pack your bags for India."

SIX

///

Flashes of white water flickered through the porthole. The ship pitched and rolled, threatening to shake their three sets of creaky triple-decker bunks from their bolts. The storm had been raging since midnight, and as the angry blackness began to fade, Julia and her eight female cabinmates were still riding it out in bed. Gripping the sides of her bunk, she was on top—the penthouse, one might say—teetering in shadowy space.

"I'm going to be sick!" Betty, looking birdlike in her husband's USN T-shirt, staggered for the head.

Julia tried to focus on the horizon line, but it kept disappearing as immense waves slammed them relentlessly. All at once, she was back on Santa Monica's Hi-Boy Coaster, with its sharp banked turns, ascents, and plunges over the crashing surf. But now there were no zips and dips, only long, dizzying climbs followed by nerve-shattering drops.

Lying prone in the dark was no way to confront the unknown. "I'd rather look my fate in the eye." Popping up, she banged her head against the ceiling—or rather, *overhead*, in nautical parlance. A pointer of light struck the ladder, but as she took hold, it winked off, and she descended blind. At the bottom, a sharp object smacked her right big toe.

"*Ow*." Julia jammed her feet into her loafers, suddenly illuminated.

"Let there be light." A pale arm slid down from the middle bunk,

and with a glimpse of cream lace, Jane pressed a flashlight into her hand.
"Don't break a leg, dear."

"Wait for me, Julia." Wearing red rompers and pin curls, translator
Rosamond Frame sprang from the bottom.

Ducking through crisscrossed lines of panties and bras, Julia opened
the door—just as the SS *Mariposa* hit a trough, flinging them against
the steel bulkhead and again into darkness. The deck reared and swayed
about them until she fumbled the flashlight back on. They grabbed
the lifeline, wobbling forward as the refitted luxury liner creaked and
groaned around them.

"I hope these rivets hold," said Rosie, a Peking-born missionaries'
daughter. "When I was eight, my family capsized on the Yangtze River.
I've been a nervous sailor ever since."

"I understand. I got caught in a nasty riptide once." Tumbling about
in darkness. The terrible unknown—which way was up? She still feared
the ocean, still loved it. "But, Rosie, what a childhood! I bet you were
never bored. That's one thing I can't abide."

"Boredom is the last thing you'll need to worry about when we reach
the front."

"Delhi's not exactly the front lines. My boss told me to pack evening
attire." Nonetheless, enemy forces prowled the open seas and skies overhead. As if to underline the point, their twenty-person OSS team had
been ordered to report to Long Beach Harbor in uniform.

She and Rosie had bumped into each other—literally—while boarding their troop ship, bound for India's eastern port of Calcutta. Onto
their packs were strapped gas masks, bedrolls, canteens, and helmets
that clattered like cymbals—sadly off the beat to the band's "Anchors
Aweigh." The GIs whistled. The arrival of nine women was an event of
much interest to the three thousand soldiers and scores of navy crew
members.

A great crack resounded through the ship as if it were breaking
apart. They froze, clinging to the lifeline. When no alarms sounded,
she and Rosie turned up the narrow ladderwell, her flashlight casting eerie shadows. Another big drop-off sent them staggering onto the

Promenade Deck. A soldier was asleep in a corner, his face covered with a paperback—*Coming of Age in Samoa*, by the famous anthropologist Dr. Margaret Mead.

Julia took a second look. "Did you know Gregory's wife wrote that? About her pioneering research into an isolated South Seas culture. I went to a girls' college, and the book had just come out, and we were all agog at her fortitude and courage." Many had begun to question their designated roles in life—teacher, nurse, charity volunteer, mother. Julia had perceived a larger future. Why settle for being a famous *woman* writer? But then, over the next decade, she had struggled to find anything meaningful to say. Until now. While writing secret reports would never lead to fame, her words might, in a tiny way, lead to something far more important: peace.

Rosie glanced at her. "I didn't know he was married."

"They did fieldwork in Polynesia. On a remote island."

"Kind of romantic. Being cut off from the world together. Where is she now?"

"Washington, I think. Different kind of fieldwork." Dr. Gregory Bateson, a Cambridge-educated anthropologist, was an OSS adviser on Southeast Asia—brilliant, witty, and tall. Julia and he had made each other laugh. It had been a bit of a blow to learn of his marital status.

As the waves continued to pummel the *Mariposa*, she and Rosie staggered up the dark, deserted deck. A faint glow emanated from the former Club Class lounge, now OSS Central. There, speak of the devil, Gregory was contemplating the portholes with Lieutenant Thibaut de Saint Phalle, a Franco-American intelligence officer. Stuffing her pin curls in a pocket, Rosie shook out her hair. Regarding her own salt-frizzled mop, Julia could do nothing but grin and bear it.

Thibaut jumped up from the table, his smooth, even features relaxing in a crooked smile. "I knew there would be light at the end of the tunnel."

Gregory lowered his pipe and pulled out two chairs. "Good morning, ladies. I see you dressed for the occasion."

As they joined the men, Julia straightened her pajama collar. "Brooks Brothers."

"I have the same pair," Gregory said with a playful look.

Reminded of always being stuck with men's sizes, she felt her clever retort about his usual wrinkled shorts and hiking boots stick in her throat. What was it about this man? He wasn't conventionally handsome like Thibaut—his nose was too large, his lips too full...too enticing. "We just saw a GI reading *Coming of Age in Samoa*," she blurted. "An Armed Services Edition."

"Margaret would not care to be entertaining," he replied quietly.

"I guess she wasn't—he was sound asleep."

As Gregory let out a roar of laughter, Rosie giggled. "If we'd known such delightful company awaited, we'd have ditched our cabin hours ago. Right, Julia?"

"Oh, you bet," she said, looking at the porthole. "Now, where is that horizon line?" As she stood, the ship pitched sharply from starboard to port, knocking her back into her seat.

"What matters is you're here." Thibaut's gaze locked on to Rosie's. "Thank you for finding us." He rose to his feet, producing a silver flask as if by magic. "In France, one takes cognac with his morning coffee. Or without." A navy man, unaffected by the rolling deck, he moved smoothly to the buffet.

Despite the rumored maharaja-bound whiskey in the hold, alcohol was banned aboard ship, but Julia didn't quibble when he returned with four juice glasses and served the illicit liqueur. This was a new day. "To clandestine operations."

As they toasted, a tentative pale light peeped through purple clouds.

"'And the dawn comes up like thunder,'" Julia said, surprising herself at the recollection. "Kipling. But I can't remember the poem's name."

Gregory nodded in approval. "'Mandalay.'"

"In Burma." Julia stared out the porthole, eastward in her imagination. A land now controlled by Japan, along with all of Southeast Asia except India, the last stronghold of the British Empire. In three weeks, the *Mariposa* would dock in Calcutta. Just across the Bay of Bengal, the Japanese Army remained hungry and on the move. It was starting to feel real.

Her cabinmates were perfectly delightful, but Julia knew that three more weeks of their clatter and chatter would drive her bonkers. All the noise and heat rose to her top bunk, where she closed her eyes and suddenly gave birth to an idea. During her senior year, she'd edited Smith's gossipy *Tatler,* which had been great fun. She could replicate that with a diverting little one-sheet, the *Daily Mariposa.* Possibly also pick up some interesting intel.

While Rosie and Betty remained in cabin 237 writing letters, Julia set off to explore the ship with Jane and Ellie Thore, a tall strawberry-blond with wide-set eyes.

"Hey. Two blonds and a redhead!" Immediately, they were bombarded by wolf whistles, gallant offers of cigarettes…and more. One intrepid sergeant volunteered to be their bodyguard.

Jane backhanded him a smile as they moved up the deck. "Did you two pack your sunbathing attire?"

"Hardly. I never thought that was part of going off to war. I'm from the Midwest, you know." Ellie gazed about in wonder. "I've never even seen the ocean."

"I'll lend you some shorts," Jane offered.

"You're on! Let's get back to our cabin—I mean, *quarters*—and round up the girls."

Notepad in hand, Julia eyed the hovering men. "I suggest we wait until these soldiers find other interests. I feel like a beetle under a microscope."

"We have as much right to enjoy the deck as they do," Jane said huffily.

"You go ahead. I'll write the story."

By the time Julia had circled the Promenade Deck, the women reappeared in swimsuits and shorts—along with Betty, Rosie, and Peggy, the freckled daughter of Army General Wheeler, now serving in India. Two other cabinmates, identical-twin brunette cryptographers, preferred to remain in their bunks, devising devilish codes for the other to decrypt. Dr. Cora DuBois, chief of Research and Analysis/Far East, had a stack of reading material to catch up on.

Julia observed the ensuing pandemonium as the men spotted the sunbathers—glistening with baby oil—in a corner of the deck. That afternoon, she grabbed her first exclusive as Captain Marks cordoned off a section of valuable upper-deck real estate for women only.

Nonetheless, war was a man's game. As Julia returned from her tour of the ship, Jane shot out of the bathroom wrapped in a towel, two pale strap marks surrounded by an expanse of red skin. "I cannot survive one more day with dirty, saltwater-washed hair!"

The women looked at one another, sharing her pain.

"Yeah," Betty said. "Why do the men get a barbershop and nothing for us?"

Ellie raised her chin. "As the eldest of nine, I learned you have to speak up for your rights."

"The boys do have sinks and proper shampoo." Former anthropology professor Dr. Cora DuBois regarded them over the top of her round tortoise-rimmed eyeglasses.

Julia lifted a clump of dry corkscrew hair. "And scissors."

Jane grinned back. "I'm on my way."

Grabbing her notepad, Julia raised an eyebrow. "But first…"

"Yes?"

"Put on some clothes."

What would become known as the "Haircut Incident" led to no end of shipboard amusement. And Julia's second *Mariposa Daily* feature.

In her dramatic retelling, the tiny barbershop had been breached by all nine female passengers after Dr. Cora announced she could use a trim. When word got out, GIs thronged around them, as many as possible squeezing inside the narrow mirrored space to view the proceedings. A few offered to aid the five barbers, who insisted they could handle the challenge on their own. Julia, Betty, Dr. Cora, and Peggy volunteered for the second seating.

In the meantime, Julia interviewed the onlookers while the other women leaned back against the sinks in blissful enjoyment as their heads were scrubbed with Fitch shampoo and cold—but *fresh*—water.

She followed up with another popular account of their toilette, describing how the resourceful women rinsed out their dainties in helmets—which, when polished, also served as makeup mirrors. The piece, especially her account of Jane jitterbugging her clothes dry on the shower floor, drew ribald letters to the editor.

———

Two days later, while the girls were tending their sunburns, Julia gazed out at endless blue, thinking of the Honolulu convoy that had come under fierce air and sea attack the other day, all hands lost to the deep. Her own convoy was guarded by two destroyers, bristling with armaments. She stared around at their accompanying troop ships—*SS Mount Vernon, HMS Raider, HMS Cumberland, HMAS Quickmatch*, and *HMS Quality*. Up against them were Japan's merciless fighters. It was luck of the draw.

She leaned into the railing, watching the reflections of clouds. One cloud tumbled off from the others, then drifted away.

As her mother had, slowly. It had been unbearable watching her fade. Always open and outgoing, sunshine herself, Caro was the heart of their family—the first to applaud Julia's every achievement, the first to wipe her tears…waiting, open armed, when she'd fled Manhattan, wounded. Only a year later, it was she holding her mother, who kept insisting she was fine, maybe just a bit tired. Julia believed her at first—*wanted* to believe. They had too much to catch up on, too much left unsaid. Her anchor to the end, Mother Caro had faith Julia could do anything she set her mind to. *Your time will come*, she'd promised.

Her fingers rippling across her pearls, Julia stared at the swelling whitecaps, the distant wake of their companion ships, their guardian destroyers.

In truth, no one outside Fortress America was safe. Last night at dinner, they'd learned Japanese troops had finally pushed across the Burmese border into Northeast India. The front lines were edging closer.

———

The following day, sunbathing resumed, along with Rosie's Chinese class, which had been hit-or-miss since the storm. Under clear skies, the language group convened on the foredeck where, on alternate mornings, Thibaut taught Français—flattering Julia over how well she pronounced his name: *Tee-bow*. But Chinese was another matter.

Rosie, though, insisted it was easier—a smaller vocabulary, only four tones.

Albeit oh so specific. And, as Julia knew all too well, her voice had a mind of its own.

"Who has a word for *horse?*" Rosie asked.

"*Moi,*" Thibaut promptly volunteered, then blushed. "I mean, *ma.*"

With his index finger, Gregory drew a straight line through the air. "First tone. That means *mother*. For *horse*, you want third tone. *Ma,*" he said clearly, illustrating falling and rising with his long finger.

She watched in admiration. "I'll defer to Rosie, but sounds good to me."

"You do have a good ear, Julia. I've heard you picking out tunes on the piano," he said in his normal BBC voice, rich and resonant.

"Music is one thing—Chinese, quite another."

"You can do it." Rosie sent her an encouraging look. "Big—the way I showed you. Fourth tone."

Julia stood, extending her arms and legs in a proud stance, and directed her voice downward. "*Da.*" Seeing Gregory's amused air, she sank back on her yellow life vest. She had felt free in the moment but now merely foolish.

"I may need some private coaching," Thibaut said sheepishly.

"Maybe a swap? My French accent…" Rosie released a despairing sigh, then smiled at Julia. "Well done. My *amah*—nanny—would approve."

"Missionaries have nannies?" she asked, surprised.

"We were up north. It was very cold, very poor. People pleaded for work. So we had servants. I couldn't pick up my dirty clothes, or I'd be depriving someone of a job. If Mother didn't hold two dinners a week, Cook would be hurt." Rosie paused. "Her name was Kuk, and she giggled when we called her Cook Kuk. The invaders shot her."

Even the slap of the waves ceased for a moment. Thibaut finally broke the silence. "When did you last hear from your parents?"

"A year ago. I love China." Rosie's voice shook. "That's why I want to serve there, wherever I'm needed. To find my parents and help the Chinese people." She abruptly stood and moved to the bow, a forlorn figure, head bent and alone.

Julia longed to console her but knew anything she said might sound hopelessly naive. Feeling disloyal even to pose the question, she whispered, "Do you think the Japanese could actually take India?"

"India *must* hold!" Gregory clenched his fists, impassioned.

Seeing the man stripped for the first time of his intellectual equanimity, she was shaken.

He stared through her, into some distant horror. "Imagine millions of Nippon troops pouring across Central Asia to connect with German forces."

As if in defiance, Thibaut said, "Give me two words for bread, Julia. *En français.*"

"*Pain et baguette.* But let's not forget *le beurre.*" Her voice warbled upward in excitement as a flock of gulls flew past in delicate formation. "Look! V for—"

A piercing alarm sent them staggering to their feet. Thibaut stumbled toward Rosie at the railing. The ship lurched, flinging Julia against Gregory's side. They looked at each other...

Sub.

"*Now hear this! Now hear this!*" the PA broadcast blared. "*General quarters. All hands, man your battle stations! Troops to assigned lifeboat and raft posts.*"

This was it. Their turn.

They strapped on their yellow Mae Wests. Julia's fingers were slippery, out of her control. Their torpedo go bags were still under their beds.

"*General quarters. All troops to lifeboat positions.*"

The four of them took off toward their station, lifeboat seven, far in the stern. Bombarded by blasting alarms...crew commands...the shouts of scrambling GIs...whips of hot wind.

They'd always known it could happen. Either a bomb or torpedo. But part of her had resisted that thinking. Maybe her will would keep it away. She'd never wanted to be weak or helpless, never wanted to admit fear—if she climbed a tree, it would be to the highest limb. Now panic swept through her. She shut her mind and went numb. Ignoring the frantic bodies surrounding her, Julia struggled toward the stern.

One of the boys opened a path for her. "Ma'am."

She glanced about for her friends...Nowhere in sight. It was only the GIs and her, over ten years older than most of them. They were too young to die. But so was she. Still unwed, her book still unwritten— even her secret reports. Julia McWilliams had left no mark on the world. Was she to leave it alone, unremembered? While she'd liked being "in the know" in Washington, living safely at the edge of power, Julia had wanted to go into the field, live on the edge of danger...*not in it*. What had she signed up for?

Despite their frequent fourteen-minute drills—the time it took to load and lower a lifeboat—chaos reigned. Blood racing, she caught up with her group, huddled at the railing. The sea was flat and metallic. Ominous.

That enemy sub could be lurking anywhere.

The waters erupted in a churning wake. With lightning speed, a torpedo skimmed below the surface, zooming toward the *Mariposa* on a perfect trajectory to hit them broadside.

She pictured its nose piercing the hull, slicing through the hold, the sea rushing in. Everyone searching for friends, lifeboats. While she, alone, choked on salt water.

Her racing blood turned viscous and pooled in her belly. Nauseous, she curled inward until Jane's red fingernails dug into her wrist, snapping her upright.

Betty squeezed her other hand. "If you make it—and I...well...tell Alex I was thinking about him."

Her husband, a naval intelligence officer, was behind enemy lines in Burma, equally exposed. "You'll tell him," Julia murmured. If she died, who would miss her? Not as a naughty sister or stubborn daughter or amusing friend, but as a lover, one's own true heart. A foolish romantic thought, yet she longed for someone to long for, a face to see in her last moments.

"Captain's positioning the stern to take the main hit," Thibaut stated with military calm.

The stern. Them.

They stared, holding back time, as the ship continued its desperate maneuver to port. Slowly, so very slowly...

"Holy Mary, Mother of God..." a voice recited in prayer.

She and God spent little time together, so Julia asked only that her beloved Caro be spared a view from above. She closed her eyes.

It was worse not to know. She opened them.

Her breath caught: the churning monster was almost upon them.

Then it raced onward—past the *Mariposa's* stern.

They had avoided catastrophe by mere feet.

The torpedo disappeared.

Julia released her breath, taking in a deep taste of salt air. She felt ill, vertiginous. The sea blurred before her eyes. She blinked hard, her chest throbbing with trapped emotion.

The group remained rooted to the spot as their destroyers circled the sub's estimated position. Barrel-like objects fired from their decks, blasting up jets of white and black water.

"Depth charges," Thibaut explained amid an explosion of boisterous cheers and relieved laughter. He lifted Rosie in the air, planting a series of kisses on her face.

Gregory pulled Julia to him in a hug that ended with his lips scalding hers. She returned the kiss, avidly, relinquishing all control. Then she stepped back and reddened, feeling every eye upon her. Until she realized her kissing a married man was the least of their concerns.

That was what Julia had wanted, back then before the sea had exploded, to admire Gregory's mastery of Chinese...and English, his beautiful voice, his full expressive lips. Theirs had finally connected, but how little that mattered compared to the embrace of life itself. She couldn't take back their kiss, but there would not be another. He had a wife, and Julia had her dreams. And a mother watching over her.

"*Now hear this! Now hear this!*" crackled the loudspeaker. "*Passengers and troops return to your quarters. As you were.*"

Thibaut smiled, his left eye winking almost shut. "Cognac, anyone?"

———

After collecting and posting mail in Tasmania, the *Mariposa* proceeded around the belly of Australia, past sheer cliffs and rocky shores. Sharks cruised alongside, silent as subs. Then it was north through the peacock-blue Indian Ocean, alive with silvery fish that leaped high, mouths agape as if as curious about Julia as she was about them. There were more fearsome creatures of the deep—striped sea snakes, a stingray with an enormous wingspan and a sharp, serrated tail. The air sizzled and steamed as they crossed the equator into the Bay of Bengal. The Japanese owned these waters, but she tried not to think about it.

She did think of Harry Chandler, serving somewhere in the Pacific. Maybe he'd already come under attack. But while her group was heading for the "safety" of land, he was stationed in these dangerous seas. She relived the terror of the torpedo strike, her mouth shriveling in thirst.

For anyone trying to survive at sea, fresh water was key. Posted to a vital navy project last spring, Julia had conducted "fish-squeezing" research to see which contained the most drinkable liquid while State Department artist Jack Moore sketched the "winners" for training brochures. She'd also cooked up a shark repellent combining copper acetate and black dye to produce a water-soluble disk that smelled like dead shark when released by a downed pilot. After she was back at the OSS, the navy added her "shark-chaser cakes" to its survival kits. Jack had also shipped out to India. She hoped he'd made it. It was too soon to know about any of them.

———

To celebrate their last weekend at sea, Julia organized a production of *Broadway on the Pacific*. Wearing oversize navy whites, her cabin-mates, including Dr. Cora, led off with "Yankee Doodle Dandy" as

Julia accompanied them on the old Steinway. For the finale, they all belted out "God Bless America." Her voice caught in her throat, but they carried it off without her. Hers was not the only sob in the house.

During the rousing applause, Captain Marks climbed onstage. "Due to political instability in Eastern India, the *Mariposa* will bypass Calcutta. I regret to inform you your voyage will be extended for several days as we sail up India's west coast—to Bombay."

The men's groans were deafening: another week at sea.

The Japanese invasion of Eastern India was threatening Delhi. Julia's heart went cold as she visualized those advancing front lines.

SEVEN

Bombay, India
April 1944

India hit her like a slap—a very wet one.

Julia's hair retreated in tight, wiry curls as the OSS team crowded onto the main deck's bow, ready to kiss the earth after thirty-one days aboard the *Mariposa*. Their ardor was met by a crushing humidity that cooked up a foul-sweet smell of rotting fruit, smoke, and diesel fuel. Orange marigolds floated on the dark waters, iridescent and slick with oil. The light was blinding.

This morning—probably every morning—Bombay Harbor was a chaotic place, a heaving mass of military and cargo ships with a hodge-podge of smaller vessels. Surrounded by screeching, swooping gulls, men in sarongs and white skirt-pants hawked pineapple and mango chunks from tiny rowboats. The raucous turmoil exhilarated Julia.

For a moment she felt like her forebears might have, assembled on the deck of the *Mayflower* after ten grievous weeks at sea: grateful and awestruck at the sight of that pristine New World. She now beheld a very Old World, with its own wonder, its own promise—but far from pristine. Then she paused; this place, too, might have once been unspoiled—a tropical paradise? She'd read of invasion after invasion into India, just as even the most well-meaning white men had invaded America. While she might grasp the ambiguities of history, changing its flow was beyond her power. Julia, for one, was ready to swim to shore.

"We made it," she exclaimed. "Over the Rainbow."

"And at Eastertime." As Rosie mustered a smile, Julia's heart opened to her, knowing she was thinking of happier holidays, her parents' uncertain fate in occupied China.

"Albeit without all the frills upon it." Jane cocked her smart pith hat.

The *Mariposa* nosed toward Victoria Docks, where bare-chested workers were loading elephants with crates and bulging burlap sacks. Victorian spires rose behind wood-planked terraces swarming with uniformed figures.

Julia glanced at the simmering yellow ball overhead. She'd thought she could take the heat, but this was something else. A dullness settled over her body; her brain was melting. She tossed her head and blinked several times. "I could certainly use a cool gin and tonic."

"Or a nicely chilled rosé," Thibaut suggested. "No need for boiled-water ice."

She laughed, recalling all the dietary warnings they'd received. "I propose we be careful, but not too careful. Besides, I've heard those spices kill off the germs."

"Good girl." Jane hooked arms. "I need a brave dining companion. Starting at lunch."

Julia winked at her. There was no one more fun than Janie when she dropped her snooty attitude. "Betty and Rosie are as brave as they come. Girls?"

"I'm ravenous," Betty said.

"Me, too." Rosie turned to Thibaut. "Never fear, I'll save room for tonight."

He gave her a scorching look. "For the occasion, I will buy you a dress."

"How do you know my size?" she flirted.

"I can estimate—but in case, I'll go one size smaller."

Jane mimed fanning herself. "In this heat, I'd advise you to go one larger."

"The monsoons will cool things down…in a month or so." Dr. Cora, who'd become Cora by now, raked her fingers through short gray-streaked black hair. "Fortunately, India has excellent weavers who produce fine cotton, linen, muslin, and voile. We'll find tailors at the markets, too. Maybe grab some food. Although that's between us—street food is verboten."

"I need to do field research in that regard." Gregory looked at Julia. "Join me later?"

She still didn't quite trust herself to be alone with him at night. "Sounds tempting," she replied, meeting his eye. "But I'll probably still be sleeping off lunch."

He gave her a keen nod. "I expect you'll be sampling street food before too long, Miss McWilliams—with me or on your own. The world is divided into those who hate India and those who love it. Knowing your bold spirit, I have little doubt into which category you'll fall."

"Why, that's one of the nicest things anyone ever said to me, Dr. Bates." Julia felt as if she'd been invited into an exclusive club. Growing up, she was always the one to lead the escapades. A favorite prank involved dropping mud pies from her neighbor's garage roof. It was a hoot…until a humorless businessman had chased her across the field, caught her by the collar, and dragged her home. Pop had viewed Julia's boldness as worrisome. Now it had been commended by a brilliant world traveler who recognized her appetite for experience.

Not all their GI shipmates were as broad-minded. Descending the gangplank, she heard complaints—*The smells! The filth! The half naked men! Animals wandering everywhere!*—but none, Julia noted with pride, from the OSS team, who marched eagerly forward.

Awaiting the group on the dock, the quartermaster, Sergeant Galvin, threw a fit over having to find "*female* housing." While the men were transported elsewhere, the nine OSS women sheltered under an immense tree with hanging roots—a banyan, Cora informed them. As they fanned themselves with banana leaves acquired from an enterprising young boy, the sergeant reappeared at the wheel of a large jeep. British right-hand drive, Julia noted as the steamy tropics rushed through the open windows. The air was liquid, and she was soon immersed in a polyphony of rhythmic languages merging in and out of a riot of sounds, a dazzle of color.

Two blocks later, they reached their bungalow—white walls, cool tile, and finely crafted dark furniture. As Cora claimed seniority for the first bath, Peggy, Ellie, and the twins threw off their damp, dirty clothing and started their laundry. Julia found the idea of calm repose terribly appealing, but so was that of enjoying a lunch not intended for three thousand troops.

Leading the way outside, Jane hailed a *tonga* cart, its driver attired in an elaborate pink turban and a plaid swimming pool–blue sarong. The blue dissolved into sweat dripping into Julia's eyes. *Wouldn't a little dip be lovely now?* How tempting the sea had been during those halcyon Indian Ocean days; how she'd yearned to immerse herself in its warm turquoise waters.

The driver clucked to his horse, who flicked his tail and set forth, creating the barest breeze, which fell upon her skin like a kiss. Her nose led the way, taking in indescribable odors. Women cooked on the roadside, using fuel patties that sent off a sweet fecal scent mixed with spices and dust. Others wove garlands of lotus flowers and pungent tuberose. There were cows everywhere, ambling about or reclining in the streets, living the life of Riley. Their droppings were everywhere, too.

The monkeys ruled the trees. She saw one smirking fellow swoop a glittery bangle from a cart. The vendor hollered, but the thief had slipped into the branches, reemerging above a mound of bananas. He leaned forward, preparing to strike. Despite the oppressive heat, Bombay pulsed with life. All kinds.

A baby tucked in her arm, a mother approached with beseeching eyes, gesturing to her mouth with a stunted, curled-up fist. Shocked with pity, Julia handed her a wad of newly issued rupees. Their driver shook his finger at her. Too late. Other beggars rushed them, including a little one-legged boy. She gasped. With a warning shout, the driver loosened his reins. They bolted forward, launching her back against the cracked leather seat.

Betty's hand flew to her heart. "It's hard to take," she said, shaking her head wanly. "We can only hope our efforts will benefit the Indian people."

"More than the *colonial* powers," added Jane. "In the interest of research, let's see how the ruling class lives."

As they rolled down the palm-lined coast, the same Arabian Sea that had delivered them to Bombay, Julia couldn't shake the image of the mother, the one-legged boy. She glanced at Rosie, who was unusually quiet.

"You never get used to it," Rosie said with a pained expression.

A gigantic arched monument rose from the waterfront. "Gateway of India," their driver told them. "Very big."

Across the way was the sprawling red-domed Taj Mahal Palace Hotel, its own sort of palace, worlds away from the beggars and even their scrawny driver. After vastly overtipping him, Julia followed her friends to the colonnaded entrance, overseen by a tall turbanned doorman who looked like a prince in his stunning white uniform.

They entered the lobby to the caress of ceiling fans. She tried not to gawk at the parade of nationalities, the military uniforms and Western suits, the richly attired Indian men and women. At the restaurant, the girls relaxed into orange silk cushions while four regal musicians sat cross-legged in a carpeted corner, producing hypnotic sounds from curious yet rather magnificent instruments. Renewed by tall glasses of thick mango juice, they ordered chicken curry "not spicy."

Famished, Julia dug right in…

Once her coughing fit subsided, she raised a glass of Lion beer, eyes glazed with tears. "To India. And the *Mariposa*. And my language teachers. *Xie-xie*," she thanked Rosie, then patted her flushed cheeks. "*Hóngsè. Red*, in Mandarin," Julia translated proudly.

"*Rouge*," Jane said. "And *brava*. I tried Mandarin once, but it got the better of me. One of the few things that ever has." She tore off the end of some hot grilled flatbread, glistening with butter. "Taste this. *Naan*."

"Oh my." Julia took another bite. "Positively *swoon*-worthy." She ripped off a larger piece and dipped it in the curry. Her eyes burned. Her taste buds saluted. *More*, she wanted more—of everything. "I grew up on meat and potatoes, never much cared what I ate. At home we had a cook; then it was dorm food, so it wasn't till New York that I learned to…" She smiled. "Well, master a can opener." She surveyed their table laden with enticing little dishes. "Manhattan was like this in the beginning. So much to sample. The world sparkled. And I was a writer."

"Ad copy?" Jane scoffed. "For a furniture store?"

"*Jane.*" Betty sent her a sharp look.

Julia couldn't disagree. But it had been the best job she could find. The *New Yorker* had turned her down. After all her dreams of destiny, she'd even failed her typing test at *Newsweek*. Honestly, she felt she'd failed New York, as if it were an advanced class simply over her head. That sense of failure had clung to her—until Donovan had plucked her from the clerical pool.

Rosie tucked her chin. "We all have to start somewhere."

"Like Nob Hill," Julia snapped.

"True, but I was a born artist." Jane had not a drop of false modesty. "My parents boasted my first finger painting looked like a late Monet water lily."

"No doubt." Julia regarded her friend, small yet powerful, sassy yet by no means cute. Jane was stylish and droll, with a self-assured presence Julia found both annoying and admirable.

Betty poured more beer. "To South East Asia Command. SEAC."

Jane lifted her glass. "A.k.a., Save England's Asian Colonies."

"The Brits are our closest allies," Betty scolded. "We need to work *with* them."

While usually siding with her, Julia knew Donovan—and President Roosevelt—shared Jane's cynical assessment of British intentions. On which she was to report, i.e., *spy*. She smiled serenely. If Jane only knew about her secret life. Maybe she would, later. Or maybe Julia would always hug the truth close, till the end of her days.

They lingered over their meal, savoring their comfort. So, upon leaving the hotel, they were unprepared for the sun's brutal assault. Dazed, they waited as the princely doorman hailed the women a taxi. Moisture enveloped them.

———

The anarchic journey across town left the friends gasping and laughing and pained deep in their hearts. While glad not to be spending all their days cloistered in the Taj Hotel, Julia found it soothing to cross the veranda and step back inside their cool, dim bungalow.

"It's too quiet here," Betty cracked.

"Don't be fooled." She regarded their former cabinmates—even the cerebral twin cryptologists, Caryl and Cheryl—clad in embroidered tunics and loose trousers, drinking gin and tonics, painting finger- and toenails around a low carved table. Ebony and ivory beads spilled from inlaid boxes strewn about the table, along with gleaming glass bangles and silver jewels. An emerald hung in the middle of Peggy Wheeler's freckled forehead. Orange and indigo scarves rippled under the ceiling fan. *India*. "We may have stumbled into a pirates' den."

"Consider it the spoils of my Intro to Bargaining," said Cora, whose round horn-rims gave her an owlish look. "They've all passed with flying colors."

Jane picked up a woven silver belt. "I'll say—"

The front windows blew in with an explosive rush of heat and light. Ear-shattering sound.

Dodging vicious slivers of glass, they dove to the floor, drinks spilling onto an OSS field manual, *This Is No Picnic*. Her insides rattling, Julia willed herself to calm. Perhaps she'd been expecting this ever since learning of the Japanese invasion. She lifted her head to survey her huddled companions. "Everyone okay?" A thumbs-up from Rosie. A nod from Cora.

But beyond these glittery, splintered window frames, red licks of fire shot through the swirling blackness. Sirens pierced the late-afternoon air. Dogs howled.

Another thunderous roar reverberated through Julia, flattened on cold tile…The explosion kept repeating, in flashing color. Smoke curled inside the bungalow, carrying a stomach-turning smell of burning rubber and oil. She attempted to identify all the noises. *Where are the bombers?*

"Bastards." Jane glared at the heavens—then at the "Old Rose" nail enamel streaming over the scarves. She scooped up the Cutex bottle, furiously screwing on the top.

"Get back down," Julia ordered. She gathered herself tightly. Unable to bear the helpless waiting, she scrambled to her feet and ducked to the door. Scarlet flames twisted through the darkness. Fire and water trucks raced toward the harbor, sirens shrilling, horns beeping. Police vehicles sped in the same direction, trailed by people on foot and bicycle riders bearing buckets and blankets. Others were fleeing the disaster in raw terror.

As the sky turned milky white, a horse cart clip-clopped toward Julia, its passenger weeping over a pile of shrouded bodies. There was a moment of eerie silence. A cowbell rang out. Then a cow stumbled past, its eyes wide in panic.

With a mad roar, the earth shook. *Again*. The veranda shuddered underfoot.

A bright-red firestorm erupted into the roiling sky. Any change of wind could send the blaze charging their way. A blast of heat hit Julia's cheek.

Suddenly, she turned cold as a high-pitched wail bore through her. Sprawled across the road was a figure clad in coral and pink. A cracked tree limb was lodged against the girl's chest. Her hand twitched. As Julia raced down the steps, a man in an ash-streaked tunic tugged the heavy branch away. His lips moving, maybe in prayer, he knelt beside the child. She cried again, then went still. He placed his palms together and bowed over her body.

Lost in the man's grief, Julia started at what felt like sharp, hot needles falling on her.

"Your shoulder!" Betty called from the porch. "Get in here. You're bleeding."

She ducked, dodging the shooting rubble. *Thunk*. A flying object thudded against her left calf, bouncing onto the dirt. Searing pain radiated around her lower leg. Wincing, she reached for the glinting projectile—the size of a Hershey bar—and recoiled from the heat. With a banana leaf, she brushed off the soot, then picked it up. *Gold.*

Betty yanked her inside and propped her against a chair. She examined Julia's upper arm, dark crosshatches blooming with blood.

Rosie spit on a handkerchief and cleaned her wound. "I don't see any shards." She frowned at Julia's singed calf, which was turning purple and black. "This is nasty. Whatever hit you?"

She opened the leaf. "Oh my." The bar was stamped *Suisse 1 Kilo Fine Gold 999.9.*

"I'll be darned," Betty said. "You struck gold—or rather, gold struck you."

Jane stared. "Remember in the harbor…your quip about landing 'Over the Rainbow'? Maybe we did."

Rosie looked grim. "This would be the first attack on Bombay."

"Sabotage?" whispered the general's daughter, Peggy.

Shaken, Julia regarded the gold bar, the foul breath of war on her face. In the past month, she'd faced death at sea and land, forced finally to confront her own fragility. It was not her way to crumble until the worst was over—but there in the war zone, would it ever be over? She peered out through shattered glass. "Or could it be *cargo*—propelled over two blocks?"

Betty studied the bar. "Our government ships gold to the Chinese Nationalists to supplement their dubious currency, which *we* print."

"Grandfather Weston used to print Chinese money." She recalled Mother Caro showing her around his Massachusetts paper company.

Clutching some documents, Sergeant Galvin rushed up the walkway. His face was grimy and sweat-streaked, his uniform splotched with dirt.

She and Betty dashed outside. "What happened?"

"The whole damn harbor exploded. A four-thousand-ton ship *disappeared*—the SS *Fort Stikine.* Everything in the vicinity burned to the ground. Military warehouses, water mains, power stations. Homes…" He stared, dazed, as if surprised to see the women. "All gone."

Julia could barely conceive the power of such an explosion. "The *Mariposa*?"

"It had already embarked for Karachi."

Her shoulders slumped in relief. "We didn't hear any planes."

"It was not the enemy." Galvin looked through her, eyes blustery. "It was *us*. An Allied ship, transporting cotton, grains, oil drums, and ammunition—"

"Such flammable cargo?" Betty exclaimed, horrified.

"With TNT in the mix! Which led to ten more vessels going up in the second blast. Others left as hulks. Eighteen fire engines and their crews sent to kingdom come. The harbor clock tower froze at six minutes past four."

They fell silent in horror. Julia's leg began to throb.

Galvin thrust some papers at them. "You must surely be VIPs. You leave this hellhole 0600 tomorrow, bound for the island paradise of Ceylon—some town called Kandy, wherever the hell that is. Sorry, ladies."

What's going on? Julia's mind couldn't work quickly enough. Far from the center of knowledge and power she'd occupied in Washington, she felt utterly destabilized, her preparations and research useless. Where was Donovan in all this—and Mountbatten? She conjured up a mental map: a small island in the Indian Ocean, Ceylon hugged India's southeast coast, quite some distance from the major cities in the north. "Our unit is attached to South East Asia Command in *Delhi*. Has SEAC also been transferred to this 'Kandy'?"

"Above my pay grade. Word is, a whole slew of SEAC brass—Brits and Yanks—headed down there last month." He glanced at the other orders. "But Saint Phalle, Bateson, and Miss Frame are still off to Delhi. I'd say you and your Ceylon-bound group are the lucky ones."

Why was their OSS team being separated? The twenty of them had developed a deep bond during their dramatic Pacific passage. She'd become especially close with her morning language group—Rosie, Gregory, and Thibaut. Now she would be continuing without them.

As the darkness deepened, insects swarmed the porch light. Their buzzing made Julia's skin crawl. She thought of the *Mariposa* being rerouted from eastern Calcutta all the way around the huge Indian subcontinent to Bombay in the west. Japanese forces had invaded the northeast. Was India's heartland next—Delhi?

Her multilingual friends might be needed to help coordinate a possible defense. But a large high-level contingent had been sent to Ceylon. Did that include Mountbatten? Or was this the end of her secret assignment?

Julia stared at the dark patch of earth where the girl had been struck down. "Excuse me a moment." She limped up the steps, then returned with the gold bar.

"What the—? Where did this come from?" Galvin examined it.

"We think it might be China-bound cargo, blasted our way," Betty replied.

"We'd like to donate it to Bombay relief efforts." Julia recalled the globe in Donovan's office. Even then, India had been only a spin away. The war had connected them all.

Tears prickled behind her eyes as Galvin walked off. She hugged Betty. They stood there a moment, surrounded by smoke and despair.

Then Betty patted her cheek. "Remember what your mama used to say."

"*Carpe diem.* Seize the day." Julia tried to smile.

EIGHT

Victoria Railway Station, Bombay

Even at daybreak, it was stifling hot. Julia pushed open the carriage window, letting in the rosy glow of dawn—and waves of smoke and dust as the train chugged off. In yesterday's explosion, seventy-five freight cars had been tossed into the heavens, smashed to smithereens, but Victoria Station—another grand edifice of towers, spires, and archways—had survived. Men and matériel could continue to flow through the land's intricate railway system. The defense of India could continue.

Jane slammed the window shut, coughing dramatically. "My hair has barely recovered from the seawater. Now this grit."

"A little dirt is better than suffocating," Betty snapped.

As if Jane was the only one with hair problems. Julia's felt like hay, and she'd been avoiding mirrors. She planned to lie low during this leg of the journey, catch up on her correspondence. After pulling out her little Royal, she rolled in a sheet of rough brown-flecked paper from the bazaar—rice paper! *D-e-a-r*...The keys left an uneven imprint; as the granddaughter of a paper manufacturer, she appreciated its home-made charm—but would Pop? Before reporting for duty at Long Beach Harbor, she'd spent a few days of home leave. Over dinners and golf, she had attempted to describe her OSS life. If her father couldn't envision why she'd left Pasadena for Washington, he was stupefied by her desire to come to *India*. If she *had* to go somewhere, why not London, where at least they had the good sense to speak English?

Now Julia had been ordered to an even more remote spot—Ceylon, which barely showed up on any map. *Where?* Pop would demand, aghast.

With her own uncertainties, she'd have to curate her news with care. She wouldn't mention the Bombay explosion for fear of his response. *What did you expect?* He'd had no sympathy when the women's military units rejected her—war was no place for a woman. What could she recount? Torpedoes at sea? India being invaded? Their abrupt change of orders? Her ambition to be a spy and live to write about it?

She stared out at the awakening day. India was already hard at work, the roads clogged with soldiers, trucks, bicycles, and bullock carts. Temples and shrines for multiarmed elephant gods and sinuous goddesses lined the way, along with straw-covered huts, village food stalls, and half naked men tilling a patchwork of fields.

The flat, dusty landscape was broken up by brilliant, even outlandish, shots of color—that was something to describe. Stately women bearing jugs on their heads. And the saris! How they would delight her little sister, Dort, a theater aficionado. The poorest woman laborer dressed as if for a ball. She squinted at an animal with cow's horns and a curving horse's belly. What kind of creatures did they breed in India? Her father might find that a distasteful detail. She watched a man urging a lethargic camel on with a stick. She wondered if her brother, John III, presumably still undercover somewhere in France, would have preferred the vast open North African desert. This terrain must be similar. But where were all the jungles?

She might write Pop about the food. Flavors that had awoken her taste buds, banishing memories of roast beef, even Caro's New England cod balls. Then Julia was ashamed. She loved Mother's cod balls... although her round baking powder biscuits were vastly outshone by India's rustic flat naan, charred and shimmering with butter! If she wrote about this marvelous food, Pop might see her as being disloyal to their family traditions. She would tell him it was different but okay.

Across the compartment, Betty was watching the world go by. Jane was scribbling away. Neither seemed worried about reshaping their experience for someone else. Why did she have to defer to Pop to keep the peace? Julia admired her handsome, upright father, a business and civic leader, but wished to forge her own path. She liked the mystery of hope, anticipating all there was before her.

After laboring over her letters, she welcomed the next stop. The station was hot, murky, and chaotic, teeming with troops, beggars, saffron-robed holy men, families lugging burlap parcels and live chickens. Departing passengers squeezed past new arrivals. Hawkers moved along the cars with goatskin water carriers. Turbaned *chaiwalas* passed tin cups of hot milk-tea through carriage windows; newspaper-wrapped food packets and rupees changed hands. She couldn't be farther from Pasadena. This was life!

Eager to explore, Julia boarded the next car. The air was humid and pungent. People sat on benches or the floor or stood between rows, which made her compartment seem airy. Everyone shared rice balls, dates, fried snacks. Whomever wasn't eating was talking. Indians were an enthusiastic bunch, she observed as she walked down the aisle, the object of curious eyes.

"Memsahib, you are so high," said a small woman in turquoise, her wispy white hair knotted in back. Seated with three generations of family, she offered some roasted cashews.

"Thank you," Julia said, glad it was nothing uncooked. How could she be rude to such gracious people?

"You are ever wearing sari?" the elderly woman asked in a singsong accent.

Impossible to imagine, so she only replied, "Yours is lovely."

Toot-toot. As a child tugged her trousers, there was another warning whistle. Julia opened the door into the connecting passageway. A uniformed dark-skinned man removed his cap. "Madam."

With a polite nod, she glanced into her car. Seeing no worried faces, she remained as the train set off. A smoky but pleasant breeze seeped in. Schoolchildren in tidy white shirts and navy pinafores or shorts held hands along the roadway.

Trim, with a small pooch on his belly, the man inquired, "You are coming from?"

"California."

"Ah. Cah-li-for-nia. I have met a few Americans, soldiers and officials. Never a woman."

"I'm a clerk with the US government."

"A *clark*," he pronounced. "You are educated woman."

"I did go to college," Julia replied, "but find I've learned much more since leaving."

"The School of Life," he said airily. "I am employed by government of India. So we have something in common."

"What is your profession, if I might ask?"

"I am a port and customs policeman in Colombo, Ceylon." He stood taller.

Ceylon. She marveled at the serendipity of their chat. "We will be traveling there by ferry. How have you fared during the war?"

"They bombed British bases in early days, now leaving us in peace. Why, exactly, we do not know. Perhaps because we are under protection of the Buddha. His holy relic resides at Temple of the Sacred Tooth in ancient kingdom of Kandy. Once a year it is paraded through city so people may give it honor."

Her mysterious destination. "You are fortunate. What is Kandy like?"

"Beautiful hill station. Cooler than Colombo. Slower and smaller. Except during Festival of the Tooth, then very sprightly." He frowned. "We pray your new Allied bases will not draw enemy fire."

"So do I. Are you Buddhist?"

He dipped his head and placed his palms together, fingertips pointing beneath his chin. "But also modern man. I am educating my twelve-year-old daughter. For future."

She regarded him closely. "What do you see in the future?"

"Japan will be defeated. And British will go home."

"Do you not like the British?"

He waggled his head sideways—*yes, no.* "While they have given us some things—you see we are conversing in their language, riding their train—they have taken much more. The days of the white plantation raj are over."

The interconnecting door slid open. The picture of outrage, Jane stepped into the swaying passageway. "Where have you been? We feared you'd been left behind." Seeing the policeman, she pressed her palms together. He returned the gesture to them both, then entered the other car.

Following Jane down the aisle, Julia had much to consider. She'd been raised to think there was a certain order of things. Although Donovan had asked her to spy on their British allies, they were still the "cousins." They shared a language and culture. Even the European history she'd studied emphasized the English experience. In their era, the sun never set on the British Empire. India was but a colony, Burma the setting for a Kipling poem, Ceylon unmentioned.

Betty greeted her with a frown. "We were worried about you!"

"I went to explore the next car. An old lady told me I was tall. Then I spoke with a policeman from Ceylon. I learned Kandy was an ancient kingdom—in the hills and cooler than Colombo. It has a temple with Buddha's tooth. He thinks it might protect us."

Jane smiled slyly. "You're off to a good start, already collecting intelligence."

Julia grinned back, pleased with her expedition. "Maybe I have the gift."

PART TWO

The Shangri-La War

NINE

—— // ——

Colombo, Ceylon
April 1944

On their rusty ferry from the mainland to Ceylon, Julia looked in vain
for the harbor policeman and was still hoping to find him when it
docked at Colombo, the island's sultry capital, ten degrees from the
equator. His absence somehow disturbed her, but she sensed this was
how it would be—the tides of war flinging people together, then apart.
It was the goal, though, wasn't it? For everyone to return to the lives
they'd known before? That gave her pause. *Where would I go? Pasadena?*

Under the boiling sun, a troop carrier jeep delivered the eight OSS
women south along a dazzling curve of coast to the posh Hotel Galle.
By late afternoon, while Jane caught up on her beauty sleep, Julia and
Betty were sinking their toes in white sand, succumbing to the balmy
breezes, swaying coconut palms, and sparkling turquoise vista. As Betty
relaxed, Julia finally immersed herself in the warm, clear water, bathing
off the dust and sweat and fear. She bobbed along, observing the coral
and brilliantly colored fish. Joining them, mindless with joy. All was
utter calm, no rough currents to spin her upside down.

Suddenly, the sea darkened, the sky. Gazing back, she saw a little
figure waving her arms frantically—Betty, shadowed in dusk.

Julia swam hard for shore, her muscles achingly alive. She stood and
strode the last few paces through the sucking surf. Hands on hips, Betty
waited, ankle-deep. Mad.

"Julia! Do you ever consider anyone but yourself? You were *way* out there. We both grew up around the Pacific! Whatever were you thinking?"

"I'm a strong swimmer. It was so peaceful—and not *that* far. Don't worry about me."

"In unfamiliar waters? I do." She swatted some gnats with a towel, shoved it at her.

Her anger surprised Julia. The movement had felt delicious, the sense of space. The solitude. But Betty's concern felt good, too. "I'm sorry. That was selfish. It's been a long time since anyone worried about me. No one ever sees me as weak."

"I don't see you as weak, Julie, but—well, we've been through a lot. And we don't know this area." She sighed. "A local fisherman just warned me about swimming at dusk. 'Very danger. Demons coming out now.'"

Abashed, Julia squeezed her hand. "Thank you for taking care of me."

"I'm only thinking of the mission," Betty said, straight-faced. "If anything happened to you, who would deal with all the paperwork?"

Although it was her nature to charge into the fray, Julia knew her friend was right. In unknown territory, caution was required.

———

"Girls!" Attired in beaded white, Jane greeted them. "You need to shake out your evening wear. And, Julia, do something with your hair."

They were soon showering themselves with champagne at the gala welcome soiree held on the hotel terrace. As a peppy combo of elderly Sinhalese musicians swung like nobody's business, Julia felt ready to scintillate, a new woman.

"You gals are looking sharp." It was that nice OSS cartographer from the ship, the one who'd been dwarfed, in every way, by Gregory. But he did have a darling Texas drawl. "Got your orders yet?"

"Kandy. What they call a hill station. Cooler, I hear. What about you?"

"I'm chucking my cowboy boots. They've attached me to a Colombo base on the coast." He shrugged happily. "Seems another Maps unit got to Kandy first—with Mountbatten's group."

Mountbatten. Julia broke into a big grin. "Well, I'll be." She was still in business!

"Say, how about a spin around this shiny dance floor? I promise not to step on your feet."

She was still smiling. "Let's give your old boots something to remember."

After a swell time with "Begin the Beguine," Julia excused herself to catch a breath of air at the marble balustrade. How grand if Jack Moore were part of the transferred Maps unit.

Gazing down at the beach, she spotted a figure in beaded white moving hand in hand with a lean, dark-haired fellow through the glimmering surf. *Jane.*

"That girl never wastes a moment," observed Betty, joining her with two icy G and Ts.

"You can say that again." Julia raised a palm. "But don't!"

Then Peggy appeared, her freckles popping out of pink cheeks. "Girls! We discovered the appetizers." She nodded toward a side gallery, where Ellie waved a piece of crispy prawn. Cora was there, too, and the twins. "If you're interested."

"Need you ask? I think my last bite was half a soggy cheese sandwich on the ferry."

"It's too hot to dance anyway," Betty said, striding forward.

Julia studied the buffet. "Oh my, this looks positively yummy." She picked up a stick with chunks of grilled chicken and a glass of limeade, salty sweet. Suddenly ravenous, they set themselves up at a little cocktail table and sampled breaded pieces of meltingly tender whitefish, delicately spiced potato triangles, peppery rice cakes, and other dishes they had no name for.

The women ate their fill and were suddenly weary. Which was a good thing, when they learned that supper would not be served till midnight. However, their bed tea arrived promptly at 4:00 a.m., which was about when Jane tiptoed in.

———

In the sticky dawn, they boarded a little blue train heading uphill under a plume of steam. The fields, tilled by sinewy, sarong-clad men, were interspersed with lively village bazaars. Then they ascended jagged mountains, serenaded by screeching monkeys and the caws of extravagantly colored birds. Giant tree ferns and shiny leaves as big as dinner plates reached inside their open windows. Wild elephants raised their trunks and trumpeted at them. *The jungle!*

"Shiva walked here," Jane informed Julia. "Others believe it was the Buddha."

"The hotel brochure says it was Adam and Eve. After they left Paradise." Julia had to agree with Sergeant Galvin—the island of Ceylon was some kind of paradise. The up-country air was moist and languid; the generous greenery bathed her eyes.

Leaving Ceylon's spectacular highlands, the "Toy Train" descended into a broad cultivated valley. At Kandy station, a stocky Bostonian GI met them in another open-sided troop carrier with facing benches. The air was fragrant. Traffic moved at a relaxed pace with as many rickshaws, bullock carts, and bicycles as motor vehicles. Long-skirted men and women carried folded umbrellas among baskets of produce and rice. Kandy Lake sparkled in the middle of it all.

From Boston Joe, they learned that US and British male officers were billeted at Hotel Suisse on the hilly far shore, while the women were quartered at Queen's Hotel, a sprawling Victorian wedding cake across a bustling lane from the lake. He pulled up under its high portico. "See you tomorrow at 0800."

Military time, Julia noted. *We're in the army now.*

The lobby was warm, its bronze ceiling fans revolving at full speed. Uniformed women moved smartly across the white marble floors, to and from the red-carpeted stairs or through the archway into a small restaurant with white columns and French windows to the street. On the other side of the stairs, an older man in a beige shirt and trousers was polishing the grille on the little mahogany-framed elevator. The front desk on their right was a similar dark wood, as were all the moldings and furnishings.

Vintage Raj colonial, as Julia might have described one of the red-upholstered ebony sofas in a W. & J. Sloane's ad.

She and Betty were ensconced in a third-floor turret—which overlooked the Temple of the Tooth! Even at dusk, a stream of white-garbed figures filed inside the white complex, white flowers gleaming, candles flickering as each worshipper paused at a trough-like stand to light one more.

Once they had bathed, and their clothing was settled in the hulking armoire, Julia pulled out a blue linen dress and white mesh shoes with tan wing tips she'd snapped up at I. Magnin's during home leave. Feeling spiffy, she sat on the pink chintz club chair—and sank to the bottom. The two dissolved into exhausted laughter.

"Cocktail hour." Jane burst in with her roomie, Peggy.

"First, I have some news, girls," Peggy said. "I don't talk much about my father because I want to make it on my own here. But I hadn't heard from him in a while and was worried. *Well.* A message was waiting in my hotel mailbox. While we were on the move, he was, too—transferred from North India, the new US military liaison to Mountbatten!"

Julia blinked. "That is some news. And to think, we knew you when." She felt in a precarious place. Unwilling to abuse her friendship with Peggy, she'd have to tread warily.

Decorated with more white walls and dark arches, Queen's mirrored mahogany bar opened to the garden. Its period atmosphere was enhanced by displays of maps and regimental silver, the vague scent of mildew. Yet half the officers were women. This was a twentieth-century war.

After claiming the last table, they ordered gin and tonics and toasted their arrival. Julia raised hers again, thinking of Rosie, Thibaut, and Gregory. "To our good friends in Delhi."

"Hear! Hear!" Jane clinked. "May they find a reliable source of boiled-water ice cubes."

Amid the tinkle of glasses, Julia was taken back to her first G and

T. In the fall of freshman year at Smith, she'd discovered the local Northampton speakeasy. Feeling terribly sophisticated, she'd prevailed upon her roommate to join her. Never in two million years would she have imagined enjoying a long, cool one on the teardrop island of Ceylon—which she could hardly have found on a map at the time. It had been cold that night in South Hadley, Massachusetts, and the ice had jangled a nerve in her tooth.

But Kandy was hot, and she hugged the ice in her mouth until it dissolved. A moment ago, during the Great Depression, she'd entered college; now she was an OSS intelligence officer during this century's second Great War. She had survived two near-death encounters; possibly the next would claim her. For the first time in her charmed existence, she'd tasted fear and knew nothing could be taken for granted anymore.

Around her, the girls chattered away. Mother Caro had longed to travel to foreign lands, but Pop wouldn't hear of it. Still, she'd raised two independent daughters—and inspired them with her free-spirited ways. After Julia was jilted and brokenhearted in New York, Caro had promised her the right man would come at the right time.

For now, it was the waiter—with another long, cold drink.

Betty regarded her closely. "What's on your mind, Julie?"

"I was thinking about fate…the lives we might have led. Instead, doors opened that none of us would have ever walked through. Maybe the opening was only a crack, the men all gone, and we slipped inside… But now we're here, and I plan to keep walking. Wherever it takes me."

She gazed into the wall of trees, their great interlocking branches. Hanging from every one were hundreds of shroud-like objects. With an explosion of movement, the pointy-nosed bats came to life.

"Flying foxes," Jane informed them.

Unfurling their massive black wings like Count Dracula, they beat them against the darkening sky with high-pitched squeals that made Julia cringe as she had when that long-ago Massachusetts ice cube struck a nerve in her tooth.

"I know what you mean," Betty said. "Becoming a foreign correspondent had seemed the pinnacle of ambition."

Julia recalled her failed literary dreams in Manhattan. "Now here we are in action—"

"In the last bastion of Empire." Jane indicated the largely British crowd. She fluttered her fingers at the reflection of a striking uniformed officer surrounded by several attentive men at the bar. The raven-haired woman returned a small red-lipped smile. "Lieutenant Clarity Hastings of the Women's Royal Naval Service—WRENS."

Peggy glanced at the stylish woman in the long mirror. "We met her at the front desk when she swanned by to collect her mail. Upon learning of my dad's connection to Mountbatten, Clarity informed me she's on his personal staff—'the Supremo,' she called him. Over tea, she gave us the lay of the land."

The Supremo. "Busy little bees, aren't you? Nosing about the flowers."

Jane winked. "There'll be no shortage of flowers. South East Asia Command is headquartered in the Royal Botanic Gardens."

"Sounds pleasant." This was a different kind of war than Julia had expected.

Peggy shook her head. "OSS is based in a nearby tea estate. We'll see it tomorrow."

"Scuttlebutt I picked up last night at Hotel Galle is there's some rivalry between US and British clandestine services." Jane zipped her lips.

Donovan would not like his people gossiping about their allies—that, Julia knew. While the truth might emerge eventually, she felt obligated not to fan the flames. "Whoever fed you that line obviously had too much to drink." She glanced at her glass. "Speaking of which, I could use a refill."

"Me, too." Jane raised her hand for the waiter, surveying the attractive men. "A pity you're married, Betty."

"If you knew Alex, you wouldn't say that," she replied coolly.

Jane smiled. "Well, Julia might get lucky."

She regarded Jane narrowly. Sometimes she wanted to smack that girl.

As a fragrant breeze wafted through the open doors—moist but pleasant, skin warm—a couple splashed around the swimming pool, tossing a ball and laughing. Betty's husband was eating roots and boiling water in the Burmese jungles while they were drinking cool gin and tonics, cosseted in colonial luxury.

But Julia had her own intelligence to pursue. Intel that might inform the decisions of the president of the United States. She pushed her glass aside.

TEN

———— // ————

At 0800 the next morning, the OSS women were waiting under the Queen's Hotel portico when GI Joe from Boston pulled up in the troop carrier. "Morning, ladies. Ready to get to work?"

"You bet," Julia said, hopping up front. "We've been journeying six weeks over land and sea for this."

The locals appeared to have been awake for hours as they set off around Kandy Lake. Egrets and herons perched on branches hanging low over the water. Taking the uphill fork, the jeep wound along a jungly road wedged between terraced fields.

"The shrubby little plants above are tea—the bread and butter of this island, until we came along. The wet ones on the lower slopes are rice," explained Joe, a muscle-bound fellow with a prominent Adam's apple.

Monkeys swung arm over arm from the branches, some pausing to observe them. An almost-hairless baby lobbed a tiny red banana at Julia. "Thanks, fella." Her eyes popped open at first bite—this was like no banana she'd ever tasted. "Hey, how about another?"

"Trust me." Joe glanced in the rearview mirror. "You will not lack bananas in your time here. Nor mangoes or papayas. But if you want a juicy medium-rare steak, you're out of luck."

"Ever tried curry?" she asked, gazing at the wide, winding river on their right.

"I prefer Dinty Moore's stew," he retorted.

Julia laughed. "That was my standby in New York."

From the river, a mass of foliage arose…then a tall iron fence.

"The Botanic Gardens," Joe announced. "South East Asia Command."

Continuing across a bridge, he turned up a rough secondary road through velvety hillsides of tea. A short cutoff ended at a gate, thick posts connecting to a barbed wire fence. The sign read *US Experimental Branch*.

Joe saluted the guard. "Your new digs."

It was like being inside a greenhouse. Leafy fruit trees and towering palms cast dappled light over the red earth. The canna-lined path led to a spacious white bungalow with a terra-cotta roof.

"Welcome to Detachment 404/Kandy." Ruddy and rumpled, General Donovan emerged from the veranda's shadows.

Surprised, then pleased, Julia felt proud to meet him in the field.

He walked down the steps. "You ladies took your sweet time getting here."

She gaped. "Sir. There were mitigating circumstances." Nor had they the benefit of a military seaplane to transport them halfway around the world.

Donovan's expression turned kind. "Indeed, I've heard of your misfortunes en route." He saluted them. "You've been baptized under fire, ladies. Then the unexpected change of HQ. But onward. Let's fight this war." He gestured to the tanned, handsome man behind him. "Your commanding officer, Colonel Richard Heppner."

"Good to see you again, Julia," said Heppner, a junior member of Donovan's law firm.

"And you, sir." They'd met last year on his return from London Station. Pale and starched then, he wore wrinkled khaki shorts and looked like he'd been soaking up sun at the beach.

"Dick, please." He glanced at Donovan. "At least, once the general leaves."

"You're in luck. I'm off to inspect SEAC—the Royal Gardens are quite impressive, according to my sources." Donovan's eyes crinkled. "Fortunately, a mere tea plantation requires less upkeep. I'll leave you in your CO's capable hands."

Waving back the major and two civilians in his party, he took a step toward Julia. "A word, McWilliams."

She followed him behind the bungalow. He trained his baby blues on her. "This is the first stop on my Asia tour, as I give your mission highest priority. I need to know what we *don't* know about South East Asia Command, so you will be my fly on the wall inside Mountbatten's headquarters. I've informed Heppner," he said quietly. "He'll assist however he can."

"Good to know, sir. How's Sally doing at the Registry?"

"She's stepped up nicely. Has a cousin in China I plan to interview. After I drop in at Calcutta and deal with intelligence rivals at Jessore airbase—one of the secret worlds of SEAC."

"If you don't mind, sir, why did SEAC leave Delhi?"

"Geography. Mountbatten is preparing the liberation of enemy-occupied lands in Southeast Asia."

Julia felt the release of some unconscious fear. "I thought the Japanese were targeting Delhi."

"Oh, they are. On the other hand, we are targeting them. That's war." He handed her a paperback of *The Razor's Edge* by Somerset Maugham.

"Thank you, sir. I haven't read this lately."

Donovan lifted an eyebrow. "It's not for your enjoyment. This is our personal codebook. Your code name is Scout; mine is 109. Our key will be based on page-line-word coordinates, e.g., two, three, five—which means…?"

"Second page, third line, fifth word. The first letter of that word begins the message. We studied this in training, sir. I got the highest marks in my class—including our ace cryptologists, Caryl and Cheryl."

"As our Chinese friends say, McWilliams, 'Silence is the source of great strength.'"

She dipped her head, acknowledging his reproach. Had he not shepherded her to this place? Of course Donovan recognized her skills. He was now letting her fly. But if she sought glory, she was in the wrong business.

"Your work is highly sensitive, and there must be no errors. When

I'm back in Washington, I need to know I can count on your reporting. The president needs to know." He strode around the far side of the bungalow.

A private book cipher with the head of the OSS. Julia placed the novel deep in her canvas musette shoulder bag. She was on her way! Dashing under a covered path, she caught up with the others in a tree-shaded garden area surrounded by several tropical huts.

"*Bashas*," CO Heppner was saying. "Meaning *thatched roof*. These are your offices."

These bashas looked like little grass shacks. But belying Detachment 404's holiday appearance, the air rang with the din of hammers and shovels, saws, drills, and machine engines, shot through with bursts of unfamiliar languages.

"Please bear with us," Heppner continued. "We arrived in Kandy only last month—by plane and four special trains. It was a lot of bother, but the British bureaucrats in Delhi were throwing balls and leaving calling cards, as if it were a hundred years ago."

Jane frowned in disgust. "Colonial dodos."

Dick suppressed a smile. "You don't mince words, Foster—"

"You can call me Jane."

Betty grinned. "It's just as well, since I neglected to bring my calling cards."

"I see I need to be on my toes around you ladies," said Dick, his eyes lingering on Betty. Then he turned to Julia, indicating a sloped-roof hut with a gawky soldier posted in front. "Welcome to your new Registry."

She stepped closer and peeked in. "Where are my locked files?"

"On order. In the meantime, it's guarded. Around the clock. As are they all." Dick indicated the two bashas lined up behind hers—Field Photography and Messages. "That's you, Caryl, and Cheryl." Then he pointed across the shady square—Secret Intelligence and Research and Analysis. "Peggy in SI and Dr. DuBois in R and A."

"Call me Dr. Cora," she said, wiping the steam off her large round eyeglasses.

His lips twisted in amusement. "Next door is Visual Display, a.k.a.

the Map Room, and then Morale Operations." Dick glanced again at Betty. "I suspect you and Jane have already cooked up some devious propaganda schemes."

Betty saluted. "You may be sure of that, sir."

"You, Ellie, will be assisting me. I understand you have nine brothers."

"Eight. That's enough. I'm the eldest."

"Then I'm sure nothing can faze you."

"And if you can get me some chocolate, I make prize-winning brownies."

Watching him shake his head and turn away, Julia thought of the OSS field manual, *This Is No Picnic*.

Farther downhill, bare-chested workers in sarongs were clearing out tea plants and building more huts for enlisted men. Below was the river and on the other side, all that greenery—SEAC-HQ.

"Besides tea, they grow spices in this region, fruit, coffee. Sometimes I think I'm in the Garden of Eden," Dick said. "Then I remind myself of the serpent."

Reluctantly, it seemed, Betty turned her gaze away from him. "What's that big meadow?"

"Nine holes next to the cricket field," he replied, rolling up his sleeves.

Weekend golf. Julia's momentary elation left her feeling ashamed. "You gentlemen certainly know how to fight a war."

Dick gave her a cool look. "A planter uprooted his family to offer this property for the war effort. Make no mistake, ladies, this *is* war—and the enemy has his eyes on us."

As they let that soak in, he jerked his thumb at a large bamboo structure behind them—the mess hall. "After lunch, we will continue this briefing in my office. Over tea."

"We expect nothing less than porcelain and silver, sir," Jane kidded.

Julia was still disturbed by the golf. "Pretty cushy for a war zone."

"Check back during the monsoons," Dick retorted. "Or when you meet your first cobra."

There was a single boarded window in Julia's would-be Registry. After finding a pair of scissors among a shoebox of supplies, she pried off the slats, releasing a breath of steamy air through the screen, a stab of light. There was no secure storage, let alone a shelf on which to hide her Maugham codebook in plain sight. Like neat rows of hairbraids, brown fiber plaiting ran up the walls—which she could probably stick a fork through.

Julia switched on the small fan and dangling twenty-five-watt bulb. Two stacks of crates supported her desk, a slab of plywood. On it was a full-size Remington typewriter, some paper, empty manila files, and a thick folder from her Message Room neighbors, which meant their radio operators and decoders were hard at it.

As she sat in her camp chair, her gaze was caught by a rectangle of color—a detailed wall map of South East Asia Command, hand-drafted with fine shading and calligraphy. India occupied the upper-left corner. There was a great amount of blue. To the east and south was SEAC territory: Burma, Indochina, Siam, the Andaman Islands, Singapore, and the Dutch East Indies—all occupied by Japan. Moving closer, she noted peninsular Malaya and the large island of Sumatra, dangerously near. As Dick had said, *The enemy has his eyes on us*.

The map, while refined, packed a wallop. Julia felt a shock of fear at the contrast between the seeming normalcy of their island world and its geographic vulnerability. While aware of the British Empire's diminished status, she could now *see* the isolation of India and Ceylon. As if to underline the point, indigenous food supplies were indicated with a warm palette…survival data should they come under blockade.

She tore her eyes away, focusing on the small bit of reality under her control. The floor was littered with masses of envelopes, packets, and sealed diplomatic pouches. A few were addressed to Detachment 404/Kandy, but most had been forwarded from Delhi—where they'd been awaiting her arrival. Many, for *weeks*.

Julia imagined time-sensitive intel on enemy actions or trapped agents.

Horrified, she cleared a space on the concrete, turned the fan her way, and dove into the paperwork she had to catalog and file—*where?*

With a sharp tap on the door, Dick Heppner walked in. "Things are relaxed at 404, McWilliams." He pointedly checked his regulation Hamilton watch. "But when I call a briefing, I expect you to attend."

Dismayed, she glanced at hers. "I'm sorry, sir. Once I started digging, I realized lives might depend on critical messages in limbo for six weeks."

"Donovan has confidence in you. However, I am your commanding officer, and you'd be wise to remember that." He stared, letting her know that he was a colonel and she was essentially no more than head clerk. "Granted, these conditions are rough…"

"Absolutely lacking in security." Frustrated, Julia indicated the mess on the floor.

"Donovan boasted of your meticulous recordkeeping and organization. Your pride in your work. I believe he wanted you to handle this. Personally." Dick turned her desk chair toward the mosquito-netted cot along the wall. "Let's have a chat."

Julia sank onto rope webbing that scratched her legs. She noticed lines etched around his eyes that hadn't been there in Washington. He was CO here. Her problems were his. "I understand we all have to make do. *Improvise*, as Donovan says."

He lifted a resigned shoulder. "I told you your locked storage was on order, but to be honest, I don't know on what slow boat it'll arrive. Or when. In the interim, I'll have our men throw up some shelves. At the end of each day, the duty guard will collect your burn bag."

"I'm supposed to coordinate communications with Mountbatten's headquarters. It's not ideal that the OSS and SEAC are separated, but I'll do my best."

"Get used to it: everything is duplicated, including radio and map rooms. The Brits are possessive about sources and signals intelligence. And curious, shall we say, about ours."

Julia gave him a wary look. "That's something I am to report on. As Donovan has informed you."

"I've served in London. We have no greater friends in the world. Yet they are embarrassed to need Yanks in 'their' empire—and seek to contain us." Dick's mouth tightened. "Twelve US and British clandestine groups are operating here alone, not counting French and Dutch units. I fear we spend more time intriguing against each other than the Japs."

Donovan had mentioned intelligence rivals at Jessore airbase, all the "secret worlds of SEAC." She met his weary brown eyes. "I apologize for my comment about cushy circumstances."

Dick shrugged. "Things are beginning to go our way in Europe, but victory is not assured, and there's no end date in sight. Out here, we're still on the defensive. You and I, we don't know where the war will take us. We need to be able to endure."

Julia regarded her CO with new respect. "Donovan gave me a codebook, said no one else was to encrypt my reports. Not even *our* Message Room. Were there any leaks in Delhi?"

"Everyone has been vetted." He got up to leave. "But who does the vetting?"

———

They all commiserated at Queen's cocktail hour. "No books, materials, or staff," railed Cora.

Julia nodded in sympathy. "No safes or locked files for me."

"The Map fellows have offered their resources," Cora said in her gravelly voice. "By the way, your pal Jack Moore says he'll meet you here later tonight."

She released a sigh of relief that he'd made it. "I wonder if he drafted the SEAC map in my basha." Julia directed her lowered tone at Cora. "Scary stuff."

"That's the point, isn't it?" She adjusted her eyeglasses. "South East Asia Command is stretched pretty thin."

"At least I have something positive to report," said Peggy, secretary to the Secret Intelligence chief. "We're holding the line against the Japanese at Imphal. And that's not classified! Let us pray we'll soon drive them back into Burma—then into the sea."

"Remind me, where's Imphal?" asked Ellie.

"Northeast of Calcutta, in the jungly hills of Assam—near the border," Cora explained.

"Lucky us. Things are pretty calm down here." Ellie glanced into the lush garden.

Cora knocked back her whiskey-soda. Seeing her dubious expression, Julia knew that the well-informed head of Research and Analysis grasped Ceylon's geographical isolation and the proximity of a pitiless enemy.

ELEVEN

—— // ——

Her mouth still burning from dinner in Kandy's old town, Julia returned to the hotel's mirrored bar, which was hopping. Pouncing on two empty stools, she looked about for Jack, then spotted him at the door with a shorter balding man, who left after a brief exchange.

As Jack opened his arms, Julia pulled him into a tight hug. "Small world."

"Good to run into my old pal."

"Ditto," she said. "Who was that fellow?"

"Paul Child. My boss at Visual Display—the Map Room."

"Did one of you draft that impressive map in my basha?"

"Paul. Quite the master of detail."

"I never considered how much effort goes into these things. You fellows put in a long day." Holding up two fingers, Julia caught the bartender's eye.

Jack shrugged. "Mountbatten had a rush job on a Burma project."

"Doesn't he have his own graphics people?"

"The Supremo is a big fan of Paul's work from Delhi. With reason."

Julia pursed her lips. "That wouldn't be the Paul Child who declined your invitation to my Halloween bash last year?"

"He had a deadline."

"Too busy to drop by and admire your smashing thirties decor?"

"He's not really the fun-and-games sort. He's finishing the Supremo's map in his quarters tonight. As for me, you know what they say—"

"'All work and no play makes *Jack* a dull boy.'" Her grin faded. "How was Delhi?"

"Washington with curry. You'd barely know there's a war going on." Over rounds of whiskey, neat, Jack regaled her with tales about SEAC's former Delhi headquarters, a maharaja's palace with countless rooms, each so treasure-laden that it was hard to find an empty wall. They'd created the Map Room out of three servants' quarters.

Julia recounted the mid-Pacific torpedo attack. "Which brought back memories of our navy experiments. My shipmates and I might have been the ones squeezing fish for drinking fluids. If we survived at all."

"I don't even want to joke about that. But," he said, "I will drink to your shark cakes."

"I worried about you out at sea, too." She smiled warmly. Jack was a cute guy, a talented artist. They'd been in the muck together, squishing fish guts and smelling dead sharks. At Halloween, by sheer coincidence, they'd shown up as Bogart and Hepburn. But she and Jack didn't have their chemistry. While things would never click between them *that* way, she adored his company. "We've come a long way, buddy."

"Here's to old friends and new lands."

They tipped glasses and tossed another one back.

———

The bats were returning to roost in the gray-blue dawn as Julia left Queen's the following morning. The sole bit of color was a line of saffron robes outside the Temple of the Tooth—shaved-head Buddhist monks sitting quietly with bowls in their palms as people filed past to scoop rice into them. The sight of food made her queasy.

Maybe it was the altitude, or maybe G and Ts, Indian beer, and whiskey didn't mix. Betty was still asleep when Julia put on her blue linen dress, pearls, and mesh wing tips, ready to shine for her first full day at work. She had awoken with a rare hangover and, hoping to air out her brain, set off for OSS Detachment 404 on foot.

The morning was quite still, humid and cloudy. People were

already bustling around the lakeshore as if unperturbed by the weather. Dripping, Julia persevered uphill. Then, on a low-hanging branch, she spotted a magnificent orange bird with a glossy dark crown and long sweeping fantail. A male, by his showy looks. He cocked his head to one side, and a bright midnight eye met hers. He began to sing. Enchanted, she yearned to sing along—a duet.

From the wells inside her sprang a deeper kind of loneliness, the kind she'd felt during the torpedo attack. Soon, she'd be thirty-two. Would she remain forever unwed, watching siblings Dort and John walk down the aisle while she became the "maiden aunt"? Julia could brush it off, crack a joke, but in the quiet of this moment arose her longing for the intimacy of life with a man.

She stepped closer to the branch. The bird paused, and they watched each other, his interest reflecting back at her. Then he continued his tender song, as if reminding her, as had Jane the other evening, that she was surrounded by men. Her odds were good.

Offering a jaunty salute, a plump, white-haired man passed in a bullock cart piled with bundles of cinnamon sticks. Flashy green parrots flitted through pearl-gray mist. So far, no sunrise. Perhaps the clouds would stick.

In a stunning instant, the skies opened to deliver a rousing wake-up call with a heavy, warm downpour. As the parrots cawed their protest, Julia understood why Kandyans all carried umbrellas. Her dress was immediately soaked, her spotless white shoes squelching through muck with each step. But it was too late to turn back.

A huge puddle rose up and struck her full force as a jeep slammed on its brakes.

Julia looked at herself, mud-splattered from head to foot, then whirled on the vehicle.

The driver turned. "Sorry," he said in an American accent, not sounding sorry at all. "Didn't see you through the rain. Hop aboard."

She glared at him, then ducked inside. "You're excused. Where are you going?"

"The base, 404. You're part of the new contingent."

The base. "And you're part of the Delhi group," she snapped. Annoyed that he hadn't bothered to introduce himself, Julia shook out her drenched hair, which would momentarily turn into a wild mop. "Thanks for stopping," she added, trying to be gracious.

"No problem," he said with the briefest glance. "Don't worry. You'll dry off soon."

As he started the engine and lurched forward, she noted his starched shorts and open-necked bush jacket, its sleeves rolled just so. Even his socks were ironed. Quite the dandy. She had a brief fantasy of splashing mud all over him.

Suddenly, the sun broke through, and the leaves seemed to sizzle. A curtain of steam enfolded her, and she was sweating almost before she dried out.

The fellow didn't volunteer any more pleasantries. Neither did Julia. Their conversation had come to a roaring halt. After they drove through the gate, the first vehicle to arrive, he turned off the engine and dropped the keys on the mat. "*Voilà.* See you around."

Wading into fresh mud, she noticed that he'd manage to park *his* side on dry earth. Scowling, she unbuckled her soggy canvas bag; her comb was covered by an inch of water. The thatched walkway led to the ladies' toilet basha. Despite a ferocious scrubbing, mudstains clung to her new blue dress and shoes. At least her headache was gone—chased away by her annoying colleague.

———

After an hour in the muggy Registry, her headache returned, but Julia tried to focus on the latest decrypts from Messages. Swallowing half a canteen of water, she spotted some small shadowy object she'd missed. She got up and reached for—a scorpion!

"*Banzai.*"

Julia whipped her head around in time to see a hard green mango fly past her eyes and smash into the scorpion.

"Just checking on you," said Jack from the doorway, a sharpened pencil behind his ear.

"Aren't you the knight in shining armor." She crunched the creature underfoot and trashed the remains. "Nasty thing."

He laughed. "Pity the next scorpion you run across."

"I have a hangover," Julia admitted. "Elephants are still tap-dancing in my head."

Jack regarded her with disbelief. "That's not the drink-'em-under-the-table gal I know."

She pulled a face.

"Speaking of shining armor, I heard Sir Galahad rescued you this morning."

"Who?"

"Paul Child, my boss."

Oh, him. "Why should I be surprised? Splashed muddy water all over me. Couldn't bother to apologize. Nor even introduce himself."

Jack lifted a shoulder. "I never talk to him before his first coffee."

"Rude. And arrogant." She scowled. "Too busy to drive you, I suppose?"

"I must admit, I slept in this morning." He winked, alluding to their long night at the bar. "Paul had to finish Mountbatten's maps. I should remind you that despite his many obligations, he found time to draft a detailed one for your Registry," he said, eyeing the drawing of South East Asia Command territory.

"It is useful. Guess I'll have to thank him," Julia said grudgingly, glancing at her mud-spattered dress and shoes. Couldn't this Paul Child have been more considerate while driving in the rain? He obviously paid plenty of attention to his own clothes but had not a thought for hers. Did he have any idea how hard it was for her to find an attractive pair of shoes that fit? "He doesn't care about anyone but himself."

"Put it this way: he cares only about his work. Paul is one of the most gifted people I know—a photographer, painter, designer. And excellent draftsman." His eyes slid back to her map, each land rendered distinctly amid a wide swath of azure blue.

The economic powerhouse of India was a bright, vibrating pink. And Ceylon was cheery yellow, shown to possess abundant sources of fish, rice, fruits, and vegetables, as if to impart some measure of hope. While Julia still admired the fine calligraphy and color modeling, the map's luster faded now that she knew it to be Child's handiwork.

Jack pointed out her small window. "Come visit our Map basha. The Supremo has us supervising a similar one for SEAC. As I said, he thinks highly of old Paul. All the brass do."

"Maybe so. Still, he's a pissy fellow. Poor you."

He winked. "See you in the mess."

"I'm already there." She indicated the floor. "The mess."

He laughed all the way out the door. Julia didn't hold it against him; she liked people with a good sense of humor. Unlike Mr. Paul Child.

Julia's eyes returned to the map. It wasn't her to remain so peeved at someone. She was always the good sport, ready to forgive and forget. She and Paul were on the same side in this war. She decided to give him another chance the next time their paths crossed.

With a shrug, she sat back down on the concrete and began sorting documents into subject piles. It was an immersive task, and again, she lost track of time.

"You look like you need a break." Betty peered down at her.

"I'm not really hungry."

"Ha. That's one for the books. However, Mountbatten is coming for lunch today. You have to be there." She handed her a handkerchief.

After wiping her face, Julia smoothed her hair and dress, to little effect. At least her head felt clearer. With a cheerful smile, she followed Betty under the covered walkway to the mess.

People were already eating. They pushed their trays down the rails of the steam table, debating between hot dogs and beans, curry, fried noodles—and other dishes she didn't recognize. Betty cracked jokes with the GI servers, who heaped the choicest morsels on her plate. With her queasy stomach, Julia settled on rice and a cucumber salad, peeled.

A sudden movement of bodies announced Mountbatten's arrival. Dick and the other American military men stood and saluted. The civilians sat tall and straight.

Wearing a smart short-sleeved white uniform with shiny gold trim, the supreme commander saluted back. "At ease. As you were. Thank you for your kind luncheon invitation. I do apologize for my tardiness, but I was detained by an urgent cable from Whitehall."

The Supremo was accompanied by two fit-looking civilian aides and three British naval officers, including the young woman in a well-tailored white blouse and navy skirt whom Peggy had pointed out at Queen's bar.

Julia was reminded of her stained dress and vagabond hair. In contrast with her casual OSS colleagues—except Paul—the Brits were a spiffy bunch. She dubbed one of them "Stuffed Shirt," for his broad chest and puffed-up air. The other navy man had reddish-brown hair and a craggy, tanned face. The woman might have stepped from the pages of *Vogue* magazine with her red lipstick and heels—how did she ever navigate the mud?

As his group moved to their table, Mountbatten approached Dick—Julia thought. He stopped before her, hand extended with a genial smile. "Miss McWilliams. How delightful to see you again," said SEAC's supreme allied commander.

There was no escape. She'd have to put her less-than-correct self on display. "Please excuse my attire, sir." She rose and shook his hand. "I got caught in the rain—or rather, it caught me."

"These are the tropics. We have all shared your experience," he said with sympathy. "Nonetheless, you continued on straightaway. I commend your diligence."

"How kind of you, sir." She bobbed her head, grateful for his considerate response.

"How is the work proceeding?" he inquired, as if she were the only one in the room.

"I like a good challenge." Then it struck her—a perfect entrée to SEAC-HQ. "As we will be sharing communications, I'd like to pop by your file Registry sometime, introduce myself."

"Our Records Room, we call it. Excellent, and I can reciprocate with a lunch invitation. I shall send a car around tomorrow after 1100."

"Thank you, sir. I don't wish to intrude any longer on your meal."

Mountbatten took a seat with his group. He spoke a few words to the rugged lieutenant, who cast a penetrating gaze Julia's way.

"Isn't he simply the dishiest?" Jane commented.

"Mountbatten? And such a gentleman," Julia replied.

"The other one, too. His lieutenant, the one who was staring at you—he isn't bad. Those green eyes! Do you think it's something in the English water?"

"You have something against American water, Janie?" asked Paul, sitting opposite.

Jane gave Paul a bewitching smile. "No offense, darling."

Julia looked from Jane, beside her, across to Paul. Was she flirting? Why would anyone want to flirt with that pretentious, nearly middle-aged man? That was Janie, of course. Perhaps simply practicing her skills—for all those *dishy* Brits. Julia gave Paul another look. He was watching Jane with interest. At least she might keep her greedy little mitts off the green-eyed lieutenant. Julia returned to her plate, on which Betty had placed a grilled coconut pancake and slice of Spam.

"I thought you needed a little more nourishment," Betty said, thoughtful as ever. "Ever tried my recipe for Hawaiian Spam puffs?"

"That sounds tasty!" exclaimed Ellie. "Did you know I won the Betty Crocker Homemaker of Tomorrow Award in high school—and two blue ribbons at the county fair. If you're up for it, Betty, we could swap recipes. Julia, too! I'm sure they'd let us use the kitchen during off-hours."

Julia regarded Ellie, radiating sincerity, then forced out a weak, "Okey-dokey." Her boarding school hadn't even offered home ec, assuming their families all had domestics. Spending time in the mess kitchen was the last thing on her mind, but she didn't want to hurt dear Ellie's feelings. "In our spare time."

Jane snorted with laughter and slapped a hand over her mouth.

Cora raised an eyebrow. "Perhaps whip up something for Fourth of July."

"You seem a little peaked, Julia," Jack said with ill-concealed amusement.

She raised an eyebrow. "I was up late. Censoring outgoing mail."

Paul stiffened and turned to Dick, speaking in a low but audible tone. "I must protest. Why was I never informed our letters were to be censored? By an inexperienced female clerk!"

Dick attempted to keep a straight face. "I'm sorry, Paul. Julia has no role in censoring. However, it seems she does have a naughty sense of humor." He stared sternly across the table at her. "For the benefit of Detachment 404's morale, I suggest you censor your own material."

"Understood." So much for her attempt to be open-minded about Paul Child. Julia tried to get down a few more bites of the grilled pancake, but it tasted dry. "Excuse me, all. Work is calling." With a nod at the gang, she got up and walked toward the door. She bobbed her head at Mountbatten's group, then left, steamed up—and not from the heat.

Did Paul Child go out of his way to be irritating? He knew nothing about her and yet had the nerve to pass judgment. Did he really think Donovan would send an "inexperienced female clerk" to run the Registry in the critical Delhi station? Fortunately, her duties would require little interaction with the Map Room. In the future, she'd deal with Jack.

Even more fortunate, Julia's secret assignment as Donovan's "fly on the wall" with South East Asia Command might require continued contact with the intriguing lieutenant. Perhaps he would show her around the Royal Botanic Gardens. She'd meet her counterpart at their Registry—or Records Room. With luck, she might even have something to report to Donovan later in their private code. *Inexperienced female clerk*, indeed.

Behind the mess, Julia saw Mountbatten's flag-bedecked blue Rover—so shiny it must have been washed since this morning's rain. She glanced through a side window and saw the Supremo's head bent toward the lieutenant. In the middle of the room, Paul was grinning across at Jane. She wanted to wring someone's neck, but she wasn't sure whose.

TWELVE

Julia awoke the next dawn in fine form, ready for anything. A knock on the door announced Taj, their room attendant, with a pitcher of hot water for bathing. Telling Betty to go first, she looked out their third-floor window—right into the big curious eye of a great gray elephant. "Well, hello," she said in utter delight.

Hello to you. And welcome, she imagined the elephant saying as he regarded her from the middle of the road, oblivious to the bicycles and carts riding around him. Sitting behind his floppy ears, a tiny man tugged his reins, directing him into the Temple of the Tooth's courtyard. She wanted to pinch herself. What a marvelous world.

Thirty minutes later, following her bath, Julia floated down the hotel's curving red-carpeted stairway. Still elated, she turned into the airy dining room, its French doors open to the lakeshore. After two years of living on the ration, Julia gawked at Queen's lavish breakfast spread, walking from one end of the L-shaped buffet to the other—and back again.

When she'd finished loading her tray, Jack patted the next seat. She laid out her omelet, a hunk of buttery grilled naan, a tall glass of thick mango juice, and a small bumpy red fruit.

When she tried to cut it, Jane explained, "You have to peel it, darling. It's a lychee."

Under the skin, it looked like a big white grape and was sweet as sin, as one of her Midwest relatives used to say. Stirring real sugar and fresh milk into her rich coffee, Julia recalled her Washington witches' brew, made with two-day-old grounds. Her eyes flew open at the first sip. "I doubt a description of this would get past the Office of War Information censors."

"We are supporting a military campaign in defense of freedom," said Peggy earnestly. "That's why our people on the home front are willing to sacrifice for us."

Julia conceded her point: Americans were not in mortal danger; *they* were. Thinking of the SEAC map, she glanced at Paul Child, who was reading the newspaper at a solitary corner table. And Jack was here, but weren't the men quartered at Hotel Suisse? Then Jane fluttered her fingers at Paul. Never mind. Julia slid a fork into her eggs, noting tiny red bits—of chili! She took a cautious taste…then scooped up a big bite. *Marvelous*.

"Time to go, gang." Paul stood abruptly. "I've taken over Joe's portfolio. He's being shipped up to the Burma Road reconstruction project."

"My father led that project," Peggy said soberly. "The whole war is depending on it."

That was a pretty strong statement, which momentarily distracted Julia from her meal. Reluctant to leave it, she replied to no one in particular, "I'll miss Boston Joe. Such a friendly guy. Good conversationalist, too."

As Jack snorted in his coffee, Jane said, "And now we have Paul, another Bostonian, to carry on in that vein."

How does she know Paul's from Boston? Already? Julia took another mouthful of eggs and washed it down with more of that heavenly coffee.

"I'll be out in the jeep. Step to it."

She grabbed the rest of her naan. There went their merry morning commute.

———

Another large mailbag awaited her at the Registry basha, with several decrypts for Secret Intelligence. The top one was from a Bangkok agent: Siamese villagers had witnessed skeletal, nearly naked POWs laboring on the Nippon "Death Railway." Bodies had been sighted, some decapitated, left behind to rot after the camp pushed west into Burma.

Julia crossed the shady square to the guarded basha. Peggy was labeling bamboo-crate file drawers. Flushed with heat, she hopped up and led Julia in to meet her stork-like boss, Dillon Ripley. Another of Donovan's Ivy recruits, he was peering out the window through binoculars.

"Intel from Siam on our POWs." She handed him the folder. "Undated."

"Thank you kindly." After reading it, the SI chief raised his head with a pained expression. "Even the Nazis treat our boys better. It is difficult to connect the refined Japanese ornithologists I've known with such barbarism. The worst of it is, I've heard much worse."

"Donovan asked me to coordinate sharing of material with Mountbatten's people. As our agent's intelligence relates to Allied POWs, I need to inform the British, too."

"Please do not reveal our source. We don't want him poached." Placing the other material on his desk, Dillon returned the file with its damning report.

"Need we be on the lookout for spies here at OSS?" Joking, Julia indicated his scratched gray field glasses on the windowsill.

"Let us hope not. As it happens, my academic focus is South Asian birds."

Donovan sure knew how to pick them. "I saw a splendid one yesterday—orange, with a very long fantail."

"A male Indian paradise flycatcher!" His eyes glittered behind rimless glasses. "Rather rare in these parts. Where did you sight him?"

"On the road from town. Early morning, before the rain."

"How terribly exciting. And how grand to encounter another enthusiast of avian species. I look forward to exchanging notes."

Dillon Ripley was quite the character. As Julia left, her mind returned to the brutalized POWs. And the rest of the day's mailbag.

———

Immersed in her paperwork, she started at three sharp taps on the door.

"Ma'am." Mountbatten's green-eyed lieutenant saluted smartly. *Handsome.*

In his sharp tropical-white uniform, he appeared solid, the very image of probity. Her father would have looked that way at his age. Solid and steady. Persevering.

"Lieutenant James Mack," he said in a lovely Irish brogue.

"Julia McWilliams." She extended her hand, which he clasped firmly. "Julia." Pop had always judged a man by his grip. She released the handshake, noticing the sparkle in his eye, which her father never had.

"Of Scot heritage, according to the Supremo," he said, regarding her closely. "As I'm Irish, he thought we might compare family trees en route to the Royal Botanic Gardens—where I plan to give you the royal tour." His rugged features relaxed in an affable smile.

Their gazes lingered, then parted as Julia picked up the Death Railway file. "I have a report to deliver to your Records Room." She unbuckled her musette bag and dropped it inside.

"And so you shall. Admiral Mountbatten has asked me to introduce you around and affirm our close partnership."

"Thank you, Lieutenant," she said politely, mindful of Donovan's warning about the secret worlds of SEAC. He might be a useful man to get to know.

"Do call me Mack." He glanced about the empty walls and cluttered floor of her basha. "Nice map."

"As you can see, the Registry is a work in progress." Not wanting him to nose around *their* secrets, she showed him out.

With a salute to her guard, Mack looked at the central garden, shaded by a red-barked tree with big glossy leaves. "Cinnamon."

She inhaled. "Mother had a wonderful old New England coffee cake recipe. You can't go wrong with butter, flour, and sugar—although cinnamon does give it a certain something."

"Mmm. Did you ever try it? The recipe?"

Although they'd always called it Caro's cake, usually Cook Milly made it. "I didn't want to mess with the magic," Julia deflected, suddenly uncomfortable admitting she'd grown up with household help. "Maybe someday."

"You have more important things to do now." He turned back to the tree. "Wars have been fought over these spices."

As they passed the white bungalow, Dick was having a cigarette on its shaded veranda. Exchanging nods, they continued to the parking area. Mack opened the passenger door of an olive drab Ford parked under a shaggy yellow acacia. He hopped in the right-hand side and switched on the engine.

"Julia is my sister's name," he said, turning downhill.

Feeling the familiar ache, Julia watched the neat tea plants give way to wilder terrain. "Where is she?"

"In our village. The schoolteacher, keeping the children under her wing."

"I hope they don't have to grow up to fight." Hot air rushed through the car, waterlogged, almost suffocating. "I was named after my mother. She always told me to stand up straight. Be somebody."

"You were lucky."

"She was young, Mack. Not even sixty. So, no. I wasn't."

He focused on the rough, winding road, then glanced at her with concern. "I am terribly sorry for your loss."

Julia nodded, staring at the river on their right. Soon, a mass of trees rose up.

"The Royal Botanic Gardens."

Four armed soldiers stood outside the double gates. After a round of salutes, Mack proceeded into a verdant world of ancient trees, flowering shrubs, and shadowy meadows. Buildings appeared, then an unfinished basha. "Our new Map Room. Designed by your chaps."

He turned up the slope and parked. Beyond the guarded gate was a two-story white-brick structure with a green corrugated roof. "South East Asia Command."

A covered walkway led to the courtyard, where smartly dressed staffers moved with intention. Mack indicated the right-hand wing. "The Supremo's offices." He nodded left. "Admin. We'll deliver your report after lunch."

Outside the main entrance, more elegant people were dashing about and saluting or getting in and out of polished vehicles—not a drop of sweat or a wrinkled garment to be seen. All the while, Allied POWs were being worked to death. "It looks like a Hollywood set."

"Do I hear disapproval in your voice?" He indicated a mustached fellow in a khaki beret who was lighting the cigarette of a uniformed young woman. "He's one of the Free French waiting to be dropped inside Indochina, part of our international force. She is a FANY."

"*FANY?*"

"First Aid Nursing Yeomanry—British frontline nurses since the Great War."

Not the best name for a unit of female nurses, but Julia made no comment.

Mack indicated a smaller white building. "America House—HQ of generals Wedemeyer, Mountbatten's chief of staff, and Wheeler, SEAC's deputy supreme allied commander."

That sounded like an even higher position than Peggy Wheeler had mentioned. Julia felt a new twinge of discomfort over spying on the Supremo. Frowning, she stared at the expansive lawn before them, now a construction zone. Several bashas were being built near an old tree with a vast umbrellalike canopy. "What a marvelous specimen."

"The java fig. This was once the Kandy king's palace, surrounded by river on three sides. A secure location—until the British came along a century ago."

She glanced at Mack, only now realizing he was a few inches shorter. He had a quiet confidence and strength that drew her. He was a village boy, unpretentious, someone who might be a lot of fun. "On the train from Bombay, I chatted with a Colombo policeman who said the days of British colonialism are over. He called it the 'white plantation raj.'"

"I'm Irish. So I do understand." He turned his perceptive tropical-green gaze her way.

They walked along the river bluff, where hammocks were slung between coconut palms, their trunks also used as tent posts. The officers' club was on a shady overlook. Facing the open deck, Mountbatten gave her a friendly nod from the linen-covered table he shared with the two American generals.

At their table, Julia recognized Officer "Stuffed Shirt" for his puffed-up chest and tight uniform jacket, which even the Supremo didn't wear. He was Lieutenant Commander Stephen Warwick of Codes and Ciphers. In the same unit, Lieutenant Clarity Hastings was the chic officer who had cozied up to Peggy upon learning she was General Wheeler's daughter.

Continuing the introductions, Mack turned to an auburn-haired civilian in a smart linen suit. "Meet your counterpart in Records, Erin Turner."

"A pleasure," Julia said as they shook hands. "I have a document to share with you."

"Likewise. Why don't you pop by after lunch, and I can show you around," she said as Sinhalese waiters in white sarongs served a cold soup, mildly sweetened with coconut.

Julia tasted it. How light and refreshing! "Quite a bit better than army chow, I must confess."

During the next course—poached river fish—the conversation turned to the big party a certain "Dutchman" was giving Saturday evening.

"Pieter von Diest," Mack explained. "A tea exporter who has lived in Ceylon for over twenty years—and knows everyone."

"Are Yanks invited?" She was ready for a good bash.

"I shall make certain of it." He pinned her with a keen look.

Julia glanced into the trees. So Mack felt it, too, whatever was in the air between them. He, too, wanted to spend more time together. Which, given her assignment, could either be productive or ill-advised—even dangerous. She needed to proceed with caution, a lesson imprinted on her by Betty at the Colombo beach. When she turned back to their table's group, she avoided his gorgeous green eyes.

"I can attest to the high style of the Dutchman's soirees," Clarity informed Julia, her red lipstick intact. "Nothing like that at home anymore."

"No more being presented at court," Erin said. "I was spared learning to curtsy."

"The coming-out season could be tedious," Clarity agreed. "Several wardrobe changes a day, endless meals, tea, cocktails, and gossip. Dancing, a bit of sleep, then more food. Sometimes I gave it to the dogs or poured soup in the potted plants."

How cruel that sounded, given the sacrifices and suffering in her homeland.

She must have noted Julia's expression. "I made my debut before the blitz, Miss McWilliams. In 1939, we thought our world would go on forever."

Never mind the Nazis already rampaging through Europe en route to France.

"How about you, Julia?" Clarity asked. "Were you a deb—back in your youth?"

With effort, she replied evenly, "I was the outdoorsy type." Many of Julia's friends had been debutantes, but it wasn't her. The parties had been great fun, though.

After a waiter took their coffee orders, Julia watched him pad away barefoot. For some odd reason, she was proud they served themselves at the OSS mess.

——————

In the Administration wing, at the end of the second floor, Julia and Mack entered a large space with tall windows. The left wall was lined with built-in mahogany shelves where clerks moved about with books and files. There were several desks to the right, and in the back, two paper-spitting teletypewriters were monitored by a sallow fellow. Erin rose to greet them.

As Mack stood by, Julia gave her the report detailing eyewitness accounts of skeletal prisoners slaving on the Japanese railway, bodies left to rot as the camp moved west into Burma.

"What is the origin of this dispatch?" Erin asked, logging it in her book.

Julia recalled Dillon's warning about agent-poaching by the Brits.

"It was part of the pile of documents awaiting me. No time stamp or date." She cast an envious look around. "It's so spacious and light here. And well equipped."

"I don't need to tell you what a difficult move it was from Delhi, but now I appreciate our good fortune. This was the reference library of the Royal Garden's former herbarium."

"My files are still on the floor." But she had an armed soldier at her door. Despite their well-guarded exterior, SEAC's records were surprisingly open and unprotected.

"We have countless boxes," Mack said. "I'd be delighted to drop some by."

"That would be helpful—in the interim."

Erin smiled. "Should you require any further assistance, please do not hesitate."

Julia smiled back, pleased by her gracious reception. "I promise to take you up on that."

Seeing the pale teletype operator hurry a printout to Erin and Mack, she moved to the sitting area near the bookshelves. After a moment, Mack returned, printout in hand. "Intercepted by Hawaii Naval Intelligence, then transmitted to our Colombo signals unit."

"You mean, *British* signals?" The paper listed schedules of Shanghai-bound Japanese supply ships—valuable targeting data for US and Chinese bombers. She felt a profound pity for all sailors, their awful vulnerability. "Odd, your people receiving it before ours."

"Perhaps a copy is awaiting you at 404," Mack suggested.

She dropped the navy intercept in her canvas shoulder bag, and they headed up the hall. "…killed. One escaped," she heard from the open door just ahead.

With her next step, Julia saw Clarity pass Stuffed Shirt Warwick a paper across their facing desks—this room would be Codes and Ciphers, the equivalent of OSS Messages.

"…*Japs waiting*," he read while clerks huddled over crackling radio receivers or typed into steel cipher machines, larger than their field units. Pointedly, Clarity closed the door.

Julia turned to Mack. "*Killed?*"

"I'll have to get back to you on that," he replied blandly.

"Mack, we're allies, sharing communications. No secrets. Remember?"

He met her eyes. "It must be a newly decrypted wireless report, which, by protocol, goes directly to Erin for logging. Given the urgency, I shall brief her myself."

Returning to Records, Julia sat again in the library area, watching Mack and Erin confer. Despite his initial effort to keep her in the dark, she had the general picture: there had been an ambush, with only one survivor. To disguise her eavesdropping efforts, she picked up a copy of *The Economist.* Underneath it were two files, *Amphibious/Burma* and *Amphibious/Malaya.* As she was about to take a peek, a Royal Marine entered with a burn bag for Erin's attention.

Mack rejoined her with a tight smile. "Best we carry on outside."

They emerged into a slap of steam heat. "Well, it's great for the complexion," she said.

Skirting the construction, they turned down a palm-lined avenue to a shaded teak bench, where Julia sat a suitable distance away. "It was a Force 136 sabotage op against an enemy ammo dump near Mandalay, Burma," he explained. "Three of our best recruits—Kachin tribesmen—were about to set their charges when the place exploded."

"Remind me...Force 136?"

"A unit of Special Operations Executive—Churchill's Secret Army."

SOE agents had procured those critical Normandy-coast sketches. "I take it the enemy was waiting."

"And killed two of them. The survivor escaped over the mountains to Assam. He believes the Japs either broke our code or were informed."

"I don't know which is worse," Julia whispered, horrified. She paused. "Would you have told us if I hadn't been here?"

Mack shrugged. "These things tend to get out sooner or later."

Later? "What if it's an informant inside South East Asia Command?" She glanced around, sick to her stomach. "One of *our* agents could be betrayed next. My friend's husband leads cross-border ops there."

"Be assured, steps will be taken." He studied her face. "You're looking a bit peaked."

On the road to Mandalay...The Kipling poem she'd quoted to Gregory on the ship. It had been just poetry then...flirtation. Julia batted a hand, then wiped a film of sweat from her forehead. "I'm fine."

"This heat can be debilitating. You must promise to rest—for Saturday's party."

"Of course," she said, trying to inoculate herself against Mack's appeal. But despite her best intentions, she found him terribly attractive. And was honestly flattered by his attention.

Yet she couldn't afford to jeopardize their professional relationship; look what it had produced so far. What if she were on to a possible leak at SEAC, secret intelligence that might impact the war? Blood flooded Julia's brain.

This was why she wanted to be in the field.

THIRTEEN

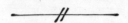

As soon as Mack dropped her off, Julia double-timed it to Dick's bungalow. Still shaken, she informed him that a Force 136 sabotage team had been ambushed in Mandalay, leaving two dead. The survivor fled to Assam, India. "I overheard two Codes and Ciphers officers discussing his dispatch, before they closed the door on me. I had to pry the details out of Mack. It's not known how the enemy learned of the op. Was it a signals intercept or a spy?"

"Lucky you were there. Your new connection with Lieutenant Mack—that's also lucky. Convenient, you might say. Watch yourself. And him." He opened his palms. "Not to pry."

Julia stared at the planter's old ebony desk, wanting to protest Dick's implied warning about any developing relationship. But she had already warned herself. As she tried to understand what was going on, her head began to spin. The elaborate carving swirled before her.

"Julia," he said sharply as she gripped the edge of the desk. "You may have a touch of heatstroke. It happens to us all. Have a seat." He poured a glass of water and passed it to her.

"I grew up in Southern California—but this humidity!" Unsteady, she dropped into a six-legged antique chair they would have killed for at Sloane's. "I'd gone to introduce myself and deliver an agent's report about the torture of Allied POWs on the Nippon Death Railway."

"Dillon briefed me." He closed his eyes an instant. "I'll dig into this at my end. You check with Messages for any related intel—and get *yours* to the boss. He'll want to know of the security breach—and SEAC's seeming attempt to cover it up."

Still wobbly but fiercely proud, Julia left. Eighteen months after entering government service, she was about to write her first espionage report to America's top spy. In code.

At the Registry, she opened *The Razor's Edge,* their plaintext reference, in search of *P.*

Four, twenty, eight. Page four, line twenty, word eight: *Paul*—as in *Gauguin*—for *P.* She began her message: *Possible leak SEAC. Sabotage Force 136 op, Burma. Dick and I to investigate. Scout.*

It was demanding work. After double- and triple-checking her cipher text, she placed it and the Japanese shipping intel into her bag. In something of a stupor, Julia walked to the Message basha, where Caryl and Cheryl, a.k.a. the "brilliant brunettes," were working under an old Pasadena pal, Byron Martin. The OSS was a small world. While some of Hoover's gang denigrated their organization as "oh so social," she found it remarkably lacking in hierarchy. Initiative and imagination mattered more to Donovan than tradition and bureaucracy.

Amid the clatter of incoming and outgoing Morse code, Byron scrutinized her encrypted dispatch while she noted the typewriter-like machines turning plaintext into code or vice versa, as she'd done manually. He raised an eyebrow. "Doing our work for us, eh?"

"I know how busy you all are." Julia shrugged. "Any new navy intel from Hawaii?" When he shook his head, she handed him the schedule of Japanese resupply convoys to China. "Useful targeting info— forwarded to *British* Signals Intelligence in Colombo."

"How did you get it?" Byron demanded.

"From a contact at SEAC. Why did they receive it before us?"

He glowered. "Let me guess: Admiral Nimitz's codebreakers didn't want to share. Navy versus air force. Lives at stake, and they treat it like a Sunday football game. Get this to Dillon."

At SI, Dillon perused the intelligence in his scholarly manner. "I'll voice my complaints to Donovan, who will echo them higher up the ladder. Louder. I shall also inform him you received this during the course of your liaison duties." He gave her a friendly salute.

Julia floated from his office. She wasn't usually emotional—maybe it was this lightheadedness—but over the years, her buoyant sense of destiny had dissipated, those high expectations…Now her OSS work had earned her respect and revived her faith in herself. However secret, her achievements were real and lifesaving.

With a giddy wave at Peggy, still organizing her files, she left SI. Struck by the dizzying tropical sun, she saw stars. When the world came back into focus, she was standing before the Map basha. Might as well get that Paul Child thank-you over with.

Blinking, Julia entered, readjusting to the dim light. While her floor was still stacked with papers, this one had an elaborate relief map of Burma in the center—where Paul was crawling around like an athlete. Jack knelt to his left in the Indian Ocean, both of them paint streaked.

"Here for the welcome tour?" Jack asked over the murmur of a BBC broadcast. "Or perhaps you'd rather tour Burma," he said, indicating their work.

Paul didn't notice her. "The distance from Rangoon's port to the sea appears off."

Julia studied the well-crafted display—Burma's green jungles and hills, ocherous cultivated areas, blue rivers and coastline. Towns and cities were shaded gray, provinces outlined in black. A vast terrain, from the remote Himalaya to tropical beaches. Staring up at Mandalay, site of the Force 136 ambush, she had a visceral sense of being there.

"As you were, boys." Still wobbly, she sat at a bamboo table, next to the radio, a small brown suitcase model she wouldn't mind having in her Registry. These fellows had pull.

"Oh, hello there," Paul said, distracted.

Julia leaned back against the chair. Larger than hers, the basha had the same concrete flooring, the same braided-fiber walls. On these hung regional maps with colored pins indicating local agent networks, order-of-battle charts, sketches, photos, corkboards of news clippings. A huge pan-Asia map, overlaid with clear acetate and marked up with colored pencils, bristled with energy. The announcer's low tone reminded her of Gregory, but that was only her dizzy brain.

As she was about to thank Paul once and be gone, Mountbatten entered with the two American generals and a dark civilian who looked like he'd once scuffled in rugby. Fascinated, the Supremo stared at the activity around the relief map.

Paul and Jack leaped up, and, with surprising effort, Julia pushed herself to her feet.

"Bravo, gentlemen. I could not run a war without you!" Then Mountbatten noticed her. "Julia McWilliams. I hope you enjoyed lunch."

"My compliments to the chef, sir. The poached fish was heavenly. And that coconut pudding! Oh my." She paused. "I'm as patriotic as they come, but your food puts the OSS chow line to shame."

With a gleam in his eye, he indicated the two military men. "Chief of Staff, General Wedemeyer. And Deputy Supreme Commander, General Wheeler. Let's see what they think."

The taller Wedemeyer tipped his head. "We need to give our people their due, Miss McWilliams, but I'm afraid you may be right."

"As we had K-rations on the Burma Road, any cooked chow is fine with me." Hand extended, Wheeler stepped forward. "My daughter, Peggy, sings your praises."

"In what key?" Julia asked as they shook.

Except for the unnamed civilian, they laughed again. Even Paul's thin lips took an upward curl.

"I must spend more time at 404. You are quite an amusing group." Mountbatten turned back to the large floor map. "I commend your attention to detail. What is your focus?"

Paul straddled the Irrawaddy River running up and down central Burma. "Topography, sir. Understanding the terrain in a new way."

Attention to detail. Julia had received such praise from Donovan. While she didn't care to share any qualities with Mr. Paul Child, he seemed to possess a solid work ethic. She noticed he wasn't exactly balding, merely had a receding hairline. So far.

"I value your pragmatism, Child. God knows we have enough woolly academics floating about." The Supremo frowned at the mountainous northern area bordering China and India—where the Burma Road reconstruction project was indicated. "While Stilwell's troops are dug in up *there*, our forces can reclaim the harbor *here*." He pointed down the peninsula to Rangoon. "'Going into the water to fight the shark,' as the prime minister calls Operation Dracula."

"Whatever the strategy, our detailed work will benefit SEAC," Paul said tactfully.

Mountbatten sent a pointed look at Wedemeyer. "Which reminds me, where are my landing craft?" He turned toward the door.

"The European theater still…" Wedemeyer's words faded as the group walked out.

Back on his knees, Paul paused in southwest Burma. "We need to build up this hilly range along the Arakan coast."

"What's Dracula?" Julia's voice warbled upward in excitement as she prepared to relay Churchill's military plans to the boss.

He sent her a disapproving glance. "I try to remain within my pay grade."

She paused, framing her words for discretion, then directed her tone lower in authority. "I am Donovan's liaison with South East Asia Command. He has ordered me to report back."

Paul replied with a sardonic smile. "Everyone's a spy here. That civilian, Peterson, is SOE—Special Operations Executive, in case you need to put that in your 'secret' dispatch."

He was patronizing her, implying she had aspirations above her station. And she didn't like it one bit. She'd learned of a possible leak inside SEAC and informed CO Heppner and Donovan.

"No one's suggesting Julia is a spy," Jack said sharply. "She has her own duties, which involve the highest security clearance."

People usually viewed her as independent and capable. But while Paul demeaned her, Jack had stood up in her defense—although even he couldn't see her as a real operative. Something moved inside; tears pooled under her eyelids. Then she was struck by another wave of dizziness. It was not like her to be unsteady and weak. Not like her to *need* anyone's defense.

"I take my orders from far above your pay grade, Mr. Child. Have a good day." She'd forgotten to thank him for the map but doubted her thoughts mattered to him at all.

FOURTEEN

After hours of primping and swapping gowns, the OSS women—except Cora, who was not socially inclined—were poised to sparkle. Filmy scarves from the local markets covered their hairdos as Paul steered the open-air jeep toward the Dutchman's mountainside tea estate. Jane was up front, while Jack and Dillon joined the group on the facing passenger benches. In high spirits, Julia admired the way her dress's scalloped hem rippled across her legs, then turned her attention to the rutted, winding road, trying to tune out Paul and Jane's annoying political discussion.

"*Gauchistes*," Paul carried on, navigating a hairpin curve.

"Left does not equal Communist." Wearing a slinky green gown made by her Kandy seamstress, Jane sounded irritated yet energized, in her element. "If it does—*sometimes*—so what? Those most committed to social change are often on the left."

Sending an eye roll at Betty, Julia craned her head after a large Buddha shrine, its pink lights winking through deep velvet foliage. The pink dissolved, smearing the night. She was glad it was too dark to look down.

At the end of a steep, narrow track, a large landscaped property opened before them with a crowded parking area tucked under a spreading tree. Julia leaped out. How good to have solid earth beneath her feet, which seemed almost delicate that evening in strappy gold sandals—another I. Magnin's find. The rose-bordered path led to an arched red gate framed by an upright unicorn and lion, whimsical characters who seemed ready to dance to the twinkly piano music wafting from the multiwinged house. Julia was already tapping her toes.

In the dramatic hexagonal foyer, their silver-haired host, Pieter von Diest, greeted them as if he'd been waiting all evening for their arrival and only now was the party complete. A barefoot servant in a fitted white tunic and aquamarine longyi offered around a tray of crystal champagne flutes. "Do make yourselves at home, my friends."

Then the Dutchman fixed his attention on Dillon. "Please allow me to show you the way, Professor Ripley." He indicated the flickering light at the end of the hall, lined with textiles and framed prints. "We have a special guest…"

"Let's find some nibbles." Ellie tugged Peggy's hand. "I'm starving."

About to follow, Julia was swept up with Betty and Paul into the cozy red-lacquered salon on their right. "Our host has a good eye," Jane pronounced, surveying the Hindu bronzes and seated Buddhas, the portraits of international luminaries, the fine carved furniture.

Then, linking arms with Paul, Jane circled back through the door. "What a divine shadow puppet. The monkey god from the *Ramayana* epic."

"Hanuman."

She pinched his cheek. "Clever, you. Shall we have a look?"

"Is that a question or a command?" Paul laughed as they moved down the hall.

Surprised at his jauntiness, Julia dropped onto a settee draped in a maroon paisley shawl. "Are they an item?"

"They have a lot in common," Betty replied, sitting beside her. "He's an artist, too. Well traveled, nonconformist…an experienced man of the world—sailor, black belt, teacher."

"That dull, pompous fellow?"

Betty smiled knowingly. "Reputed to have quite a taste for the ladies."

"But do they have a taste for him?" Julia said dismissively.

"I've heard tales."

Paul Child? Ladies' man? She winced. "Never mind. Spare me."

Betty cocked an ear toward the music. "How about this enchanting Cole Porter?"

"'I Love Paris.'" The champagne had gone to Julia's head, the pinks, oranges, and reds rippling behind her eyes.

"Wouldn't that be a kick? Maybe someday."

"There was a job opening in Paris, after Smith. But Pop would have never…I'd like to taste a baguette, though." Julia looked around—all those fluid colors…not a morsel in sight. "Remember, in Colombo, where they didn't serve supper until midnight? I need some food now."

"That makes two." Betty stood and reached out a hand.

Anticipating a lavish spread of hors d'oeuvres, Julia allowed Betty to pull her up, then led the way down the hall. The fizzy piano music drew them toward the glowing archway. Her hunger was forgotten as they entered the artfully lit room of beautiful people. "This man knows how to throw a party!"

"Definitely not a potluck," Betty observed.

The crowded teak bar extended toward French doors opening onto the candle-dotted terrace, where more elegant guests glided about with long icy glasses or short ones of amber whiskey. Across the room, famed British performer Noël Coward was striking the tune's final chords on an ebony baby grand.

"How dreamy," Julia said. "To be able to play like that."

A playwright, composer, actor, and director, Coward was also a society figure widely viewed as flamboyant, even frivolous. Yet she had been privy to some of the intel he'd collected during his musical tours around the front lines. He was in Ceylon now to entertain the troops on the *HMS Victorious*. For all Julia knew, Coward could be spying on a guest here, this evening. Not that she'd put herself in his league, but she admired him. He did his duty despite personal risk.

Dashing in his white dress uniform, Mack walked over. "If it isn't the Yanks."

"Betty MacDonald, meet my friend, Lieutenant James Mack." As they shook, Julia added, "Should you ever need a tour guide at SEAC, this is your man."

"Lovely," Betty said. "How did you come to meet our host, Lieutenant?"

"Mack, please. Upon the Supremo's arrival, he threw a welcome party. This one is rather more intimate." His eyes searched her face. "You're looking a bit flushed, Julia." Mack lifted a tentative hand toward her cheek, then lowered it, and his warm gaze left her. "It seems I am being summoned. I shall see you ladies anon."

With a relaxed yet determined stride, he moved toward the end of the bar where Mountbatten was the center of attention. Julia imagined playing tennis with Mack or going for a swim. She imagined his warm gaze remaining on her a little longer.

"An Irishman?"

"Hmm?" Then she nodded, still watching him move.

"You seem to have made quite the impression on the guy."

Mack joined the smart group of military and civilians, including Dillon Ripley and the Dutchman. Charismatic as a movie star, the Supremo looked superb in his formal white uniform, gleaming with medals and trim. But Mack, Julia felt, held up well in comparison. Wheeler and Heppner were in khaki army-dress attire, very fit and all-American.

Now it was her, watching Betty, watching Dick. She had noticed the spark between them from the beginning. "Our commanding officer is rather nice-looking, don't you think?"

As Coward segued into "I Get a Kick out of You," Betty replied, noncommittal, "He cleans up well."

"So do you," Julia observed. "The gown suits you far better than it did me as a bridesmaid. I'll never forget that bouquet flying my way—a conspiracy of the bride and Harry. I eased another friend in its path just in time."

Betty laughed. "You look lovely yourself. That blue."

"It was my mother's." Pop had left her closet untouched, and during home leave, she'd stepped inside a space suffused with Caro's presence, her scent, her generous spirit. *Take my sapphire gown, Jukie. It will fall to your lovely calves. Show yourself off to the world.* She cast another glance at her scalloped hem, knowing it would never go away, this longing.

Looking up, Julia felt a bit woozy and wobbled toward a cushiony daybed along the wall. Betty followed, plucking fresh drinks from a passing waiter. *But...not even a peanut?* Gratefully, she sank down. Lowering her glass on a brass side table, she gazed at the long teak bar, the glittering guests, bottles, and crystal. What a splendid soiree!

Then her gaze returned to Mack, who seemed rather attentive to Clarity, attired in a sleek, long uniform skirt, her raven hair in a tidy chignon. Julia was irked by the woman's intimate smile.

Betty glanced at her. "Quite a favorable ratio of men to women here, wouldn't you say?"

"As Jane has commented, more than once," she replied tartly. "You're not looking?"

"Certainly not." Then Betty's voice changed. "I haven't heard from Alex for months."

"He's stuck in the jungle. Remember, absence makes the heart grow fonder."

"Not always." She flinched as Noël Coward segued into "Every Time We Say Goodbye," then took a long drink—her eyes, Julia could have sworn, on Dick.

After a burst of applause, Coward took his bow and embraced Mountbatten. He raised a champagne flute. "To SEAC's supreme commander. May he get us safely home. Soon."

"To the man who portrayed me in his immensely popular and inspiring film, *In Which We Serve*."

"Not even Hollywood's best makeup artists could transform me into the ship's heroic captain."

Mountbatten clapped him on the back. "That's why they call it acting, old boy."

Into the conversational hum arose the blend of exotic sounds she'd first heard in Bombay, this time performed by a trio sitting cross-legged near the French doors with their beautifully crafted instruments. Despite her music minor, Julia had never heard such harmonies. Now she was swaying in her cushioned seat like a mesmerized cobra.

At the bar, the Codes and Ciphers officer, Stuffed Shirt Warwick, turned toward Clarity in the manner of a sunflower. Their sleek host, Pieter von Diest, also seemed interested. She had an air of mysterious reserve that only hinted at an inner heat.

When the Dutchman was called away, Warwick whispered something to Clarity. She shook her head, gliding a graceful step backward. All at once, Mack was at her side. As the two walked onto the terrace, Warwick refocused his bedroom eyes on tall blond Ellie. Or were they on one of the pair behind her, Caryl or Cheryl—or both?

"That man reminds me of Charles Boyer in *Gaslight*." A villain they'd hissed at during last Saturday's screening in the mess.

"Poor Ingrid Bergman. Shall we intervene?" Betty asked as Dillon joined the girls.

"He'll look after them," Julia said. "Just as well. I need some air." All the party sounds were creating a discord in her brain, which seemed connected to a penetrating ache in her upper back. A reflection from the glass door pane struck her, shimmering and sliding across her field of vision. The difficulty of trying to refocus left her flushed and sweaty.

"You're not well." Betty placed an icy palm on her cheek. "Come on."

Mack was having a cigarette at the lotus pond beyond the swimming pool. By himself. He looked up and caught Julia's eye. A wave of molten energy passed between them. As he stood, Betty led her to a wicker pool chair.

Then Jane and Paul appeared. "I love these Asian nights." She looked positively bubbly.

Or was it the air itself? Things were unstable; a chill ran through her. Feeling hot again, she knelt on the flagstoned terrace and dipped her hand…The dancing water moving closer…

"*Julia.*" Paul, maybe.

She jerked back and pushed herself up, embarrassed. "Sorry, I—I'm a little out of sorts."

"Oh God, I hope it's not malaria—" Jane sounded worried.

"No. No. I'll be fine. I'm never sick," Julia protested. "I'm healthy as…"

Her knees crumpled, and a strong hand gripped her upper arm, aiding her back onto her chair. The world was still spinning. "Oh my," she said weakly.

"You poor dear. I should have known—those flushed cheeks." The Irish lilt was Mack's.

The hand on her arm moved to her forehead, its fingers calming and sure. Julia turned: Paul, searching her face. Concern, she saw. Fear.

"Don't worry about me," she wanted to reassure him, but his hand remained.

"We do," Mack said on her other side. "Let's get you to hospital."

"*Really?*" she scoffed, attempting to regain control. "I only…need a few moments." But they were already helping her to her feet.

"I'll drive," Paul said firmly.

Lacking the wherewithal to resist, Julia let them lead her on.

FIFTEEN

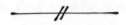

A fair, auburn-haired woman in a khaki uniform opened the curtain around her bed. Julia squinted—all at once, there were two of her at the window.

Assaulted by the light, she shielded her face with the sheet, an effort that sent shuddering pain through her body and left her drenched with sweat. She collapsed deep inside the mattress, feeling as if she'd been wiped off the face of the earth.

"You've been out twelve hours, Miss McWilliams," said a man in white. "I'm Dr. Lewis. And this is Lieutenant Olivia Mitford, First Aid Nursing Yeomanry Corps."

"What's wrong with me?"

"You're suffering from dengue fever. Also known as breakbone fever."

"No kidding." Julia struggled to pull her body up from the mattress while some kind of reverse gravity from above was pushing her down. Her right arm seemed immobilized. The nurse placed a cool cloth on her forehead and daubed her cheeks, then gave her a sip of water—so metallic tasting she tried not to gag.

The doctor doubled for an instant before returning to himself. "Your body needs rest. You'll be fine."

The room spun. "I am pretty achy," she croaked, noticing the hydration drip in her right arm. "I'll stay tonight. Then I need to return to work."

"Coconut water," he said. "An excellent substitute for IV solution. Your fever has come down rapidly. Another week or so, and you shall be able to resume your duties."

"A *week*? Or *so*? Impossible." The Mandalay ambush…Donovan…
Her brain went fuzzy.

"We shall monitor your condition, continue hydration, and discuss
this again."

"Where there's a will, there's a way. I promise you a swift recovery."

"Your determination is heartening. Let us hope our other patients
have your spirit." With a grave smile, Dr. Lewis walked off as Nurse
Mitford placed a thermometer under her tongue.

———   ———

"Don't you look perky." Jane showed up the next day, placing Julia's
canvas shoulder bag on a shelf beneath the wicker bed table. There was
only one of her—thank goodness! "At least you've been spared malaria.
And Delhi Belly."

Julia laughed. Then groaned. "My ribs still ache."

"I've had breakbone. But *after*, you're immune. So enjoy your R and
R. Don't worry: Peggy is overseeing the Registry." Jane squeezed her
knee; Julia almost kicked her.

"*Ow!* Tell everyone I'll be back soon. Please thank Paul and Mack."

"I'm meeting Paul this evening and shall pass the word to the others.
Tootles."

After she left, Julia wondered again about the two. Jane must have spotted something she'd missed. She glanced at the sky, the coconut palm, its
swaying fronds. What would Paul, as an artist, see? What he would see
differently? The pastel blue, the tree's graceful curve, its deep-green fronds.
She felt the hot, moist breeze on her face. The humidity made her so drowsy.

The breeze seemed to turn drier, crackly. What month was this?

———   ———

The Santa Anas came like clockwork every September. Indian Summer,
her favorite season. Julia was lying in the dim, cool living room, reading
Death on the Nile, a twenty-ninth birthday gift. The Agatha Christie
novel was an altogether satisfying adventure with missing pearls,
murder, drugged wine, and romance. Her mother would have loved

it—and, with another husband, possibly embarked on her own Nile cruise. Instead, she explored through literature. Julia, while combing Caro's shiny red hair, loved to listen to her read Beatrix Potter and Frances Hodgson Burnett—famous *women* writers—then later, from her ladies' book club selections. It was Caro who'd taken her to the library and bookshops, she who had encouraged her youthful writing and theatrical productions. She with the loudest applause.

A copy of the *Los Angeles Times* under his arm, Pop strode in with his assured gait. "It's cooling, so I thought we might enjoy a round of golf at Midwick. Then some of your mother's New England cod balls. I've asked Milly to give them another try."

"Poor Milly. Nothing comes close to Mother's." The feelings were inexpressible, so she could only sigh. "Good idea." Golf was the bond between them. Sometimes he asked for her aid on a charity event. John McWilliams Jr. had a firm sense of duty that she admired.

Swatting down the newspaper, he sat straight-backed in his armchair. "Roosevelt's still angling to get us into war."

"Don't you want to help England?"

He sent her a fearsome glare. "It's bad enough John III is over there. Leave the Europeans to sort out their own mess. They've been going at it since recorded history. No one here cares to get involved—except Roosevelt and his ilk. That man is a traitor to his class."

"No one cares to fight Nazi evil?" Then, there they were, off to the races.

"It's Britain's business. Which your pinko 'intellectuals' would do well to recall." His familiar rant. "Fortunately, we don't find that sort out here—except in Hollywood."

Julia stood and took his arm. "I need you to help me on my golf swing, Pop."

———

The coconut palms were swaying violently.

Thump.

She sensed a presence. A bent figure. "What's that?"

A pale, blue-veined hand reached for her wrist. "Our resident

monkeys shaking the branches." It was the auburn-haired Lieutenant
Mitford, delicate fingers taking her pulse.

Another cannonball-like thump crashed upon the roof, thudding
onto the ground. There was an outraged shriek—maybe one of the
scallywags had been hit. After a clattering on the roof tiles, three more
monkeys leaped onto the trunk and scrambled down out of sight.

"You are doing well, Miss McWilliams." With a soothing nod, the
nurse made a note on her chart. *FANY*, read her little red lapel pin. She
had a clipped British accent and crimson lips like Clarity's, but fuller
hips curving below a tightly belted waist.

"Haven't I seen you at Queen's?"

"Quite likely. Marvelous relic, isn't it?" She smiled and left.

The monkeys rampaged through the palms. They were working
in teams, with a partner catching the coconut and hurling it to the
ground, where Julia pictured a third picking through the cracked shells
to collect the spoils.

With a fingernail-scraping rasp, a lizard slithered into action from
the window frame. She watched, rolling to her side—and groaned.
Deciding to lose herself in a good read, she reached for her musette
bag, which she could have sworn was buckled when Jane delivered it.

Inside, she found pajamas, toiletries, her hairbrush, undies, and a
dress. How thoughtful, uncharacteristically so. But how could one visit
the hospital and not bring a book?

Julia settled back to watch the monkeys. *A Little Princess*, by Frances
Hodgson Burnett, came suddenly to mind, beloved equally by her and
Caro. A monkey leads to the rescue of Sara, an impoverished orphan
in England who was born in India and is in reality an heiress. Maybe,
deep down, that was where *her* dreams of India had come from…Maybe
her mother had planted those seeds deep in her soul. She dozed again.

———

Thursday morning, right on schedule, Julia was ready to be released.

Nurse Mitford handled her discharge. "A gentleman will collect you
straightaway."

Was that Paul being dutiful—driving her here and now picking her up?

With a blast of sultry air, the front door opened and slammed shut. It was Jane, dragging herself in, Paul at her side.

"I thought once you've had it, you're immune," Julia said in surprise.

"Yet here I am," she groaned. "I think it's the hotel drains. Mosquito heaven."

"You do have immunity, for a few months." Paul patted Jane's shoulder. "On the other hand, we could have been sent to support our intelligence bases in Iceland."

Hurt that he hadn't even asked how she felt, Julia watched them move to the admissions desk. Then the door opened again—Mack. *The gentleman.*

"There you are! You had us worried, Julia, but I believe you've made a record recovery. I am leaving for China tomorrow and hoped to see you first." He looked handsome in his fresh white uniform. "Would you care for some tea?"

She turned to Jane and Paul. "Enjoy the R and R, Janie. Then it's back to war."

They passed from her mind as Mack took her elbow with polite concern—and a warm pressure of his fingertips that felt a little more personal.

SIXTEEN

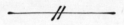

A sheer curtain of warm cinnamon-scented rain drifted around the thatched walkway as she and Peggy headed for the Registry the next morning. While eager to be back at it, Julia dreaded the awaiting chaos.

"Feeling better?" the guard asked from beneath the basha's sloping, extended roof.

"Better than ever." Her heart gladdened at the sight of labeled boxes aligned in neat rows with separate sections for China-Burma-India Command and South East Asia Command. Beaming, she turned to Peggy. "You are simply aces."

"It was fun." Peggy indicated a large parcel near the door. "This must have just arrived."

Inside was a mailbag from Burma, addressed to Betty MacDonald, Morale Operations. "I'll drop it off—after I walk you to your basha and thank Dillon for sharing you."

There, Julia again found him peering out the window through his old field glasses.

"More undercover activity, Dillon?"

The ornithologist spy-chief pressed them into her hands. "I've spotted a marvelous blue-eared kingfisher. Look at his beak. He's a fisherman, you know."

She lifted the weighty binoculars to her eyes. "I've never seen such a blue."

"Glories abound, Julia." He regarded her with concern. "Forgive me for not asking after your health. It appears you have beaten back the dreaded dengue fever."

"Takes more than a fever to get me down."

"However, you will need to take it easy. I know. I had dengue during my year with the Karoon cannibals in New Guinea. As there were no doctors, I figured I'd be useful one way or another, collecting bird specimens if I survived—or providing a festive village dinner. One develops a fatalistic attitude out here."

She blinked, not certain if he was joking or marvelously mad. She handed him the binoculars. "What's happening at Imphal? Still holding the line?"

"Not just holding it," Dillon began in quiet triumph. "We're turning the Japanese back. The Indian subcontinent is safe." There was an abrupt movement behind him—a spotted gecko on the wall with half an orange dragonfly in its mouth. They stared until the iridescent wings disappeared. He grabbed a pencil and jotted down a note.

"You're a rare bird." She didn't realize what she'd said until after she said it.

He let out an appreciative laugh. "I'm off for Trincomalee Harbor. Perhaps you'd care to join me? It's a spectacular drive over the top of the island; you could be my lookout. Ceylon has around two hundred-fifty avian species—migratory or permanent. I've spotted forty-two so far and plan to see every one."

"I'd love to—when I get caught up." Sometimes it hit her, the unrelenting flow of paperwork.

Dillon gave her a kind look. "Cora's new assistant arrived with Jane on the Colombo train the other day. Perhaps you're next."

"Wouldn't that be swell. Odd. Jane didn't mention it when she visited me at the hospital. Now she's a patient. The girl's had a busy week."

"Possibly Colombo was one of her Morale Operations." He opened a drawer and handed her a Leica camera. "For your own bird-watching. You must record anything unusual or noteworthy."

Birds? His scholarly demeanor was good cover for a spy, just as Maugham's writing obscured his WWI work for Britain's Secret

Intelligence Service. Noël Coward gadded about the world, entertaining the troops like Marlene Dietrich, both using their glamour to deflect attention from their clandestine activities, willingly putting themselves in harm's way.

"Thank you, Dillon. I shall certainly do so."

Next stop: MO, where Betty was fit to be tied. "Get this. Nippon Radio claims their army is marching through India."

"But Dillon said we're pushing the Japanese out."

"This is propaganda, to pump up their troops. And the waiting families." She narrowed her eyes. "We need a counterpunch."

Julia handed her the mailbag. "Taken during a raid of one of their Burma bases."

Betty riffled through dozens of soldiers' postcards—cards to be sent home to Japan, all with handwritten addresses, an Imperial Army star, and a censor's chop. "These must be young recruits, by the simple language and rough characters." She passed Julia one of the cards.

Julia regarded it, an idea dawning. "They're in pencil. And I bet you have an eraser."

A quick smile lit Betty's face. "The censor has approved them, so they're ready to be dispatched—after my little rewrite. We'll get an agent to mail them at an occupation post office." She handed Julia some paper. "Be creative."

"I really need to get back to work. Ten minutes."

After Betty erased the first card, Julia looked at the address, trying not to imagine an anxious family at home. "How's this? *Where are our supplies? Why are we starving in the jungles? Better to surrender than fight without bullets.*"

Betty lifted a finger and traced a wavy tear down her cheek, then wrote her message in Japanese characters. "*Don't tell our son I died for a lost cause.*"

Even though they were the enemy, it was painful. "War's a dirty business."

Erasing another postcard, Betty said, "I heard that cute Lieutenant Mack picked you up from the hospital. Beyond the call of duty, I'd say."

"I was surprised," Julia replied truthfully. "Why would he go out of his way?"

"Maybe you had some kind of connection?"

"Actually, Mack reminded me of my father—only younger, and nicer. I didn't even notice I was taller than him."

Betty smiled in sympathy.

She knows me, Julia thought, plucking out another card. Betty understood how she suffered from towering over all the men. But there was more she couldn't understand. How Julia was spying on Mack's boss, her confused feelings…She'd always been so open in life, so unguarded. Now she had to measure every word—even with her best friend. She was betraying Betty, too.

No one at this base but Dick Heppner knew of her SEAC mission—work so sensitive Donovan had ordered her to report in a private code. In pursuing her patriotic duties, she had fallen into a troubling conflict of interest: her unexpected rapport with Mack, her target's aide.

Before they could continue, Jane entered the basha with a damp watercolor. "Paul did the most clever drawing for one of my projects. That guy is such a darling." She smiled slyly. "Kind of cute, too, in his own way."

Julia tasted something sour, as if she'd just bitten into a lemon. "*Cute?*"

"You have to get to know him," Jane said with a mysterious air.

"You have the knack, Janie." Betty smiled. "With men, I mean."

Holding her tongue, Julia gathered her folders. "I'd better be going. See you girls at lunch." She waved her fingers and walked out into the steam bath. *Cute,* she repeated to herself. *A dear. Clever?* Jane was living on another planet.

She thought of the unpleasant, humorless man she knew. With his receding hairline and beaky nose. His pretentiousness and fussy, superior manner. Who would ever iron his socks? Like Mack, he was shorter than her. But with Mack, she hadn't even noticed. Looking down on Paul gave her a peculiar pleasure.

Eager to check in with Dick, she crossed the garden square, where the mapmaker himself was photographing the tall red-barked cinnamon tree. With her next step, Julia noticed Paul focusing on what looked like a necklace of oval maroon leaves strung across the tree's midtrunk. It was shady, and she almost tripped on his L.L.Bean camera bag. He didn't look up, oblivious to her presence. One would think he'd at least inquire about her health, after failing to do so yesterday when she was finally released from the hospital.

But, to be fair, he was the one who'd insisted on driving her there. The first to catch her before she'd fainted into the Dutchman's swimming pool. She recalled his concern for her; he had paid attention then. Something in his eyes…his *eye*. The one that stared deep inside her. The other seemed to gaze past her, although it could have been her feverish state.

As at the hospital, Julia tried to see what he saw: the delicate, leafy "necklace" against the rough red bark. She would have liked to pause, take in the beauty, but her responsibility came first. And she couldn't wait to hear the latest from Dick.

"Look at those rosy cheeks." Ellie jumped up and hugged her. "Aren't you just the image of health! We've missed you." She nodded toward Dick's door.

As Julia entered, he turned from a Burma wall map. "Good to have you back."

"Not much can get me down. Anything new?"

He pointed at the central plains—Mandalay. "The Kachin survivor of the blown Force 136 op confirmed that his unit had followed wireless-security protocol and not engaged in any insecure or plaintext comms. So the enemy penetration wasn't at their end."

"Could the breach have possibly been here at OSS?"

"Byron's been monitoring Messages closely. I've followed up on my own. Nothing. Either the Japanese have broken our code or there's a penetration within SEAC."

Julia shook her head. "Mack and I just happened to be walking past Codes and Ciphers when the report arrived."

"They're keeping it quiet." Dick let out a heavy sigh. "Upon

Mountbatten's return, he and I will each receive an *Eyes Only* cable about an American arms drop behind Burmese lines."

"A fake one, you mean? A decoy?"

"You could put it that way."

"When will the drop take place?"

"July seventh. Seven-Seven."

Her eyes widened. "If the enemy shows his ugly mug, we know SEAC is the leak."

"Correct. Not even the Supremo will be informed of our suspicions— until we have further proof."

"Their HQ is well guarded. It's hard to figure how an outsider could get in. A Royal Marine incinerates their waste. However, their files are unlocked and exposed. Like mine."

"Yours are guarded around the clock. The Registry shelves should be up soon. As to safes…" He opened his palms. "This is where we were ordered, with no infrastructure in place. Things are ad hoc; we must be pragmatic. But no matter where, breaches occur."

"Who will the cables be from?"

"Wild Bill himself. No one else is to know. Only Bill, me—and you, our point person. What do you suggest we call your operation?"

Julia thought a moment. "Operation Friendship?"

"Very naughty." Dick tsk-tsked. "But apt."

Point person. Your operation.

Leaving his office, she noted how quickly her ambitions had over-come her qualms about spying against their friends. On the other hand, one of their friends might be spying against them.

———

One didn't bounce back quickly from breakbone fever, Julia realized the next morning. Trying to generate an appetite, she dragged herself down the red-carpeted stairs to Queen's breakfast buffet, where the scent of temple flowers drifted through open French doors. She claimed the empty seat beside Jack. Returning with some fruit and naan, she spotted Paul in his corner nook reading the *Ceylon Times*. "Mr. Personality."

Jack grinned. "While you were ill, Jane began joining him with her own newspaper. They settled right in like an old married couple, rarely speaking."

"That's our Janie, marching in where angels fear to tread." Had she possibly had her eye on him from the beginning? By the second day, she'd known Paul was from Boston. Julia stirred her coffee. There were infinitely more important things to worry about.

"For example, the *thalagoya*, a cross between an iguana and a large lizard," she heard Cora say from across the table.

"How is it prepared?" Peggy asked.

"First, you bend its head under its throat and slam the nape with your fist."

Ellie put down her chai.

"Then chop the tongue and serve it in curry," Cora said, straight-faced.

Julia laughed out loud. "I would have enjoyed your anthro class, Dr. DuBois!"

Chatting over their teacups, a nearby group of women looked at her. Two were in British khaki, including FANY Nurse Mitford. Erin, from Records, wore another trim linen suit.

Struck by that familiar feeling of being large and gawky, Julia modulated her willful voice. "Perhaps we could barbecue it," she said to Cora. "For our Fourth of July picnic." Rather than slumping, she sat taller in defiance. To heck with prim and proper.

Clarity walked toward the British table with a tray of tea and one piece of toast—obviously still on her debutante diet. And wearing that alluring red lipstick.

She had a way of drawing everyone's attention. "In Washington, they've declared makeup 'necessary and vital' to the war effort," Peggy said.

"We need to ramp up production of Victory Red," Jack proclaimed.

"Have a bond drive." Julia glanced back at Clarity, whose lips might have launched a thousand warships. In Codes and Ciphers, she would soon receive their decoy cable about the fake arms drop. What would she do with the information? Where would it go next?

A busted cipher could at least be changed. But a spy?

Not that Julia suspected Clarity. It could be any of them—someone she'd looked in the eye or hadn't even met.

———

As they arrived at 404, Dick raced down his steps. "We did it!"

He was blinking hard as they drew around. "The Normandy invasion has begun—while the Germans were expecting us at Calais!" Dick cleared his throat, pumping everyone's hands. "Now, into my office for some vintage Calvados I've been saving for just this occasion. We shall celebrate our imminent liberation of Paris."

Gunfire burst up from the Botanic Gardens. The Brits had heard the news.

Julia's chest tightened with hope. And fear, for all that might yet go wrong.

SEVENTEEN

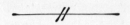

The following Friday, Jane returned from the hospital with Paul in time for cocktail hour. They joined Julia and Betty at a quiet garden table where they were already cooling off over cool drinks. "You look wonderful, Janie!" Julia exclaimed. "The rest did you well."

With a bit of a Bette Davis air, Jane turned to Paul. "Be a darling and get me a tall G and T. I have developed a powerful thirst."

When he was out of earshot, she whispered, "I'm in a situation, girls. Paul and I have a movie date later. However, someone is unexpectedly in town. Can one of you go in my place?"

Julia raised an eyebrow. "Might this *someone* happen to be connected to the Colombo trip you forgot to mention?"

"He's off to the field tomorrow," was her no-answer answer. "Tell Paul I'm not fully recovered."

"I have a dinner tonight," Betty said.

"With whom?" Julia asked.

"Dick."

"As in, our cute commanding officer, Dick Heppner? My, my," Jane purred.

"We're discussing my Burma-postcard op." Betty glanced into her drink.

"Security, darling." Jane eyed Julia.

"The op was actually Julia's idea—while you were in the hospital."

With a flash of pride, she regarded her friends. They all had their secrets, their secret lives. Secret worlds. Yet something deeper bound them. "Which leaves me. Greater love hath no woman than to spend an evening with Paul Child. The least you can do, Janie, is tell us about your mystery man."

"Since you're twisting my arm…" Jane said. "Manly's with Detachment 101 inside Burma. He's here to brief Dillon about the Arakan network he built to support the Allied offensive. One of his agents is a postman's daughter—Myong, I think. She'll mail the cards."

Julia visualized the long, narrow strip of Burma's west coast as depicted on Paul's relief map. "How long have you been carrying on with this Manly?"

"We met at the hotel party, our first night in Colombo. It was…" She snapped her finger. "*Hot.* And I don't mean the weather." She lowered her voice. "This is on the q.t., girls. Very hush-hush. He's married."

"I understand." Julia decided to level with her. "Remember Gregory Bateson?"

"Of course. A little conceited for my taste."

Takes one to know one. "I think I was infatuated by his brilliance. He liked me, too. He kissed me, once, after the torpedo attack. But there was nothing between us, and I decided to end it before it was too late." Shaking her head, she took Jane's hand. "Be prudent."

"I will. After tonight. Maybe." Her eyes gleamed.

———

Following tedious attempts at conversation, Julia and Paul reached the Regal Cinema, which was screening *Ten Days in Paris.* Something about one of the entry posters caught her short—its subtitle was *Missing Ten Days.*

"What?"

She stared at the shadowy street scene. "I had a college chum, an artist who set sail for Paris the day after graduation. Ten *years* ago—" She drew in her breath.

As she released it, he sighed, almost as if they were breathing in unison. "Goes quickly, doesn't it?"

"It does. We lost contact after the Occupation. Now my friend's

missionary parents have gone missing in China. My brother's undercover in France—with no word for months!" A rush of desperate anger
filled her. "I'm proud to be entrusted with the Registry—but I *need* to
do more."

"I understand, Julie," Paul said kindly. "And we're all doing our
parts. Maybe all of us want to do more." He glanced at his watch, an
OSS Hamilton with a nice umber strap; hers was basic beige. "We'd
best take our seats."

She was peeved at having revealed her personal ambition to him—
only to be put in a pot with everyone else. Then she noticed the sheaf of
newspapers under his arm. Did he plan to read before the movie started?
Granted, she lacked Jane's witty repartee, but...how rude!

The newspapers had another purpose, she soon saw as he layered the
seats with them—protection against tropical bugs that inhabited cane
and wicker. "Body warmth brings them out," he informed her. "I've had
my legs covered in welts. You notice I'm wearing trousers."

"Thanks for the warning." Julia tugged her skirt down past her knees.

After the cheerful opening music, she flinched when a man was shot
in the first scene. What kind of "entertainment" was this?

Paul patted her arm tentatively, but that ominous opening clouded
her focus. The images drifted over her—and when the lights came up,
Julia had only a vague sense of the plot. She busied herself collecting the
papers, hoping to avoid any discussion. She didn't want Paul to think
less of her intellect than he already did.

But he, too, was elsewhere. Driving back, he told her about his years
in Paris, painting and photographing, making stained glass, drinking
wine along the Seine with his late lover. As his voice cracked, he pulled
off the road, the jeep's right-hand drive putting him next to Kandy Lake.

Paul stared into a shadowy shrub growing out of the water. "She
taught me about art and good food, helped educate my eye, my sen-
sibilities...all my senses. She was everything to me. Then...I lost her.
And the light went out of my life. It took the war to shock me back. I
was given work that matters—it's all I have. I have nothing to return to."

Julia had never seen Paul Child as a man of deep feelings. A hard worker, yes, but a passionate one? No. She collected her thoughts. "I wouldn't want to go back. To be honest, I was something of a social butterfly. With ambitions but no follow-through. This war put me on a path. Who knows where it'll lead?"

"Then we have something in common. We have no ties that bind." Paul turned to her. An oncoming car illuminated his one focused eye, while the left appeared to see in all directions. "Something else. I sense we're both hungry to encounter the world."

"That's why I turned down a respectable guy who might never leave California—but also might end up running it."

Both eyes shimmered, in their own ways. "Lucky you. I suspect you have bigger fish to fry."

EIGHTEEN

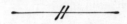

Donovan's encrypted *Eyes Only* cable arrived for Mountbatten the afternoon of his return from China and India. The identical one to Dick ended: *Burn after Perusal.* The message alerted both leaders of a big arms drop to take place on *Seven-Seven.* This advance notice was to give a possible leaker two weeks to inform his or her contact of the OSS plan.

Mountbatten's receipt of the cable would put Operation Friendship into motion.

Adding it to her SEAC folder, Julia left Dick's bungalow and was about to requisition a driver when she saw Jane and Paul chatting outside her MO basha. After they parted, he strode away, several map rolls under his arm.

Following last week's movie "date," their exchanges had been slightly more cordial. So she thought she might request a lift. Hurrying toward him, she tripped on a root. Papers scattered over the red soil. Without a word, he knelt, helping her gather her docs and shake them out.

"Oh dear. Thank you, Paul!" Julia exclaimed, mortified.

With a shrug, he picked up his map rolls and stood—dirt on his shins, even his creased shorts, the first time she'd seen him less than immaculate. He had a smudge of red she wanted to brush off his cheek but didn't dare. Paul looked like a boy back from collecting beetles to sketch. Not mischievous like she'd been, rather purposeful. "You're a mess. Sorry, didn't mean it that way."

"How did you mean it?"

As they laughed for no reason, their eyes held for a moment. "I don't want to put you out any more, but any chance you're going to SEAC?"

"The Supremo wants these China maps for his 1700 staff meeting." He checked his watch, swept himself off. "I'm running late. If you're coming, let's go." His old gruff self.

As he walked away, Julia stared after him. She had no choice. She needed a ride.

———

SEAC was hopping. Passing under the portico, they entered Mountbatten's white-columned wing. "We'll meet in a quarter hour or so," Paul said. "Then I'll drop you at your hotel." No questions about her plans. With a self-assured nod at the desk officer, he opened the inner door.

Moving against the flow, Julia crossed the courtyard to Admin, feeling as if a scarlet *S* for *spy* were emblazoned on her shirt. She dashed upstairs and handed the encrypted cable to Erin. "*Eyes Only* from Donovan to the Supremo."

"Thank you." With a glance at the clock, Erin logged it in and stood. "I have a meeting to attend. Let's drop this at Codes and Ciphers on the way." As they reached the next office, Clarity was leaving. "*Eyes Only* for the Supremo."

"Ta, darling." Clarity turned and passed the cable to a clerk. "Highest priority," she instructed, then caught up with Erin.

Julia followed and waited in the courtyard for Paul. "If it isn't my favorite Yank. What are you doing here?" Mack's face opened in a wide grin.

She'd forgotten the delights of his Irish brogue and felt an electrical zap. "A delivery. How was your trip?"

"Fast-paced. I can tell you about it over dinner. If you recall, we have a date."

"It's your first evening back."

"A man's got to eat. A woman, too. I shall collect you around eight. Save your appetite." He paused. "Sorry, but I'm expected at the meeting." Mack paused again. "Do you need a lift afterwards?"

"There you are," Paul said sharply as he emerged from Mountbatten's offices. "Ready?" Holding the door open for Mack, he looked at Julia.

"See you tonight," she told Mack, then turned slowly, vexed by Paul's brusqueness. "Yes. Thank you." She doubted Mr. Child directed those moods toward his superiors.

Never mind, he wasn't worth dwelling on. Julia tapped her knuckles against the courtyard wall for luck. The trap had been set. Soon they might catch a rat.

———

A little early, Mack arrived at Queen's. "It's good to see you, Julia—and looking so fit."

"I feel well. Better now." She smiled.

"It's a lovely evening," he said, meeting her eyes. "The breeze seems to have chased away the mosquitoes. I suggest a stroll." He touched that special place on her elbow.

Outside, a dog napped, oblivious to the passage of sandaled feet, the swirling rainbow of sarongs and saris. After they turned up the lakeshore path, Mack told her about flying "over the Hump"—the Himalaya mountains—to China. "We shaved several peaks, so close I could have reached out and touched them. I saw the wreckages of too many planes, impossible to retrieve."

"My friend Rosie was born in China. She speaks eleven dialects, is desperate for a posting there. But last I heard was still cooling her heels in Delhi." She thought about connecting and disconnecting. Being close and then pulled apart. Becoming close with new friends.

"I doubt she's *cooling* them." He smiled through cracked, sunburned lips. "The China theater needs her. It's treacherous, though. Even allies are at loggerheads."

Julia glanced at the sickle moon rising over the hills. "Hard to believe. Mountbatten could not be more gracious. He was terribly kind the day your group visited our mess—*I* was the mess, all mud-spattered, while you Brits were so nicely turned out."

"I grew up amid constant rain and rubber boots. No one was expected to be 'nicely turned out' every moment. Not in an Irish village."

"Yet you manage." What drew her, though, was his rugged earthiness, so different from the polished Ivy League and Stanford types she'd known. "Have you heard any more about the Force 136 ambush in Mandalay?" she asked, uncomfortable at her duplicity with a man who seemed so genuine.

"Our investigation continues." He gazed at her through grave eyes as clear as a mountain stream. "I propose we expand it into the dives of Kandy."

Leaving the lake, they wandered into town, losing themselves in narrow, airless lanes of food stalls, dazzling temples and Buddha shrines, shop-residences with balconies and roof terraces. And people, so many people. Julia had walked these streets before, but it was different with Mack, more fun. The congested atmosphere enfolded them. They were alone, together.

Hot and sticky, they paused under a bookstore arcade. Across the road, a vendor was selling drinks from a three-wheeled pushcart, glistening bottles displayed on an iced riser. They watched him pour drinks into glasses. "Join me for some cold ginger beer?"

"We've been warned off street food. You never know what kind of water those glasses were washed in."

"Of course. You have been ill. Best not push it."

Julia gazed at a bullock plodding past with a towering load of coconuts. A tiny monk carrying a great black umbrella. A tinsmith flattening a can into a metal sheet, which became a cup. And back at the pushcart, those enticing chunks of ice. "I guess this is the moment to break free."

With a thumbs-up, Mack bought the drinks. Julia took a big thirsty gulp, then stared into the murky brownish liquid. "It's spicy."

"Fresh ginger," he said.

"I've never tasted it before. Betty said it's good with Spam."

He grinned. "Not sure I'm keen to try that."

After they returned their glasses, the vendor's helper dipped them in a tub of dirty water and, with a vigorous shake, placed them right back on the pushcart display.

Julia's eyes popped open; then she burst into laughter, which he joined merrily. She shrugged. "So much for being careful."

Mack pulled a long face. "I'm a bad influence."

"Well, I could have stayed in Pasadena." Patting her belly, she recalled the pride she had felt upon their arrival in Bombay when Gregory Bateson predicted she'd soon be eating street food. He had meant that as a compliment; he admired her bold spirit. Julia flushed with pride. That was who she was—a bold spirit, intrepid, adventurous. Embracing the new. "Let's think of them as welcoming bugs, shall we?"

"That's how I feel."

As they continued through the old streets, Julia fell silent, basking in his comfortable presence. She paused before the hanging sign of a leather-worker stitching a pair of sandals. "Don't they look cool and comfortable!"

Mack glanced inside the narrow stall. "Let's give it a go."

The shoemaker bade them sit on a low bench. "Some tea?"

"Thank you, no." Julia pointed at her loafers, feeling all at once exposed and less than feminine in Mack's eyes. She should have returned later, on her own, but it was too late. "Can you make me some sandals?"

Within moments, he'd traced her feet on paper. The chalk was damp and warm, the outline embarrassingly large. "Tomorrow, this time."

"I could use new boots," Mack said.

"I will be finding fine leather piece. Come back tomorrow with wife."

Julia flushed, struggling to slip her sweating toes back into her men's loafers.

———

After duck curry washed down with tepid Taj Mahal beer, Mack hired a tonga to drive them up to the great seated Buddha, an enormous white figure visible from every angle in Kandy. "Locals call this 'Devil's Hill.' Not to scare you off."

Julia craned her neck. Under the luminous curving moon, the Buddha seemed more ethereal, a floating mass of light, getting nearer and nearer. After they pulled into a view site, Mack offered the wispy-haired driver a cigarette and told him to have a smoke.

"We've been invited to your July Fourth bash."

"It is rather awkward, celebrating a military defeat." She regarded him gravely. "Oh, but you're Irish. So you might be quite pleased to join in."

He laughed, tossing an arm around her shoulders. "I like your spirit, Julia."

"Me, too. I mean, yours. You know how to have a good time." It was so easy between them—which deepened her inner conflicts. With today's cable, they'd launched a deception op against their closest allies…against Mack. It was not proper that she—

Unexpectedly, his lips were on hers. Still sunburned and rough, they moved down her throat, sending new sensations through her body. "Oh my."

"Oh my, what?"

She felt his mouth smile behind her ear.

"I don't know." No one had kissed her like that since Tom, her hand-some two-timing Manhattan beau. A soft wind tickled the back of her neck. "*Mack.*"

He cupped her face in his hands. "Julia."

Somewhere far away, she heard Dick warning her to be wary. She heard her own warnings, and Mack's. *Even allies are at loggerheads.* The air turned still, clammy, unsettling.

And yet, there they were, necking on Devil's Hill. The horse began shuffling his feet as if ready to go. She should be, too. She was, of course. In a minute.

But now, she threw herself wholeheartedly into tonight's final embrace.

NINETEEN

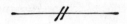

Ten days later, descendants of the American Revolutionaries and British Red Coats enjoyed a bang-up Fourth of July barbecue, grilled hot dogs, and bangers along the Mahaweli River. Whatever their past—and present—differences, they shared a delirious celebration of the Allied success in pushing the Japanese back into Burma.

After they ate, Julia ambled up a shady knoll with a cool drink. Gazing at the broad, flat waterway, she recalled yesterday's letter…smudged envelope, an unfamiliar scrawl. She'd steadied herself against the hotel front desk. This was wartime, what good news could it bear? She sank into an armchair…then slowly opened the backflap, only to see another envelope—that one addressed by a well-known hand—*brother John*. There wasn't much he could say other than he was safe and being debriefed in a censored location. Not to worry. He'd be home soon and write in more detail. In the meantime, he wanted her news from Shangri-La. *Ha ha*, she tried to laugh, then burst into tears, right in the middle of Queen's lobby.

Looking up, she noticed Lieutenant Commander Warwick on the other side of an overgrown clump of tea plants. Turning away, she sank back in her camp chair and watched the sunset catch fire over the hills. The decoy arms drop in Burma was to occur in three days—Seven-Seven. Her eyes roved from guest to guest, any of whom *might* be the SEAC traitor. Even Mack.

Anxious, Julia glanced at her red toenails and new sandals, which she'd collected alone. Her insides turned to jelly whenever she thought of Mack's lips on her, the quiet mountain road, the tonga rocking, the horse shuffling. The warm wind giving way to disquieting stillness. She worried her affection for him might get in the way of her judgment. And she didn't like lying.

She wasn't the only one entangled in romance. In a secluded view spot, Dick was whispering in Betty's ear. Upriver, Jane and Mountbatten's muscular aide—Special Operations Executive, according to Paul—were rehearsing a scene for SEAC's elite Shakespeare group. Julia was still irked that despite all her theatrical experience, she hadn't been invited to join. But Janie had her ways.

Hearing a murmur of male voices, Julia saw a red-faced RAF colonel join old Stuffed Shirt. Warwick began going on about his estate, conscripted by the government for training purposes. "Lady Warwick is making do with a third-floor suite and single ladies' maid."

"What about meals?" the colonel asked, refilling their glasses from an icy martini shaker.

"All ranks and civilians dine together. It took rather a bit of getting used to, but my wife insists we must pull together. And yours?"

"She's with the children in the country—Sussex. Our place is but an old family pile, of no use in the war effort, unlike your wife's property."

"Nice sandals." Pulling up a chair, Mack gave her a questioning look. "That poor man, with his fine piece of leather, waiting for me. Was it something I said? Or did? Or didn't do?"

Julia tried her darnedest to control the rush of blood to her cheeks. The guy had cornered the market on charm, but that was no evidence of deceit. However…"I've been really busy."

"I can imagine. It's a grand evening." He held up a bottle of aged Irish whiskey. "To the woman behind it all," he said in his delicious brogue. "For a proper toast, I propose we take this down to the riverbank."

As he was reaching out his hand—and she was about to take it—the skies opened. Laughing, they turned their faces into the downpour, as people were doing all over Ceylon.

———

Dawn light slanted through her bathroom window as she watched water trickling down the drain. Jane had warned her that Queen's Hotel was a breeding ground for mosquitoes, the probable cause of their dengue fever. Julia scooped up some of the treacherous water and slapped it on her face. Had the enemy known, the day after the barbecue would have been an effective time to attack. They'd all overindulged. But once in a while, they had to let down their hair. In her case, it was about to turn into frizzy chaos.

No longer warm and gentle, the summer rains attacked with a vengeance. The hard-packed red dirt turned to sludge. At least they weren't soldiers slogging through it. After two sleepless nights, Julia awoke to a feeling of dread, hoping her operation flopped. The decoy arms drop would take place, and no one would know about it, which meant—no spy. She busied herself by moving files out of boxes onto her new shelves as she awaited word. None came.

The next morning, she inspected her thatched roof and plaited walls. Still no leaks—here. The cloudy skies cracked open with thunder, the winds roared, insects buzzed. Swatting away a pack of vengeful mosquitoes, she unsealed the latest pouches and packets.

During a lull in the downpour, Julia heard a familiar voice and peeped out her window.

Donovan. Back in the field for the denouement of Operation Friendship.

A study in contrasts—crumpled and supremely crisp—he and Mountbatten were taking the covered walkway behind the Registry. She sidled back against the thin coconut-fiber wall.

"…our pilot observed the enemy intercept what was a bogus arms drop. Apologies, Admiral, but my cable held operational details intended to draw out a possible leaker. McWilliams saw it logged in by your Records head, then taken directly to Codes and Ciphers. Other than you, me, and Heppner, they're the only…" Their voices drifted off.

Taking no solace in the "success" of their op, Julia waited for the boss's visit. He finally appeared later that afternoon. "How much did you hear?"

"I wondered if your route was for my benefit."

"Need to know, McWilliams. I sent you here to be my eyes in SEAC, with a focus on British imperial initiatives. Instead, you uncovered a penetration of SEAC itself."

"And reported Mountbatten's push for an amphibious Rangoon invasion—Operation Dracula." Then she wanted to bite her tongue. *As our Chinese friends say, McWilliams, "Silence is the source of great strength."*

"For obtaining this intel, you may boast—but only between us." He smiled. "What a benefit to British prestige if they were to liberate Burma's capital before the Yanks. FDR was amused. Now, about your op…"

My op.

"We've pinpointed the leak to Codes and Ciphers. According to the Supremo, Clarity Hastings hired their eight-person staff, including Warwick. It seems she's a viscount's daughter, so can 'doubtless be trusted.' These blue bloods," he scoffed. "Mountbatten will continue SEAC's probe into the sabotaged Force 136 op as a smokescreen for your investigation."

"Yes, sir." She cleared her throat.

"You need to uncover the penetration agent. Get any help you require, but it's on you, McWilliams."

Stunned, Julia watched Donovan exit into a haze of vapor rising from the sodden ground. She was honored by his confidence—but was he overconfident? Who was she to pit herself against a ruthless fascist spy in their midst?

Her shoulders sagged. She thought she'd shed her old self-doubt, but here it was, waiting to undermine her. Closing the door, she leaned her head against the wall and slid down to the floor. She was exhausted from being the brave, gung ho Julia. She longed to be weak, just for once. Maybe she should have married Harrison Chandler.

Maybe her mother had been wrong about her potential.

Don't you dare, Caro said softly in her brain. *I gave you my name so you could go where I couldn't. This is the only thing I've ever asked you. Stand tall, complete your task. Do it for me, Julia Carolyn McWilliams. And yourself.*

TWENTY

———— // ————

So Julia had to carry on. She would never admit she'd come *this* close to giving up. Her mission remained: *You need to uncover the penetration agent. Get any help you require, but it's on you.*

As she was pondering where to get that help, the monsoon picked up steam. No one escaped making a pun of it. The air was filled to bursting with 100 percent humidity. Everything turned moldy, and paperwork dissolved before her eyes. Fungi burst through the floorboards of Dick's lower file area. The bugs reported for duty en masse, and nerves were frayed.

After the garden outside Queen's bar flooded, it was determined that *le sacré* cocktail hour would continue at Hotel Suisse, across Kandy Lake. That evening, while she and the girls waited beneath the portico for Paul and Jack, Julia was caught up in a swell of voices, horns, and drumbeats. As the rain seemed to sway along, people gathered before the temple, their white garments and flowers gleaming under the streetlamps, black umbrellas fading into the darkness.

Then, sheltered by great gold umbrellas, three elephants emerged, caparisoned in jeweled satin. The middle one, bearing a glowing shrine, resembled the elephant who'd greeted Julia outside her window the first day. Maybe it was him. Or *her*. She waved. "You sure don't see that in Washington!"

The jeep pulled up, and Jack leaned out. "Hop aboard, ladies."

Paul maneuvered smoothly through the animated crowds, the garlanded motor vehicles and animal carts. The road flowed with water, but they eventually rounded the lake and turned up the drive to the hotel, overlooking the misty town.

Heads bent against the torrent, they dashed inside the columned lobby and climbed the broad, curving mahogany stairway. Every person in the packed bar and restaurant, including staff, was standing.

"...Bastille Day, 14 July." In ringing tones, Mountbatten addressed the crowd: "While Allied troops battle their way to Paris, our French brothers and sisters dared join their voices in the streets—forcing the Nazis and Vichy collaborators to listen." His chest expanded. "*Allons, enfants de la patrie...*"

A lump swelled in Julia's throat as their ardent voices rose in thrilling harmony. "La Marseillaise" had become *their* anthem, expressing their unity in this brave worldwide struggle. Well before the end, everyone was blinking madly and choking back tears.

"To victory!" Jane stepped forward. "*Vive la France.*"

Betty hugged Julia, who pulled Jane into their arms. Julia loved her passionate spirit...and Betty's generous intellect. She loved their friendship. Who knew when she came to Washington to do her part what a gift she'd receive? Glasses were pressed into their hands. She raised hers. "To the Three Musketeers." They clinked, then Jane kissed her cheek.

After more toasts and cheers, Mountbatten slipped away. Armed Forces Radio Services picked up the slack as Judy Garland launched into "The Trolley Song," upbeat and bouncy.

People returned to their tables, and Paul waved the girls to his. Glancing about for Mack, who was nowhere in sight, Julia saw Stuffed Shirt Warwick making a move on a blond bombshell in a black sheath. She had long dark lashes, high rouged cheekbones, and burgundy bee-stung lips.

Paul caught her stare. "Donna Desmond. Just arrived. She's ours. Secret Intelligence."

"I doubt she could disappear undercover," Julia observed.

He bit back a smile. "In Delhi, she was known as 'the Black Tulip.'"

"What does that mean?"

"You know, the Dumas novel," Jane replied airily. "Set in Holland during the tulip mania. During a competition to develop a black tulip, the intrigue turns deadly."

"No need to go back in time for deadly intrigue." She'd never read Dumas but wasn't about to let Jane get to her. Still stirred by "La Marseillaise," Julia swept her gaze about the room. "Here we are on a remote dot on the map, our own little *Casablanca*. While none of us may amount to a hill of beans in a world at war—it sure feels good to stand up together." Then, embarrassed, she dropped her eyes.

"I had the same feeling." *Paul.*

Her cheeks grew warm even before she looked up and saw his fond expression.

"Only who's our leading man?" Betty mused. "Our Bogart?"

"Mountbatten's too gorgeous," Jane said, all innocence. "Dick, maybe?"

As Betty blushed and turned away, Julia thought of Bogart's gruff character—Paul certainly had his gruffness. But a heart of gold?

Jane was studying Donna. "I'd like to get my hands on that girl's Elizabeth Arden mail drops."

Julia was more interested in Warwick, his starched white uniform seemingly impervious to rain and humidity. While he was unaware of their top secret investigation, everyone at SEAC knew of Mountbatten's highly visible "smoke screen" probe into the Force 136 leak. Yet Warwick appeared unruffled. Either innocent—or a very good actor. Definitely not Bogart.

Equally calm, Clarity was surrounded by men at the bar. A viscount's daughter.

The radio segued to Vera Lynn's "You'll Never Know."

An apt title, although Julia preferred the more upbeat orchestral—

A great roar shook the room, throwing her back against her seat. Cries rang out. Betty and she stared at each other…Between them raged the charging torpedo, the fiery Bombay blast…Then, turning to assess the situation, Julia saw the light-filled smiles of their waiter, the barmen. The glistening rain falling upon the terrace, the lake, the town…The dazzling white temple. The festive crowds. The shrine on the elephant's back—

"The Festival of the Tooth!" she exclaimed, hearing the Colombo policeman speak of Kandy, existing through the ages under the Buddha's protection. *His holy relic resides at Temple of the Sacred Tooth…Once a year, it is paraded through city so people may give it honor.*

The drums and horns picked up, and everyone flocked to the broad French doors. The rain had given way to a huge golden moon.

Julia opened her arms. "The Miracle of the Tooth."

Paul smiled. "No one could beat you for enthusiasm, Julie."

She blinked with pleasure. "*Allons, enfants.* Let's join the parade."

TWENTY-ONE

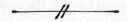

The next morning, July 15, the Germans still occupied Paris. According to OSS reports, the Allies were closing in. But no one could breathe easy until they chased the jackbooted thugs all the way back to hell.

Hearing a knock on the basha door, Julia slipped her Codes and Ciphers investigation file under some unclassified paperwork. "Yes?"

"It's Mack."

"Come in." She remained seated. The air between them vibrated.

"Did you see the parade?" He sat on the rope cot.

"Memorable. Very theatrical. Where were you?"

"Working, up at the Supremo's residence. The cannon shook the floorboards."

Julia nodded. "I dreamt the Japanese Army had swept through India—and won the war. Our base was a prison camp, and we were sent to slave on the Death Railway."

"You need to clear out the cobwebs. I've an errand at Trinco Harbor. Thought we might enjoy a picnic afterwards at Polonnaruwa."

"Polo—what?"

"Some stunning ruins. On a lake. Less than two hours away."

Dillon had mentioned a lovely drive over the hills to Trincomalee, on Ceylon's east coast.

"Brilliant!" Mack applauded, looking around. "Shelves. Labeled folders. Index card boxes. Even books."

Among them, Donovan's codebook. "It's a relief."

"You deserve an escape from all this toil."

"I confess to being sorely tempted. But there is a war on, Mack."

"I could say you'll be more effective after a change of scene." He gave her an unnerving stare. "Everyone needs to be naughty once in a while. It *is* Saturday."

"And no rain…I don't know when I last played hooky."

Mack appeared puzzled. Then he grinned. "Oh, you mean, *skived* off."

All at once she wanted to shut out the world, be a normal woman with a guy who knew how to kiss like there was no tomorrow. No one could deny the Americans and Brits were allies. "Right. Let's ditch this war for the moment. I suspect it will still be around when we return."

———

They drove up the mountain north of Kandy. After a series of tea estates and villages, the jungle took over. Flashy birds darted about, using yellow acacias and multiarmed banyans as landing pads. Pointy-eared macaques and pale, black-faced langurs swung loose-armed through the green canopy. Magenta orchids parted for the snout of a giant boar. A spy in their midst.

Julia glanced at Mack's craggy profile, his wiry russet hair. He caught her staring, and she flushed. Both from his charged look—and her lingering mistrust.

Perfumed with sandalwood and cinnamon, the road continued downhill through palm groves and cultivated lands. Farmers worked in the shade of lavish flame trees.

Soon, a sign in English and the swirly Sinhalese script announced Trincomalee. They turned north along a palm-lined curve of blue coastline filled with graceful little fishing boats.

Despite the bristling warships beyond, the scene was as pretty as her brother probably imagined it when he'd asked for her news, thinking she had all the luck. Easy duty. "Do you ever feel we have the Shangri-La war?"

"The enemy bombed this harbor once, Julia. They can return any moment."

The torpedo racing closer… Praying her mother would not witness her fiery end.

"Fort Frederick," Mack said as he drove under a stone archway inscribed *Anno 1675*. "Built by the Portuguese, later passing from Dutch to British hands." The old ramparts were lined with forbidding cannons, the sapphire sea crashing below. "Imagine being imprisoned here. The sound of the waves reminding you of the world you'd lost."

As Julia shivered in the heat, he showed her to the red-tiled building on their right. "Naval Intelligence."

She was pleased. A guilty man would not likely bring her on an intelligence errand.

Inside was the usual hubbub of typewriters, wireless receivers, cipher machines, and male voices. Mack approached a uniformed man with slicked-back hair and a pipe. After their grins and backslapping, he said, "Please meet Julia McWilliams of the OSS. Peter Fleming."

"The travel writer?" she asked as they shook.

"You might say."

"Donovan lent me your books. I feel I've traveled with you through Central Asia."

"Lucky you. No need to repeat my journey." He flashed a wicked grin. "Would that I'd had such a delightful companion. Instead it was me and some nasty camels who'd spit as soon as look at you. Once in a while, Providence would send me a donkey."

Mack removed a packet from his bag. "Replacement cipher text."

Fleming cocked his head. "Need we worry about security breaches?"

"Normal procedure," Mack replied.

Normal? It was the leak that had necessitated a new codebook, but apparently Mountbatten wanted to keep the threat under wraps. Seeing Mack dissemble with such ease—to a fellow Brit—Julia felt her hopes for trust between them fade.

———

A rough track ended at a mossy brick ledge, where Mack parked his jeep under a sprawling fig. Across a narrow stony beach lay a vast shimmering lake.

"Man-made. Rather splendid, I think." He got out and opened her door. "Built a thousand years ago by the king of Polonnaruwa as a reservoir for irrigation." He nodded north. "His palace ruins are there—government buildings, bathing ponds. Temples."

Squinting through the dense greenery, Julia could make out jagged, time-darkened walls. After all that enterprise, Polonnaruwa was deserted, not a sign of human life.

Mack looked southward. "The ancient library."

This, she had to see—for her book-loving Mother Caro.

There was but a faint breath of heavy, saturated air. Her thin white blouse stuck to her skin. She shimmied it free, then sensed his gaze. She felt transparent.

"I promised you a picnic." Stepping over the shady ledge, he lowered his pack and smoothed a patch of ground next to the fig's broad trunk. Sweat glistened on his brow, the V of his chest.

They spread out the blanket, the food, then relaxed against cool brick.

Mack opened his champagne with a triumphant pop. "To the liberation of Paris!"

Julia joined his toast. "To Paris." She twirled her glass, watching the bubbles rise and fall. His body was warm, the rumble of his breath rushing through her.

Shifting away, she unwrapped a banana leaf, handing him a sandwich. "Life is strange, isn't it? One day you're having a picnic in…How do you say it again?"

"Po-lon-na-ru-wa."

She repeated it twice. "I hate to admit I've taken little effort with their language."

"Few of us have."

"The West thinks it was us, that we 'enlightened' them. You see the world differently out here. I…"

He inclined his head, waiting as she clarified her thoughts.

"I really had no idea." She gazed at the ancient reservoir-lake. This had been their land long before the British came. She'd gained a new perspective from the Colombo policeman. And from their room attendant,

Taj, whose calm presence uplifted her every day. Who, when asked about the weather, would reply, *Same-same. Too much sun, too much rain. But no bombings.* Placing his palms together with a gentle smile. *We are under protection of Lord Buddha.* These good people deserved liberty, too. "We believe there's no returning to the status quo."

"If you mean the British Empire, I have to agree."

Turning to him, Julia was too aware of his open shirt collar, his smooth tan skin, the smattering of golden hairs. She looked back at the lake, almost silvery in the unrelenting flat light. "What does your boss think? Or his boss?"

"Churchill cannot conceive of Britain without Empire."

"Mountbatten?" She took a long, perilous sip of champagne, her limbs loosening.

"He is the supreme commander. He follows the PM's mandate." Julia felt him shrug...the movement of his ribs. "Our dollars finance your strategies."

"Speaking of strategy—your op regarding the Force 136 ambush? Dropping cow patties on the waiting Japs was a good touch."

"I'm not aware of that." She rubbed her thumb over a smooth stone. How did he know of their decoy drop—which the Supremo had agreed to keep quiet? And why did he let her know that *he* knew?

"Probably one of the few things you're not aware of. Between us, our positions offer an eye on much of what's going on. There was a nasty mess in Burma last year when one of our units and one of yours fired on the other while pursuing the same objective. If you and I were to liaison, unofficially, it might facilitate communications."

"You mean, a sort of back channel?" She stiffened, ancient brick scraping her back.

"Something like that. For example, we shared the Japanese shipping intercept with you," he said, his gaze piercing right through her.

"It was much appreciated. But I'm just a file clerk." Julia watched a cloud breach the clear blue sky, then opened another banana-leaf packet. She ate a golden slice of mango, the juice dripping down her lips.

Mack wiped her mouth with an index finger. He curved his arm around her. "Julia?"

This time she kissed him first. They lay back on the blanket, legs intertwined, picking up where they'd left off two weeks earlier under the Buddha's beneficent gaze. Their limbs slipped right into place. A hot wind brushed over them, and the leaves fluttered.

A warning bell inside rang, a deep gong, a terrible push-pull. Unprofessional. Dangerous. But *oh my*. Julia buried her face in his neck, her mind going soft focus. Another gong shocked her back. As she rolled away, the ancient lake appeared metallic, even sinister.

Mack stroked her arm, then lifted her palm and kissed it. "I can taste the mango."

She shivered, the secrets between them sizzling like dry ice. That gong again: *My duty. Donovan.* Although her body resisted, she willed herself up, smoothed her skirt, and reached for her Leica. "Care to explore?" she asked brightly.

"I count on your detailed report, darling." He lay back and closed his eyes.

His breath evened and smoothed. So easily he had fallen into the sleep of a child. His face so innocent—but how did she know what lay underneath? Julia felt loopy.

With a last glance at Mack, she stepped over the low lakeshore wall onto a parallel path that ran north to the palace complex and south to the library. Away from his magnetic presence, her head cleared. Working together to "facilitate communications"? She didn't buy that. One thing not subject to doubt: the sparks were real. Julia stiffened her spine. She was an intelligence officer serving her country in wartime and needed to control her emotions.

As she approached the palace ruins, the path turned muddy, overgrown by a profusion of trees and vines. Slipping through, she spotted a fiercely carved lion on a dais, a blue kingfisher perched atop his head, and took a picture for Dillon. Roofless stone columns were occupied by several haughty monkeys, who ranted at her as if annoyed at her intrusion.

"It's all yours, fellows." Farther on, a serene Buddha faced her from inside a temple where the Sacred Tooth had once resided, according to a plaque in Sinhalese and English. What would remain of her era in a thousand years? Van Gogh, Tchaikovsky? Democracy, she hoped. The Eiffel Tower, soon to be freed of its brutal tourists. The Statue of Liberty, a powerful symbol. But what about the Buddha and all he symbolized? The temples and sculptures, pulsing with life. The Taj Mahal. The music! The ancient culture of the East had already endured.

As the sun drilled into her brain, Julia turned south, moving through jungle brush past Mack's jeep. It was quiet, only some monkey chatter, a mosquito's buzz.

The buzz became a rumble…as another green jeep approached the crumbling, mossy brick walls of the ancient library.

Beyond it, a small tan sedan nosed out of a narrow lane. It parked in the shadows of a dome-shaped structure, one of four surrounding the curved central ruin. A backlit figure emerged in a fitted khaki top, skirt, and shoulder bag, a large straw hat.

Squinting into the sun, Julia observed a second backlit figure exit the jeep—a large man. Both walking toward the library, rather than each other. No hugs or hellos. He moved through a patch of dappled light, carrying a small box.

It was an odd encounter. Instinctively, she reached again for Dillon's Leica and snapped a few photos until the pair disappeared behind a half wall. Was it an illicit rendezvous in an area with few hotels or places for privacy? But with no one around, why hadn't they greeted each other?

Julia moved deeper in the concealing overgrowth. A former gate opening offered another angle into the ruins. She caught a glimpse of sun-struck golden-red hair. A back clothed in a snug white jacket. A heart-shaped blue box. Perhaps a gift. Some candy?

Then came a pounding so great it shook the earth under her feet. A thunderous roar coming from the lake area.

Explosion? Earthquake?

As she whirled back into the brush, there was another roar, a multi-octave trumpet. She crept over the low brick wall, peeping through the foliage.

Flourishing his trunk, a huge elephant lumbered up the shore. Ahead, other elephants were splashing madly, wild and free. As he joined the group, they sprayed him and one another, sending great showers of water skyward. Tails and trunks swayed as if to their own musical beat. Their joy was palpable, infectious. Julia felt a moment of awe.

Hungry to share it, she glanced at Mack, sleeping under the fig tree. Yet something about the mysterious assignation still gripped her.

She ducked back toward the library just as the man opened his jeep door. He was still carrying the blue box. She squinted—at Stephen Stuffed Shirt Warwick!

In the shadows of the curved wall, the woman was lowering the straw hat over her gleaming hair—darker now, more auburn. After his jeep disappeared in the trees, she headed for her tan Hillman—wearing a fitted khaki uniform. Julia was stunned to recognize the narrow waist and rounded hips of FANY nurse Lieutenant Olivia Mitford.

She and Warwick must be having an affair. Yet their rendezvous was awfully quick—for *romance*. Though why else would they meet so far from Kandy?

As Julia walked back to the low lakeshore wall, her mind was everywhere—the secret meeting, the melancholy grandeur of a bygone civilization, the majestic elephants reveling in this earth. A little one rolling in the mud. A mother spraying it clean. Caro, both at her side and forever lost.

Propped up on an elbow, Mack sprang to his feet. The same shock of connection drew them together. "Aren't they magnificent?" Grinning with boyish excitement, he took her hand. "What else have you discovered in your adventures?"

"The ruins were beautiful and disturbing. I—" About to mention the couple's tryst, she caught herself. "I felt sad, such an advanced society and then…"

"There's a lot more to see. Next time." He folded her in his embrace, his mouth against her ear, two-stepping her back to the tree's broad trunk.

Their bodies stuck together, and it was difficult not to sink down upon that dangerous blanket. She gathered her breath, composed herself. "Night falls quickly in the tropics."

He glanced at the blanket, the sky, and, with a regretful nod, pulled away.

After they left for Kandy, Julia spoke little, puzzling over the afternoon's events. Had Mountbatten told Mack of their top secret decoy op? Otherwise, how did he know? And what did he mean about an unofficial exchange of information, which could be a slippery slope to an attempted recruitment? Then there was the couple, Stuffed Shirt Warwick and FANY Nurse Olivia. Why would they arrange a rendezvous so far from town—and part so quickly? Was it romance or something else?

And why did he leave with his blue "gift" box?

TWENTY-TWO

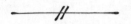

The next morning, Julia reported the events to Commanding Officer Dick Heppner—their unexplained delivery of the replacement cipher to British Naval Intelligence, the picnic, the peculiar encounter between Olivia and Warwick.

"Warwick is married, we know." She frowned. "Yet their behavior didn't feel amorous."

"Couples have fights," Dick replied. "He got ticked off and left. Not to be graphic, but maybe he expected more than she was willing to offer."

"That must have been a doozy of a fight if he took back the gift. No doubt our SEAC investigation puts me in a suspicious frame of mind…"

He drummed his fingers on the carved planter's desk. "Get your film to Field Photographic. Who knows? You might have discovered something, at least about the blue box."

"Thank you. By the way, I heard we dropped cow patties at the Burma site." Although the op had been deadly serious, the image still made her want to giggle.

"A creative touch by our air force crew, which I don't recall mentioning." He gave Julia a quizzical look.

"Mack told me at the lake. I wondered how he knew—after the Supremo promised to keep the operation secret. Maybe he has another source, or…"

"He was letting you know that Mountbatten trusts him. Maybe he wants to gain your confidence." His brow furrowed. "A SEAC breach is a risk to us all. Let's start looking at everyone with access. I'll see what I can find on Warwick and the nurse."

"On my way."

In the course of her first op, less than a year ago, she had received a Minox camera with history-changing intelligence. In her second, the Leica had produced a possible lead to uncovering a major SEAC breach.

"Stephen Warwick and Olivia Mitford," Dick agreed later after viewing the prints.

"And a heart-shaped blue box, no other identifiable marking."

"They went to great pains not to be observed. Your instincts are good, but..."

"I know, it's probably two lovers who had a fight," Julia said. "Yet one of them oversees messaging at Codes and Ciphers, whose security has been compromised—as proven by Operation Friendship. It's not impossible they were exchanging intel."

"You must keep an eye on Warwick—and Olivia. While investigating the rest of that unit. This operation is ongoing, and you remain my point person."

She looked down, trying to hide her pleasure—and anxiety. To beat back that nagging voice of doubt.

"Some of your surveillance will take place in the evening. To avoid unwanted attention as a single woman, I'd advise working as a couple—someone on *our side*."

"You mean, Mack and I should 'break up'?" Julia could feel his rough lips on hers, his sure fingers grazing her spine. Yet her wave of relief spoke of the troubling conflicts between them. "I'll tell him I need a breather."

Dick made no comment. "Of your possible 'dates,' Dillon and Byron are both linked to intelligence. To avoid any red flags, I suggest Paul—"

She grimaced. "How about Jack? He has the clearance."

He ignored her words. "Paul is low-key but seasoned; he has navigated Washington and Delhi politics, he's familiar with who's who in Kandy...Even more than you."

There was no point arguing. This was an order, and Julia was expected to stand up and salute. "Thank you for your support." Despite this honor, she left with a sense of alarm at the idea of working with the arrogant Paul Child…and that he might try to take over her operation.

———

During Queen's cocktail hour, she bought Paul a drink and, at a secluded garden table, issued a dry briefing about Polonnaruwa, their joint mission—and the heart-shaped blue box.

"Why did he leave with it?" Paul peered inside the bar, where Julia had already noted the absence of Warwick and Olivia. And Mack.

As dusk deepened, lights flashed on around the swimming pool. Secret Intelligence chief Dillon Ripley stood across the garden, his binoculars pointed into the trees.

"In the beginning, I thought being a bird-watcher was simply good cover," Julia mused.

"Maybe it's the reverse. The war gives him cover to pursue his passion."

"I envy that passion." She watched Dillon. "He knows who he is. I'm still looking."

"I understand the feeling." Paul put down his glass. "Why did you leave New York?"

"To be with my ill mother. Anyway, things weren't working out for me there."

"What didn't work?" He wouldn't let her off the hook. "What did you want to happen?"

"To be magically brilliant," she said with a wry smile. "To be accorded a position at the *New Yorker* and be witty and drink cocktails at night." As it had been with Tom Johnston, that one magical moment in Manhattan.

"Timing is everything."

"That's such a cliché," she replied, annoyed at being forced back to her humiliation.

"I'm a late bloomer, too."

Paul was over forty. How long would it take for her to bloom?

"In France, I learned something about wine." He regarded her thoughtfully. "The finest wines take their time."

Julia gazed at the swimming pool. He had rescued her from another glistening pool. She imagined going under…sinking…struggling for air…Then she took a long inhale. No one would ever accuse Paul Child of being the life of the party. Yet when he spoke, his words had substance—and this time, even warmth. What she'd seen as arrogance and pedantry was his meticulous, resolute nature. Although his flaws were still evident—his too-long nose, receding hairline, short stature, and advancing age—he was a solid guy. Someone she could work with.

She turned to him just as he was turning to her. "I suggest we shift our surveillance operation to Hotel Suisse."

She and Paul found a table in the cocktail lounge where they'd sung "La Marseillaise." On the terrace, General Wheeler was dining with daughter Peggy. Julia focused on their targets. Warwick was alone, sipping a scotch. Clarity huddled at the bar with "Black Tulip" Desmond.

"Mind if I join the fun?" Jane sauntered up with her catchy smile, then sat down.

Julia eyed Paul, who blinked his assent. After they ordered drinks, stuffed samosas, and spicy cashews, Jane began a story about smuggling a baby panda out of China.

"You've had more lives than a cat," Julia marveled. "When was that?"

"After I dumped my husband in Java. More of my checkered past. If I had stayed, we'd probably be stuck together in his POW camp."

"Janie! How horrible. You never told me."

"I suppose I have a little guilt about moving on." Jane picked up a samosa. "As I was saying…My traveling companion's husband had captured Baby Su-Lin in Sichuan, planning to sell it to the Chicago zoo. Then he died. With panda exports banned, we needed sympathetic air transport, which meant the Flying Tigers—controlled by Generalissimo and Madame Chiang Kai-shek. He speaks no English, but she does. She interceded for us."

"I'm sure that didn't come cheap," Paul replied dryly.

"You said it." Jane's attention shifted to the bar. She waggled her fingers at her lithe scene partner, Peterson. Mountbatten's aide, whom Paul deemed Special Operations Executive.

"How's Shakespeare coming along?" Julia asked archly.

"It seems no one has time to learn lines, so we read sonnets—and drink whiskey."

"Maybe Shakespeare is cover for a drinking club." Julia grinned at Paul.

His face creased as they shared the joke. "He ever try to probe you for intel, Janie? You know they call SOE the Ministry of Ungentlemanly Warfare?"

"As his unladylike counterpart in Morale Operations," she said aloofly, "I can out-fence and outfox him. I'm trained in black propaganda, pot-stirring. And *counter*intelligence."

Jane Foster was a spy, too!

Then Dr. Wilson and Nurse Olivia Mitford strolled in, moving to Warwick's table. Julia kicked Paul in the shin. The doctor introduced Olivia—she and Stuffed Shirt shook hands.

As if they'd never met. Paul and Julia eyed each other again.

Her uniform was tightly belted, her auburn hair pinned up. Curvaceous yet delicate and fair, Olivia listened to the men with deference, a slender hand smoking a cigarette.

That long-boned hand moving up my bedside…reaching for my wrist, taking my pulse with slim, pale fingers.

"Anyway." Jane turned back to Paul. "With that kind of corruption—"

"What kind?" he asked, bemused.

"General and Madame Chiang Kai-Shek."

"Back to the Chiangs, are we? Sadly, we need them as much as they need us."

As the two went at it, Julia viewed Olivia and Warwick interact with a formal reserve, evidently meant to disguise their relationship.

Seemingly bored with her rant, Jane noticed Julia's attention on the pair. "That man."

"Who?"

"Warwick. He bought me a drink one night, said if I'm ever in England after the war, he'd give me a private tour of his ancient estate."

"I bet." Paul squinted as if at a map. "It is a fact that most men are skirt-chasers."

His "ancient" estate belonged to *Lady* Warwick, as Julia had overheard at the barbecue.

"Fortunately, there are a few gentlemen left." Jane gave Paul a teasing smile. "In this treacherous world—how about escorting two innocent damsels back to Queen's for dinner?"

"I've seen enough here," Julia said. "Besides, octopus curry is on the menu tonight."

He cocked his head. "You're stepping up, gal. That's one thing I've never tried."

"Escorting two innocent damsels? Or tasting octopus curry?" she asked.

He laughed. "Put it this way: I've never escorted two such *exceptional* damsels."

Julia was feeling saucy and free. "Otherwise, you've done it all?"

"I wouldn't say that, exactly, but I have lent my hand to a few enterprises, tasted a few dishes, bent my arm at a few bars."

"Save a few stories for later, Paulie." Jane stood, slapping some rupees on the table. "We've got a long evening ahead."

Julia thought of Jane's complicated private life. Maybe Paul was simply her good chum. Anyway, who cared? As he'd said, she had bigger fish to fry.

TWENTY-THREE

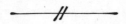

Julia dreamt it was Valentine's Day, and Paul gave her a hand-drawn blue heart—which became a heart-shaped box. Then there were *two* of them, passing between two sets of hands. When her eyes flew open at dawn, she pictured Olivia arriving with a heart-shaped blue box in her khaki shoulder bag and *exchanging* it with Warwick's. What were they up to? Something about Paul's skirt-chaser comment needled her yet remained elusive.

Equally elusive was her recollection of Nurse Olivia bending over her bedside. Had she been searching Julia's bag? It had contained nothing secret. But it could have.

At breakfast, lavishing mango chutney on a potato-stuffed rice pancake, she tuned out her friends' chatter. Across the room, Paul and Jane were reading their newspapers, sharing articles, and chuckling. *It is a fact that most men are skirt-chasers*. Then Julia recalled Betty mentioning Paul's reputation as a ladies' man. *It takes one to know one*, she thought, annoyed all over again. Yet she was impatient to hear his thoughts.

After he drove them to HQ and everyone left the parking area, they moved under the yellow acacia tree, where she relayed her suspicions.

He angled his head, his good eye regarding her straight on. "It's only circumstantial."

"As a longtime mystery reader, I know you must beware of such evidence. What if he's not a skirt-chaser? What if it's for the money? I heard him say his estate belongs to his *wife*. Maybe she controls the purse strings. And he's eager for…financial independence."

"To be his own man." Paul gazed somewhere beyond her vision.

"After my father died, we were penniless. The businessman on whom my mother depended favored my sunny brother—and sent *him* to Harvard. I'd have given anything for my own dough."

"*Betray* your country?" Julia was pained for him. His *sunny* brother. Paul, the somber one.

"Of course not. But you've proposed a believable motive. Let's go see Dick."

———

"I've known more than one blue blood with champagne taste and no cash," Julia told their CO. "Maybe Olivia was dangling money before his eyes. What could she be after?"

"Let's see what we have. We have the auburn-haired woman in khaki—Olivia Mitford, the FANY nurse." Dick held up his thumb, ticking off the first point. "Two." His index finger. "We have the man in the snug white uniform top—Stephen Warwick, head of Codes and Ciphers." Middle finger. "Three. Here comes your speculation: we have him arriving with a blue box he *possibly* intends to swap with an identical one in her bag." Ring finger. "Four, we have Warwick, not as a lusty Romeo but a man living off his wife's resources and *possibly* desirous of independent funds." His eyes were dark and challenging.

Julia held up five fingers, then closed them. "What we don't have *yet* is hard evidence. What was inside the heart-shaped blue box—or boxes? What is Olivia's role?"

Paul frowned. "And why did they behave as if they didn't know each other at Hotel Suisse?"

Dick tapped his desk. "Wild Bill is due in tomorrow night. You will report to him at 0800 the following morning."

———

Despite the humid weather, Dick's door and windows were shut tight ahead of their hush-hush meeting. While their CO did paperwork, Julia sat in nervous silence. Paul studied the maps.

Eyes ablaze, Donovan pushed inside. "People have taken to the streets in Paris. The German garrison is retreating!" He and Heppner pounded each other on the back.

Jumping up, Julia threw her arms around the nearest man—Paul. He returned a powerful hug.

There might never be such a moment again, and they meant to savor it. But once they wiped their eyes, they were still in this world. This war. And still investigating their own allies.

Julia delivered her report. Donovan listened from the antique six-legged chair, arms crossed. After she finished, he stared at the shuttered window, rubbing the bridge of his nose. "I wonder if it's too early to confront Warwick."

"Does that mean you think I have something?"

"You've built a preliminary case, McWilliams. I'll have his quarters searched. *If* they find anything, we shall have a chat. Did you happen to know that FANY nurses are also trained in codes and signals—for possible fieldwork?"

"So she has the background," Julia said, elated they were taking her conclusions seriously. "Byron could mock up a cable 'revealing' some fake intel."

"Let's not put the tonga before the horse," Donovan cautioned. "We'll watch them both for a while. Dig deeper into her background." He nodded at Paul, indicating the door.

After they left, she sat down, afraid to be proved a fool before these men she so admired. What if, as Paul had suggested, her "case" was merely circumstantial?

"On another note." Dick smiled. "I have a gift for you—"

"Nothing in a heart-shaped box, I hope."

"Much bigger. You'll forgive me if it's not wrapped—your new assistant, Patricia Norbury, direct from DC. I told her to sleep in. You remember that journey."

Julia beamed. "Poor dear."

———

After lunch, Dick stopped her outside the mess. "Olivia is from an old, landed English family. Single. Served at the 100th Station Hospital in Delhi before arriving here late March—shortly before Warwick. A skilled field officer, well positioned to collect intel."

She gazed down at a terrace of shaggy, untended tea. "Maybe she got wind of SEAC's move and arranged a transfer." Julia was heartened he didn't refute her. "She wanted a well-placed target—susceptible to seduction. And/or in need of money."

"We live in a dark world." He walked away.

Later, Donovan dropped by her basha, intention blazing from his eyes.

She shot to her feet.

"They found your heart-shaped box. Taped under Warwick's armoire. You can tell right there he's not a pro. We're going to Hotel Suisse. You, me, and the Supremo."

Julia's heart soared.

The right side of his mouth curled up. "What are you waiting for, McWilliams? We have a spy to catch." He opened the door and ushered her out.

You, me, and the Supremo.

TWENTY-FOUR

———— // ————

The blue box was on the table of Lieutenant Commander Warwick's quarters while they awaited his return, seated on various chairs behind it.

Warwick entered, stiffened when he saw them, then saluted.

Mountbatten left him standing and did not return the salute. He glanced at Julia. "Is this the man you saw meeting FANY Lieutenant Olivia Mitford?"

"I have photos of the event." She held up the envelope.

"Did you see them exchange a heart-shaped box?"

"Yes." Julia had not actually witnessed the swap. But Lord Stuffed Shirt needed a push.

Mountbatten pointed at the box. "Is this it?"

"It appears so, sir."

The Supremo trained his steely eyes on Warwick. "Our search team discovered it taped under your armoire. We counted five thousand-pound notes."

A gamut of expressions crossed Warwick's face, ending in despair. "I…"

"You will be court-martialed for treason and shot. Or you can cooperate, and perhaps escape the firing squad. Which will it be?"

"It was Olivia," he blurted immediately. "She said how desperate she was to learn the whereabouts of her brother's unit in Burma. Her *only* brother. I wanted to help her."

As they regarded him in stony silence, Julia wondered what else he wanted from her.

Warwick looked around the room as if searching for the correct answer. Spotting two armed MPs at the door, he deflated further. "I located his unit, hoping it would relieve her mind."

"Your intel led to the Force 136 ambush. The loss of two good men." Donovan's mouth twisted. "Nurse Mitford doesn't have a brother."

Warwick grimaced. "I should have known! She insisted I accept a monetary gift, her expression of gratitude. I declined, but, well, my marriage is not what one would wish, and I thought a cushion might give me options. Then Olivia needed to know something else. When I refused, she threatened to turn me in. That woman *trapped* me!" he said indignantly.

While she had no doubt used her wiles on him, Julia was certain the skirt-chasing lieutenant had been easy prey.

Mountbatten gave him a withering stare. "You lied and betrayed your family…your nation…the free world." His voice dripped venom.

"I'll cooperate to the full extent. I will." Warwick hung his head. "My father died in the Somme. I was the *second* son, inherited nothing. By then, the sale of Seated Titles was banned, so I was forced to purchase a title that did not include land."

Julia thought of Paul, whose "sunny" brother got the love and Harvard education. Although there were no titles in America, they did have their own nobility—of which she was part. Paul inherited nothing. Unlike Warwick, he didn't poor-little-me but worked hard.

The traitor lifted his head with a pleading look. "I had to borrow money from my wife! She has never let me forget it. But she's happy enough to be Lady Warwick, now, isn't she?"

His sigh told the tale of a loveless business deal masquerading as a marriage.

"I will help you. But please…"

Donovan gave him a nasty smile. "We appreciate your offer of *cooperation*. What did Olivia 'need to know,' and what did you pass her?"

Warwick raised his chin. "First, I'll tell you what I learned, which may be of value. The Japs are planning a sort of local Radio Tokyo—Free

Ceylon. The first broadcast will 'reveal' America's anticolonial initiatives, to drive a wedge between our two services."

"No wedge," Donovan insisted. "I'll repeat my question. What did you pass to Olivia?"

"They also have plans to incite our Indian plantation workers against us." With a hopeful expression, he looked at Mountbatten, who regarded him as if across a bloody battlefield.

Warwick cleared his throat. "She wanted operational secrets. I discovered a clandestine printing unit outside Kandy, run by Jane Foster and Betty MacDonald. Olivia demanded more on Betty, whose husband runs secret radio ops in Burma, and Jane—a Communist, she said."

"Kee-riste," Donovan said.

Although she knew better, Julia was stunned by her closest friends' duplicity—or rather, tradecraft, she corrected herself with a certain pride in their professionalism.

"More of their 'wedge' material, I would assume," Mountbatten said grimly.

"Who's handling Olivia?" Donovan asked in disgust.

"I don't know," Warwick asserted.

"Do your best to find out. Let me be clear: you are working for us now—your fate is in your hands. If Olivia has any further 'requests,' you must inform us immediately." Donovan picked up the blue box. "And thanks for your contribution to the Allied anti-fascist campaign."

Mountbatten pinned him with an arctic stare. "You understand the penalty for treason?"

Warwick drew himself up. "Yes, sir. You can count on me, sir."

After the MPs saluted, the three of them walked out.

"'You can count on me,'" Julia repeated sarcastically.

Pausing at the top of the stairs, Mountbatten regarded her. "We can certainly count on *you*, Miss McWilliams. First-rate work."

She flushed bright red.

"Now, get back to it," Donovan ordered. "I'll meet you at the Registry."

—————

Shortly after the night guard took over, the boss arrived. "Olivia is under twenty-four-hour surveillance. We need to learn who's running her and the mechanics of their exchange."

Julia perched on the cot in case he wanted her desk. "Did you know about Betty and Jane's secret MO unit? Did the Supremo?"

"As you're aware, the United States and Great Britain are engaged in a quiet campaign over the fate of postwar Asia and which system will prevail—European colonialism or American self-determination and free enterprise. Your friends produce leaflets to educate native peoples about their choices. So no, Mountbatten did not know."

"Of course Jane's a leftist, but—a *Communist*?" Whatever would Pop say?

"It doesn't matter. She's effective, energetic, and clever." Donovan began pacing.

"She'd laugh at the accusation. But Betty would hate compromising her husband." Each bore secrets, unable to share; how empty their letters must have felt. Julia had been present in the Messages basha during one of their silence-filled radio communications.

"The identity of Alex MacDonald is well-known. His jungle broadcasts have made the Japs lose terrible face. He is a courageous leader."

At the price of his marriage. She understood that the couple's geographical separation was not the only cause of estrangement. Their business was based on secrets. "What now?"

"We'll offer something of extremely high value." He paused at her SEAC map.

She thought quickly. "A British source reveals Churchill's mistress has something damaging on him."

Donovan turned, his lively blue eyes meeting hers. "Which might force him to resign."

Julia jumped to her feet, crackling with energy. "Leaving a power vacuum the Germans could take advantage of."

He twinkled. "Now Byron can mock up that cable you suggested. You will deliver it to SEAC tomorrow."

"What if Clarity receives it?"

"She'll be in Colombo with Donna Desmond—her new best friend," Donovan said with a wicked smile. "Warwick will demand ten thousand pounds from Olivia for intel that could change the course of the war. After the transaction, we follow her to her handler."

As Julia let out her breath, envisioning the scheme, he asked, "Anything else?"

"Over the course of my SEAC liaison work, I developed a friendship with Mountbatten's aide Lieutenant James Mack. As I reported to Dick, Mack recently suggested we swap intel to 'facilitate communications.' I was disturbed and even wondered if I was *his* target."

"I would think. You need to monitor him. Be careful what you say."

"Of course. Dick ordered me to conduct my surveillance with Paul Child."

"I've found Child's insights to be quite reliable."

"He's solid." And hadn't yet tried to take over the way some men might. "To support our cover as an 'item,' Mack and I broke up. But I'm careful around everyone these days."

"As it should be, McWilliams." Donovan walked to the door, then turned. "Good luck with your op."

She was being thrown in with Paul. Like it or not, they were a team. But it was her op.

TWENTY-FIVE

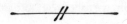

It was midmorning by the time Julia collected Byron's mock cable with the Churchill dirt and corralled Paul. A hot, muggy breeze blew through the jeep as she briefed him on the interrogation and its aftermath with Donovan—including the bogus intelligence she would soon be delivering. The skies were a dull-gray scrim over the monstrous sun.

"Impressive work," he said, steering between muddy potholes that had gouged out the road. "To be honest, I used to think you were a little too...frothy to run the Registry."

Anger welled up inside. What about his vaunted diplomacy? Or was that only for the brass? Still, Donovan had recognized her. And Mountbatten! "I've been a leader since I was a girl, the one who made things happen." Hearing her voice warble with emotion, Julia willed it lower. "I stepped into Donovan's chaotic file room and organized it as a functional Registry at the heart of the OSS. Then he entrusted me with a high-level, classified operation. That doesn't sound very *frothy* to me." She surprised herself, but every word she'd said was true. *This one's for you, Caro.*

Paul turned, his features compressed in that narrow-focused way. "Now you have stepped into another difficult environment. And transferred your skills with aplomb."

She tossed her head at his offhand praise and didn't speak again until they arrived at SEAC.

Mosquitoes dive-bombed the jeep as they drove through the dripping greenery of the Royal Botanic Gardens. Without a word, she and

Paul parted. While he went to deliver some maps to the Supremo, Julia walked to Records with the file bearing their falsified intel about Churchill.

She handed the cable to Erin. "Just in from DC. Attention: Codes and Ciphers/SEAC."

Erin lowered her pen onto some index cards. "I'll log it and deliver it straightaway." She opened her ledger, noted the cable's arrival, then set it back at her right hand.

As an advantage to being tall, Julia had a bird's-eye view of her desk. Near her were two narrow catalog drawers from the library file cabinets. One drawer, labeled *Burma*, was open to a typed divider, *Arakan*. The coastal area with Manly's network.

"Nice. My index boxes are cardboard."

"It's endless, isn't it?" Erin indicated the other drawer, labeled *India*. "I have been updating these cards and find no entry on Jessore." Her voice as crisp as her fine linen suits. "Any related material you could share, Julia?"

Why would Erin query her about a secret airbase outside Calcutta? Expressionless, she shuffled through her memory. Donovan had spoken of competing intelligence groups at Jessore. Since then, she'd mentioned it to only one person—Mack.

It struck her like a gut punch. Knocking the wind out of her. What else had he passed on about her? She placed her palms on Erin's desk, firmly, desperate not to give herself away. "Is Jessore a person or place?"

Erin raised a finely shaped eyebrow. "A place. India."

"I'll get back to you." Julia smiled.

"Ta." She smiled back. "You must join me for a drink one evening soon."

"That would be peachy." She left, frantic not to run into Mack.

The air in the hall was charged, all her feelings bouncing off each other. Her eyes cast downward, she was surprised to notice Paul's feet... then the rest of him waiting before the stairs. His face was closed off; obviously something was on his mind. But she had her own problems.

At least there was no need to make conversation on the way back.

She had enough to consider following Erin's unintended revelation of Mack's treachery. Just as she'd been assigned to infiltrate SEAC-HQ and learn what she could, Mack had a parallel mission. They were spying on each other. And shared the guilt of deceit. Yet something real had existed between them.

Two days after their lake picnic, just before cocktail hour, Mack had shown up at Queen's. Julia told him she had dinner plans, but he only wanted to walk with her to the outdoor market. She agreed, knowing this would be her moment to handle the breakup. They carried on a light conversation until he paused at the second stall, a fan seller.

She smiled softly. "When I was at Montessori preschool, I made a folded paper fan for my mother's birthday. She tucked it in the mirror of her dressing table. It's still there."

He squeezed her hand, briefly. "You have a birthday coming up, don't you? I'll buy you one."

Julia couldn't help but be charmed. Some were delicately carved from sandalwood or bone, or painted on rice paper—but she found herself smitten by a gorgeous peacock fan with a shiny mahogany handle. Watching her expression, he bought it without bargaining.

She thanked him but, as soon as they turned onto the lakeshore, said she needed time apart. The press of work, etcetera. His face fell, but he didn't try to change her mind. She'd felt guilty all the way back to the hotel, wondering if she could have handled things differently. Or had their relationship been doomed from the start? There was no way to reason her way through it. It was all true, and it all hurt.

It still hurt. Even amid her immense anger.

A bell tinkled. And a horn beeped—in what order, she wasn't sure, but Paul was gingerly passing a water buffalo who'd wandered onto the road.

"I never meant to disparage your talents, Julie."

He called her by a name used by close friends, and she wasn't sure how she felt about that. "I'll take your word for it," she replied with dignity. She did not need to compel his recognition.

After several more moments of silence, Julia glanced sideways and noticed his dark aura had lifted. He was chuckling to himself, apparently pleased as punch.

"Who'd have thunk—a spy mission? Things are never dull around you."

"I was also known as the Organizer of Fun," she said, then immediately flushed and looked away. What kind of accomplishment was that? Yet, surprisingly, her own darkness began to lift.

"Still are, according to my sources." He glanced at her with a roguish smile. "I could certainly use a little fun in my life—and you're the gal with the know-how."

She knew Paul was trying to soften her up. And it was working. "Not too *frothy* for you?"

"Just the right amount to liven things up. Care to join me for some bazaar chow tonight?" he suggested. "If you have an appetite, I can suggest an outstanding Javanese curry, *rijsttafel*."

His face was creased with warmth. His nose no longer seemed too long, nor did she mind the mustache. Or even his taciturn nature. Julia felt certain that, unlike Mack, he would be straight with her. "Whatever it is, my appetite is up to the task."

TWENTY-SIX

——— // ———

"*Imagine*. I thought Washington, DC, was exotic!" exclaimed her new assistant, Patricia Norbury, as they set off on their morning commute. "I even peeked inside the temple. You can forget there's a war going on."

A dimpled Texan with a pixie haircut, she had not stopped chattering since entering the jeep. "I know the feeling, Patricia," Julia said dryly as Paul turned the vehicle uphill out of town.

"Oh, please call me Trixie." She spun around, gawking at some mango-tossing langurs. "I keep thinking, *Wait till I tell my fiancé!*"

"Where is he?"

"Roy's a flyer—Lieutenant Roy Wentz Jr., Tenth Air Force," she said, still looking away. "His plane was shot down over Rangoon. Everyone's given him up for dead. But me. I see him in my dreams, waiting. I took this job to be as close to Burma as I could."

Julia noticed Betty, on the opposite bench, close her eyes. "You're in the right place, Trixie. Everything passes through the Registry."

"I know someone will pick up his trail. Someday." She gave Julia a bright smile. "Oh, those darling monkeys. I—"

"Sorry to intrude," Paul said brusquely. "Through general agreement, we've instituted a reign of silence in the morning."

Trixie's lips quivered. Poor dear, to come under Paul's scorn her very first morning.

As soon as they got out of the jeep at HQ, she bounced right back. "In Colombo, I bought an adorable little monkey god. For our office."

"If Julia doesn't want it," Paul said with a slight smile, "I'm sure our CO will be delighted to take it off your hands."

"Not *it*. Hanuman. One time, he thought the sun was a mango and tried to eat it, preventing an eclipse scheduled by some other god. I bet that got him in a fix."

"Welcome, Patricia," Dick greeted them from his veranda. "I'm going to borrow Julia for a moment; then she'll show you around." He gestured her up the steps. "We searched Olivia's quarters but came up cold. No wireless equipment or concealed intel."

"She's either hidden it elsewhere or has already passed it."

He nodded. "To be continued."

The tour took longer than Julia expected, as Trixie stopped to marvel at the river view, a cinnamon-colored frog on a cinnamon shrub. And, of course, the monkeys.

"I've heard they make great pets. What do you think, Julia?"

"I think we'd better begin that training."

———

There was a tap at the basha door. Donovan.

With a glance at Trixie, he said, "McWilliams. Let's take a walk."

Acknowledging the guard's salute, he led her across the quad. "Olivia's brother-in-law—a commander in the Naval Air Service— happens to belong to England's Right Club and the Link, which coordinate profascist and antisemitic activities. Surprisingly—or not—the groups have quite a following. This connection doesn't mean anything in itself. But it doesn't *not* mean anything."

He gave her a nod that thrilled her heart.

As they entered the Map basha, Paul even looked up at her from a topographic map of southern China he was sketching. Jack was off somewhere.

"Warwick set a sunset rendezvous tomorrow with Olivia. At the big white Buddha in the northern hills." Donovan gazed off, as if visualizing how it would play out. He turned back with a wink at Julia. "He'll be passing Byron's sizzling cable, which he believes to be an intercept from a high-royal source, to Lord Mountbatten himself. Very gossipy, I'm sorry to say. Damaging to Mr. Churchill."

Paul widened his eyes briefly. "I imagine that would be valuable intel to our enemies."

"Priceless," the boss sneered. "However, our spies settled on five thousand pounds up front, the equal balance to be paid once it checks out."

"Fortunately for Mr. and Mrs. Churchill, it won't." Julia tried to be professional and master her wayward voice, but the location brought back complex emotions about her romantic interlude with Mack.

Donovan's face hardened. "Well, before then, Olivia will have led us to her handler."

She heard the "us" and waited.

"One thing I've learned about field ops," he said gruffly, "you can't plan for everything. Warwick may have spilled the beans. Or Olivia's handler may have sensed us closing in and prepared an escape via a Jap sub. There may be collaborators—armed. What I'm saying is we need to expect the unexpected." He cleared his throat. "Your training is limited, McWilliams."

Julia felt sick, to be sidelined at the very last minute. "I grew up duck hunting, sir. And target shooting." She stared at Donovan's closed face. "And Paul's a black belt."

He glanced at Paul. "That true, Child?"

"I'd like to do my part. If you'll have me. If Julia will."

"We'll stay on the sidelines, boss."

Donovan narrowed his eyes. "The other thing about field ops— there are no sidelines."

TWENTY-SEVEN

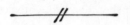

Late the following afternoon, Julia and Paul left Detachment 404 for the police compound rendezvous. Donovan had been noncommittal about what would come next. Her mouth was dry as they parked, the enormous white Buddha looming overhead.

Paul's eyes swept the area. They were the first to arrive. Maybe the plans had changed. "You can see that fellow from all over town," he said, making conversation.

"They say ancient demons lived there before Buddha. Locals call it Devil's Hill." She caught herself. "I guess that's kind of negative, considering…"

"Impressive, though. Not many of us have taken the trouble to study their culture."

Julia frowned, unwilling to take credit for Mack's cultural knowledge. "I have to confess something." She glanced up at the Buddha. "I had a crisis a while back. Donovan kept calling it 'my op,' and suddenly I was afraid. I didn't want to fail him. He had so much confidence in me—or at least, the gung ho Julia. But she got cold feet. Then I heard my mother telling me I had to complete my task. 'I gave you my name so you could go where I couldn't.'" They were both Julia Carolyn McWilliams, she explained, her voice quavering. "She was already Caro, so I became Julia. She wanted to travel, but women had to follow their husbands, and she was trapped…by and for those who loved her most. That's why she wanted me to be independent. She said being tall…gave me freedom." She bowed her head, tried to swallow her sobs.

Paul put a gentle hand on her shoulder. "Julia."

"I'm sorry. Don't mean to burden you. I'm okay now."

"Hey. Do you believe I'm not fearful about tonight? Bursting into a den of fascist spies?"

"He hasn't even invited us yet. Maybe we'd be a hindrance," she said, collecting herself. "They don't really need us."

His hand still on her shoulder, he pivoted toward her. "That is certainly true, but don't you think your mother would want to see your success? This *is* your op, Julia McWilliams."

She blinked wildly, and Paul appeared in a shimmer before her. "No, Paul. It's ours."

Donovan and Dick pulled up in an open-sided two-person Willys, followed by three larger military-police jeeps, a few unmarked cars. Paul and she got out and approached Donovan. He gave Julia a thumbs-up, and that was that.

Everyone was smoking and chatting quietly—as if their targets might hear them a mile away. All the men were armed, including General Donovan and Colonel Heppner. Dick adjusted the antenna of his handheld radio transceiver and set it on the hood.

By 1700, the sky was turning hazy gray. A brilliant yellow shone through for a glorious moment, then disappeared. Heavy with moisture, the air soon released a soft rain. Not enough for umbrellas, almost refreshing.

Dick's handie-talkie crackled, and they converged around it. "Sal here. Reporting with Bob from the monastery grounds just below the big guy. Testing."

"Loud and clear. Do you read me?" Dick pushed the button to talk, releasing it to listen.

"Affirmative. We'll get back when we have something. I'm in a blue Austin two-seater, fairly common in these parts."

When Sal went silent, they heard monks chanting through the H-T's open channel. Everyone resumed their pacing, matches sputtering in the damp air.

As Paul handed Julia a poncho, Sal said, "We're on! Female target in khaki is exiting tan Hillman Minx near entrance steps. Red hair visible beneath headscarf."

After a pause, he reported, "From a jeep uphill, male target in Royal Navy white is heading toward female target with bouquet. She drops gift card into her shoulder bag…hugs him—and slips an envelope in his pocket. They admire the view…wave goodbye. Now returning to their vehicles."

As a rainbow cracked open the dark skies, there was a rumble of engines. "Bob will tail Warwick," Sal said. "I'm on her. Heading down Pushpadana…Crossing Peradeniya."

"Let's go," Donovan ordered. "Paul, you bring up the rear, after the MPs." He passed Julia another black handset.

She aimed the antenna out the window as Paul followed in the jeep.

Bob: "Male driving east through hills north of town."

Sal: "She's passing the market…now the mosque."

Donovan: "We're on the move."

Sal: "Turning up Rajapihilla…past Palace Park."

South of the lake, the road hairpinned upward amid minimal traffic. Rounding a bend, they saw Donovan's team closing in on Sal's dusty Austin. His brake lights flashed. Paul downshifted; they all fell back.

Bob: "Warwick's entering the Royal Bar on King Street."

"Slinking in, more likely," Paul sneered.

Julia stared at a Buddha shrine surrounded by pink lights. "Isn't this the way to the Dutchman's…?"

"This is the road," he said, shifting calmly around the curves.

Sal: "Passing Mahamaya Girls' College…entering residential area."

They followed the team into the school's carpark and got out. Dick again put the handie-talkie radio on the hood.

Sal: "One kilometer past school, target is turning right up narrow drive. Keeping my distance."

Breathless, they heard his engine crunch uphill.

Sal: "I'm in a turnout with line of sight. Target walking to red gate."

Julia pushed the button. "With a white lion and unicorn?"

Sal: "Affirmative. Standing by, awaiting orders."

"*The Dutchman.*" She felt her heart burst open. "Pieter von Diest."

Dick's eyes flashed understanding. "Twenty years in Ceylon and our guy knows everyone. Imagine what intel he's scooped up."

Donovan grabbed the H-T. "On our way." Glancing at Julia, the radio. "You two remain at the bottom. We still don't know if they'll be waiting for us." *Armed*, he didn't add.

Dick's engine was already in gear. The caravan sped off.

Julia and Paul arrived in time to see the last MP jeep turn up the drive. She clutched the radio, hearing their vehicles slide to a halt.

Donovan: "Open up."

Julia grasped Paul's hand, waiting for a burst of gunfire.

There was a click, the rush of the OSS team. The door slammed.

Paul squeezed back.

Donovan: "I'll be taking that 'gift' off your hands, Pieter. You are both under arrest."

Von Diest: "For what?"

Donovan: "Espionage."

Olivia: "Nonsense. I'm a British military nurse—"

Von Diest: "I am a businessman with many friends." There was the snap of handcuffs. "You and the *fokken Engelse* will be hearing from the Dutch government."

Donovan: "The *real* Dutch government is in exile. With the Allies marching in any day, your Nazi-loving rulers will be running for the hills."

Julia slumped against the seat. Paul raised a fist of triumph.

Olivia: "My Anglo-Saxon ancestors go back to—" Another snap of handcuffs.

Donovan: "You'll have plenty of time to reflect on history, Olivia, during your voyage home for trial, unless a torpedo gets you first. Did your brother-in-law recruit you?"

Olivia: "What nonsense! He is a *commander* in the Naval Air Service."

Donovan: "And a staunch member of the Right Club—those proud English supporters of German fascism."

Olivia: "One can appreciate High German culture without

supporting Hitler. The entire world acknowledges their great philosophers and artists. Nietzsche. Rilke. Beethoven, Mahler."

A guttural sound of disgust, then Dick: "Mahler was Austrian, *not* German. A Jew. We helped his wife escape over the Pyrenees—from your Nazi 'philosophers.' Carrying the composer's last song-symphony."

Olivia's next words were unclear.

Von Diest: "We have no Jewish problem in the Dutch East Indies. No politics. We are merely a trading nation."

In the moment of silence, Julia could imagine the arrows of anger darting about.

Olivia: "This man tried to seduce me in Delhi—to help him."

Von Diest: "You should have stayed there, doing the *female* work—in bed. Better I had handled SEAC alone. I have the contacts!"

Had, Julia furiously corrected him in her mind.

Donovan: "As an attorney, I always enjoy watching two conspirators turn on each other. Let's continue this little chat en route to Trincomalee prison."

Those ancient walls, the crashing sea below…

Paul's face broke into the biggest, most open grin she'd ever seen him wear. "Sounds like they've got things under control." He switched off the H-T. "The end of Operation Friendship."

Julia closed her eyes, seeing the Dutchman's red gate…the enchanting house, the art, the music…Mack…a glittering evening, cut short by her illness. "You were very kind that night."

"You would have done the same for me."

Her throat tightened. "I would. I sure would," she said, grateful for his steadiness. Thanks to Paul, she could now admit her fear. Not only of physical jeopardy but also of letting everyone down. Of looking foolish. Failing. After all those years of drifting, she had dug her heels in and finally proved herself. She'd made a difference and was esteemed by men she honored.

He patted her hand. "Well, *partner*—if I'm not overstepping…?"

She shook her head, the tension draining from her body.

"Wonder what our next case will be."

Julia hadn't really thought of that. She'd wanted to be a spy, but...
would there be a next case? Would it be with Paul? Did she even desire
that? She looked at him, trying to find a response.

He stepped up again. "I propose a drink to celebrate the successful
conclusion of our operation."

And, maybe, the start of something else? *That* was too soon to know.
But one could always celebrate the end of hostilities. "I'm buying."

TWENTY-EIGHT

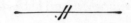

The following week was her birthday—a girls' night out. For the occasion, they'd had frocks made by Jane's virtuoso seamstress, Devi, shopping her bolts of jewel-colored silk with photos from *Vogue*, courtesy of Jane's mother. Two days later, they marveled at the dresses—Betty's, a green paisley that accentuated her dark hair; Jane's, a knockout magenta. Jane and Devi collaborated on Julia's, a deep indigo blue with a curving hem that highlighted her best feature.

"Movie-star legs, if I ever saw them." Jane beamed, regarding her in the glass.

Betty whistled. "Betty Grable, look out!"

The woman staring back at Julia was not a thirty-two-year-old spinster but a worldly sophisticate. Her mother's pearls glowed.

On her birthday, she went to work as usual. The girls urged her to leave early, and by late afternoon, all gussied up, they set out for a lakeside stroll. A sweet breeze was rising.

"That SOB got off too easy," Betty said bitterly. "It could have been my Alex ambushed in the jungle because of him!"

Like her, everyone remained shocked about the espionage case that had played out under their noses. "Have you spoken with Alex?" Julia asked as the sun's rays slanted lower.

"Two weeks ago." She shrugged. "We joked about how bad radio comms are. Then agreed it wasn't the radio. We had nothing to say to each other. It's over." Betty smiled with a false brightness. "So is the spy drama."

"I would imagine SEAC was happy to keep it quiet," Julia said in innocent speculation.

There had been a swift court-martial, during which Warwick pleaded guilty to treason and, in an apparent attempt to regain his honor, requested a sentence of death. FANY Nurse Olivia Mitford—in Julia's view, the guiltier party—was shipped home to life imprisonment.

"I'd give anything to see the welcome Little Miss Fascist receives—in a British prison." Jane's silver bangles jangled as she made a fist. "I wonder how the Dutchman is enjoying the hospitality at Fort Frederick." Her eyes glittered with fury. "I hope he rots in the dungeon."

Imagine being imprisoned here, Mack had mused during the visit that led to her discovery of the conspiracy. *The sound of the waves reminding you of the world you'd lost.* "He's far better off than our prisoners of war," Julia said heatedly.

Betty's mouth tightened. "Another blow to the 'Greater East Asia Co-Prosperity Sphere.'"

"And three cheers for that." Julia hooked arms with them. "One from each of the Three Musketeers." She held her secrets close and was no longer hurt by being excluded from theirs.

"Fancy meeting you ladies." Paul pulled up in a four-person Willys. "Care for a lift?"

Despite their détente, she'd been looking forward to a girls' night out. "Thanks, but we're enjoying our stroll."

His hopeful look faded. "Sorry for the intrusion."

"Give the poor guy a break." Jane opened the jeep's front door and eased Julia inside, while Betty got in back. "Keep him company."

"How about we catch a nice sunset?" he suggested, setting off around the lake.

"Sounds lovely," Betty said, breaking away from a chat with Jane about some blouses Devi was making.

As they turned uphill, Paul glanced at Julia. "It's been a helluva week."

"*C'est la guerre,*" she replied with equal casualness. They shared a private smile.

"You ladies look swell. That blue is terrific on you, Julia."

"It's my birthday."

"How grand, to celebrate in Kandy!"

Then she recognized the turnoff to Detachment 404. "Hey. I'm off duty tonight." But it was too late to protest. After they parked, Paul escorted them toward the river overlook.

"Oh, darn," Betty exclaimed. "Looks like someone left the mess door open. I'll close it so the snakes don't slither in."

They headed back, and as Julia was wondering why Betty entered the mess rather than simply close the door, Paul and Jane each took an arm and led her inside.

"*Surprise!*" a chorus of voices called from the darkness.

When her eyes adjusted, Julia stared at Betty and Jane. Paul. Their faces wreathed in smiles. She blinked rapidly, recovering from the shock of being descended upon by her nearest and dearest. A scene filmed by one of the boys from Field Photography while cryptologists Caryl and Cheryl recorded sound. "Not a single leak. One would think you were a bunch of spies."

Balloons bobbed from the pitched ceiling. A tropical mural covered the rear, with *Happy Birthday, Julia* written in cursive green vines. Darling Jane.

Paul's palm, on the small of her back, pushed her forward. "Seems you've been part of another secret operation, Mr. Child," she said severely.

He grinned. "Mum's the word, Miss McWilliams."

Armed Forces Radio swung into Duke Ellington's "Ring Dem Bells." Half the tables had been cleared for a dance floor. Jane must have scoured the base for eight-by-tens and movie-magazine covers brought over in trunks or gifts from home. The bamboo walls were covered with images of Marlene Dietrich, Gary Cooper, Rita Hayworth. Ginger Rogers and Fred Astaire. John Wayne wearing a flight jacket and pistol in *Flying Tigers*. Bogie and Ingrid in *Casablanca*.

Cora and Peggy presided over the food line—with its rice, curries, and condiments—while Ellie acted as kitchen liaison.

"*Rijsttafel*, we call it in Java," Jane said.

"'Rice table,'" Julia recalled. "Paul and I ate this at a Kandy hole-in-the-wall."

"I took him there," Jane said. As a fleeting something crossed Julia's face, she shook her head. "Remember my married Manly? To keep it quiet, I dated other fellows. There was never anything between Paul and me. We are truly 'just' good friends."

"Nice of you. But Paul's personal life is none of my concern. How's Manly?"

"He's in Burma—most of the time…" Jane closed her eyes.

Betty pointed to the French flag hanging over *Happy Birthday, Julia*. "Hope you don't mind sharing, dearie. We're also celebrating the liberation of Paris."

She beamed. "Now that's the real icing on the cake."

"Which is chocolate," Jane said. "For which you can thank Ellie. And her three layers of butter, sugar, and flour."

"You can never go wrong with that."

Paul offered her a plate that looked like a painting, with an arty assortment of food. "As I recall, you were fond of these dishes."

He remembered! She was touched. They sat down to enjoy their *repast*—as he, in his formal manner, called it. Then it was on to the dessert table.

Ellie had decorated the cake with chocolate coconuts dangling from a palm tree on a sandy beach. And Julia beneath it, arms piled with papers. *Happy Birthday* was spelled out, each letter on a tiny manila folder.

"It's too pretty to cut," Julia said.

Paul raised his camera and moved in close. "I'll record it for posterity." Then he shot one of Betty lighting thirty-two candles plus one for good luck.

"Let's get to it," Jane said. "We have the hungry masses to feed."

After she wrangled the group, they burst into an enthusiastic rendition of "Happy Birthday." Julia blew out the candles on the first try.

"Looks like a lucky year ahead." Paul popped the champagne.

Feeling the warm breeze, she looked up…Mack, standing at the door. A month since Bastille Day—July 14—and the Festival of the Tooth. And, the following afternoon, their lakeside picnic, which had led to…well, everything. Including her discovery that Mack had been reporting on her. Julia gripped the knife and slashed into the cake.

Betty raised her glass. "To the life of OSS!"

"Hear! Hear!" everyone chimed in.

"The best damn nature photographer in Kandy," Dillon toasted with a private look, no doubt referencing her Polonnaruwa espionage.

"To Paris." With a pensive expression, Paul lifted his glass.

"Liberation!" Julia added fervently. "And the future democracies of Southeast Asia." Feeling Mack's gaze, she resumed her cake-cutting while Paul passed the plates forward.

Glenn Miller and his Army Air Force Band were up next. Then came the opening bars of Dinah Shore's sunny-sad rendition of "All I Do Is Dream of You."

After Betty and Dick led off, Dillon asked, "Ready to kick up your heels?"

"Always," she said, passing Paul the cake knife.

Dillon swept her across the dance floor, proving himself quite a good dancer. As they were laughing over a small misstep (hers), Paul tapped him on the shoulder.

He whirled her about until she was breathless. Paul was a smooth dancer, strong and graceful. Julia enjoyed his physicality, his ease in his body. His ease with her body, the way he held her. She felt his breath on her throat. She closed her eyes.

When she opened them, Mack was waiting. She stiffened, and Paul released her. She barely noticed, locked into the raw emotion radiating from Mack. She took a steadying breath.

"Don't tell me you were only interested in my Irish allure," he said, calm on the surface.

Touché. Julia glanced away. "I did like you. Very much."

Mack sent her a pained look. "Conveniently. While you were spying on SEAC."

She thought of Olivia's fake brother. "Do you even have a sister named Julia?"

"I suspected your duplicity just as you suspected mine. But I cared for you. I wanted to protect you. Sometimes, when things go bad, they need a fall guy—or girl. At the lake, I tried to warn you that the Supremo had his own means of sussing things out."

"Plots within plots. Did Mountbatten send you after me? Or maybe you and Olivia were a team? Or you're playing your own game? An anti-British Irishman—in league with the Axis?"

Mack shook his head in disgust. "You could find conspiracy in a trash bin."

"You were the sole person to whom I mentioned Jessore, India." That betrayal still hurt.

"You were a naive young woman manipulated by Donovan. I don't take it personally."

"All's well that ends well—we shut down the Dutchman's network. My work helped us all. You Brits had the security leak. I found it. So go fry an egg, Mack!"

He raised an invisible glass. "I'm being transferred to China."

"As a reward—or punishment for not recruiting me?"

"I came to wish you happy birthday. But never mind the cake." He turned to go.

"Mack," Julia said. He paused. "I was glad it wasn't you. The leaker."

Emotions crackled between them; then he moved for the door. As she caught a glimpse of the magnificent sunset, it slammed behind him. Their parallel missions had led to true feelings—which opened them both to true hurt. In her ambition to be a spy, she had not understood the inner costs of lies and deceit. She stood alone, head bent, ashamed of her foolish hopes and dreams.

But she had her work. Her duty. And self-respect. She would be honest with the next man in her life—if there were to be one, and he would be honest with her. No more lies.

Inadvertently, she glanced at Paul, who had helped plan her surprise party and support her operation, and held her close on the dance floor.

Who was still mourning his true love. She was simply another woman to flirt with.

The music segued to "We'll Meet Again," Vera Lynn singing with a lyrical purity that brought tears to her eyes. Soon after going to work at the OSS, Julia had seen the movie, in which the beau of the Vera Lynn character falls for her best friend during the London blitz. The song stirred up too many emotions to sort out. Swallowing hard, Julia yearned to disappear through the floor on which she had danced, the belle of the ball, but it was unyielding concrete.

"Hey, birthday girl." A slinky arm wrapped around her; then Jane put a champagne flute in her hand.

She regarded her distorted reflection. Her indigo silk was wrinkled. She was thirty-two, a file clerk, and an old maid.

"We're waiting on you," Jane said. "Paul finished slicing the cake. Between you and me, he looked pretty grim during your tiff with the Irishman. Poor Paulie needs some sweetening in his life. So go taste the cake, will you? We're starving."

Julia felt their hearts connect in a sisterly kind of love, their differences part of that love. Then she looked around at all her friends. She was lucky that way. And she had another year until she was thirty-three, the age Caro married. A lot could happen in a year. She straightened her pearls. "As my mother used to say, 'A party without cake is just a meeting.'"

"What about champagne?"

She smiled. "It can't hurt."

They finished her glass, together, then, pinkies linked, rejoined the party.

TWENTY-NINE

———— // ————

The monsoons arrived the next day, severe and unrelenting. Protecting her papers was a nightmare. The electricity went out periodically; thick mists darkened the skies.

California didn't have summer rain, not like the East Coast thunderstorms that cleared the air and squeezed it dry. These rains never stopped. There was never a moment of relief; the air was never cleansed. They lived under a constant battering of unknown forces, as if subject to a battle in the skies between all those gods. Julia wondered why there was no god or goddess of the monsoon. She would make lavish offerings.

On their way to lunch, she and Trixie huddled under the thatched walkway. The wind launched naillike pellets of rain at her sideways, drenching her skirt. The path was slick, and she slipped, her left foot landing at a vicious angle in the muck. As Trixie grabbed her, she wrenched it free—and yelped at the surge of pain shooting up from her ankle. Mud blackened her foot and sandal, splattering her leg. She brushed herself off uselessly.

"Lean on me," Trixie said while they made their way to the mess.

Julia limped to their table amid the hum of mostly male voices and the clatter of utensils.

Betty put down her fork. "What happened?"

"Nothing, really. Just slipped." Rather annoyed at herself, she appreciated the gazes of sympathy from her friends—except Paul, who was glowering into his plate.

He looked up sharply. She thought their eyes met for an instant, but before she could be sure, his gaze traveled down her legs—which made her more flustered. Why should he be paying attention now? *Now*, when she had proved herself ungainly and ungraceful?

Paul scooted over, closer to Jane but making space for her. "Sit, Julie."

Her ankle was throbbing, and she didn't even think to question his brusque command. She was uncomfortable about the tropical mud smell clinging to her.

He dipped a napkin in his water glass, leaned over, and took hold of her foot—bigger than his hand! As she sat in helpless embarrassment, Paul cleaned it. Gently, every toe. His fingers. His sure touch.

Julia started as the napkin turned bloody. "But…I only twisted it."

With a terse shake of his head, Paul propped her calf on his thigh. Adjusting her skirt, she tensed at the intimacy, cringing over her unshaven legs. His features squeezed in concentration, he bent closer, running his thumb over her ankle and behind it.

"Matches," he ordered.

"Here you go." Trixie produced a matchbox from the first aid kit in her bag.

Julia tried to yank her foot away, but Paul's grip was like iron. She was too conscious of his sinewy, taut thigh muscles.

He flicked his index finger at a red-black worm with orange dots.

"What the heck is *that*?"

"A leech."

She recoiled as he struck the match and thrust it at the inch-long leech burrowing into her flesh. Engorged with blood, the shiny, ridged creature reared backward—a tiny thing, yet so monstrous. It dropped to the floor, rose up on its posterior sucker, gyrating in a death dance. She watched in horrified fascination as Paul smashed it with his boot.

The wound felt fiery. Her leg was still on his thigh. Julia longed to remain like this, but he was already shifting away, businesslike. He reached for the first aid kit.

The drama over, their friends began chatting around them. In silence, he dressed and bandaged the wound. They were in a bubble, the two of them, and she wanted time to slow down.

He wrapped her ankle, then gently lowered her foot—without any comment on its size. "Paul," she said, touched again by his kindness. "Thank you."

He brushed away her words with the same hand that had tended her. "You wait here while I get us some chow."

Julia was still lost in a strange mix of emotions when he returned, their two meals on a single tray, wearing the tight, remote look she'd mistaken earlier for a glower. He probably had no idea how off-putting he was when preoccupied.

"How do you know about leeches?"

"Some things you pick up along the way," Paul said, as if this skill were one of too many to count. He frowned at the piece of stringy meat on his plate, then looked at her, fully, as he had when she arrived. Even his walleye seemed trained on her. "How does the ankle feel?"

"A little sore, but not as sore as I am at being clumsy."

Paul tucked his chin, studying her. "You're pretty tough on yourself, Miss McWilliams."

"Independent, that's all."

"You do know how to run an op." Respect shone from his face.

"I had a first-rate partner." As the burning from her wound rose to her chest, she moved the food around her plate. "There are a lot of things I wouldn't know how to handle on my own." Julia indicated the leech's smashed corpse. "I must admit, it felt good being in experienced hands." She blushed and looked away.

"I grew up pretty independent, too." Paul took a long breath, turning inward again. "So we're both resourceful. Life is a lesson in humility, so much out of our control. Now, with the war…" He shrugged. "Next year the Allies will invade China en route to Japan. I expect to be transferred soon." With precision and grace, he laid his utensils across his chipped plate.

Julia saw finality in the gesture. His suntanned fingers against the scratched metal. She could still feel those fingers on the small of her back as he'd whirled her about the dance floor. And around her ankle as he'd burned off the leech. Her skin had grown hot, too, from the match—or his deft touch.

Now she went cold; longing dug at her ribs, hollowed her insides.

Their Kandy life dissipating into the mists. Their little family separating. "China is a big country. They'll need a lot of maps." Their eyes connected.

"That, they will." He exhaled. "Jack says he's always wanted to see China, so he's ready. I'll be ready when I get the call. In the meantime, there's an ancient cave site at Dambulla I've been meaning to photograph. A splendid Buddha. I thought you might wish to accompany me. If your ankle allows."

Oh, it will.

———

The following Sunday dawned miraculously clear. "'You are my sunshine, my only sunshine,'" Paul hummed as they drove up the mountain.

Then, together, they sang the song again. He harmonized with her soprano, and she applauded at the end. "Not bad. I usually keep my singing voice to myself—but back in the day, onstage, I could really belt them out. Did you know I used to write and direct musicals?"

He laughed. "Music. We have that in common, too. After Father died, my mother took Charlie and me—the twinnies—to salons around Boston. We had the society lineage but no dough. She had a beautiful voice. You might say, we sang for our supper."

Julia felt another surge of pity. "I think you're the most gifted person I know."

"These are not gifts, Julie. I'm a workhorse. Nothing comes easily."

"This song did." She smiled. *We have that in common, too.* What did he mean, besides running a spy mission together?

"My Pollyanna." He lapsed into dark silence, which she didn't dare break.

Farther uphill, they stopped before some steep granite steps—slippery and uneven.

"Let me know if you need help." He tightened his faded L.L.Bean knapsack.

"I shall." But she wouldn't. It was not her to be the helpless dame. And why depend on someone who was leaving?

The air was so thick and wet it was hard to breathe—to move, even. But they finally made it to the top, turning to admire the sweeping view. The foliage was lusher than ever. Everything here was magnified—the rains, the bugs, the colors—their every experience heightened by the intensity of war. And its transitory nature.

Julia looked at Paul. He was sharp and clear, yet the edges of the world were blurred, iron-gray clouds gathering around them. Then the clouds let loose. He grabbed her wrist, and they dashed under the terra-cotta archway, sculpted with guardian figures.

The only fools to believe the promise of a clear monsoon morning, they entered the long, narrow cave—and came to a full stop, awed by the great stone Buddha reclining on his carved bed. Draped in an undulating robe, he had dreamy eyes, a beautiful mouth. One hand rested between his pillow and head; the other held a lotus flower.

Paul studied the great gilded figure, perhaps fifty feet long, from various angles, using a flashlight for detail work. "Impossible to capture his impact."

"How about these tootsies?" The Buddha's feet were red, with intricate gold designs. "They're bigger than mine!" she exclaimed, shocked at how relaxed she felt with him.

His laugh was submerged by the hammering rain. "Take a look at his ears. They're big, too. Elongated from wearing heavy jewels in his princely days. Once he renounced that life, the Buddha's long ears gave him an openness to all beings." He paused, shining his light at the closer ear. "Maybe you can view your feet in another way now. They take you places."

Speechless, Julia stared upward…both of them sharing the wonder.

Then the flashlight died. "For want of a battery, the battle was lost." He dug in his bag for a candle. But the matches sputtered out. "Fortunately, I have fast film—for low light."

While screwing on a wide-angle lens, Paul said casually, "I ever tell you I'm blind in my left eye? When we were seven, Charlie poked a sewing needle in it."

"*No*," she gasped, grasping the tragedy behind his walleyed look.

"I don't dwell on it. Don't want any pity." He loaded the film. "It was an accident. I'm fine, but poor Charlie never got over it. I learned to compensate, which sharpened all my skills. As a teacher, I could empathize with my struggling students. As a sailor, I forced myself to climb a schooner rigging in a storm. In Paris, I learned to make stained glass windows and studied perspective with photographers Cartier-Bresson and Steichen. It helped my drawing, too."

"Good practice for becoming Detachment 404's official driver."

He winked with his good eye. Julia considered him in a new light. Paul Child had mastered photography, painting, martial arts, sailing. Had loved a woman fully and taught eager young minds. Lived his life without a drop of self-pity.

All she'd had to contend with was being tall. As he snapped pictures of the golden figure, she wandered about, dizzy from the intense color and detail. The cave was empty yet pulsed with energy. Every nook and cranny was painted or sculpted, every space covered by intricate story frescoes of Buddha's life. It was like being inside a fever dream.

"It's funny. That seated white Buddha on the hill left me cold, but this thrills me. Imagine the artist-workers, their dedication."

"You're wasted in the Registry, Julia McWilliams."

She swallowed. "I take that as a compliment, Paul Child."

"You should. You have a creative spirit that needs to be fed."

Moved, she stared at the curtain of watery green. "Seems like we might be here awhile."

"I have lots of film, two more Zeiss lenses. Water, bananas, cashews, rotis, boiled eggs. And two ponchos that zip together."

Julia heard the smile in his voice and glanced at him. For the first time, she saw none of his defects. "Then let it rain."

The downpour continued. Despite the humidity, a penetrating chill set in. They nestled under the ponchos, shoulder to shoulder, as the world dissolved before them. It felt oddly peaceful, until he curled an arm around her waist and turned her toward him. She shivered.

"Julie," he murmured, "there is something between us I can't quite figure out. I want to, but I'm leaving soon. You never have as much time as you expect." He sighed like an old man.

Not old. Older. Worldly. Seasoned. She longed to figure it out, too. But the war, in its intensity, shaped all their experiences, including this *something*. Maybe it was simply a passing moment. At least she and Paul had had time for friendship. It was starting to feel like a beautiful one.

THIRTY

— // —

One thing seemed permanent: in November 1944, Franklin D. Roosevelt was reelected to his fourth term in office, a rousing mandate as the Allies continued their advance into Germany. A boisterous celebration erupted that evening at Queen's bar, where, among her OSS compatriots, Julia was buoyed by pride and patriotism. She felt Caro's presence, their shared memory of dressing up and walking to their polling place in 1936 after Pop had left for work, and daringly casting their ballots for FDR's second term. Pop had disdained the president's radical new policies, but Julia and her mother saw only the way he was lifting the nation out of the Depression. Fewer people came knocking on their back door for food—that was a fact.

"Did we miss anything?" An animated Peggy burst in, followed by her boss Dillon and CO Dick, who wore a frazzled look and nodded at Paul.

Then Byron appeared with his five-person Messages unit, including Caryl and Cheryl, festive in red lipstick. "We couldn't miss it, but the comms are flying, and we only have time for a quick toast," he apologized as Betty passed around fresh flutes of champagne.

Cora lifted hers. "To the codebreakers!"

Amid a round of *Hear! Hear!* Dick slipped away. After another sip, Paul got up and wandered over to the display cases, as if really interested in regimental silver of the old Raj.

With rising unease, Julia watched the Messages team wave their goodbyes. Then Jack cleared his throat. "Heppner's been promoted to head Detachment 202/Kunming in China's far south. He's taking many of his team."

Despite Paul's warning of the coming changes, the reality gutted her. It was too soon. Julia gazed into her champagne. The bubbles had gone flat.

He returned to the table and dropped into the opposite chair. "We'll be posted there. After New Year's."

Less than two months. Her throat squeezed shut. "To your new Map Room," she croaked. Her fingers tightened around the stem of her glass, but she couldn't lift it. She didn't trust herself to look at him.

"To something other than curry." Peggy raised her drink cheerily.

Into the bar's jangle and clatter poured Dinah Shore's liquid lament "I'll Walk Alone."

"It's the fifth time they've broadcast that tune tonight," Betty snapped.

Her breakup with Alex was still painful; she lashed out sometimes. On the other hand, Julia had seen her light up around Dick. Only later did she learn that Dick had a wife at home. The war had taken its toll on them all. Yet the song was also about emotional resilience, being fine with one's own company. "It's a hit. Armed Forces Radio must be getting a lot of requests."

"You'll be in the center of things, Paulie," Jane said with enthusiasm.

"No doubt. Kunming base might as well have a red bull's-eye painted on it." Paul removed a manila envelope from his pack. "Japanese Zeroes are making forays."

Bombers. Julia searched for something positive. "New terrain. New elevations. New food to taste."

"That's one way to look at it." As the waiter, Krishna, approached, Paul gave him a large buff envelope. "Photos of your baby." He held up a hand to stop the man's effusive thanks.

With a pearly grin, Krishna patted his chest. "Next champagne is on me."

"My felicitations to your wife," Paul said quietly.

It was a humble gesture, generous and kind. His image glowed before Julia.

Jack jumped to his feet and reached for his glass—empty. After Peggy handled the refills, he declared, "And one more to our president. The man who's led us in the war to end all wars."

For that toast, they all stood.

Then: "Here's to adventure." Jane tipped her glass against Betty's. "I've put in for Java. I want to do my bit to keep those nasty little Dutch clogs off the island."

"I've heard rumors. I may be Kunming-bound, too," Betty said.

Nooo! Julia's heart wailed. She couldn't bear to lose her dearest friend. But of course she would bear it. She had to.

"I'll be off to Thailand," Dillon said. "We have Allied airmen to rescue. And the jungles contain birds never seen by the Western eye," he added with fervor to Julia.

She nodded, overwhelmed with loss.

Paul turned, staring into the garden with that closed, focused look. "I get the feeling the easy part is over—for us all."

"Except yours truly. No doubt I'll still be filing reports from Shangri-La," Julia said, aiming for a lightness she did not feel.

Then Bing Crosby began "White Christmas" for the first time that year.

And, all of them dreaming, they fell utterly silent. She believed they shared the same thoughts, dear friends who would soon be moving on. War threw them together, then ripped them apart. There was a chance she and the girls might stay in touch, and Jack maybe, but would she ever see Paul again? What did they have in common except a remote posting, an accident of geography?

A beaming Krishna returned with his bottle of champagne. "Happy Christmas, my friends. I am wishing us blessings of peace in the New Year."

Betty's chest heaved, and Julia placed an arm around her, touching heads. Her quiet best friend–sister. Like Caro, she was Julia's cheerleader, with her no matter what. Jane was Jane, the competitive sister who energized them all.

From across the table came a festive pop, then a burst of laughter from Jane—and Paul.

"Paulie, you are so naughty." Jane giggled, insensitive and self-centered as ever.

Julia didn't hear his reply, but something snapped in her. Angered at her false feelings and hopes, she decided to cut Paul from her life. She wished the best for him, that he continued to do good work, that he survived. But the two of them were done, their intimacy. No need for her to worry about Paul Child. *He'll be fine*, she thought as Bing Crosby crooned to the end. But really. From out here, a white Christmas was hard to imagine. And in the middle of war, whose days could possibly be merry and bright?

Soon they'd be moving on to "Auld Lang Syne." She would be fine, too. Like Paul, she had a curious, willful side. Tormenting her adorable little sister, Dort, for her own amusement. Julia was ashamed of herself now. She glanced up and saw Paul watching her. She looked away.

———

A week later, Donovan arrived from the front. When he showed up at the Registry, Trixie left to deliver some mail. Julia stood to greet him, but he waved her back down as he sat on the cot. She turned her chair.

"Our forces are on the move in Burma," he announced with an upbeat air. "We've retaken the northern half of Ramree Island off the west coast. McWilliams, I need you to establish a basic Registry at our airbase there and train the Cambridge fellow who'll run it."

She felt a rush of excitement, until reality set in. "*Basic?* There's nothing basic about setting up a Registry." At the front!

"*Here*, you've got not only SEAC and China-Burma-India Command but communications from the Pacific, Washington, and London. Ramree-HQ will focus on Burmese operations, including our agent networks in the Arakan."

Julia visualized Paul's Burma relief map—and *him*, moving nimbly on the floor. The Arakan, she recalled, was a narrow strip of mainland off the Indian Ocean…and Ramree must be one of the coastal islands. "What about SEAC and the Supremo's amphibious invasion of Rangoon—Operation Dracula?"

"His landing craft are on the way. However, Operation Capital, our infantry push from the north, will likely beat him to Rangoon. But let him have his moment." Donovan lifted his shoulder with a dubious look. "Mountbatten has reassigned Lieutenant Mack to China."

"As a demotion? For not recruiting me?"

"China is critical to the British postwar strategy. So perhaps more of a promotion—a trusted, well-vetted man on the scene."

"I wonder if the Supremo thinks I'm due a promotion," she asked lightly.

"Rather the contrary, I would assess. Perhaps Mack's transfer is also a message to us not to send anyone snooping again."

It's nothing personal. But… "Mountbatten commended my actions in exposing the leak."

"He had every reason to. You performed like a pro, McWilliams. At the same time, one might say that your cover has been blown."

Of course. Julia cringed. The leak had resulted from a security weakness at South East Asia Command she'd stumbled upon during her fly-on-the-wall duties. Mountbatten couldn't very well ban General Bill Donovan from SEAC, but Julia McWilliams was no longer welcome— and had thus lost her special value to the boss. Would he even need her anymore? She clutched onto what was offered. "How long would I have to organize a 'basic' Registry and train this fellow?"

"Two weeks, max. However brilliant, I doubt he could get it going without you—or has your savvy and street smarts."

At least he valued her "street smarts" over Cambridge brilliance. "When do I go, sir?"

"You have till the end of the month to prepare your assistant, Norbury. December first, it's off to Calcutta, where your handler will prepare the way. You'll be back before Christmas."

Then what? She needed to consider her options. "Dillon mentioned openings in Secret Intelligence. I thought I'd raise my hand."

"You are eminently qualified, McWilliams. Unfortunately, you're a memorable woman, difficult to place as an asset."

Too tall, damaged in Mountbatten's eyes. "Will I still have a job?" She tried not to plead.

"The Kandy Registry—and all of us will be awaiting your return."

Faint words of support. "I was worried I'd never get my hands dirty here."

"Burma is a very muddy place." Donovan's sharp gaze seemed to lose focus. "Like the trenches in WWI. I was a young man then—your age." He stood, steadying himself against the fiber wall for an instant. "I suspect I'll be returning to Europe before long. To see what's left of civilization and bring about what justice we can. In the meantime, let's get on with it, shall we? Once we liberate Burma, it's on to China—the endgame. Will you help me win this war, Julia?"

She lifted her chin and met his weary eyes. Then he left.

From the door, she watched Wild Bill square his shoulders and walk off. Probably to rally more of his troops. He'd never called her by her first name before. Nor had he ever spoken so personally or admitted how the war had aged him.

She owed this man—everything. She couldn't let him down. Yet it was a terrible time for her to leave her friends. She didn't care about Paul anymore, but the others. Their last few weeks together. Things changed rapidly during wartime. Would they still be here when she returned at Christmas?

PART THREE

A Very Muddy War

THIRTY-ONE

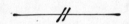

Calcutta, India
December 1944

It was her first plane flight, eleven hours in a camouflage-green RAF Dakota. The night was foggy, the tarmac outlined by the lowest of lights as they landed at Dum Dum Airport, the indoor-outdoor terminal milling with every nationality and uniform, every language blasting from the loudspeaker. Despite having spent half a year in tropical Ceylon, Julia gasped at the sweltering humidity.

"Welcome to Calcutta."

Through the hubbub came a familiar voice with a *soupçon* of French lilt. "Thibaut de Saint Phalle! What a coincidence." She opened her arms for a three-cheek kiss, then pulled him close for a hug. "I haven't seen you since Bombay. I guess you heard they sent us to Kandy. And you and Rosie—still in Delhi?"

"She is." He tapped his chest and murmured, "China."

"What about *Rosie?*" She regarded him curiously—instead of sharp navy whites, he was wearing plain khaki.

He brushed a hand over his sandy hair, longer now. "China is unsuitable for women—per the US ambassador who didn't want to bring his wife. Which accords with Delhi's desire to keep her, a skilled translator. But Rosamond is determined."

"Sometimes you can be too good in your job—especially a woman who wants to move out in the world. It happened to me." With a shake of her head, Julia glanced around.

"Looking for someone?" His left eye crinkled shut in that breezy grin of his.

The light bulb went off in her brain. "So this isn't a coincidence?" She tucked her chin. "Don't tell me. Wild Bill."

Thibaut lifted his eyebrows. "I'll bet you're hungry."

His dirty yellow Austin was parked nearby. "What are you really up to, *mon ami*?" Julia asked as soon as they headed into town.

"I was shipped to an airbase in southern China—Free China— Kunming, Yunnan Province."

Paul and Jack's new posting! Where Japanese Zeroes were making forays. *Kunming base might as well have a red bull's-eye painted on it*, Paul had said. These were the front lines.

"Japan is starving China via sea and land blockades," Thibaut continued. "When the new Ledo Road from India connects with the old Burma Road in Yunnan, we'll finally get the supplies we need to survive until the Allied invasion. I'm attached to a Sino-American covert unit dug in above the South China coast. Reporting on Japanese ship movements."

"You're in the middle of things." She paused. "Wait, what are you doing here?"

"You're also in the middle of things," he replied as they reached Calcutta's long, grassy Maidan.

Julia was shocked to see an airstrip down the middle of the park, marked only by dim amber lights. "I'm so sorry you and Rosie had to be separated."

"*C'est la vie.*"

"*La guerre*," she commiserated as the city crowded about them.

Thibaut pulled up before a brick barrier. "Blast walls—to protect against shrapnel. Fortunately, no bombs have fallen for some time."

"How reassuring."

With Calcutta on war footing, Julia was astonished to enter Firpo's, a haven of crystal chandeliers and black-tie musicians. They discussed the Burma operation over a five-course meal that concluded with gâteau mille-feuille.

"A little out of touch, do you think?" Julia observed. "I guess this is what our people complained about in Delhi—that blind clinging to tradition. Colonial nonsense, Jane would surely rail against if she were here," she said as coffee and cognac were served.

"While enjoying it immensely." His face darkening, Thibaut tipped his glass against hers. "To my *oncle* Alexandre, a wireless operator with the French Resistance. He's gone missing."

"May he be found," she said fervently. What was that movie she and Paul saw in Kandy? *Ten Days in Paris*. She didn't quite recall the ending, but its subtitle, *Missing Ten Days*, implied the character had been found. There was always hope. Look at her brother! "Has Rosie heard from her parents?" When he shook his head, she pushed back her chair, repelled. "Let's get out of here."

———

The dingy safe house had peeling wallpaper and stank of mildew. They were greeted by a slight man wearing a white oxford shirt and coffee-brown sarong.

"Julia McWilliams," Thibaut said. "Please meet Teacher Si Paw. He will accompany you to our base in north Ramree and attempt to make contact with Manly Fisher."

Jane's *Manly*? How many could there be? He had an agent there…a young woman…someone's daughter?

Si Paw placed his palms together and bowed. "I am at your service."

He was two heads smaller than Julia, but there was a largeness about him. "I hope to learn more about your country."

"We have a daylong journey, during which I will do my best to instruct you."

As a teletypewriter clattered somewhere behind them, Thibaut disappeared for a moment, returning with two canteens and field kits—packed with silk maps, a compass, a Zippo lighter, two knives, medical supplies, and, in Julia's, a small dictionary. "The cases are waterproof."

Si Paw offered a grave smile. "Should there happen to be rain."

"Tea and toast before dawn, then off to the port," Thibaut said briskly. "Your PT boat will hug the Indian coastline as you proceed east. Once you near occupied Burma, the skipper will push out into international waters. Due west of Ramree Island, he'll make a quick run north to our base. You are to radio me immediately upon arrival."

Julia stared at Thibaut, a navy man, her *Mariposa* shipmate. He knew what it was to be attacked at sea. What he was sending her off to do.

While preparing for the operation, she had tried to lose herself in work. Every day had been full, no time for contemplation. She'd studied Cora's briefing material, picked Dick's brain—and brushed off Paul's conversational attempts. She was too busy not facing what was to come.

Now, staring at her field kit, Julia had to face it. While the risk of confronting desperate Nazi sympathizers in Kandy had been real enough, she and Paul had been part of an experienced team on home turf. Here, her only backup would be a gentle teacher—in an actual war zone. She tried to conceal her sudden shock of fear. "A relaxing tropical cruise."

Thibaut met her eyes. "Just in case, your boat is fast and well armed."

THIRTY-TWO

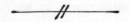

As Thibaut sped south through the darkness, headlights low, Julia's heart fidgeted in her stomach. She glanced at him, an experienced intelligence officer, yet sensed his own disquiet—how hard it must be to mix duty and friendship, to launch a close friend into danger. As if perceiving her thoughts, he turned and shot her his dear lopsided smile.

As they passed the Hooghly River, her eyes watered. Julia sniffed. "Fire. And flowers."

"The ghats," Si Paw said. "For Hindu cremations. The family will garland the departed and chant—to release the soul."

"My mother was cremated." There had been scentless flowers at the service and bland hymns. Pop kept her ashes in a blue ceramic urn. She heard him murmuring to her sometimes. A taciturn man, he'd always perked up in his wife's presence. Now he seemed so alone. She shared his loss. She and Caro used to talk constantly...never a period in their sentences...Their words were like a river. But the river was dammed with everything she'd never had time to say.

Si Paw's look was kind. "This is a good thing. Next life will be better."

There wasn't a glimmer of pink in the sky when they reached the docks, some still charred or shattered from earlier bombings, others bustling with sailors and burlap parcels.

Its engines running, their camouflage-painted PT boat was equipped with a machine gun in the bow—one on each side midship—torpedo-launcher tubes, and a cannon on the aft deck. Far from being reassured, she felt their puniness in the face of the enemy's more powerful munitions.

Si Paw jumped aboard with her duffel bag. He wore a compact knapsack, his kit and canteen belted around his sarong. Hers were secured over her bush jacket and trousers.

Thibaut embraced her, cheek to cheek to cheek. He smiled tightly. "*Bon voyage.*"

Bon courage, he could have said. But didn't.

Si Paw helped Julia board, passing her a yellow Mae West. She held it, lost in memories of the *Mariposa*, the friendships, the attack. The vastness of the sea. He watched her, waiting patiently until she adjusted the straps and cinched up the life vest. Then he put on his own.

At the rusty iron-rope railing, Julia waved goodbye to Thibaut. She stood there until he disappeared from view, leaving her with a lasting image—his unwavering hand upheld in a V for Victory. As she sailed off into the unknown.

They motored downriver, passing a big fort to the east and ghats that stepped down both banks into the water. Embers of funeral pyres floated past washerwomen and people bathing fully dressed.

A tall dark-skinned man in a navy cap, life vest, and floppy white shorts brought her a chipped mug. "Chai?"

Sipping her sweet milk-tea, she gazed at the wooden warehouses, multicolored temples, shacks on stilts. The verdant green.

A year ago, she was surrounded by towering file cabinets in a pea-green Washington office, aching for adventure. Yesterday, she'd flown over the endless ocher plains of India, and today would be sailing one of the seven seas into war.

Julia went topside to meet the skipper, a fellow Californian from San Diego.

"Make yourself at home," Lieutenant Stewart said. "My stateroom has a private head, if you'd like to freshen up." Wearing a vest, pistol, and knife over his uniform, he eased the wheel to port. "I'll try to make this trip quick and painless."

"Thanks for the trouble." She peered down into the chart house, where a man was tapping on the transceiver.

"That's what we're here for. To support your mission."

Continuing her survey, Julia spotted several depth charges, which she'd witnessed in action from the *Mariposa*. Farther toward the bow, Si Paw was chatting with a few South Indian crew members, all brown and stick thin, with gleaming smiles. All wore the same loose white uniforms with various weapons under their Mae Wests.

Indra, the tall man who'd brought her tea, unfurled a bamboo canopy over the foredeck as the sun rose behind the feathery palms lining the shore. Two seamen turned over the life raft, secured it to the bulkhead, and patted its bottom. "Sit-sit," one said.

She and Si Paw relaxed, watching the morning awaken. "I always like the dawn."

"You are an optimistic woman. Seeing the good."

Paul had called her a Pollyanna. "I try to. These days, it's more difficult." For all the glory of dawn, they were riding an armed boat, its engine powering them closer to enemy territory. Her head throbbing from the roar, her jaw tight, she turned her face into the spray.

By 0800, the fast-moving Hooghly brought them into the Bay of Bengal, the northern waters of the Indian Ocean.

"As to this boat," Si Paw began with an earnest air, "it is going forty knots per hour, which equals forty-six miles per hour. Our entire journey is approximately four-hundred-fifty nautical miles, should you wish to perform the time–distance calculation."

"I see you are a demanding teacher."

"How else can I prepare my students for their future?"

"Since I slept little last night, I wonder if you might perform the calculations."

"In the best of all possible worlds, this would be a pleasant day's journey." He offered a sad smile. "As we know, our world is far from the best possible. The occupiers control the last fifty miles of coastline. Our detour will bring us to landfall after dark."

"I traveled across India by train. I loved watching the world pass by."

"You might also take a few moments to observe your inner world. If you excuse me, I will do so now." He recrossed his legs and closed his eyes.

Lulled by the warmth and bobbing waves, Julia relaxed, watching the jungly coast drift past. Palms swayed over the clear-blue bay. It was as if man had never set foot upon this land.

After some time, Si Paw opened his eyes. The sun was higher, and she appreciated the canopy's shade. She looked up as Cook Mohammed brought two small round tins and spread an oilcloth before them. The top container held a red-brown curry. The deeper section was filled with fragrant white rice.

Using his right hand, Si Paw rolled a bit of rice and curry into a little ball and ate it. "Please try. You will find it enjoyable."

Julia had seen locals eating this way, and flung convention to the wind. Making a rice ball, she dipped it in curry and tasted the sea-freshness of the fish, the piquant spices. She washed the food down with salty-sweet lime juice, a combination that made her senses sing.

She imagined rolling the rice ball, dipping it in the curry, and placing it in Paul's mouth. His eyes on her fingers—or her mouth. She thought of his able hands, his strong body. Sinking into the fantasy, she curled to her side, just for a moment…

But no, she was done with Paul Child. She jerked awake. "What time is it?"

Si Paw glanced at the sun. "About two—1400. The hottest time. Best to sleep some more. Once we reach base, there will be much to do."

Shifting her field kit, she rolled to her other side, eyelids drawn shut as if by glue.

When Julia reopened them, the sun was lowering, the light pastel soft. A red ladder took her to the tiny galley where Mohammed had conjured their lunch. The bulkheads were indented with bunks, decorated by family photos and goddess-like pinup girls in saris.

Her jaw clenching against the relentless throb of engines, the revolting gasoline smell, she ducked into Stewart's stateroom. She splashed water on her face, then saw a half-finished letter on his desk, a wide-bottomed inkwell. A gun rack with rifles, machine guns, machetes.

As Julia ascended the ladder, the sky behind them was warming into coral pink. Which meant they'd made the eastward turn toward

Burma, still a warm indigo blue…A lyric soprano wafted through her brain, an ethereal smile…Jeanette MacDonald singing "Beyond the Blue Horizon" in *Monte Carlo*. Julia had seen the movie before going off to college, where, the song promised, a beautiful day awaited her. She hummed along…

But then, the refrain returned "beyond the blue horizon"—to a rising sun. Meant to be a hopeful image, it could now only mean the Japanese flag. She feared their brutality. If this boat swerved off course, they might land somewhere in Ramree's south—still enemy held.

Anxious, Julia rejoined Si Paw. "What if…?"

He pressed his palms together. "Our karma takes us where we must be."

The engine roar increased. Jittery, she paced around to the stern. Indra stood, wide-legged behind his autocannon, its barrel pointed upward. Why was he on alert?

The PT boat accelerated…pitching her toward the surging wake. The corroded railing edged into her belly. She pushed hard, falling back on a metal storage box.

Catching her breath, Julia turned her gaze south toward Ceylon, that teardrop off the coast of India. She took out her compass.

Then the sea erupted, a thunderous cascade of fire and smoke.

THIRTY-THREE

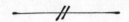

Bay of Bengal

Waves shot up, sending the boat into a tailspin, tossing Julia back against the flimsy, rusted railing. A roar resounded through her, an awful slap, shaking her mind out of her body.

She opened her eyes to salty darkness. Gasping and coughing, she surfaced amid a sea of gleaming red. When she looked back, there was only fire.

Submerged to her nose, she watched a Japanese Zero swoop off, its stubby wings flashing red rising suns…She ducked under, fearing the plane would circle around.

When she peeped out, the air was foul with smoke, burning fuel, rubber, and who knew what else. She didn't move for several eternal moments after the plane disappeared.

"*Si Paw?*" She call-whispered over the crackle of flames, the slap of waves.

Afloat in the life vest he'd insisted she wear, she paddled around the smoky void. Searching for survivors. Finding only debris…a spiky wedge of wreckage shooting at her belly. Catching and flipping it—the mahogany hull?—clutching it as ballast and shield.

"*Anyone there?*" They couldn't all be dead…could they? A tin lunch bucket bobbed past. The nonspill inkwell. An inflated yellow Mae West—empty. Where was the man who'd worn it?

A pale L-shaped object drifted toward her. Moving to push it away, she quailed.

An elbow. Shards of gleaming white bone attached at each end.

Julia screamed, then smothered her cry. Then gagged. The smell.

What else was circling? What creatures? She pictured the sharks cruising the belly of Australia, giant stingrays with enormous wing-spans, serrated tails propelling them forward. And whipping about these dark waters, sea snakes, ready to wrap around her legs and pull her under.

Demons. The perilous dusk the Colombo fisherman had warned Betty about as Julia swam blithely off the coast. *Very danger. Demons coming out now.*

Stop.

She was afraid. Pure mindless fear.

Instinct took over. As day faded around her, she dog-paddled in place, watching the fire's fury die, the smoke dissipate, a thick fog blot out the world. The vast ashen emptiness created its own claustrophobia. There was too much of nothing.

Her eyes stinging, she inhaled, trying to draw back her courage. She was a strong swimmer, accustomed to rough California currents. Hugging the piece of hull, she stared into eerie whiteness. As a girl, she'd survived riptides, hiked and fished, sometimes disparaging herself for being a tomboy. Now she was grateful for being tall and strong. Her long arms and legs could cover more territory.

She didn't have the choice to give up. She'd seen Donovan's weary blue eyes, his flagging energy. Then the way he'd squared the shoulders that bore the weight of their nation's defense. He had asked for her help, and she'd promised to give it her all. She had an obligation to her family, too…her friends, her wartime sisters, Betty and Jane. How they would all be crushed by her death. Maybe even Paul, confronting another loss.

Julia took inventory, patting her field kit. The *compass.* Gone.

She paddled slowly, three hundred sixty degrees. No sign of life. Here was a green palm branch she hadn't seen. Where had it come from? There was a terrible risk of swimming the wrong direction—losing herself in the Bay of Bengal, being pushed south by powerful currents into the vast Indian Ocean, the third largest in the world.

She gazed into the opaque heavens. After minutes…or hours…or perhaps mere seconds, the sky blazed open, an infinity of light overpowering the fog. She marveled at the Milky Way…a shooting star. Then found the North Star. And turned east toward Burma.

The water was not warm but tolerable. She tied her thin chukka boots to her waist. Her canteen was lost with the ship, and the realization roused in her a powerful thirst.

Then she shut down her mind—at least, that part of her mind—and she swam.

———

A faint light flashed in the distance. Was it only inside her eyelids or her mind playing tricks?

Again, the light. She was nearing the Arakan coast; there were towns, with electricity.

The light blinked out.

Now there was another. Maybe her eyes had grown accustomed to the dark and she could see more, farther.

A silver fish darted past—a source of liquid. She reached out, but the fish eluded her grasp, and the next, and the next. Finally, she caught one, tipped back her head, and squeezed every drop of moisture into her parched mouth.

After drinking three more, she extended her right arm, then her left, kicking toward the light.

But was that light in Allied or enemy territory?

THIRTY-FOUR

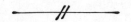

Burma

At the first gold of dawn, Julia crawled onto dry sand. And collapsed.

She'd been nauseous at the end—backstroking, paddling, floating, barely conscious. Sometimes buoyed from hopelessness by another flash of light.

Her eyes opened on a little green webbed foot. And wings! No, flippers. A baby turtle…several of them, crawling to the sea. *Get going, guys.*

Burrowed in the sand, she watched the last of the turtles paddle into the ocean. In the morning's radiance, their survival seemed as miraculous as her own.

Behind her, the sun peeped through a fringe of palms. Was this Ramree, another island, or the mainland? Who was behind those swaying tree trunks?

Manly had agents along the Arakan coast. A Ramree postman's daughter…*M*-something. Julia needed help to find her—someone she could trust.

With trembling fingers, she buried the bright-yellow life preserver, then unbelted her field kit. Its contents were dry. But like her compass, her watch was gone.

They were all gone. Si Paw, who would not find peace through cremation. The California skipper who'd supported their mission. Mohammed, who'd cooked for them. Indra, who'd made her chai. All of them, bombed into nothingness. She stared at the sea that had claimed them.

The terrible thirst returned, but Julia recoiled at the idea of venturing out there again for fish. Throat raw, lips cracked, she clawed the sand, pushing herself to her knees—and then crumpled.

Her last sight was the sun, shiny as a new penny. The sand embraced her, and the warmth felt sweet…

Then the sweetness was gone. Battered by the heat, she shrank into a ball.

Squinting her eyes open, she gazed into deep shade.

Coconut palms. *Food. Water.* She sprang up, then fell back beside an etched trunk surrounded by coconuts. Dr. Lewis had used coconut water in her IV. She shook a green one next to her, almost fainting with desire. After working her Woodsman's knife inside the husk, she twisted the Swiss Army corkscrew into the stem end. Milky liquid splashed into the sand.

Julia watched in despair, parched, breathless in the humidity. She tried again, slowly. And finally drank. Her brain coming alive, she selected a ripe brown coconut for its fruit. She set one upright and slammed a large rock onto it…Then again. By her fourth blow, dripping sweat, she saw cracks appear. At last, the shell surrendered! Nothing had ever tasted so good. She devoured two more, then three mangoes.

Move. Hugging the trunk line, she found a red-dirt path that turned inland. The air buzzed with mosquitoes and gnats. Trees and creepers pushed in, dimming the light. A red heliconia beckoned, its hanging blossoms resembling bunches of parrots' beaks. In a dazzling blue-yellow flash, a long-beaked kingfisher swooped into a glimmer of pale water—a stream. She knelt and sampled it. Fresh! As she drank, two fat dark toads side-eyed her. She felt other eyes…from the opposite bank. Leaping to her feet, she turned, ready to flee. But where?

"Hello," said a round-faced girl with dark braids, white chalky powder on her cheeks. Lowering her bucket, she hiked her purple sarong, kicked off her sandals, and entered the stream.

Julia stiffened yet felt no threat as she watched her draw closer… then step out.

The girl gestured: *Follow me.*

THIRTY-FIVE

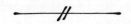

The lush foliage parted for a quiet settlement, a few scattered bashas with coconut-husk bases. Shadowed eyes peeped through bamboo-slatted windows, along cloth-hung doorways. A child gawked, dropping her ball on the red dirt. A mangy dog ran off with it.

Exposed and powerless, Julia could do nothing but follow the girl in the purple sarong. As they emerged into an open area, street vendors and customers paused midtransaction, their grains, soap, squawking chickens forgotten. People stopped sorting rice, weaving baskets, and mending nets. But the girl never spilled a drop from her bucket.

Silence again fell as they reached a marshy field dotted with young green shoots. Another field was terraced above it, shimmering with water. Above, uncultivated hills rose—jungle.

The world vibrated with menace. And she was alone in it.

In the shadows of a low, sloping roof, a lean, gray-haired man in a faded sarong watched her approach. "You are coming from?" He had one tooth missing, front and center.

He seemed harmless, which made her distrust him more. "You speak English?"

"In Burma, many are speaking. British Raj." He nodded to the girl. "But Cho Yi youngest daughter, no more money for school." The man regarded her with an equal measure of suspicion. "Why you are coming to Chindaung?"

"Is this an island?" Darts of danger prickled her back. Any moment, she would be seized.

"No. Arakan mainland."

"Are the Japanese here?"

"They come, they go," he said. "Our village is too small. I am Aung Nat."

"I am Julia McWilliams." She swallowed to generate saliva. "American."

His gaze never leaving her face, he gestured toward the low door. "Some tea?"

She hesitated, her options closing in on her, then ducked inside. The hut was airless, dim—no one visible. The smooth dirt floor had bamboo sleeping platforms on each side. As Cho Yi carried her water bucket behind a hanging yellow cloth, they sat on mats in the middle.

This man could betray her—or save her life. She looked at her hands, still wrinkled from the sea. "My boat to Ramree was bombed," she whispered. "I swam to shore."

He did not react. "Ramree is not far," he finally said. "Not too far. There is river to follow, then fingers of sea, then again river. When it ends near Yebok village, you will find road to Tat Tuang port. Here, you must get boat."

It sounded straightforward, but it was not. She would be alone. Vulnerable. *You're a memorable woman,* Donovan had said. *Difficult to place as an asset.* "How long?"

His eyes were quiet and dark. "Before they take our elephants, one short day. Now, maybe one long day."

"'Maybe'?" Thirsty. So thirsty.

"If no rain—or no Japanese. If yes, then two, three, maybe four," he said.

Her heart leaped when Cho Yi emerged with tea. "Thank you." Julia took a grateful sip, thinking of jungle trails—and finding them. *Solo.* She had to risk it. "I've heard there are friends in this area, people who don't like the soldiers who took your elephants." Maybe someone would know Manly's agent—*Mong*? Or maybe someone would arrest her.

"If such people were, I could not find," Aung Nat said as Cho Yi joined them on the mat.

Understanding his caution, she opened a map. "Can you show me the way?"

He shrugged. "Tell me why you go to Ramree."

"America wants to free Burma. I am going to our base in the north—to help."

"In Tat Tuang, Japanese are also taking boats—to south Ramree."

"How do you know these things?"

"Everyone knows. Where is safe. Where not." He stood. "Come."

Julia searched his face, then folded her map and followed him through the rice paddy.

They reached a hut with mud-brick walls that stopped shy of its straw roof.

Aung Nat opened a rough bamboo door. Was she about to be captured? Raped? Killed?

In the darkness, Julia saw only the glint of a revolver—pointing at her. "Don't shoot!"

Aung Nat pushed after her, waving his palm back and forth. "American."

The gun did not waver. The arm holding it belonged to a thin, dark-skinned man sitting against a bamboo center post, his left leg and bandaged ankle extended on the ground. As her eyes adjusted, she noted his tattered green uniform shirt, worn sarong. Brown shawl.

"American," Aung Nat said again. Then, to Julia: "Indian Army."

Slowly, the man lowered his weapon. Aung Nat pulled up two mats.

She sat, releasing her breath. "Do you speak English?"

He lifted his chin in brief assent.

She met his wary gaze. "I'm Julia McWilliams. I work for the US government. We were going from Calcutta to Ramree when a Zero sank our boat. I'm the only survivor."

"My sympathies," he replied, with a crisp British-inflected tone. "I am Jemadar Deepak Binoy of the Fourteenth Army under General Slim."

She glanced at his leg. "What happened?"

"Our unit was overrun in central Burma. Prisoners were sent to railway work-to-death camps. At the Irrawaddy River, near Thayet, we were assigned a bridge."

"Repairing?"

"Building. With dull, rusty tools, wood cut from the jungle. Even the sick and injured must work—even in monsoon. Only maggoty rice to eat. I escaped."

"How?"

"I swam the Irrawaddy and ran toward India. Then I fell into a ravine, cut my ankle. Infection set in." The soldier coughed, and Aung Nat gave him water. He coughed again, tightening the brown shawl about his wasted body. "I crawled to the next town, Ahn."

"Many Japanese there. Take our rice. Our women." Aung Nat looked away. "My cousin found this man hiding behind cooking shed and carry him in buffalo cart."

"To your too-small village."

He gave her a hard stare. "Tallest elephant grass get stomped down first. We have tended him with our medicines. Six days in hiding. Maybe enough."

Enough for recovery or village safety? Julia looked at the injured soldier. He spoke English, knew the region—and might possess valuable intelligence. They could help each other. "I have maps and medicine for your infection. Can you travel?"

Jemadar Binoy put his Enfield revolver in his belt. "Tomorrow."

Again, she asked Aung Nat, "Any anti-Japanese groups nearby?"

"Never here." He scowled. "You must beware. Some of our people do not like *farang*. Not British, not Japanese. Americans, they do not know."

———

In the predawn chill, Aung Nat slipped goatskin water bags around their necks. He gave Jemadar Binoy a stout walking stick. "Mango wood. Strong."

Cho Yi handed Julia a woven bag with boiled eggs, peanuts, bamboo tubes of steamed rice. After Julia slung it across her body, Cho Yi draped a tan shawl over her shoulders. The soldier's sarong had been replaced by ragged trousers, tucked, like hers, into his boots against leeches. She had a brief image of Paul striking a match, feeling its heat against her ankle.

When the darkness softened into gray-rose, they walked to the river. The previous night, they'd spread her maps on the floor and plotted their course on the detailed Arakan view. They would follow this river to an inlet, avoiding the occupied town of Mawhun. South of the inlet, another river would take them to Yebok, where they'd find the paved road to Tat Tuang port.

And a boat. Julia hesitated. "In Ramree, there is a postmaster's daughter?"

"It is many years since I've been to Ramree," Aung Nat said with bland opacity. "You may ask Tat Tuang postmaster."

She knew the man had helped them at some risk to himself. She could tell he was now eager to see them go, protecting his family and village from enemy retaliation. And he might yet betray them—an American spy and Indian fugitive.

"Go quickly." Aung Nat's eyes slid across hers. "You must watch for daytime snakes—kraits are most dangerous. Sometimes they are still as a stick, sometimes hanging from trees. Cobras are everywhere, day and night. Also crocodiles in mangrove swamps."

Julia glanced at a low branch. "We'll remember. Thank you."

As she was about to shake hands, Jemadar Binoy folded his palms, fingertips high in respect, and bowed his head. She made the same gesture. He saluted, then dug his stick in the mud and stepped forward. She followed.

When she looked back, Aung Nat and Cho Yi were still standing at the river. Was he calculating their worth?

THIRTY-SIX

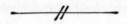

After a while, Julia didn't feel the biting insects. It was so humid her sweat never dried. Hyperalert, they made their way along the spongy rivershore, over stones and roots, under dangling vines—her eyes ever alert for cobras and crocodiles.

They pushed through bamboo thickets and tall dripping grasses so sharp their hands bled. Briars slashed their sleeves and trousers. Their pace was slow. It seemed they'd been walking for hours, but the sun was still low in the east.

Jemadar Binoy drove himself, making every effort to conceal his pain. He did not seem feverish, so she hoped her antibiotic cream was fighting the infection.

"*Ow.*" Julia slapped aside an overhanging branch that scratched her cheek.

As he turned, index finger to his lips, she tripped, almost falling into his back.

He steadied her, pointing at something brown and twisty on the ground.

Cobra? She jerked back as he poked his stick into the snaky object—a woody liana vine, rooted in the soil and tangled into the surrounding vegetation.

Plucking a leaf, he dabbed her cheek, wiping off some blood, then limped on.

By midmorning, they'd circled the inlet and found the river south to Yebok. He signaled a stop. As she scrutinized a mass of hanging vines for snakes, a huge orange-striped leech dropped next to her foot. Emulating Paul's easy power, she squashed it into the mud.

"Tiger leech." Suppressing a grimace, the soldier squatted along the muddy riverside.

She squatted beside him and whispered, "Your wound?"

"I am well." He refilled his goatskin, then splashed his face with water.

Julia rinsed her hands, cleaned her scratches, and drank her fill. "What shall I call you?"

"Deepak."

"I thought your name is Jemadar Binoy."

"Jemadar is my rank," he said quietly. "Like your lieutenant."

Feeling foolish, Julia batted away a biting fly, then a swarm of them.

"You are brave woman."

"Not really. My boss sent me to do a simple job." She gestured helplessly.

"You survived an attack at sea, swam to shore, evaded capture, and are helping an injured officer return to duty. Not so simple." His brown eyes softened.

"You're brave, too. Fleeing the camp, hacking through jungle. With intel?" As he drew back, she saw his mistrust. "Do I look like a Japanese spy?"

"You are too big," he blurted. "Sorry, perhaps that was impolite."

She smothered a laugh. "Definitely impolite. Or I might be a German sympathizer."

"I could be a soldier of the anti-British Indian National Army."

"Are you?" Julia studied his high-cheeked features, his sharp eyes.

"I am not," he said with quiet dignity. "But I will join the freedom struggle—after we defeat the greater enemy."

Deepak dug his stick in the muck and, with the briefest wince, pulled himself up. They continued down the uneven river trail, his limp becoming more pronounced.

The vegetation thickened around them. They pressed on hard through midday, eating half their rice and eggs. She opened her goatskin—empty.

Soon after, they came to a backwater where seawater mixed with fresh—undrinkable, he warned. As they walked on, she wondered about Deepak's family, his education. Indians and Sinhalese had made her food, served her, but other than the Colombo policeman, she'd never spent time with one—as an equal. For all their avowed anti-colonialism, her OSS crowd had remained separated from the real world.

She recalled the Indian major who'd been tossed out of the DC bar the evening she was assessing Sally Lu as her possible successor. Sally Lu had feared making herself a target, so Julia didn't defend him. She still regretted her silence. She should have spoken up for them both.

———

Later, when the river again flowed fresh, Deepak indicated a smooth rock. "We will rest."

After they refilled their pouches, he squatted, staring in the water. "One day, in a hurry to move camp to the Irrawaddy River, the guards burned the barracks of cholera patients."

"*Alive?*"

"There, they drove us harder, feeding us only cooking water from rice, which they ate. Working us dark to dark. If we fell asleep on our feet, they beat us more. If we dropped, they used us for bayonet practice. If we were lucky, we found rats to roast—if we found dry matches. People traded their clothing for food. Wearing only banana leaves."

Julia stared. Sometimes you thought you'd heard it all. Then you heard one thing more.

"While taking my compass for rice, a farmer whispered of Allies in Ramree, one hundred kilometers away. Word spread. People found new will." He closed his eyes. "An Aussie ran. They fed him to the crocodiles. Guards took bets how long he'd live."

She clutched her throat.

"Yet I had to try." In a flash, he reached into the river and retrieved a silvery fish. With brisk efficiency, he slammed its head against the rock, then laid it down.

Julia regarded him with admiration. "Impressive."

"I am a fisherman's son. I was raised in Sundarbans—wetlands like this, with rivers that flow into the Bay of Bengal."

"How did you get your education?" she asked.

"My uncle attended Dehradun Military Academy in North India. He secured my admission."

She looked at the plump, shiny fish. "Can you cook it?"

"Japanese eat it raw. So far, they've survived."

He smiled, surprising Julia into her own smile, her first since the PT boat. She liked this man.

THIRTY-SEVEN

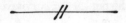

The first raindrops felt refreshing, but by midafternoon, they had not reached Yebok—let alone the paved road to Tat Tuang—and were still slogging down the muddy river shore, stumbling over rocks, roots, decaying vines. Wind sliced through the branches, rain fell like darts. Under a banana-leaf umbrella, Julia could only think of weakened men building the railroad in such conditions. *Work-to-death camps.*

Wiping his brow, Deepak stared ahead as if into a minefield. "Maybe it will clear. If not, we must sleep here." They finished the rice and peanuts, saving the last two eggs.

Taking shelter beneath a rocky overhang, they watched the ceaseless rain, the barely visible river, wavy with mist. A screeching flight of bats announced day's end. They collected the driest brush into two mats. She spread out her shawl.

With some damp brush, Deepak swept the area, setting off a mass exodus of lizards. Then he slumped against the granite knoll, closing his eyes.

Exhausted, Julia lay down, sensing his unease at their physical closeness. "Thank you."

"Thank me after we are on the boat."

"Aung Nat says the Japanese also take boats from Tat Tuang—to south Ramree."

"They are everywhere."

Like the wild animals she imagined encircling them in the inky night. The wind rose, whipping the trees. Then, as if she'd conjured it, there was a crashing through the foliage. Deep, echoing grunts. Terrible, high-pitched squeals that ended abruptly in dread silence.

Trembling, she reached out her hand. "I like to be strong, but…"

"In battle, I am always afraid. Fear can be a good thing."

Like Paul, he was reminding her there was another kind of bravery, to go on despite fear.

"Besides," Deepak whispered, "I have prayed to Ganesh, elephant god of good fortune. He will look after you."

"Us, you mean."

"We are on the same path." After another moment, Deepak extended his arm, the side of his hand a breath away from hers.

How sick is he? Julia was inspired by his efforts. In the darkness, his image combined with Paul's, although Deepak had finer features and an even more formal air. Both the fisherman's son and Paul had hard, wiry bodies shaped by a lifetime of physical work. Both had sudden, surprising smiles.

The wind settled; the skittering noises subsided. The rain lulled her to sleep. When she awoke, his shawl was lying over them both. And resting atop her hand, his—burning hot.

Hastily, he rolled away and stood. "We must go."

Under dripping foliage, the warm, moist night enfolded them. Deepak planted his walking stick with confidence. The ground was softer now, more unstable. He glanced away, but she saw him flinch. Saw his flushed cheeks. Had felt his fevered hand.

———

At the first hint of dawn, they washed and drank, filling their water bags. Julia finished her last egg, but he declined his. They ate mangoes and gathered bananas. The grasses had grown seemingly overnight, and she almost tripped over a tree stump smothered in green. Her brain closed in. She had no thoughts but the next step, the next danger.

By early morning, the river skirted a village field. A man was planting tiny rice shoots in the shimmering water.

"I will ask about Yebok." Deepak limped off.

As they spoke, the man kept glancing at her. Indicating they should wait, he gave her a toothy smile and walked away. She opened her map.

Deepak returned with a worried look, his eyes darting about. "We have reached Yebok. The rice farmer said his son will take us to Tat Tuang road."

His discomfort mirrored her own. Something about that man. She pointed to her map. "At Yebok, the river turns southwest, and the road to Tat Tuang heads southeast."

He gripped his stick. "We will find it. Alone."

They returned to the river, testing the mud until their feet landed on the promised paved road. Deepak set off on a pace she knew must be excruciating.

Bordered by tall leafy trees with exposed, fingerlike roots, the road descended through swampland, smothering humidity. "Why did you also mistrust that man?"

"These are hard times, and villagers are cautious around strangers. He seemed too eager. I feared he would sell us to the enemy."

"I feared that about Aung Nat, too. What do you know about him?"

"During war, we cannot know about anyone. But he did not sell me when he had the chance. Nor you."

Not yet. Her sweaty body prickled. The stinging insects and lurking snakes, the other unknown perils. And the known...Aung Nat, the Yebok farmer. Japanese soldiers heading to Tat Tuang port. Deepak's fever and halting gait.

The jungle canopy thickened, gnarled branches protruding from unexpected angles, ancient roots thrusting upward, light dimming into a soupy green gloom.

"This land is much like my home," he told her. "With wetlands and mangrove trees that can grow in mud or seawater. But we are lucky—no tigers."

"What about those crocodiles?"

He made a weak movement of his shoulder. "Maybe."

There had been those blood-curdling cries in the night. Julia was grateful not to be alone. "I've never had an Indian friend before."

"I've…I've never had a white person touch me."

"Deepak, we're in this together. Before we're through, you might need to lean on me. Or I on you. Think we can break through the old ways?"

"I will try." He scanned the terrain. "My ankle is very bad, my fever…I may have to rest. You must go on."

"I couldn't leave you alone."

"You have no choice. My report will save many lives. It is the reason I fled."

"Tell me." Julia saw his sheen of sweat, his glittering black eyes.

"I learned why the sudden urgency to finish the bridge. A convoy of Japanese supply trains and troop reinforcements bound for south Ramree Island will travel this route twenty-fifth December."

Blood pulsed through her brain. They had to get this intel to the Allied base on north Ramree—or their troops faced certain slaughter. *A Christmas massacre.*

"That's only three weeks," she said. "We need to bomb the Irrawaddy Bridge."

THIRTY-EIGHT

The mangrove-lined road narrowed again, shutting out the midmorning sun. As Julia focused on her footing, a low drone arose behind them.

Voices. Japanese. A barked order so vicious her insides congealed.

"*Hai*," came the equally vehement response.

She tugged Deepak off the path into a mass of tangled roots and branches. Two langurs squawked angrily overhead, awakening a fretful jungle. They dove under some shrubs, burrowing into each other—his body burning with fever.

The voices grew louder, harsher. A rush of birds took flight, creatures rustled around them.

Bodies smashing through undergrowth…overgrowth.

Then stopping.

Through the brush, Julia spotted khaki leg wrappings—the kind worn by Japanese troops in *A Yank on the Burma Road*, a movie she'd seen early in the war. Back then, how could she have conceived being *here*, those uniforms searching for *her*?

Sweat dripping into her eyes, she rubbed in the sting of dirt. Frantically blinking, she flinched at the whoosh of a blade. And another, as the soldier slashed deeper into the mangrove thicket. He smelled of mud and sweat. Possibly their own scent, by which he was tracking them.

Deepak took her hand. She squeezed hard, but he opened her fingers and placed his Enfield 2 in her palm. He flattened her to the ground. Then, with a final look, he leaped up. She reached to stop him, but he was too quick. Where did he find the strength? *Why?*

Deepak crashed loudly through the thick creepers—away from the road. Away from her. At the end of a small clearing, about fifty yards, he disappeared into dense foliage.

With a surge of angry grunts and yelps, the soldiers charged after him. Now she understood. His revolver scalded her palm, its six chambered rounds for her survival—not his.

A guttural call of triumph was followed by a burst of gunfire.

Deepak's piercing cry drew a further volley of gunshots. A swarm of green and yellow parrots burst up from the trees.

Laughing, the soldiers stomped back past her to the road as she sank deeper into the saturated earth. She gripped the weapon, watching their shoes disappear.

Long after the jungle resumed its throbbing quiet, Julia waited, immobile. So far, the only attack came from dive-bombing mosquitoes.

Finally, desperate to find him, she crawled through the mess of thorny undergrowth, dashed across the clearing, and ripped through a wall of vegetation.

She reached another clearing…dim green. A twist of glistening red vines.

And Jemadar Deepak Binoy lying there.

She ran to him. A bullet had pierced his throat, knocking him into the embrace of a great mangrove—the tree of his boyhood. Still clutching the revolver, she crouched over him, placing her left palm to his open mouth. There was no release of air, no movement of his chest. She closed his eyes.

My ankle is very bad, my fever…I may have to rest. You must go on.

I couldn't leave you alone.

You have no choice. My report will save many lives. It is the reason I fled.

Aware his body was giving out, Deepak had sacrificed himself so she could deliver his horrifying report. Julia cupped her raw, scraped hands around his still-warm cheek. She longed to give her warmth back to him, but it was too late.

Trembling, she focused her hearing. If the rice farmer—or Aung Nat—had betrayed them, the Japs would have returned for her. But they'd continued down the paved road.

She hugged herself to stop shaking, then pulled out his metal ID tags—one green, one brown, each bearing the British flag on the back. His service number, name, rank, and religion were inscribed. *Jemadar Deepak Binoy, Hindu.* She pocketed his chain and tags to return to his family.

At least she had been with her mother when she died. Been able to say farewell with words and tears. Mourn her amid loved ones. For Deepak, there was no one to perform the rites—to garland him in blossoms, to light the fire and chant. To help free his soul so he could return to the good, peaceful life he deserved.

Julia draped him in flowering vines, bowed her head, and wept. Hearing his voice, his gentle command. *You must go on.*

It was no consolation that she was following his will. Leaving her friend for the jungle to embrace. Alone. They were all alone in this murderous world.

Devastated, she crept back to their shrubby cover. As she burrowed underneath, her fingers hit a smooth piece of wood—the walking stick. She clasped its handle, gnarled and patinated with many lives, among them Aung Nat's. A hot wind rushed over her…Deepak willing her forward. After several more moments of silence, she stood and moved on.

———

Forging a path parallel to the mangrove-lined road, Julia concealed herself in the jungle. Oriented by the sun, a haze-covered ball not yet at its height, she pushed southeast, branches tearing her clothing, a thorn ripping her chukka boot. Her spirit, too, was shredded. Deepak's greatness of character made her feel small. Yet he had trusted her to complete his mission.

Her mind left her body, roaming through her life. Caro urging her to see the world before settling down. Pop telling her to work hard and contribute to society. She and her OSS sisters firing handguns at spy school. Donovan challenging her on. Paul striding beside her…on a map he'd made with hands that could do anything—burn a leech from her leg, cut her birthday cake, zip her into his poncho, teach her about the Buddha and good food. In her delirium, he was hand-feeding *her* a ball of curried rice. *She* was licking his fingers, savoring every last taste... before he left for China.

But no, he was here, talking about fishing in the Seine. He started teaching her French; then it was Rosie giving the lesson while Thibaut taught Mandarin. There was no sky, only liquid green. There was no ground. Now it returned—the road. She stopped hard.

Around the bend, a stocky Japanese soldier was relieving himself amid some tree stumps.

Dropping the stick, Julia pulled her gun. He might be Deepak's killer—if so, where were the others?

He whirled and saw her. Moved for his rifle.

"*Drop it.*" Her hand tensed around the grip.

He let his weapon fall. Immobile, they eyed each other—he, fiercely incongruous, a gaping open button below his belt. Maybe she saw their old Pasadena gardener in his face, but she couldn't do it. She gestured with her gun: *Go*.

After a surprised glance, he fled. Julia took his rifle and slung it across her back—a far cry from the shotguns they'd used duck hunting in Bakersfield. She retrieved Deepak's stick and stuffed his Enfield in her waistband. She was a good shot but preferred firing at targets. Now she was the target.

She raced into the trees and away, losing track of space and time. Pausing, she struggled to catch her breath, feeling smothered by this tangled green blackness...every view the same.

Heavy clouds had overtaken the skies. No sign of the sun.

She feared the merciless jungle would swallow her.

Or that the stocky soldier she'd foolishly spared would pounce from behind.

As she checked her Arakan map, a blast of stifling wind ripped it from her fingers. The sky opened in a torrent. She stood in the pouring rain...lost. Sinking into the sodden ground.

Julia leaned against a rough trunk, inhaling several deep breaths of calm, as Si Paw would have advised. The rain ceased.

Her eyes opened to a canopy of mangroves pierced by rays of light. One of them pointed to a patch of dirty gray—the tree-lined road to Tat Tuang.

THIRTY-NINE

— // —

A whitewashed temple. Two orange-robed monks entering a faded-gold door.

Then a little thatched house with a front porch—past it, an open-sided shed radiating glorious smells, rice, onions…meat? Julia's knees weakened.

A low gong resounded, sending her deeper into the shadows of a flowering teak. She needed no mirror to apprise herself of her disreputable condition. Corkscrew hair, scratched face, battered hands, ripped bush jacket and boots. Even she would be terrified. Filthy and *armed*! She hid her gun and the Japanese rifle behind the tree, then gaped into the open kitchen.

There was only one visible occupant, an elderly woman in a yellow top, scooping rice into an earthen bowl. About five feet tall, with pulled-back white hair and brown skin, she carried her offering out toward the temple. Seeing Julia, her eyes grew wide as saucers. She stopped in her tracks.

Julia stared at the bowl, like one of the desperate souls who used to knock on their back door during the Depression. Milly had fed them—sometimes families, or a pregnant mother—before sending them on their way. Probably still starving.

Her face creased, leatherlike, the old woman stepped closer, craning her neck up at Julia—a towering female *farang*. Entirely at her mercy, Julia waited, until a curt tilt of the head indicated the open-sided shed. The woman sat her in the kitchen and placed the rice bowl before her.

She ladled curry into another bowl, poured a cup of water, and gave Julia a cloth.

Dazed, she rolled a ball of rice, dipped it—and ate. *Oh my.* Jolts of sensation shot from mouth to brain. Feeling a resurgence of life, she devoured every grain, beyond caring about manners or how she looked.

She wiped her hands, then pressed her palms together against her chest. "Julia."

The old woman in yellow bowed. "Su Chi."

"Tat Tuang?"

Su Chi bobbed her head, a movement that could mean anything.

"Do you know the Tat Tuang postmaster?"

Su Chi took out two cigars and lit them, handing Julia one. "*Cheroot.*" She inhaled.

Despite her distaste for cigars, their smells and soggy nubs, she thought it prudent to go along. She took a delicate puff, tasting a hint of pineapple and mold. She coughed.

The old woman's features dissolved into a crinkle of merriment.

After another tentative inhale, Julia got the hang of it, and they smoked together.

"Briteesh?"

"American."

Su Chi stared, her mind evidently clicking away. When they finished their cheroots, she held up a palm, then pointed at the sky.

Wait? Till night? Was there another option?

The old woman got up. "Chai?"

———

Deep chanting from the temple punctuated the afternoon. Su Chi hid her in a storage space smelling of rice, cooking oil, and mildew. Knees to chin, Julia crouched on hard-packed dirt, peering through slats in the rough door.

With nightfall came the creak of wooden wheels and squelch of hooves. Drawn by two horned buffalos, a cart pulled up to the main house, where Su Chi waited on the porch. A bald old man stepped out—her husband?

They commenced a long conversation. With a sharp nod, he got back in the cart and drove away. Su Chi disappeared inside, leaving Julia's mind to weave narratives of guile and treachery. She considered fleeing, but it was night, and where would she go?

The silence was so complete that her ears picked up the animals' snuffles and shuffles long before Su Chi's hand reached down to her. She led Julia to the table where the bald husband sat with a middle-aged man in a mismatched brown suit.

Failing to return her smile, the man studied her. "Tat Tuang postmaster," he finally said.

"I'm looking for the Ramree postmaster. Or his daughter…Mong? A friend."

"Americans very tall," he stated, stone faced. "You are like man."

She ignored his rudeness. "You speak English."

"British Raj," he replied as Aung Nat had. He exchanged a few words with Su Chi and her husband. "Can go on mail boat tomorrow—as local man." He plucked his tunic and loose trousers, then pointed at Julia.

She'd been mistaken for a man more than once. Now she welcomed it. "Go where?"

The postmaster drew a map on the earthen floor. "Here, Tat Tuang. Here, Ahn River." The river flowed into a waterway. On its other side was an island.

"Ramree?"

He made a dot on its shoreline. "Pyindaung." Farther west across another inlet, he drew a larger island. "Ramree."

She opened her remaining map, a regional view. Comparing it with his sketch, she had a good picture of the low-lying coastal terrain. "The mail boat will go to Ramree?"

"Only Pyindaung."

She stared. "Then?"

"Mail goes…" He made a vague gesture west. "Better not to know."

In case, was his implied message. In case the Japanese captured her.

Julia slept on a mat in the kitchen hut—or tried to sleep. All night, she worried about enemy-troop movements through Tat Tuang to their base in southern Ramree. About being sent to a work-to-death camp, Deepak's sacrifice for naught. As the sky turned silver-gray, she slipped away to retrieve her weapons from beneath the sheltering teak.

———

Before dawn, Su Chi gave Julia straw shoes, a white shirt, and loose blue pants. Popping a bamboo hat on her head, she adjusted the cord beneath her chin and smudged dirt on her face. Regarding her closely, she finally smiled: Julia could pass as a local man. Her eyes widened as Julia presented the Japanese rifle to her, then placed the Enfield in the small of her back.

They bowed to each other. "Hello?" she said.

"Goodbye," Julia replied, raising her folded palms high. "Thank you." Then, gripping Deepak's walking stick, she joined Su Chi's husband in his bullock cart bound for the small port.

Tat Tuang's postmaster met them at a faded dinghy. He tossed in two mailbags, helped her board, and introduced the pilot: "Ban."

After they spoke, the postmaster said, "Japanese soldiers also traveling today."

"*Did* travel? Or *will*?"

He only nodded. She lowered the hat over her eyes as the postmaster entered the cart, and they drove off without farewell. She didn't know Ban, didn't know this area nor speak the language.

The rain began, hot and steamy.

With a roar of his outboard engine, Ban shot down the Ahn. She clung to the gunwale.

———

By midmorning, under a light mist, they docked at Pyindaung, a tiny fishing village with ramshackle houses built on stilts along the water.

The few visible people wore sarongs and local dress, no uniforms. No one paid them any heed except a similarly dressed white-haired man, to whom Ban gave the smaller mailbag. The man hoisted it and walked down the muddy main road.

A wiry, barefoot boy in ragged pantaloons also waited at the dock, holding the lead of a great grayish-black elephant. As Ban handed him the larger sack, the two spoke, glancing at Julia. Then the boy scrambled up the animal's long speckled trunk with the mailbag.

"Ali," Ban informed her. He returned to his boat and chugged away. She'd been handed off again—to a turbaned boy and his elephant.

"Ganesh." Ali uttered a quiet command. The elephant knelt, left rear leg extended.

Her throat tightened. Deepak had prayed to Ganesh—*elephant god of good fortune*—and here he was. She pressed her palms together and bowed. "My friend told me to expect you. Thank you!"

The majestic creature regarded her with a big glassy eye as if sharing her emotion, then fanned her with his delicate pink ear. Moving closer, she placed a tentative palm on his rough wrinkled skin. He seemed to smile.

Taking Julia's hand, Ali helped her climb from Ganesh's rear leg onto a padded mat secured by a leather belly strap. She settled behind the mailbag, tucking her stick through the strap. The boy climbed back up the elephant's steady trunk, perching behind his head.

Upon Ali's command, Ganesh lurched upward, one massive foot at a time. Julia felt his quiet force beneath her body, his steadiness, the sure rhythm of his movements. Inhaling his grassy scent, she found her exhale matching his. Then her belly tightened. This was no time to relax—in unknown territory, in the hands of strangers.

Julia adjusted her hat and lowered her head. Soon the mucky road was lost in mangrove terrain. It was still early, the sun behind them, which indicated they were heading west toward Ramree—but to the Allied zone in the north or the Japanese-controlled south, she could not know. Caught in the middle, the Burmese, as Aung Nat had warned, did not like any *farang*.

They tromped through jungle carved by estuaries and rivers. Mosquitoes feasted on her sweaty neck. Although the drizzle had ceased, she was sopping wet.

They were rounding a shrubby curve when a shot rang out. Harsh shouts.

Two Japanese soldiers. Bayonet-rifles pointing their way.

Ganesh thundered and reared.

While Ali held tight, Julia lost her balance. Her straw shoes slithered off her feet.

Slipping backward, her hat flying off, she fell into rotting foliage, clutching the mailbag. A sharp pain radiated up her spine—the Enfield. She screamed.

A stocky man wearing tattered khaki leg wrappings aimed his rifle at her, planting a territorial boot on her hip.

She lay there, the gun jabbing her back. Better to fight than be captured—or worse. *This* time, she would shoot. Julia went ice cold, awaiting her moment.

The taller soldier pointed his smoking weapon at Ali, then the ground. After the boy shimmied down Ganesh's trunk, the soldier grabbed the scruff of his neck.

Shifting slightly left, she prepared to seize the Enfield. Her right heel dug in. Then she powered her foot toward her captor's groin, reaching for the gun. At the same moment, with a grunt, he thrust his bayonet at her stomach—sunlight flashing off its tip.

Blinded by eternity, Julia closed her eyes.

They were jolted open by a dull thud—as the blade caught in the mailbag. Cursing, the stocky soldier booted it aside.

Roaring in fury, the elephant pawed the ground. The taller man lunged for Ganesh's lead. With brutal force, the great creature wrapped his trunk around him, shook wildly—and tossed him against a tree. The soldier hit with a loud thump.

His body crumpled to the ground, then went still. Ganesh stood over him, flapping his ears in agitation. Patting his flank, Ali crouched toward Julia, a finger to his lips.

Still flat on her back, she again tried to maneuver for the gun. Enraged, the stocky soldier prepared another thrust—this time, at her throat. His rifle freezing in midair, he stared at her long and hard.

Their stares deepened as, stunned, they recalled yesterday's encounter—when she'd spared his life.

With a growl, he slashed his bayonet across the mailbag, then stomped through an eruption of letters to his unmoving comrade. He looked back at Julia, laying down the rifle.

Dashing to her side, Ali grabbed the revolver—and fired into the soldier's head.

His eyes flew open, met hers with a look of surprise; then he collapsed on a pile of mail.

The man was undefended, she wanted to protest. *This war is an ugly beast*, she heard Paul say.

Shoving the gun into his waistband, Ali crooned sweet words to Ganesh, calming his charge into a kneeling position. Once Julia had climbed up, he gestured for her to lie flat on her belly, then clambered aboard. They pressed on, the wet earth littered with mail to remain forever undelivered.

All she could see was the elephant's back, all she could hear was his heart. Or was it hers? They'd faced the same threat, the same terror. Yet he resumed his steady, swaying gait. Each powerful stride taking them deeper into the mangroves. While she awaited more gunfire.

Dazed, she stroked Ganesh's leathery skin to calm them both. Hearing the lyrical birdsong, she rolled her head—toward a flash of orange in the trees. A paradise flycatcher. Her spirit lifted. But she could not relax. Where was this boy, who could shoot like a man, taking her?

FORTY

———— // ————

Julia did not have to look up to know the sun was nearing its height. She was liquefied, dissolved into the elephant.

Then she felt the quality of light change as the foliage around them parted.

Ganesh lumbered into a clearing and stopped, kneeling for her to descend. Like an apparition, a grave young woman in a sarong floated out from a basha.

"Myaung," Ali said.

Myaung. Could she be the "Mong" Julia had been seeking, the postman's daughter mentioned by Jane? Manly's Arakan agent?

A suntanned man in shorts, a bamboo hat, and round tortoiseshell glasses followed.

Julia shook her head slowly. "*Manly?*"

"You certainly took the long way around," he said blandly. "Gave everyone a fright. Thibaut radioed at eight that evening. By ten, we heard from Wild Bill. When you didn't check in by midnight, they ordered an air and sea search of the Bay of Bengal. The next morning they found fragments of your PT boat."

To the question in her eyes, Manly replied, "I'm sorry. There were no survivors. Thibaut notified family members."

She looked from one to the other. "Why are you here?"

"The appearance of a tall American woman could not go unnoticed— especially one who'd swum the Bay of Bengal." He released a low whistle.

"Only the coastal waters," she said with unnecessary humility. "Did Su Chi report me? Or Aung Nat?"

"He's our radio operator in Chindaung," Manly explained.

"Why didn't he tell me?"

He opened his palms. "You appeared out of nowhere—during a Japanese squeeze that made it dangerous to use his wireless. In the end, Aung Nat took the chance of trusting you."

"Did you know he was hiding Jemadar Deepak Binoy?" Her voice broke.

"Only that an injured Indian POW was recovering there. Aung Nat has sent his recent reports through the postal underground—including that of your survival."

"Deepak didn't make it. He saved my life." Julia buried her face into Ganesh's body, spread her arms across his wrinkled skin. And let go.

They fell silent as she wept. Then the great animal blew into her ear. She laughed and cried until she was spent. Myaung patted her shoulder softly.

When she'd collected herself, she kissed Ganesh's trunk. "Are these two good souls part of your local net?"

"I recruit Mahout Ali." Myaung smiled. "And he recruit Ganesh."

Julia saluted Ali. "Then we will definitely win this war."

"It's a good team," Manly said simply. "But where's the mail?"

While she recounted the events, Ali and his charge left to bathe in the river. Myaung found her replacement shoes and hat. Then they sat under a palm tree. Julia sank back and closed her eyes as a tender tropical breeze soothed her bruised body and spirit.

"Some tea?" Myaung asked.

Her heart swelled with emotion. "Wherever you go in this land, they offer you tea," she said, batting back more tears.

Manly tsk-tsked. "Helluva thing, having to break it to the guys about their mail."

"That mailbag saved my life. My intel will save many more." Staring into the mangroves, Julia wiped her eyes and told them about Deepak— and the enemy's planned Christmas attack.

Manly's unruffled demeanor cracked open in rage and relief. He exhaled before speaking. "May I express the gratitude of forty men at this base, plus countless locals."

"Deepak sacrificed for all of you—all of us." She didn't want to take one drop of his credit.

As Myaung rushed inside the hut, Manly gazed at Julia with sympathy and respect. "I've lost people close to me, too. You never get over it."

"I won't." She heard the clatter of their message being transmitted on the field radio.

"You are a real pro, lady. Janie's always talking about you."

As she was digesting that startling news, Ali and Ganesh returned, dripping clean. Manly and his agent exchanged a few words in the local dialect.

"They're leaving now," Manly said. "We mustn't be seen together."

Another farewell. Julia stared, holding them close inside.

Ali stepped forward and gave her Deepak's revolver. She clasped it for a moment, then passed it to Manly.

"Thank you, Ali," she said with a bow. Raising his right palm toward his face, the lithe mahout bowed back.

She touched her forehead to Ganesh's side. "And you, my brave friend." He raised his trunk with a flourish.

As Myaung reappeared with a quiet nod, Ali shinnied up the elephant's flank.

Hand on her heart, Julia watched them disappear into the jungle.

"I also report Deepak's loss to unit," Myaung told her. "Request family details."

"Thank you."

"And you." She folded her palms and bent her head. "Soon we are free."

"Let's get to base." Manly hurried them onto a rusty fishing boat beyond the trees.

———

By dusk, Donovan sent his congratulations. An RAF airstrike had taken down the Irrawaddy Bridge at Thayet, eighty miles east of there. The POW camp was not bombed.

Although glad to have done her duty, Julia was in no mood to celebrate. She clung to Deepak's walking stick.

Their K-rations were a far cry from Kandy cuisine. But the food that had sustained her travels stuck with her—the curry Si Paw taught her to eat with her hand, the coconuts she split open, the fish Deepak caught with *his* hand, the rice Aung Nat and Su Chi shared.

After dinner, the three of them walked to Kyaukpyu, the island's deep-water harbor. They cracked some warm beers and sat against a row of empty oil barrels. The slender moon sent glints of silver on the bobbing waves.

"Sharks out there," Manly commented.

"Now you tell me." Julia took a long sip of beer. Finally, she understood what Jane saw in him. Despite his offhand persona, he was a sensitive, committed man. His respect moved her.

But even after her shower, even as they soaked their feet in the evening-cool sea, she felt sticky. Unclean. The spirits of her friends hovered, clinging to her. She knew that would not be their intention. It was her. *Her* clinging to them. She did not want to let them go. Yet knowing their traditions, she needed to release her friends. She closed her eyes and said goodbye. Tried.

A fresh breeze, from nowhere around there, brushed over her.

Was Deepak pushing her away? Or sending her another gift? Julia reached for his walking stick, still holding on to him. More tears were forming. She suppressed them but could not prevent the tremor in her voice. "Si Paw tried to teach me time and distance calculations. So patient."

"His code name Wise Man," Myaung murmured. "He stay after family escape to Assam."

"And Deepak?" Manly asked her.

"The son of a Sunderbans fisherman who became an officer. He intended to fight for Indian independence after we win this war." Julia closed her eyes, seeing her proud, brave companion. She felt the closeness they had attained in two short days. "Deepak was a hero. He deserves a medal, and I will do all I can to ensure he gets one. I hope to stand with his family."

"They will be honored," Myaung said.

"And I'll check the refugee registers for Si Paw's family. I need to tell them his story." Julia gazed at the glimmering indigo waters. "I guess that's what war is—countless human stories, most of which we can never know. But their stories are now mine. Mine to carry."

Manly tipped his can against theirs, eyes soft. "I'm carrying a few of my own."

"You going back to Ceylon?" They both knew Julia was asking about Jane.

"Janie is one of a kind. But I'm based here for the duration. She'll be off to the East Indies. Nothing permanent about war."

She nodded. "Except the memories."

"We'll be feeding off them the rest of our lives." He finished his beer, opened three more. "There's a Catalina flying boat can take you back in the morning."

Julia glanced at the starry sky, imagining possible bomb attacks on Ramree-HQ, or an invasion from south Ramree, more terror and death. She thought of relaxing in her bath, sleeping in fresh sheets, having cold drinks with friends. Paul. "It's darned tempting. But Donovan sent me here to set up a Registry and train some smart Cambridge chap to run it. He promised I'd be done by Christmas. Then I'll take you up on that Catalina." She smiled. "The boss is counting on me. I haven't let him down yet."

FORTY-ONE

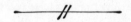

Kandy, Ceylon

Two days before Christmas, Julia's flying boat touched down at Trinco Harbor, where Mack had driven her so long ago. Paul was waiting… with a bear hug. He pulled her under a great flame tree that enclosed them in filtered coral light. "We were worried about you, Julie." He cupped her face between his palms with a tenderness that almost broke her.

A dazzling blue butterfly flitted between them. It flew away, then swept back and landed on his shoulder.

Julia wanted to weep and never move from the safety of his arms. To say that thoughts of him had propelled her forward. That she'd seen him in her fevered dreams. The intimacy had only been on her end, though. So she shifted away, hiding in the bare facts. "Burma wasn't quite the walk in the park Donovan made it out to be. But I'd asked to go into the field, so…"

"He told me in confidence that the Irrawaddy Bridge bombing was your work."

"It was Deepak, the Indian soldier who escaped a Japanese POW camp. It was his intel."

Paul studied her in his attentive manner. "He didn't make it?"

She looked down, struggling to master an onslaught of emotion.

"You completed the task he had entrusted in you. He would be proud of you. We are."

What about I *am proud of you?* Turning, she placed Deepak's walking stick in the jeep.

Although Paul didn't prod her further, her volcanic feelings had a deep need for release. As Donovan had informed him of the op's successful conclusion, she felt able to recount the rest.

"I'm sorry for your losses," he said halfway over the mountain to Kandy. "I respect your resolve. And I salute you for the lives you saved."

We are content to work in the shadows, the boss had told her long ago. Meaning, *don't expect glory from your job*. Still, Paul's recognition meant something. But that didn't soothe the wounds she bore. Julia looked away, gripping the rough smoothness of the mango wood.

———

Later, at Queen's bar, her friends peppered her with questions. Julia deflected most of them, saying only that she'd been ordered to deliver some secret files to Calcutta. "Let's talk holidays. Last year, we celebrated in snowy DC."

"*This* year, in tropical Kandy," Betty said, a little too upbeat. "Janie's been decorating the mess for a blowout Christmas party." Her cheeriness fading, she leaned over to hug Julia. "It seems I'm going to China, too."

With Dick. While happy for Betty, she thought of his wife back home, alone for another Christmas. But maybe the Heppners had never been close, or maybe those long years of separation and secrets had come between them—like Betty and Alex. Julia was swamped by a pitiless wave of loneliness. She had appreciated being able to share confidences with Paul during their SEAC investigation. And in her personal life, with Betty.

She tried to remain matter-of-fact. "And you, Peggy?"

"Some of us are staying. After Dillon left for Thailand, I began showing Byron the ropes in SI—he's also in navy intelligence, did you know? And here's the best news: Caryl and Cheryl will be running Messages."

"Brava. They're finally allowing a woman to step up. Two of them." Then Julia's grin faded. "What about SEAC? And the Supremo?"

"They're here." Jane pursed her lips. "Mark my words: Churchill is still set on Mountbatten saving their Southeast Asian colonies."

The two had spoken privately about Manly. While pleased at Julia's positive assessment, Jane was ready to move on. An affair with a married man had a shelf life. This one had expired.

Now Jane turned to Paul, whispered something, and he laughed. Julia froze. They were still at it, discussing mythology or history, French cinema or surrealism. Her face shining in delight at some witticism, Jane reached up, accepting a drink from Krishna without a glance or a word of thanks.

What a hypocrite. For all her platitudes about social justice and revolution, she remained a spoiled society girl from Nob Hill. And Paul. Mr. Charm, able to make any woman fall for him. Julia's doubts were realized; he was just another skirt-chaser.

———

The Christmas party was a boozy, emotional event centered around a beautiful conifer adorned in liana vines, orchids, and flickering candles. "Where did you get it?" she asked Jane.

"The Botanic Gardens," came her reply—with an angelic smile.

Julia was horrified. "You *cut* it down?"

"My associates," she said airily. "It was for the cause."

"What cause?"

"We had to have a Christmas tree, didn't we?" Jane gazed around the transformed OSS mess. "I considered it more democratic to steal from all the people. I also came up with mistletoe—and champagne." She glowed with pride.

It was no time to scold her. Armed Forces Radio was playing a tribute to Glenn Miller, who had crashed in the English Channel ten days earlier, en route to entertain the troops in France. The very next morning, Germany launched its counteroffensive, the Battle of the Bulge, which had Allied forces slogging through snow with no overcoats, due to overoptimism in some quarters. Out here, brutal warfare continued in Burma and China. While in the long run, the Allies were headed to victory, no one expected it to be quick, or painless. Last summer's euphoria could not be recalled.

Appropriately enough, the music of another selfless performer wafted through the night—Dietrich's "Lili Marlene," a song that seemed to bear all the mud and hunger and heartache of the season.

The lyrics tore through Julia, the rawness in Marlene Dietrich's voice, her husky German accent conveying another level of grief. Lost in melancholy, she stared at the poor uprooted tree.

"Merry Christmas, toots."

Merry? How insensitive. Stung by Paul's enduring closeness with Jane, she coolly handed him his Christmas gift—the Zippo lighter he'd mentioned in the Buddha cave.

"Julia McWilliams! You remembered. Where the hell did you get it?"

"My Burma field kit. I'll throw in my Swiss Army knife. For China."

All at once, he planted his lips on hers with a thrilling intensity. Her body took over, and she responded with abandon. She couldn't help it.

"You are a surprising woman," he said when they finally came up for air.

Her head spinning, she gave him a wicked grin. "Sometimes I surprise myself." Taking his hand, she walked under the mistletoe and kissed him again.

The party flowed around them, and then their lips parted...their bodies.

Falling back to earth, she looked at Paul. Still dizzy, she reclaimed her will and slipped from his embrace. "Merry Christmas," she said in a breathy voice out of her control. "See you later."

Preserving the sense of his mouth on hers, Julia floated to the screened window, surrounded by vines of starlike night-blooming blossoms. The river seemed so sinuous, two banks yearning for each other. A tropical breeze glided through the room, mingling the scents of jasmine and pine, burning candles, coconuts, and curry. In a world of suffering, there was still a place for joy. Her heart was full; she finally had the holiday spirit.

She turned back, filled with fondness for her friends, nostalgia for all they'd shared. Then the light went out of the room as, unable to turn away, she watched Paul embrace Jane under the mistletoe. The same mistletoe. His mouth on hers, his hands cupping the narrow curve of her waist. The perfect couple—Jane, so blond and petite, and Paul, *taller* than her.

Now they were laughing. Jane's curly blond halo encircling both their faces, Paul's wreathed in smiles, no doubt at one of her clever remarks.

Tom Johnston had kissed Julia at a Christmas party. Then she'd kissed him on New Year's Eve. Part of it had been the wonder of Manhattan. The crystalline towers, the sparkling river and champagne. How superficial they'd been, skating over the Depression in pursuit of a good time, a carefree interlude before they took their foreordained places in society.

Julia wrenched her eyes away. Under the lowering clouds, the river looked muddy, its banks probably teeming with cobras.

"Would you care for some cake?" Paul held the plate between them.

Did he know she'd seen him and Jane, or was he not even aware of her feelings? He had to be; he was too smart. "I'm not hungry." She shifted to her more distant foot.

"The heat and humidity. Absurd, isn't it? Christmas in the tropics." He laughed, still holding the plate. "It was thoughtful of you remembering the Zippo. That was quite a day, wasn't it? The hike, the rains, the stunning art, sharing the last egg—"

Deepak had given her his last boiled egg. He had sacrificed everything. "Sometimes things happen in the moment," she replied distantly.

Paul scooped up a forkful of cake, lifted it to her lips, now closed and protective. If this were an apology, she wasn't interested.

After eating it himself, he carried on reminiscing with no response from her. Finally, he persuaded her to have a bite. The cake was fine. After all, they had butter here, sugar and eggs. She thought of his reference to them sharing a single egg, swapping bites, taking in the moisture of his mouth, him taking in hers. Everything was moist here, moldy and moldering, but her skin had never been better. And she'd enjoyed the best meals of her life. Sometimes Julia wondered if she'd ever tasted food before that first curry in Bombay. So, this cake was fine, but it wasn't memorable. What was memorable was Paul kissing Jane under the same mistletoe as her. Kissing Jane *after* her—as in, saving the best for last.

———

She didn't see Paul much the following week and hardly cared. Then it was New Year's Eve. Those left in Kandy sang "Auld Lang Syne" with deep emotion. The OSS mess had a barren look. As if Jane had already moved on to Java. All things end.

Two glasses and a champagne bottle in hand, Paul took Julia off to the corner. "In case you hadn't noticed, I kissed a number of women under the Christmas mistletoe. It's the custom, usually doesn't mean a thing. But with you, it did."

She gazed across the room…Betty and Dick swaying to Frank Sinatra's "I'll Be Seeing You." Julia had nothing to say.

"We've been through a lot together," he mused. "Certainly your brilliant secret op—which you kindly invited me to share—but also the way we're able to brace each other up when things are hard. We're quite different, you and me, Julie, yet I believe we've developed a real friendship. I admire how you throw yourself into life with such passion. Your marvelous spirit. Not to mention your way with a tune." She heard the warmth creep into his voice. "That was some day. Those caves. The company."

"Memorable," she said from some distance. Then, compelled to turn back, she saw his face crinkled in a big smile. Even unforgettable, but she couldn't quite give him that.

Whether or not he'd remember every little thing, she knew she would. The great gilded Buddha, laughing over his big feet and big ears. The stunning revelation of the accident that had left Paul with only one good eye, comprehending his courage. The flashlight going out. The green rain sealing them inside the cave…inside the two zipped-together ponchos. *There is something between us I can't quite figure out,* he'd murmured. *I want to, but I'm leaving soon. You never have as much time as you expect.*

Julia felt herself softening. What was it about Paul Child?

He regarded her with eyebrow raised. "Friends?"

So he had been aware of her bruised feelings. She nodded. "Friends." For now, she'd go for what she could get.

He poured two glasses. "To our adventures in the spy trade."

They clinked. And oh, the music it made. She listened till the pure ringing tone died out. Their shared experiences had bonded them. She would miss having him around.

"We were a damn good team, Julie. It was tough going back to the Map Room."

"And me to the Registry." Julia almost choked when Armed Forces Radio segued to "We'll Meet Again," Vera Lynn's angelic voice expressing all the longing in the world. While her own longing had to remain unexpressed. "Paper sorter *par excellence*."

"Don't downplay your talents."

"You're the talented one!" she said.

"I am a worker bee. Except perhaps once in a blue moon—"

"The moon can appear blue anytime, Mr. Child, depending on many things."

His sudden, endearing grin broke through. "Is that so, Miss McWilliams? Then one can always hope." He embraced her, and this time, there was no mistletoe in sight.

It may have only been the New Year's champagne. But maybe it wasn't.

———

The next morning—January 1, 1945—Dick, Paul, and Jack departed for China with more staffers, including Betty, to follow. Julia waved as they drove off, but her smile was forced, her heart heavy. Whatever was between her and Paul was too unformed to stick. She knew the long odds of reconnecting somewhere in the misty future. Thick foliage closed behind their jeep.

What's wrong with me? Seeking romance in the midst of all this suffering and death? While Paul left to serve in the last great battlefield

of World War II, she had no right to mope. She hurried back to her
Registry, prepared to catch up on work. And tonight, on her letters
home, especially to her sister, Dort, who had so generously dedicated
herself to their father's care with Julia off at war. Her family was together,
safe in Pasadena. She had much to be grateful for.

The following week brought several large parcels, a backlog of
material delayed by the holidays. Thanks to Trixie, they weren't too far
behind. "Any word on your fiancé?"

"Soon, I'm sure." Positive as ever. Then she drooped, like a sunflower
facing the wrong way.

"You're a brave girl." Julia hugged her. "But, as my mother always
said, 'You must keep your chin up and move forward.'"

"And look at you." Trixie squeezed back, hard. "You're my hero, Julia."

She smiled sadly. "I'm just fumbling my way through like everyone
else, trying to do my best. One thing I learned—well, two things: Work
hard. And never give up."

Trixie's spirit lifting before Julia's eyes, she said, "Let me buy you
lunch."

Under a pale-golden rain, they approached the mess. At the door,
Donovan boomed, "There you are, McWilliams." He nodded toward
the covered walkway.

She waved Trixie on. "Nice to see you, sir. We have your briefing
material for the Chungking talks."

"I hear your assistant has been doing a credible job." He sent her
that blue-eyed Irish grin she'd seen turned on many a friend and foe.
He was softening her up. "I won't beat about the bush. No matter what
scuttlebutt you hear, Detachment 404/Kandy is winding down. You are
no longer needed, McWilliams."

She recoiled, as if that bayonet had finally found its mark—only the
blow had been delivered by a man she trusted and revered. Flooded with
rage, Julia rallied every fiber in her being to protest the injustice. But the
betrayal was beyond words to express. She stood there, mouth open, a
fish about to be squeezed to death for its last drop of liquid.

"However, we do need you in China."

"I...I..." She was still alive. She brought in some fresh air. Her lungs expanded. Her heart. *We'll Meet Again*...She wanted to be cool and professional; she wanted to soar. "Oh my."

"Sorry I can't send you as an operative." Donovan grinned, pleased as punch at his little gag.

Some joke! She was embarrassed at having revealed her deepest self. She had her pride! Using all her acting skills, Julia replied casually, "Don't tell me. Your new Registry."

"Detachment 202/Kunming."

"I haven't said if I accept the position."

His blue eyes turned probing. "Well?"

Was there a choice? She and the boss had been through this crusade together—and it wasn't over yet. And of course...*Paul*. "I guess you might need a little hand up there."

"Is that a yes?"

She pretended to consider it. "Would any ball gowns be required?"

Donovan laughed. "Dick Heppner? What do you think?"

"Any spies to ferret out?"

"You'll be tripping over them." He turned dead serious. "Until we reopen the Burma Road, Free China depends on our air resupply. The outcome of World War II itself depends on it. However, too many goods are going sideways. I'm depending on your sharp eyes—as ever."

"General Donovan, you're a military man. But I prefer the civilian way of life and will do anything to put this damned war behind us."

"*Anything* is exactly what you may be facing. I always say a good OSS operative should be like Lawrence in Arabia—able to improvise, deal in any terrain. I expect more of the same."

A good OSS operative! Lawrence in Arabia! You couldn't get better than that.

"Briefing tomorrow at 0800. In the meantime, you can inform Norbury she's promoted."

"Yes, sir. Next stop, China. Thank you!"

"Let's see if you wish to repeat that after you and Betty fly over the Hump."

PART FOUR

War and Peace

FORTY-TWO

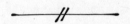

Chabua, Assam, India
February 1945

"Welcome to Station Six, Air Transport Command, India–China wing. Don't get many ladies up around here." Lowering his paperwork, the baby-faced quartermaster regarded the two women as if they were some quirky species from another planet.

"It's good to see you, too," Julia replied cheerfully. "Seems we made it on the last plane out of Calcutta for a while." They'd skidded onto the runway just as a thick, dripping fog fell over the highland town of Chabua, set in a narrow finger of Northeast India that poked into China's southwest—where Kunming was their final destination.

"Happens all the time. Something about the Indian monsoon colliding with Himalayan weather fronts," he explained.

"We saw those mountains." Betty glanced out the open-sided supply basha with awe. "Jagged walls of ice going on forever. Which country are they in?"

"The lower ones are in India, believe it or not," the young man, a corporal, said.

"Snow in India," Julia marveled. "Wouldn't Pop want to know about that!" Swiping the sweat off her forehead, she watched tendrils of mist slide inside. "He'd probably say, *Just go to Yosemite.*" She laughed. "It's different, though. Maybe you have to have been here. Put it this way: there's a lot of scenery."

"Beats New York any day." The quartermaster released a world-weary sigh. "You'll see more on your way out. You were trained to jump, right?"

They exchanged anxious glances. "No!"

"Just joshing. No worries. You've got a seasoned pilot ready to go as soon as the clouds lift. I'll get you prepped." He indicated the lashed-together shelves crammed with folds of pale-blue silk, olive drab canvas bags, flashlights, K-rations, and all manner of military odds and ends. From these shelves, the quartermaster issued their survival kits and parachute packs. "Last but not least…" He handed them each a blue envelope. "Your blood chits."

Julia removed a thin piece of rice paper with Chinese characters. "What?"

"*This foreign person (American) has come to China to help the war effort,*" he recited. "*Soldiers and civilians, one and all, should save and protect him. Reward.*"

"Wonder how much we're worth," Betty mused.

"The price of dinner, if you go down in headhunter country," the corporal replied, straight-faced. "Ladies." He raised an index finger to his brow, then returned to his inventory list.

———

Two mornings later, they were still socked in. Their feet barely visible through the fog, Julia and Betty paced the airstrip. All that lay between them and Kunming were five hundred miles of skyscraping white peaks—the roof of the world. The Aluminum Highway, the military called it, for the many skeletons of planes that would rest there for eternity.

Muffled sounds traveled across the field—voices, the thump of equipment and cargo, the beep of vehicle horns, the rumble of an elephant. Otherwise, they felt quite alone.

"Standing orders are, if you can see the end of the runway, takeoff is expected," a disembodied voice boomed.

They turned to see a Cheshire-cat grin emerge through the sticky mist.

"Sergeant Sam Booker." The barrel-chested man thrust forward a broad hand. "Army Services of Supply, Kunming. They call me SOS Booker."

"I'm Julia," she said as they shook. "We're heading up there, too. This is Betty."

"It's a great pleasure. You gals would be warmly welcomed at our nightly sporting event—involving wagers and the best moonshine this side of Kentucky."

"What's your game, Sergeant?" Betty asked.

"Blackjack, poker, mah-jongg. But I must warn you, I'm on a roll."

"Sounds delightful, only we'd hate like heck to take any poor soldier's dough," Julia said. "Especially yours. Or the pilot's."

He replied with his wide, mischievous smile…which lingered as he disappeared in the gauzy gray haze.

———

The din was deafening. In the 0500 darkness, vehicles were racing from one plane to another, supplies being loaded under lights clamped to bamboo scaffolding. One of those Hump workhorses was theirs, identified on its tail as a Curtiss C-46 Commando.

Sweating under duffel bags, parachute packs, and lined jackets, they waited on the tarmac near the only stationary figure, a driver smoking in his jeep. Mesmerized, they watched an elephant transfer a barrel from his trunk into the double-cargo hatch. Another loaded a very large crate, then three small ones. Meanwhile, two mechanics worked on the left engine.

Betty watched anxiously. "Last-minute repairs?"

"Normal maintenance," said a male voice behind them. A familiar voice.

Julia whirled around—Thibaut de Saint Phalle.

"In daytime, that metal can burn your hands off…"

"*Thibaut!*" Betty exclaimed, walking into his open-armed embrace.

Julia regarded him with some dismay—she had not shared details of the still-classified Burma op with Betty. "Imagine running into you here."

That small crooked smile. "We have some catching up to do."

"Love to. But we're on our way to Kunming."

"Fancy. Me, too." Seeing her dubious look, he added, "This time really is a coincidence."

"Don't tell me." Betty tipped her head. "He's the one you delivered papers to in Calcutta?"

"Small world, isn't it." Julia placed a finger over her lips, giving Thibaut a little shake of her head.

"Never mind," Betty said with a worldly air. "Need to know. Where's Rosie?"

Thibaut's face lit up. "Julia got her transferred to China. With me."

"I told Donovan I couldn't organize the Kunming Registry without Rosie Frame. Has she arrived yet?"

"The other day, I hear. I've been in Calcutta on a supply run." He took Julia's hand. "I—we—are very grateful. And I have good news."

Betty's eyes widened. "I hope I know what it is."

He nodded happily. "On an earlier trip, I organized a champagne supper at Delhi's Red Fort. Perhaps it was the full moon, but for some crazy reason, Rosamond accepted."

Julia beamed. "I imagine we'll have plenty of rice to throw in China."

That was the end of Thibaut's jovial mood. Stepping away from the jeep and driver, he bent his head, and they moved closer. "Sadly, we have plenty of *nothing*. While our mission is to report on enemy-ship movements, my Sino-American unit has to scrounge for rice from farmers around the South China coast—rice they've hidden from the Japanese."

"You're the only non-Chinese in the unit?"

He nodded. "Great fellows. Tough. Funny. Never a complaint about cloth shoes, threadbare uniforms—or the lack of war matériel, including batteries. Our camp is a crumbling old hillside monastery with a pagoda/watchtower vulnerable to location tracking."

Julia exhaled in a big puff. "That's why you fly to Calcutta every month."

"To collect our goods, personally." He scowled. "Sometimes I'm too late. Two days ago a critical order vanished from Cal's Services of Supply depot. It was logged in, I learned, then disappeared. Never got to see it."

Our agenda—yours—is to help plug the leaks in our supply pipeline to sustain China, Donovan had said, *and us all. I need you to keep me informed.* Julia's shoulders clamped around her neck. "What?"

He surveyed the tarmac again. A truck sounded its horn, an elephant trumpeted; everyone was rushing about. No one paying attention to them. "There are covert bases like ours dug in all over occupied China, so secure comms are essential." His voice dropped to a whisper. "I had the idea of camouflaging a transmitter-receiver inside an actual broadcast radio. An older table model, nothing flashy—but with state-of-the-art components. Our Washington Communications group built me three prototype transceivers housed in 1935 RCA walnut cabinets, the vertical design."

"My pop has one like that—with a brass dial in the middle marked *RCA Victor.*"

"Similar." He nodded grimly. "The transmitter fits in a false bottom. I wasn't able to save my uncle, but maybe I could protect our people."

"Oncle Alexandre?" The man they'd toasted in Calcutta.

"He was a wireless operator with the French Resistance."

"Oh, I'm so sorry," Julia and Betty both said, clasping his hands.

He glanced at their Curtiss Commando. "On our honeymoon, I hope to take Rosamond to Paris for a family memorial. Some day in the future. If we have one."

Julia was shocked at his pessimism. That was some intelligence she didn't want to report.

As the first ray of dawn glittered off the pilot's port window, Betty read the red-lettered phrase across the plane's nose: "Is This Trip Necessary?"

"Besides batteries, I'm carrying radio fuses, tubes, crystals, other spare parts. So yes, it is necessary—if we want to keep this war going." Thibaut indicated its scalloped dirty-white underbelly. "Camouflage, for flying through snow and clouds."

Besides battling the Himalaya, their lumbering aircraft would be a sitting duck for any Japanese Zero on the hunt. Julia closed her eyes, smelling the PT's burning fuel and rubber, seeing the hungry red flames, the empty yellow Mae West, the floating white elbow. Then she opened them, staring at the hulking cargo plane in a vain attempt to inoculate herself from fear.

Before long, the work lights shut down. Takeoff was getting closer.

Three uniformed men strode to the C-46 wearing boots and shearling jackets, oxygen masks clipped to their baseball caps. The taller one, Chinese, had a .45 on his hip.

"First Lieutenant Lim, Kuomintang Air Force," Thibaut said. "His copilot and radioman are American. We're all part of SACO—the Sino-American Cooperative Organization."

"They look like Flying Tigers," Betty exclaimed. "You know, the John Wayne picture about American flyboys in China. That volunteer group from the thirties."

"Later merged into the US Air Force under General 'Old Man' Chennault, who, for a time, served under Generalissimo Chiang Kai-shek." Thibaut laughed. "We're all entwined."

"Wouldn't you know Jane once smuggled out a panda on a Flying Tiger plane," Julia remarked as they watched the pilot and his officers climb into the cockpit. Their flight jackets were emblazoned with the Nationalist China flag, a twelve-pointed white star on a blue square in a field of red, and America's red, white, and blue. Beneath the crossed flags, a series of red characters rippled across their backs.

"Chiang's guarantee of a reward to anyone who rescues them," Thibaut explained.

"All we have is a letter," Betty cracked uneasily.

After being ushered aboard, they settled into jump seats along the port fuselage, stowing their gear underneath. Closest to the hatch, Julia locked her legs around her duffel bag, carrying a top secret item critical to their success in China—and a parcel from Paul.

The center of the tunnellike cabin was a mass of lashed-down cargo—the large bamboo crate and three smaller ones, jeep tires, fuel drums, assorted containers. Beyond, seated among a dozen or so sol-diers, was the SOS card shark. "Still on a roll, Booker?" she called.

The sergeant raised his thumb. "Here's hoping my luck carries us over the rock pile."

Luck. She sank into her hanging hemp seatback. Life was a crapshoot for any of them. A loose screw, snowstorm, or enemy fighter was all it took.

Amelia Earhart had spoken one year at Smith. Julia had been cap-tivated by the famous aviator, with her short hair and confident smile. She'd encouraged the girls to test themselves. Said they could do more than society expected. Amelia and her plane had disappeared somewhere near New Guinea; the news was reported three days after Caro died.

To distract herself, Julia counted the passengers and crew—seventeen, plus the three officers up front. She asked Thibaut what else he was transporting.

"Those crates. Two of the smaller ones hold Nationalist currency printed in the States, worth over a million," he replied quietly. "The third is gold for payroll or payoffs. From Fort Knox via Bombay."

She felt the force of the gold bar crashing into her leg. "And the big one?"

"Madame Chiang Kai-shek's baby grand."

To a country desperate for food and supplies? Her eyes flew open.

Then the twin engines began revving and the propellers spinning.

The crew chief passed out oxygen masks and demonstrated how to connect them to tube lines dangling from the ceiling. "At thirteen thousand feet, I'll put out the alert."

With a clink of hooks and D-rings, everyone shook open their para-chute packs. Thibaut showed Julia and Betty how to secure the harness around their chests, cinch their leg straps tight, and fashion the sky-blue silk into a cushion. "I hope you had a light breakfast. Prepare yourselves for five hundred miles of bad road." He handed them earplugs.

"We expect clear sailing," Lieutenant Lim announced in an American East Coast accent. "In about four hours, we shall land at the US Fourteenth Air Force base, Kunming, China. Enjoy your flight."

FORTY-THREE

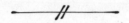

Over the Hump

With a thunderous boom, the C-46 shot straight up. Julia's head flung back against the webbing, snapping her teeth together. The reverberations pounded through her body. She grabbed the hanging strap, deafened by the roar. The temperature dropped. Rapidly.

Frigid air penetrated multiple layers of clothing to her very core. The lashed-down center mass shifted ominously toward them. Then the plane leveled off, and the cargo resettled in place.

She visualized the shiny piano inside the large dusty crate. Madame Chiang Kai-shek, the generalissimo's glamorous wife, was celebrated in the States, even featured in *Life* magazine, but Jane scorned her avarice. Donovan had spoken of the white-glove treatment the couple required. Nonetheless, Chiang's Nationalist Kuomintang Army was tying up over one million Japanese soldiers—and America needed to keep the KMT on the right side.

Twisting her earplugs in deeper, Julia peeped out her little square window at elephants and rhinos wallowing around India's marshy Brahmaputra River. Then she settled into *Lost Horizon*, which she wanted to finish before starting one of Paul's gift books. This novel was about a mythical Tibetan valley, Shangri-La, where people lived in peace and harmony.

She glanced back at the jungly terrain—cut through by the snaking red-brown Burma Road, soon to reopen to Kunming-bound American convoys. Bypassing enemy-held territory, the crucial supply route had been reengineered to begin in Northeast India, a hellish project that had claimed many lives.

The next time she looked up, plumes of mist had overtaken her port view. They drew together in silvery clouds that turned gunmetal purple and swallowed them.

How could their pilots see anything?

After several sickening minutes, the clouds parted to a smudged landscape of lichen and twisted pines. The first dustings of snow. A line of migrating geese flew north past her window, oblivious to the rough skies. She admired their savoir faire.

Suddenly, the plane banked hard to the right…startling Betty and Thibaut awake. Julia gripped her seat, breathless and dizzy, her insides jelly. Outside, she caught the silver flash of another plane—too close.

"Masks on," the crew chief ordered.

Julia connected her tube to the oxygen supply and felt immediately intoxicated, euphoric. Clearheaded and ready for anything, she watched the otherworldly scenery.

The next time she looked, there was only white. Snowy white, sharp and glittering. Then a softer white as they bounced into a cloud, the engine rumble amplified by the fluffy nothingness.

So much for the pilot's "clear sailing." Or maybe this was the best you could expect on the notorious Hump route, but it was the price of admission to China's byzantine theater of war.

———

"Main thing you need to know is—it's complicated," as Donovan had begun her predeparture briefing. "In China, our navy is allied with Generalissimo Chiang Kai-shek's security chief, General Tai Li—a man who knows where all the bodies are buried and put many of them in the ground himself." He raised an eyebrow. "Couple years ago, Tai Li and Captain Milton Miles bonded under enemy fire in a rice paddy. They shook hands on the Sino-American Cooperative Organization—SACO."

"What's the US Navy doing on the ground in China?"

"Weather patterns move west to east—from the Gobi Desert in Central Asia to the Pacific. We wanted weather-reporting stations and intel on Japanese coastal activity, while Tai Li wanted arms and training." Donovan lifted a forefinger. "The OSS cannot operate in China without Chiang, Tai Li, and Miles, now a navy commander. I've an old family Bible for the generalissimo, a devout Christian. You are to deliver it to Tai Li—and watch your back."

Thus would she meet Generalissimo Chiang Kai-shek's dangerous spy-chief. "I will. Sir."

"Some might say the main event is Japan versus Free China. Others understand it to be the ongoing civil war between Chiang's Nationalists and Mao's Reds." He ran a hand over his thick white hair. "Then there are other factions, all vying for rice and supplies. American goods intended for the battlefield are being stockpiled or diverted to the black market."

"What about the Chinese people?"

"For them, we can only try to achieve peace." He released a long exhale. "Our job is to hold our ground until one hundred thousand American troops land later this year on the South China coast. This is the endgame, McWilliams—the launch of Operation Downfall, the invasion of Japan. Our agenda—*yours*—is to help plug the leaks in our supply pipeline to sustain China, and us all. I need you to keep me informed."

"Will we use the Maugham novel for our codework?"

"A word of advice, McWilliams: never be predictable. Knowing your predilection for mysteries, I've obtained an unpublished manuscript by cryptologist Herbert Yardley, *Crows Are Black Everywhere*—set in the capital, Chungking. Same code names, but you pick the key this time, again based on page-line-word coordinates."

"Eight, one, five. My birthday."

"Too predictable."

"Seven, one, nine. My mother's."

The pilot swerved sharply, launching her forward. Her lips clamped hard around the tube as she gulped down oxygen.

All at once, a glittering white mountain loomed out her window.

Engines straining to clear the peak, their plane angled upward.

A sudden downdraft sucked them lower. The more air she inhaled, the dizzier she felt. That clearheaded sensation was gone; so was the euphoria.

With mighty effort, the C-46 cleared the "rock pile"—barely. Amid nervous laughter, Booker circled thumb and forefinger. Two airmen took off their masks and had a smoke.

Julia thought of their volatile cargo—and the devastating Bombay explosion. "Hey, fellows," she hollered over the roar. "*No smoking.*" She received only cocky grins.

Before she could sic the crew chief on them, they were again plummeting through space, as if on a free-falling elevator. Icy peaks rushed by her window.

The next thing she saw was the red rising sun on the belly of a silver Zero. Diving toward them. The C-46 bucked as if kicked from the side…spiraling down and down.

Terrified, she relived the PT boat assault, the Zero's wings flashing red rising suns. She clutched Thibaut's arm.

Straightening course, pilot Lim accelerated into clouds that muffled the fighter's growl. Mesmerized, she watched massive white peaks lurch by…the misty valley narrowing around them, a glimmering granite point growing closer…until at the last second, they slipped past. She closed her eyes, and it was some time before she realized theirs was the only roar she heard.

The Zero was gone. Shaking, Julia attempted a normal breath.

Then they were above the clouds, filmy enough to reveal the expanse of craggy snowlands below. Men had frozen to death here. She touched her cushiony parachute, which, by a whim of fate, might become her shroud. She had been lucky in the Pacific…lucky in Bombay. In peaceful Ceylon. And Burma. How much more luck did she hold in her account?

With a stricken look, Betty reached past Thibaut and nudged her hand—the port engine was running weak and ragged. Either the all-night repair had not done the trick…or they'd been hit. Panic spread through the cabin, a palpable thing.

The C-46 dropped into another spiral. The lights flickered and died.

They sat in eerie silence, too dazed to react. Julia sucked on her oxygen, harder, as the flow diminished. At least the starboard engine seemed okay.

With a shudder, the plane leveled out.

Then fell again. The craggy mountains getting closer.

The port engine choked and sputtered, the bone-chilling fuselage vibrating against their backs.

After a shouted consultation, two flight officers leaped up, slashing through the piano crate's tethers. As they shouldered it free, the crew chief threw open the cargo hatch—on Julia's right! The Shangri-La novel was ripped off her lap, into the ethers. Papers whirled about. Icy fingers tugged at her, her safety clips, pulling her toward the void.

As she struggled against this terrible force, Thibaut hugged her close, his fingers digging into her side. All the while, her entire lower torso was muscling around the duffel bag with the Bible intended to cement their alliance with Chiang Kai-shek.

Frigid air howled through the cabin. Screams rang out. Curses. Murmured prayers. Jaws frantically worked their chewing gum. A man vomited in his cap. Violent chords pounded through her brain.

With a final push, Madame Chiang's piano was launched into swirling space.

Followed by one of the smaller crates.

SOS Booker craned his neck toward the window. "The *gold*?"

"Mark that spot," joked the fellow beside him.

The flight officers and two soldiers leaned into the door, fighting enormous outer pressure, ferocious gusts of wind.

As the men collapsed against the closed hatch, Julia released her deathlike grip on the duffel bag. Her feet were numb, calves and thighs racked by horrible cramping. But she joined everyone in ripping off their masks and cheering their crew, their valiant pilots. Their survival.

The C-46 soldiered on, skimming the frozen mountaintops. Close enough to touch, as Mack had once said.

Her hand clammy, Betty patted Julia's arm, as if to make sure she was really there. "*Is This Trip Necessary?*"

She forced a smile. Apparently so, if things were so bad that a baby grand might help win the war. Or a Bible—more necessary than ever, now that Madame Chiang's piano was gone.

"We're over the Hump," the crew chief announced. "But we've lost an engine."

The rush of voices, the clink of hardware. The smell of fear.

She watched the dirty-white hillsides coming closer. Her mother's face formed before her. She thought she might join her, but Caro shook her head. *No. Not your time.*

Brown foothills sloping into a muddy river. But which river? And where?

FORTY-FOUR

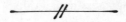

A terrible jolt shot from her ankles to her knees. Her neck whiplashed back and forth as the C-46 thudded down, knocking her head against Thibaut's.

There was an ear-splitting silence. Then people began to inventory their injuries.

"Out. *Now*," the crew chief ordered, releasing the cargo hatch with a blast of cold, moist wind. "Ladies—*go!*"

In a rush of movement, they unclipped their harnesses. Seizing her duffel, she jumped onto the river shore, followed by Betty and Thibaut with their gear. Men poured out after them and through the emergency exits over the wings, clutching bags, hats, or nothing at all. One wild-eyed guy brought only a large silver flask.

The tall Chinese pilot emerged from the crew door in front of the propellers, two of which were sunk in the mud.

"*Move it*," the chief called in angry fear.

With a glance at the damaged engine, they dashed downriver, then, gasping, surveyed the scene through the dimming light. The plane had bellied into the east bank, nose partially submerged. The area was remote and bleak, no sign of life, ringed by saw-toothed white peaks. Miraculously, they hadn't crashed into one, or even a slushy foothill. Or the river itself.

"Looks like we bypassed headhunter territory," Betty said.

"How do you know?" Julia looked at Thibaut. "Do you have any idea where we are?"

He shook his head. "There are three great rivers up here. The Salween, Mekong, and Yangtze. The first two might place us in Burma, possibly occupied territory. But if this—"

Whoosh.

With a burst of red-blue light, the left engine exploded in a roar that resounded through the mountains. Ravenous flames gorged on the plane's ammo, fuel, and oxygen.

Julia took a quick head count and reached nineteen. There had been twenty of them. "Who was the last one out?"

"I don't know," Betty said. "The last words I heard were *Move it*."

"The crew chief. He made sure we all escaped first." She stared at the fire. In one of the small silent groups, the copilot was crossing himself. In horror, they watched the flames burn out. Taking with them one human life—and the rest of the day's light.

Weapons drawn, Lieutenant Lim and his copilot made forays to look for help. By the time they returned from their fourth trip, empty-handed, it was pitch-dark.

And freezing. Gathering some embers, a few men made a small fire at the tail section, skeletal but a good windbreak. Everyone moved in. Nearby, SOS Booker and another fellow rummaged through the debris.

As the supply chief scooped up a handful of ashes next to a charred piece of bamboo, Thibaut said, "The currency."

"We dumped the *gold*." Booker shook his head in disbelief.

"I hope some poor peasant wasn't beneath it," Julia said fervently.

"But what a way to go!" Booker's eyes gleamed in the firelight.

Betty patted her bag. "At least I saved my opium."

"Your *opium*?"

"I was advised some sources prefer payment in nice thick slices of the stuff. Which I'll need to store in your Registry safe."

If she had one. Julia could see China was going to demand maximum flexibility.

There was little the explosion hadn't consumed. People huddled together, awaiting the dawn under jackets, odd bits of clothing, empty gear bags. Thibaut had thought to bring his silk parachute. Nestled under it, she remembered Deepak, his shawl covering them both the night before he gave his life to save so many others.

Beneath a sky pulsing with light, she thought of the other items in her bag—the Kunming map Paul had drafted for her new post. As if that weren't dear enough, he'd included two books for her to read. *Dream of the Red Chamber* would be an introduction to Chinese culture, with its themes of fate and love. *The Letters of Vincent van Gogh*, whom they both admired, would show her the struggles every artist goes through to find his or her voice.

Julia was supremely flattered Paul saw her as a creative being, so she didn't mind that he wanted to take a hand in her education. Although she had the Ivy League background, he had the brains and worldly knowledge. If this gifted, self-taught, self-made man wanted to make her his personal project, she was all for it. Maybe she wasn't his type. But fate had brought them together—with luck, for the purpose of love. Fate and love. She decided to read *Dream of the Red Chamber* first.

She must have fallen into her own dream, because in the middle of kissing Paul under the mistletoe, her eyes flew open to a pinkish river to the east. A gleaming-blue bird with an orange belly landed on a bare branch. He surveyed the scene, then abruptly dipped his long beak in the water, reemerging with a shiny silver fish. She gasped. A kingfisher.

The bird made her think of Dillon. Mack. Si Paw. Deepak. People whose lives had intersected with hers, whom she would never forget. Now she had crashed into a new crossroads of war.

Jolted by a sharp *skreek*, she looked north. Three men on horseback were crossing another waterway at the head of a string of small horses, each bearing a pair of baskets.

After speaking with them, pilot Lim explained, "We have landed on the ancient Tea Horse Road to Tibet—*cha-ma-dao*. *Cha* is our word for tea—like *chai* in India. These men are traders and will take us to a nearby unit of the Sino-American Cooperative Organization. Perhaps they have extra rice to share. The women will ride, and the rest of us walk, but the ponies can carry our gear."

"I will radio Kunming-HQ from SACO," Thibaut said.

Julia didn't want special treatment. "We'll take turns riding and walking."

"You must not challenge these men. They must not lose face. So you *will* ride," First Lieutenant Lim ordered. "They speak a strange dialect, but as I understand it, we bring luck to their caravan. By great fortune, we missed the Tiger Leaping Gorge and instead touched down at the first bend of the Yangtze River as it goes north."

The two rivers she'd seen were but curves of the famous Yangtze. "Which means…"

Lim bowed his head. "Welcome to China."

FORTY-FIVE

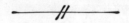

Western Yunnan Province, China

Shivering in the icy dawn, the C-46 passengers and crew—minus the heroic crew chief—squeezed onto the rough benches of two right-hand-drive Dodge trucks, their tires bald and patched. As they rolled out of the base, Lieutenant Lim rode in the cab between two SACO men, the Chinese driver and an American. Both wore plain khaki with round hand-sewn sleeve patches—the crossed US and Nationalist flags overlaid by a white pennant bearing the symbols ???!!!***. *SACO* was embroidered on top of each patch and *US Navy* on the bottom.

"What the heck?" Julia asked Thibaut as they sloshed down the road.

"You mean, *What the hell?!*" He grinned. "Everyone's response to finding the navy entrenched inside China."

"You said you're with a Sino-American unit, on the coast." Julia was beginning to grasp just how enmeshed the OSS was with SACO and the navy—and thus, Miles, Tai Li, and Chiang Kai-shek.

"It's complicated."

Donovan's words exactly. "So I hear."

He shrugged. "At least I got through to Kunming-HQ. Seems they spent an exorbitant amount of aviation fuel hours conducting the search, led by CO Heppner."

She caught Betty's blush.

"Assisted by translator Rosamond Frame. Using maps by Paul Child."

Julia's throat squeezed her vocal cords, so her words escaped in a shrill warble. "You'd think they'd have better things to do with their time."

Further downhill, they lunched on noodles and meaty fried mushrooms at Dali Lake, then continued their descent past tidy fields dotted with white tombstones. The rocky, uncultivated land was covered with stands of bamboo and eucalyptus. The calm silence felt eerie, given the proximity of the front lines, soldiers dying only a few hours north.

By late afternoon, terraced hillsides appeared, smoke curling from thatched cottages. Then, in the middle of a broad, dusty plateau—a sprawling dun-colored town.

"Kunming." Thibaut's left eye crinkled shut in his lopsided smile.

They turned south to the US Fourteenth Air Force base. "Chengkung Airfield, where we usually land," he said as the men hopped off to report.

SOS Booker rubbed his five-o'clock shadow. "You can drop me at Services of Supply," he told the SACO driver.

At the end of the field, the depot was a huddle of metal airplane hangars. Some were open, revealing everything from jeeps to fuel drums to bamboo crates like those jettisoned over the Himalaya. All those supplies, she thought. Easy pickings.

China is no place for the Timid, read a sign over the door. Mindful of Thibaut's radio transceivers that had disappeared from Services of Supply/Calcutta, Julia followed Booker inside the Quonset hut. Clerks in shorts and boots were logging, stamping, and notating paperwork.

"Didn't I promise to bring you luck?" SOS Booker winked.

"You were right," she said. "That was some rock pile."

"One of these days, we must toast the Hellacious Hump over a beer—say, the Servicemen's Club, up the road from the OSS?"

"One of these days." She enjoyed the hearty sergeant, a Midwest go-getter like Pop, recognizing her own let's-get-on-with-it attitude.

The truck headed north past mud-brick huts, grazing goats, vegetable gardens, and fields of young green rice. The brisk cold wind carried a nasty odor their way.

"Human 'night soil'—traditional fertilizer," Thibaut explained as they bounced through tracks created by the wooden wheels of donkey-drawn wagons.

Two handsome long-haired men strutted past in black robes, turquoise and coral beads. They resembled Native Americans, and there, on this vast brown plain, she could easily imagine herself in the Wild West.

Instead, she was in the Far East, setting up another OSS Registry while preparing to wade into a black market morass that was hindering the final days of World War II.

———

Kunming, Capital of Yunnan Province

Through the dimming light, a dramatic three-tiered pagoda roof with winged corners appeared. "The city gate," Thibaut said.

Entering the towering archway, the SACO driver nudged his truck down the cobblestoned street—a free-for-all of men in traditional gowns and Western suits; women with babies strapped to their backs; ragged soldiers; laborers bearing yo-yo poles across bent shoulders; stringy drivers pulling rickshaws, animal-drawn carts, bicycles, and motorcycles. As the shops closed, curbside merchants remained crouched behind bins of eggs and greens, peanuts, dried mushrooms. A sidewalk barber was still at work, and a dentist bent over his patient's open mouth. The odors were potent, and Julia was reminded of her first day in Bombay. Overwhelmed again, she felt giddy and almost laughed out loud. Another new land.

How dull and unworldly she'd been before this war. Again, she imagined trying to describe the scene in a letter. Nothing that would put her father off, like a sidewalk dentist, but what about some charming, picturesque sight?

When they turned up a canal, the smell of sewage intensified. Narrow sampans rode low, laden with burlap sacks and chickens that flapped their wings as it began to rain. The rain became a drizzle and gradually gave way to a luminous sunset glimmering over a large body of water, golden, pink, and weeping willow green. Pop would surely like that. Perhaps Paul might take a picture to send home.

"Green Lake," Thibaut told them as they passed between the lake-shore and faded-yellow stucco walls topped with cypress and bamboo. "The French Quarter during our days of empire."

"It's lovely." Betty smiled. "But we know what Jane would say. 'Down with colonialism.'"

He opened his palms. "That era's over, so I can only say, 'Up with France.'"

"Hear! Hear!" Julia tapped the bench, trying not to be in a tizzy about seeing Paul.

Leaving the lakeside road, they entered a lane bound by the same high yellow walls. Thibaut craned his neck, as if Rosie might step forward any moment to greet them.

Before the truck ground to a full stop, he leaped out with a brief salute at the two American soldiers manning a large red gate. She and Betty followed him through a small garden and inner gate. The court-yard was bordered by three stone buildings with scalloped, gray-tiled roofs and carved wooden eaves.

"Detachment 202." Thibaut squinted into the columned loggia on their left. It was dark and empty, which sent his face into free fall. He gestured to the right. "Naval Group China and SACO. And in the rear, behind that large ginkgo, British Special Ops—SOE."

Julia thought back to the Force 136 ambush in Burma, which had led to them uncovering the British leak. How was their security this time?

Exiting SOE with a very large man, Heppner strode down the peel-ing red steps. "About time," he said gruffly, his eyes on Betty. "Everyone's gone home now—including Rosie, who's waiting to receive you ladies. Driver Tung will escort you there." He turned to the crestfallen Thibaut. "I promise you'll see her bright and early tomorrow. In the meantime, I'll take you to bachelor-officer quarters. And buy you a drink."

They returned through the red gate, where Driver Tung, a lanky middle-aged man in a fresh white shirt, showed Julia and Betty to his jeep. Following the lakeshore north, they watched colonial buildings give way to simple wooden shops and dwellings where amber lights were flickering on. Piles of refuse dotted the dirt roads. But as they entered a posh hillside district of white stucco compounds, the flower-lined roadway became clean and paved.

From inside a modern, wisteria-draped villa, Rosie ran out to meet them, radiant with joy. "Thank God. We were terrified!" She flung her arms around Julia. "Thank you for reuniting Thibaut and me. You're a miracle worker." Her eyes glistened with tears.

So did Julia's. "I missed you, Rosie."

Then Betty stepped into the hug. "Miracles happen. The three of us girls, back together."

As Rosie looked around with a big question mark on her face, Julia had to deliver the bad news. Dick had taken Thibaut to the bachelors' quarters—kicking and screaming.

"Let's see that engagement ring," Betty said. They oohed and aahed as the stone caught the first starlight.

"The lives we've lived." Julia inhaled the brisk air. Her lungs opened and closed with ease. For a moment, the world felt normal. "Peaceful here. Feels like I'm back in Pasadena."

"I know. Very *Meikuo*. American." Rosie lifted a shoulder. "But we're lucky to have shelter. Welcome to your new home, *Mei Yuan*—Beautiful Garden." Then she showed them into the front room, furnished with carved woods and full-length parachute-silk curtains.

"Looks like you have indoor plumbing," Betty cracked. "After a night in the open, we need a bath."

"I hadn't noticed." With a smile, Rosie led them upstairs, where their room was next to hers. While Betty bathed, Julia followed strains of Billie Holiday singing "I'll Be Seeing You." At the end of the hall, on the floor, sat a portable 78 record player. She slid down the wall beside it and watched the spinning maroon label. Tomorrow, she'd see Paul.

During a dinner of rice, vegetables, and bits of gristly pork, Rosie introduced them to their new roommates, a few of whom worked at the

OSS, while others served in various civilian and military offices around town. Then they recounted their adventure—unclassified. Some of the girls shared tales of their own near misses. Most hoped not to return over the Hump but to sail home in peaceful, postwar waters.

Later, Julia asked Rosie if she'd had any news on her parents.

"This poor country," was all she said.

FORTY-SIX

Thibaut was pacing outside the gate when they arrived at Detachment 202 the next morning. While Rosie rushed to his arms, Julia hurried up the faded-red loggia to the Map Room, carrying the tube with Paul's Kunming map. She had visions of his relief at seeing her, his elated bear hug. After a distracted nod, he returned to his sketch. It was Jack who gave her the hug.

"Boy, is it swell to see you, Julia," Jack said. "You seem to attract adventure."

Deflated, she attempted a breezy "All's well that ends well." Feeling like a punctured balloon ground underfoot, she recalled how she had studied the map, prepared to impress him. Turning away, she took in the tidy space, with its typewriters, pens, pencils, and brushes, its white-washed walls covered with photos, maps, charts, sketches, borders indicated by yarn and pushpins. As if nothing were amiss, she said to Jack, "I hope my Registry is half as nice as this."

"It may need something of your magic touch," he replied in a tone that prepared her for the worst. "We in the first wave got lucky." The men's Kandy shorts had been replaced by trousers—his crinkled, Paul's clean and starched.

A short-haired young Chinese woman in a pink shirtwaist stood. "I am Sally Lu's cousin, Lu Mei," she said carefully. "Thank you for hiring me, Miss McWilliams."

"You can call me Julia," she said, feeling their mutual connection. "But it's General Donovan you must thank. He's very impressed by the way Sally has taken over my old job." She remembered Sally speaking about her relatives here, with barely any rice to eat after the landlord or the Japanese had finished with them. She couldn't imagine Lu Mei's struggles.

"Thank you for helping her rise in your government. Our family is very proud." She caught her breath, as if exhausted by her speech, but added, "Please call me Mei."

"Doesn't *Mei* mean beautiful?" She thought of their quarters, *Mei Yuan*, Beautiful Garden.

With a flush, Mei indicated the other clerk. "May I present Miss Kung Ai-ling—esteemed niece of Generalissimo Chiang Kai-shek."

Slender and fine-boned, yet shapely, Ai-ling had a regal aura. She extended her hand, pointedly looking up at Julia. "I'm honored to meet someone of your standing."

"Nice to meet you, too." She shook her cold, limp hand, unsettled by the thought of Paul working with such a beauty. She could smell the creamy magnolia tucked into her bun.

"These girls help explain the lay of the land," Jack said. "We found the existing maps woefully inaccurate, while *we* were woefully ignorant of Chinese history and geography."

Paul finally lowered his pencil. "The borders and front lines are extremely fluid." He briefed her on the Japanese Ichi-Go offensive. Following its lightning sweep through Southeast China, it had pushed inland, gobbling up Nationalist, Red, and warlord-controlled territory. "They are advancing as swiftly as they can march." His face drawing in upon itself, he gazed out the window at the filmy blue sky. "There's also the matter of weather. Snow and slush, freezing rain, floods, mud as sticky as glue. Meanwhile, the poor, underequipped Chinese soldiers slog it out, defending their little scraps of land." He cleared his throat. "What small part can our maps do to help them?"

She could read Paul Child by now. How like him to launch into a brainy analysis in the face of troubling emotions. But she heard the anguish beneath his rational, self-possessed exterior. She saw how consumed he was by their tenuous circumstances, even distressed. Things must indeed be dire. Compared to all that, Julia's near death in a plane crash was low priority. Yet even though it was only *her* story, it mattered to her, and she would have thought to Paul. Concealing her hurt, she said, "I see you have your work cut out for you."

He frowned. "When your C-46 went missing, Ai-ling found an old atlas to assist us in mapping the far reaches of Yunnan Province. She and Lu Mei were a great help through a truly grim night." Paul looked at her with real concern—but how could she trust it? Then he returned to his sketch of the South China coast. Where Thibaut would soon slip back behind enemy lines.

Julia eyed Ai-ling, her swanlike neck rising from small shoulders draped in red silk. As a girl, she was always struggling to be a pretty person, ideally petite and delicate—like Ai-ling—the kind of woman who drew men without a thought. Now she wanted to take her gawky self elsewhere. And did.

Like the Map Room, her office was whitewashed with dark beams, clean but stark, a few shelves with tidy rows of folders. Rosie was sorting mail on the scratched black lacquer floor, as Julia had done during her early days in Kandy. At least this Registry had a locked cabinet, where Betty intended to safeguard her opium.

Whatever had been between Paul and her now felt as fleeting as the clouds blowing in from the mountains. Maybe all she had left was his Kunming map, so painstaking and precise. And a supposed friendship that she didn't really understand. She unrolled it.

"How lovely," Rosie said. "Did Paul Child do that? Or Jack?"

"Yes," she replied shortly, reaching for a small box of tacks.

"Nice guys." Rosie was bright and breezy, buoyed by her reunion with Thibaut.

"Their secretaries seem very competent." Julia shoved in the last tack. "With a lot of local info. One of them, Ai-ling, is Chiang Kai-shek's niece." She turned. "Have you seen Paul and them together at the mess, or…?"

Rosie gave her a curious glance. "It's not like Delhi, with all its hier-archies. Everyone sits together here."

She heard her, softening the truth: Paul was lunching with Ai-ling.

Still seething at his dismissive response, Julia looked at his meticulous work, which she now saw as finicky and show-offy. She ripped the map from the wall, tacks clattering to the floor, and held it a moment, corners slashed, tainted. Then tore it into small pieces and tossed them to the wind.

"Julia!" Rosie leaped up in alarm.

What had she done? As she stared at her friend with helpless embarrassment, CO Dick Heppner walked in. His eyes were dark and sunken, his Kandy tan replaced by an ashen look, reminiscent of his appearance on returning home from London in its darkest hours. He gazed between them…at the scraps of paper strewn everywhere.

Then two blue-clad workers carried in a table, on which the third set a beat-up typewriter. "You arrived at a helluva time," Dick said sternly. "The war is a few mountain passes away—and getting closer."

"I've heard." She attempted to collect herself. "Paul just delivered a lecture on the situation."

He tucked in his chin, regarding her—severely, she felt. As if he had no time for childishness. "You need to assemble a go bag of docs—lists of agents, covert and sabotage ops, etcetera. In the event of retreat."

Julia looked around the naked Registry, barely habitable, barely anything to retreat with. She was angry at herself for giving such power to Paul, allowing him to spin her off her axis. And shocked at Dick's defeatist tone. "First, we have to inventory what we have—and don't."

"And won't," Dick snapped. "We need to prepare for the worst. Save your optimism."

She thought of Thibaut's alarming pessimism. "But what about the American landing later this year?"

"That will take place—whether or not Kunming is in enemy hands." As her eyes widened, he added, "The good news is, we're in the beginning of the end." Without comment, he left.

Shaken, she stood there, staring blankly at the tidy shelves. "You've made headway."

Rosie took her hand and led her to a chair, then pulled up the other one. She seemed to be searching for words, but Julia saw the deep feeling on her face. "Remember on the *Mariposa*, how we kidded about being eager to get to the front? Well, here we are. Now how do we survive— not only the two of us—*all* of us? I don't know Paul yet, but whatever's going on between you must be strong."

"There's nothing going on between us. We conducted a big project together. We're friends, that's all."

"Friendship is good." Rosie nodded. "You befriended me on the ship. You were my first friend in the war. When your plane went missing, I almost fell apart. You and Thibaut! I had to put my mind on something else—which was *this*. I kept at it until he radioed the next morning."

"He's found himself a great woman. Something good had to come out of it all—right?" She picked herself up. "Now, show me what you've done around here."

Work was her refuge, and she plunged into it.

———

Shortly before noon, she and Rosie dropped in at Morale Operations. Betty sat at a scarred rosewood table with a bespectacled Chinese artist, Yung Kai. "Dick hired him last month—to do his worst." She proudly showed them his leaflet with graphic images on how to disable Japanese vehicles by urinating in the gas tank.

"Clever work," Julia said. "Let's go to lunch, you two."

At the mess, they joined Paul and Jack, seated in the middle of the former villa's dining room. As they sat, Rosie nudged her, indicating Ai-ling and Lu Mei at a table near the buffet. Given America's tenuous position in China, she realized her worries about Paul and Ai-ling were irrelevant. She had to accept that the affection he'd expressed in Kandy stemmed from champagne and holiday spirit. Paul might view her as he did Jane: a close friend he could kiss under the mistletoe—however "meaningful" the kiss—then go on his way in search of his second true love.

With a brave face, she heaped her plate with a sort of sloppy joe stir-fry.

"The worst of all worlds," Rosie said.

Paul grimaced. "In the name of 'safety,' we are banned from eating off base."

"The Kandy brass tried to restrict us—and we know how long that lasted. I bet you can enlist Dick to bend a few rules," Julia suggested to Betty, who blinked coyly.

"That's my girl." Paul regarded her across the table. "Dinner tonight?"

My girl. For an instant her heart sang. But really, *Hey, girl* was how her family called their dog. Or *Good girl.* She honestly didn't know where she stood. These were tense times, and she'd seen Paul's obsession with his work. Maybe he did have feelings for her. Or maybe she was a faithful companion, like an old dog.

———

"The Hump route," Dick toasted them with *baijiu* at Ho-Teh-Foo, a family-run restaurant recommended by Paul's secretaries. Clinking ceramic cups, they drank to survival.

Heat flooded her chest from the dizzying, clear sorghum liquor. All dolled up in her mother's pearls and a slinky bias-cut dress, Julia grinned wildly. "Anyone for going home over the Burma Road?"

"*Ganbei* to that. Means *dry cup.*" Paul tipped his drink against hers; then they tossed them back.

"To friendship." She smiled around the table, avoiding any more intimate looks with Paul.

Thibaut picked up the earthen jug and refilled their cups. As a plate of crunchy spring rolls was served, he proposed another toast. "*Bon appétit.*"

"*Màn man chī*—eat slowly," Rosie said. "Meaning *enjoy your meal.*" With chopsticks, she picked up a radish carved into a little rose. "Red. *Hongse.* First tone, high and level."

Thibaut and Julia, her dutiful *Mariposa* students, repeated, "*Hongse.*"

Rosie regarded the others. "Your turn." After they pronounced it to her satisfaction, she said, "In Chinese culture, red represents luck and happiness. And the Communist Party. Smart of them—maybe that's why they're winning."

Astounded by that bombshell, Julia blurted, "I thought the Japanese are?" Which led to a harsh look from Dick.

But Rosie was intent on the latest platter, pointing out each item. "Fried caterpillars, centipedes, and maggots."

Without batting an eyelash, Paul dove in with skillfully wielded chopsticks. Lacking his life experience, Julia spooned up one of the mysterious tidbits. It was crunchy, and she didn't really care to know what she'd eaten, while he was in his element, tasting his way through a new land.

Dick poured another round before the next dish—a plate of pillowy stuffed dumplings.

"To adventures in Chinese cuisine." She looked at Betty and Thibaut. "I'm still salivating about those thick Dali noodles. And the mushrooms. As good as meat."

"You see?" Rosie insisted. "We don't need to fly in steak and potatoes for the boys."

"Our SACO guys have developed a fondness for peanut butter, though," Thibaut teased.

"We've always grown peanuts in China," Rosie retorted, love flying between their eyes.

"Speaking of supplies," Betty said. "Yung and I are planning a yen-counterfeiting op. Units like Thibaut's can circulate them in enemy territory to destabilize Japanese currency. I've ordered a printing press from India."

"*Ha!* That'll be the first thing jettisoned in the next Hump drama." Julia turned to Thibaut, lowering her voice. "We need to have SOS Booker check his logs for your missing shipment. Just in case."

"You know I'm leaving soon." Forehead furrowed, he reached for Rosie's hand. Stroking her arm. "If I can't make it down there, please follow up."

"Will do." She felt the magnetic pull between the two, their pain at another separation. Pushing away her twinge of envy, Julia saw Paul add hot sauce to his dumplings and place one on her plate. The flavors burst across her tongue.

He smiled fondly at her reaction. She smiled back with reserve. It was a roller coaster with him, dangerous for its ups and downs. She needed to concentrate on her duty.

One thing she would certainly do, though, was learn to use chopsticks as well as Paul Child.

FORTY-SEVEN

———— // ————

Welcome, Julie, she read from the Registry doorway.

The note, written in Paul's elegant script, was pinned between two maps—a *new* one of Kunming and another of Greater China. She moved closer: *In case your map disappeared in the crash, I dashed off a new one. Along with the big picture. You'll need it! Yours.*

She cleared her throat. Paul Child never dashed off anything in his life. On the other hand, he hadn't even noticed the map tube in her hand during yesterday's visit.

"Looks like your guy beat us in today."

Julia reddened, avoiding Rosie's look. "I told you, not my guy."

"He sure put in a lot of care into this."

"Naturally. To help our work. Prepare us." With a rich palette, Paul had illustrated the enormous strategic importance of Kunming, located near China's southwest border—and the Burma Road. As seen on the country map, Japan controlled the north and entire east coast, so he'd made the China Sea a luminous blue, as if beckoning the Americans… *Hurry*. Other regions were delineated by color-coded yarn, according to which power was in control—at the moment. His skill had imparted a three-dimensional quality to their new world. While maps were viewed as pragmatic tools, Paul Child seemed compelled to add beauty to his work. To create art. Deep inside, she knew that by destroying his earlier map, she'd shown a wrongful disrespect.

Rosie walked over to the wall, pointing north toward the Russian border. "This is where I grew up—my parents' mission."

Julia watched her shoulders rise and fall, not wishing to intrude on her silence. Rosie's fingers moved east, tracing the coast south to Thibaut's undercover camp, which was suffering a shortage of the most basic tools. The battery shortage meant their surveillance intel might be outdated by the time their reports got through. Their primitive radios meant they were vulnerable to location tracking.

Thrusting a dispatch at her, a beak-nosed carrottop from Messages rushed in. "From SACO Unit 10/Kweiyang." He turned on his heels and strode out with the same urgency.

According to the Greater China map, Kweiyang was three hundred kilometers north of Kunming—their sole land link with the genera-lissimo's capital, Chungking, located almost four hundred kilometers farther northwest. Julia logged the decrypt, which informed them of Operation Ichi-Go's rapid advance on this critical crossroads town. She hurried down the gallery to Dick's office. "One mountain pass closer."

"Meantime, Chiang Kai-shek is refusing to cooperate on a coun-teroffensive with the Reds—or even Governor Long Yun, a reformed warlord who commands a large loyal force here."

It seemed that Paul's "warlord-controlled territory" might include Yunnan itself. "Donovan wants me to deliver his Bible to Chiang—via Tai Li. Where can I find him?"

Dick raised an eyebrow. "Next door. And good luck."

Back at the Registry, Julia opened the safe and reached for the Bible. Thinking of her first message to Donovan, she tapped their codebook, *Crows Are Black Everywhere*, a mystery about encryption and spies. There were also stacks of various currencies and, in the corner, a little black packet marked *Property of Morale Operations*—the opium. "I see Betty's been here."

"She just left," Rosie said. "Where are you off to now?"

"Special delivery."

Julia followed the high yellow wall to the next compound, where one of Tai Li's armed guards stepped from the gatehouse and escorted her through a garden, a second wall, and gate. Another guard dashed ahead to announce her arrival. Then a tall bony man ushered her to the reception room and a dark velvet armchair facing a crimson door.

Framed by two calligraphy scrolls, the door opened for an imposing figure in a plain blue uniform and black riding boots—Chiang Kai-shek's security chief. She stood, holding Donovan's gift Bible.

Ramrod straight with dark hair and broad features, he fixed her with penetrating, wide-set eyes. "You are one of the new Americans from Kandy," translated his robust aide. "I am General Tai Li. Welcome."

"Julia McWilliams, on behalf of General Donovan."

The translator placed a hand on his chest and bowed. "Colonel Gong Peng."

She presented the gift to Tai Li. "As a sign of deep esteem, the general wishes to give his cherished family Bible to the generalissimo. He'd be grateful if you would offer it personally."

Tai Li smiled a flash of gold. "It is my honor," he said through the translator. "I will present it to him on General Donovan's behalf tomorrow in Chungking. Upon my return, I hope you will honor me again with your presence so I can prepare some of my special aged Pu'er tea."

———

Camera bag over his shoulder, Paul was pacing the loggia when she returned to HQ. "Where were you?" he demanded.

None of your business. She didn't like his sharp tone and brushed off his query. "Oh, and thanks for the new maps. Sorry about the other one." Ashamed of destroying it, she didn't correct his assumption that it had been destroyed in the crash.

"I wanted to help you get oriented to a complex theater of war. So you can function."

"Your maps are always useful," she replied coolly. "If you must know, Donovan asked me to deliver his Bible to Tai Li as a gift for Chiang Kai-shek." Starting back to the office, she turned. "Did you want something?"

Paul took her arm and—without asking—headed for the carved entry gate.

Julia wanted to shake off his hand...but didn't. "Where are we going?"

"To make the unknown a little more known." He led her across the flagstoned lane, where a row of budding trees led them to Green Lake. Reflections of clouds mixed with carpets of lotus pads. A few brave blossoms swayed in the breeze.

"Have you begun *Dream of the Red Chamber*?"

As brusque as ever. "Not yet. Fortunately, your books survived the Hump." She met his eyes, not neglecting the unseeing one, as she felt he saw with them both, in different ways.

"Not light reading, I understand. However, I thought you'd appreciate them."

She softened, understanding his compliment. "Once we get settled, I'll have more time."

Paul paused before a deep-pink lotus bud atop a long green stalk. "China is a difficult world to penetrate. Challenging. But I suggest we give it a go."

We. It was good to share a history with someone. "Beginning with the food."

"Top of the list! We have a great deal on our plate." He winked his blind eye.

She had to smile.

He returned his gaze to the flower. "Next is art. And culture. What do the people value? In France, it's an allée of chestnut trees, an ancient church, refinement of dress and manner. Here it might be a well-designed rock garden. A calligraphy scroll mounted on fine silk. A graceful woman with an elongated neck and sloping shoulders. Ai-ling, for example."

His petite secretary. Towering above Paul, on an ultra-long stem, Julia felt another jab of hurt. She stepped back, her sense of their closeness gone. "Maybe she'd be more feminine with bound feet."

He gave her a reproving look. "They're a new generation, modern career girls."

"How's Lu Mei doing?"

"She's very diligent. They both are."

Diligent *and* a delicate flower. "I need to write Sally Lu to commend her cousin," she said evenly. "Do you think Chiang Kai-shek placed his niece in our midst?"

Paul stopped, turning his back to the path. "That's why I wanted to talk to you. Be careful of Tai Li. He's connected to a Shanghai triad boss who works all sides."

Julia cocked her head. "Sounds like a good man to cultivate."

"I don't like Donovan using you for access to such a devious person."

"He's used me for access before."

He regarded her severely, his face etched with concern. "This is vastly different than nosing around SEAC—where they may stab you in the back, but no one's going to kill you! Tai Li has spy networks throughout Asia. Nothing slips his view. So he knows people are dealing in the black market, taking payoffs—and smuggling, even pilots. He's also a womanizer."

"There was no chemistry between us," she replied slyly.

Paul swatted the air. "Don't joke. This is life and death for them. After Japan invaded, Chiang and Mao declared a truce—which everyone knows is temporary."

"Donovan told me the generalissimo is stockpiling arms."

"Cached in local caves. The Central Bank of China has vaults up there."

The boss had not mentioned *that*. "I see it can be hard to know who's on whose team."

"Speaking of which, Sunday is the season's opening softball game, led by the 'Pitching General,' Claire Chennault. I'll take you."

That sounded like a *date*. She felt inordinately delighted, until he reached for his Leica. He focused on the long-necked lotus flower, shimmering in the gentle late daylight.

As they strolled on, Julia wondered what he saw, how he saw it. Everyone there seemed faded and worn, like their clothing. Masking their fear so they could go on. How could they not be afraid when people were starving, fighting, and dying across China?

Seemingly detached from it all, Paul continued photographing flowers, the lake, the young soldiers, the haggard mothers and plump, red-cheeked babies wearing no pants. The women in elaborate headdresses squatting behind baskets of tea and roots. She'd always admired his discerning eye. But where was his heart?

"Don't you *feel* it?" She burst out. "Everyone wondering when the war will hit Kunming. A bomb could fall on us right now, and we'd be scrambling along with them. Yet we're not hungry and weak. Worried about our children starving."

"Life is not fair," Paul replied, holding up his light meter with that aloof expression.

Where did this detachment come from? She thought of his passion for the arts, his dedication to helping soldiers, all of them, with his maps. For all his aloofness, Paul Child was a sensitive man. Aloof—and scarred. Had he ever felt safe? Raised by a flighty mother who'd used her boys to "sing for their supper," playing second fiddle to his twin brother, whom he'd not blamed for half blinding him. Nor for gliding through Harvard, while Paul attended the School of Life, as the Colombo policeman had put it. Struggling to relearn how to *see*. None of that had been "fair." Yet he'd persevered in becoming an artist. Julia understood, but couldn't he turn some of that sensitivity on her? Had he ever tried to understand her the way she did him?

At the far side of the lake, Paul hailed a pony cart.

"*Xie-xie*," she thanked the driver, climbing aboard.

The passenger space was small and cozy, two patched cushions on the bench. Julia held herself apart, wanting something more from him, something she wasn't getting.

It was what he didn't say, how he didn't sit, didn't put his arm around her. How he had the driver stop so he could take another picture, as if the city were simply local color for his art. How he was so proud of his secretaries, molding them into twentieth-century career girls.

"Your Mandarin is coming along nicely."

Now, after openly admiring another woman—for everything *she* wasn't—he was patronizing her. "Too bad more of us don't make the attempt. Don't you feel selfish living high on the hog? All the rice you need, while these people have nothing."

"It's not so simple. We have a job. We're helping them."

Oh, she was simple, was she? Julia gripped the seat. "You don't even consider the basic truth of what I said. Has anyone ever told you you're an arrogant know-it-all?"

"Many times," Paul said simply. "I've never been the lovable sort—like you."

Surprised, she glanced away. "I always thought your life made you broad-minded—and aware. I thought we were kindred spirits," she said, her voice rising in emotion.

"We are. We know each other."

Taking a long breath, she saw him seeing her—not a delicate flower yet lovable. She forgot her pride and took his hand, moved by his sweet smile. "Donovan wants me to look into the black market. I could use your help. I'm sure he'll approve."

"I accept with alacrity." His face brightened. "Let me show you something." He spoke a few words to the driver in the local dialect. So he had taken the trouble to learn.

As the tonga swayed around the corners, Julia allowed the space between them to relax, their hands still joined. Curving rooflines and projecting upper stories reached for each other over narrowing lanes that enfolded them.

A marketplace appeared, a blur of pungent wares. "Kunming is known as the City of Eternal Spring," he said as the air turned swoony with fragrance. "The Flower Circle. Often, when I haven't slept, I come here to remind myself that beauty still exists despite it all."

From glum to professorial to arrogant to soulful and poetic, Paul had as many facets as a diamond. He tapped the driver's seatback, told him to stop.

Instead of lifting his camera again, as she'd expected, he turned to her, gripping her forearms. "When your plane disappeared over the Hump, I felt a blackness I hadn't known since…" His good eye bore into her. "I couldn't bear to lose you."

Her heart melted. Paul had suffered too much. "Your maps would have found us."

Maps. Then, her skin still tingling, Julia turned away. From her first day in Kandy, she had admired his mapwork. His artistry and precision, his dedication to fighting the war his way. Turning the unknown into the known. She had respected him even before she'd "liked" him. Yet she still hadn't confessed her folly in destroying his map. After the scene at her party with Mack, she'd vowed to be honest with any man she might become close with in the future. She looked at Paul. They were close—physically in this moment, and in some other deep way. She wanted to set him straight...but not now, as the light dimmed, and a hint of rose gold appeared over the western mountains—and his arm curled around her shoulders.

Paul pointed out the tall white pagoda of an ancient kingdom, the French railway station that had linked Kun Ming with Ha Noi. The crowded old Muslim district, where a haunting vocal cry made her shiver. "Their call to prayer," he explained.

They fell into easy silence, his strong body pressing against hers, as if they were other sides of the same seam, even though made from different fabric.

At the end of the street, hundreds of birds were landing on the golden lake waters in a radiance of motion and color. "Look. A pair of mandarin ducks—*yuanyang*, they're called. The male with that glorious plumage and the female, such a velvety gray lavender. In Chinese culture mandarin ducks are a symbol of fidelity—they mate for life," Paul said wistfully. He removed his arm from her shoulders.

Julia felt the same wistfulness, wishing to be one of those two ducks. Being part of a pair. Connected to him, made larger by his soaring mind. But it was their friendship he valued. Maybe one lifetime mate was it for him.

While she was hoping he'd ask her to dinner, they arrived at Detachment 202. As the girls piled into Driver Tung's jeep for the ride home, Betty called, "Hop in. Rosie's with Thibaut. He's going behind the lines in the morning."

Poor Rosie. Although expected, his departure was a personal reminder the war was closing in further.

When she turned to wave at Paul, he was gone.

FORTY-EIGHT

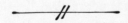

The airfield had its own baseball diamond. As Paul pulled up in the jeep, the fifty-six-year-old Mound King of the Rice Paddy League, Air Force General Claire Chennault, wearing white shirt and gray trousers, was going into his windup.

The ball flew toward the plate.

The green-trousered batter for the Army Grunts swung—too late.

"Struck him out. 2–0 Tigers," the announcer called.

Paul and Jack strode toward the bamboo stands. Under the bluest skies she'd ever seen, the dreamiest clouds, Julia linked arms with a subdued Rosie and followed.

The Grunts poured onto the outfield, and Chennault's Flying Tigers moved to the dugout. First up, and on the first pitch, the general hit a line drive and jogged to first.

From the highest riser, a handsome, placid-faced man in khaki gestured to Paul.

"Miles," Paul informed them in an undertone.

My lucky day. Julia recalled Donovan's pronouncement that the OSS couldn't operate there without Chiang, Tai Li, and Miles.

"Sir," Paul greeted him after they climbed the steps. "Head of Naval Group China and SACO chief, Commander Milton Miles. Jack, you know. My OSS colleagues—Julia McWilliams and Rosie Frame."

"Thank you for your service, ladies." He extended his hand.

On his arm was the round Sino-American patch with the crossed US and Nationalist flags and the unforgettable symbols: ???!!!***—*What the* *hell?!* as Thibaut had translated after their rescue. "In my opinion, sir," Julia said as they shook, "SACO wins hands-down for this war's most artistic emblem."

"Mine, too." The navy commander winked. "'What the hell?' indeed."

"Hit 'em hard and run 'em out," the general called to the batter from first.

Chennault had served under Chiang Kai-shek during the wild and woolly Flying Tiger days. So, now, did Commander Miles. As Thibaut had said, *We're all entwined.* Allies.

Shifting his gaze from the ballfield, Miles brushed back his wavy light-brown hair. "How are my invasion maps coming along, Child? Or are you angling for your own coastal survey?"

Julia tensed at the hint that Paul might be following Thibaut into enemy territory. An image of the work-to-death POW camp in Burma burned through her mind.

"I like Kunming well enough, sir." Paul grinned in that easy way he had with authority. "We've had some rush mapwork for the Kweiyang defense—the reason for our tardy arrival—but US invasion prep remains our priority."

"Good. We must be prepared to greet the fleet come Christmas."

"Wouldn't that be the best holiday?" Rosie said with an awakening smile.

"Strike two," the announcer called.

"Rosie was born in China," Julia boasted, shaking off her dark cloud. "Speaks eleven dialects, plus Russian."

"Then you know this is not America." Miles's lips tightened. "Some of your naive colleagues see the Reds as social reformers—and are spreading anti-Chiang propaganda. Anything that weakens the generalissimo, weakens our own war efforts."

The Flying Tigers' batter connected. And took off.

"That man swings a wicked willow," Jack observed.

"And Chennault slides into third."

"After our Hump flight crashed near the border, a SACO unit got us here," Julia said. "You have good men under your command, sir."

"Sounds like you've seen a bit of the real country. Anytime you want to see more"—Miles included Paul in his glance—"you're welcome to borrow my new Plymouth. Its springs are a lot better than in our Dodge trucks."

Crrr-ack.

Julia flinched, gripping Paul's knee. He patted her hand, smoothed her fingers open. She tried to smile. "Sorry, I—"

"Only blue skies today," he said gently. "You've been through it, Julie, haven't you?"

She sat up, hoping Miles hadn't noticed. "No more than a lot of people," she replied, embarrassed by her fearful reaction to the familiar sound of bat against ball...at her momentary weakness.

The cheers rose. "A line drive past second...And that will bring the Pitching General home!" called the announcer as the other men rounded the bases. "5–0 Tigers."

"Old Man" Chennault went the distance, pitching all nine innings, and completed a one-hit shutout. As Miles went to congratulate him, Paul looked at Jack. "If we don't want a trip to the war zone, we'd best get on that mapwork. We'll drop you girls home." He got up, heading for the jeep.

She had hoped to confess about the Kunming map over dinner. Instead, she and Rosie would console themselves with Chinese food. "Drop us at Ho-Teh-Foo."

———

They were seated on the second floor overlooking the courtyard, where it seemed the entire family was cooking—sending up the most heavenly smells. Fortified by two spicy buns, Julia concluded that the black market crisis required Rosie Frame—and her language skills. As Rosie had been vetted by Donovan, she leaned closer with a whispered briefing about their leaky pipeline of supplies, including Thibaut's missing transceivers. Her surprise told Julia that he, too, could keep a secret. "Any intel we ferret out will help support our troops and shorten the war."

Rosie's jaw set in determination. Seeing Lu Mei and Ai-ling enter, she waved them over—the very ones who'd recommended this place. "They're nice girls, Julia. You'll see."

Sally's cousin, Lu Mei, suggested they try the hand-pulled noodles, being made before their eyes. Taking a mound of dough, the cook stretched and twisted and pulled it into noodles the length of his body and width of his outstretched arms. He tossed them into a kettle of water and, a few minutes later, stir-fried them with mushrooms, garlic, and spices.

The noodles were heaped on a platter and served.

Seeing Lu Mei sprinkle hot sauce liberally on hers, Julia picked up the bottle. "*Hongse*. Red." Her eyes watered after tasting it. "Sensational. As good as Dali Lake noodles."

Lu Mei kept eating with steady focus.

Ai-ling plucked a plump black mushroom from her plate. "A Dali specialty. I always take dried ones when I visit my uncle in Chungking." The generalissimo, she reminded them.

Julia smiled cordially. "You must tell us where you buy them."

After daintily nibbling the rich morsel, Ai-ling put down her sticks. "The outdoor market. The mushroom sellers lane is two past Thieves Row—three past the Flower Circle."

"Thieves Row?" Rosie asked while Lu Mei continued wielding her chopsticks as if there were no tomorrow.

Ai-ling made a small embarrassed smile. "You understand, we have some problems in our economy, so many people trade for what they need."

Julia nodded encouragingly. "How are these goods obtained?"

"Perhaps I have many knives in my kitchen," Ai-ling began. "If I receive a new knife as a gift, I might take it to someone there. Possibly she will buy it, or possibly I can trade it for something else. A new teapot, perhaps."

"Oh my. Seems like a useful spot." Julia noted she'd avoided the *thieves* part. Returning to her noodles, she contemplated what else besides knives and teapots one might obtain there.

FORTY-NINE

—— // ——

The early-spring rains had brought the familiar humidity. The Registry, too, was feeling familiar, lived in. Kunming itself was becoming a familiar place, and so were the names of the regional towns—towns being overrun by the Japanese Imperial Army. The air crackled with threat. Julia's Registry and personal go bags were packed and ready. They were deluged with sabotage reports, urgent requisitions, and messages from far-flung agents in the field. They'd put out the word on Rosie's parents but had heard nothing yet.

As she opened the latest diplomatic pouch from Chungking, Paul entered with a pinched, anxious air. "Miles wasn't kidding about that coastal survey. Luckily, we finished the Kweiyang maps last night. While Jack holds down the fort, I'm leaving tomorrow at dawn with a SACO truck convoy. For Camp Six—"

"Thibaut's base!" Rosie interrupted.

But while Thibaut had fought in North Africa and Italy, Paul had never worn a uniform. An artistic, bookish man launched into great peril. Julia thought again of the Japanese death camps. "You can see Miles's 'real' China," she joked, masking her fear.

"I plan to. I've packed two cameras and quite a bit of excess air force film."

"I bet *Life* magazine would love your pictures," she trilled with forced enthusiasm. "Or what about your own book? *Paul Child's Asia.* I could help edit it after…"

"You're my best fan, Julia," he replied flatly, then looked at Rosie. "I'll bring back an eight-by-ten of Thibaut."

"You're a dreamboat." She hugged him fiercely, then broke away. "Excuse me. I'm off to the canteen to beg, borrow, or steal some goodies for him and boys."

Julia told Paul about their dinner with Ai-ling and Lu Mei—and the Thieves Market intel. Before they could discuss it further, Betty burst in with handbills for him to distribute en route—depictions of Chinese villagers carrying a downed US pilot. The message: Americans were their friends. The subtext: US pilots were being attacked every day.

———

The next morning Rosie found a rickshaw puller to take them to the Flower Circle.

"I hate having a skinny old man pull me around." Julia felt weighed down by Paul's departure. The fog…and uncertainty.

"You are helping keep food in his mouth. His family's."

Ahead, a young-old mother was nursing her baby on a canal footbridge. "*Wait.*" Flooded with emotion, she jumped out and gave her a wad of CN—Chinese Nationalist money, depreciating every day. The mother's weary black eyes met hers in an instant that almost brought her to her knees. Then the woman transferred her baby to one arm and bent to kiss Julia's feet.

As if scalded, she backed into the rickshaw, remembering the Bombay mother who'd approached their tonga, baby tucked at her side…gesturing to her mouth with a curled-up, stunted fist.

Rosie patted her arm. "I know. My parents always say we must endure, for *them.*"

She was still blinking as a dazzle of color pierced the mist—the Flower Circle. The driver lowered his poles, and they climbed out. "*Shi-shi,*" Julia thanked him, tripling his minuscule fare. Bathed by nature's tender fragrance—*these sweet peas!*—she understood why Paul came here to be revived by beauty.

The air remained fresh as, per Ai-ling's directions, they walked two lanes beyond Thieves Row and bought a bag of dried mushrooms, some fresh ones, and a wicker basket.

Thieves Row turned out to be the hub of a maze of side lanes. As they rounded a corner, a grizzled man in a straw hat was examining a pair of army-green trousers. Julia nudged Rosie as he gave some money to a broad-shouldered vendor with beefy arms and stringy gray hair. She passed him a can of Spam. He put both items in a cloth bag.

There were also folded parachute silks, cans of Heinz baked beans, and packs of Lucky Strikes. How did those American goods get here?

Trying to retrace their steps, they found themselves before an open hut where opium smokers sprawled on cots. It was a pitiful scene. Julia understood how people might want to escape the horrors, but what hope could she offer them? She stood there, helpless…until Rosie tugged her away.

Around the next corner, a throng of young protesters were waving placards and banners.

"They are supporters of Governor Long Yun," Rosie explained, reading the signs. "He's a former warlord turned advocate for Yunnan independence and free speech—unlike Chiang. Students admire him."

Some banners were red with gold stars or images of Mao. "Communists, too," Julia observed. To avoid getting mixed up in a factional street scene, she led Rosie away from the crowds, turning down an uneven cobbled lane.

A distant rumble resounded from the east—an approaching storm? As Rosie looked around for a rickshaw, a dark-blue Buick stopped. A soldier flashed his Nationalist blue and silver badge. "Tai Li," he said.

Were they being followed? Or did the second-most powerful man in China simply want to safeguard them from bad weather? They ducked inside the car, which sped away.

———

The bony aide led them through Tai Li's gates, the reception room, and a camphor-scented hallway. Another door opened onto steep steps carved from cold stone.

In darkness, Julia steadied herself between narrow walls.

"*Julia?*" Rosie whispered, touching her back.

"It's okay," she reassured her. But was it?

A dim light met them at the bottom of the steps—the basement.

"Welcome," Gong translated for Tai Li, who nodded graciously, as composed as ever, from the table he occupied with Gong. Other staffers huddled on stools or the floor.

After Julia introduced Rosie, Tai gestured to two empty chairs. "I promised to offer you my special aged tea. Although my home is a tea-growing region, Pu'er is—"

A thunderous roar rocked the room. Julia almost fell into her seat. This was not a storm but a military assault. Was it happenstance that Tai Li's man passed by in time to pick them up? And did their American–British compound have such a shelter? What about all the people out on the streets? *Paul*, exposed on some open road?

Seemingly oblivious to the battering, Tai prepared his Pu'er tea. While the black leaves steeped, Julia tried to match his calm demeanor yet could barely breathe in the crowded, airless space. Gong lit a cigarette, adding to the smells of sweat, garlic, and dust. The rough, low ceiling pressed down on her. She linked fingers with Rosie.

How she wanted this hellish war over. But she remembered her desperation at the thought Donovan had fired her. How could she ever find such gratifying work? Such friends? Who would she be? The future was obscured, as if by a sheer map of parachute silk, Paul's image moving in and out.

The next explosion again spared the ceiling, but tremendous vibrations rose from the stone beneath them. Shock waves sent her knees shuddering. No point musing on a future she now saw as purely speculative. *Some day in the future*, Thibaut had said. *If we have one.*

Tai Li proceeded to serve perfectly brewed tea, recounting the history, cultivation, and varieties of Pu'er. Despite what seemed like endless cups, Julia's mouth was parched with fear.

"We were bombed every cloudless day in Chungking. Here, it has not been bad so far," Tai Li said through Gong.

So far. "Should we keep our bags packed?"

Tai Li cocked his head and spoke.

"Sometimes we withdraw for tactical reasons," Rosie translated boldly.

While Gong showed no reaction, Tai Li questioned her with a smile.

"My *ah mah.*" She smiled back. "I learned *má jiàng* from her, too."

After a snap of his fingers, the table was cleared. Tai Li opened a small drawer to his left and passed them each thirteen ivory tiles. He removed a pack of cigarettes and set out ashtrays.

"Three suits," Rosie explained. "Dots, Bamboo, and Characters."

There were also Winds—East, South, West, and North. As she reached the Bonus tiles—Flowers and Seasons—the bombing grew heavier. Under the sustained pounding, their tiles clattered defiantly.

Amid the swirling smoke, Julia felt like Alice when she was very tall. She rather expected the White Rabbit to appear at any moment and join their game. Rosie, on the other hand, was at home.

Behind them, a radio crackled on, sending forth a stream of soothing traditional Chinese instrumental music. Julia glanced back—at an old RCA table model, walnut with a brass dial in the middle. Vertical in design. Polished nicely like her father's—but with better sound quality. *One of Thibaut's?* Her throat tightened. Impossible.

When the attack ended, they climbed shakily upstairs. "Thank you for looking after us, General Tai. And for your delicious Pu'er tea."

"You are always welcome."

They exchanged somber smiles.

Emerging into the garden, they took great gulps of damp air and hurried to their compound, where everyone was pouring from a side door at SOE. Relieved to see no damage, she grasped Rosie's wrist. "That radio! It was the kind that went missing from Thibaut's special Calcutta order. High-power transceivers camouflaged inside three ordinary brown table models."

"Tai Li *is* a general," Rosie said. "Naturally, he'd have military supplies."

"But not prototypes designed to protect our operatives from location tracking inside enemy territory. Thibaut needs that radio for his safety. SACO's. Paul's."

———

Everyone returned to their offices, awaiting the next attack. Only rain fell from the skies.

An hour later, on her way to brief Dick about Thieves Row and Tai Li, Julia passed the Map Room, where Jack and Ai-ling were facing a large wall map. A mass of red-topped pins represented the Japanese spearhead toward Kweiyang. If they took the crossroads town, where would they push next—northwest to Chungking or southwest to Kunming?

Julia's knees were wobbly. Still feeling the bombardment, like aftershocks of an earthquake, she asked, "I guess we weren't the main target. Did they hit our airbase?"

"The boys scrambled in time, but two loaded C-46s were destroyed and several fuel barrels. They missed the supply depot, though." Jack shifted a red pin. "Four maintenance men were killed, two GIs, and two Chinese civilians. Several huts were leveled. We were lucky."

Pondering their "luck," Julia glanced at Lu Mei, busy typing. Her nerves ragged and throbbing, she continued up the gallery. The courtyard ginkgo was leafing out in what looked like frilly heads of lettuce. Spring, normally such a hopeful time. What if a bomb had smashed that tree to bits? All of them?

"The Kweiyang defense maps are gone," Dick announced as she entered.

Her mouth opened. Jack hadn't mentioned it. "When?"

"After Paul left yesterday, Lu Mei reported them missing. Donovan has been notified."

"He interviewed her. Her cousin Sally Lu is running the Registry in Washington."

He rubbed his forehead. "And Kung Ai-ling is the generalissimo's niece."

"She knows about Thieves Row, where the black market operates in plain sight," Julia said. "Rosie and I witnessed a man buying a US Army uniform and Spam."

"It's an open secret."

"An open sore, you mean. Supplies 'falling off the truck' in plain view."

Dick looked pained. "The Chiangs are dependent on America for their regime's survival. They would not undermine us."

"But they want to know what we're thinking. Maybe Tai is behind the Map Room theft?"

"He may be sending a message that this is his country, and there are no secrets."

"One of his men followed us earlier. We'd just left an anti-Chiang protest." Seeing his outrage, she hurriedly explained, "It was an accident. We got lost at the market."

"You could have provoked an international incident! Our entire Japan strategy is predicated on General Chiang Kai-Shek remaining a firm ally."

She glanced down. "We were driven to Tai Li's bomb shelter, where he taught me to play mah-jongg. Rosie already knew."

Dick barked a laugh. "I suppose he served his special aged tea?" His mirth faded. "We don't know where your digging will lead—or to whom. I don't want you wandering about on your own. Even with Rosie."

"In the back of his shelter, Tai Li had a radio similar to the RCA transceivers Thibaut ordered for covert units—the first such shipment to China. Three state-of-the-art prototypes arrived in Calcutta, but disappeared before he could claim them."

"Tai Li is Chiang's Number Two in China. Perhaps he believes he has priority."

"More than his own SACO men—risking their lives to report from enemy territory?"

"Inform Donovan," CO Heppner said. "Then, carry on."

Troubled, Julia plodded back to the Registry. This was why Donovan had sent her.

She was also troubled by her bad conscience about Paul. She needed to admit she'd destroyed his original Kunming map. *Why?* he would ask. Even now, she hung her head: *Jealousy. But why?* Because she'd never been a petite pretty person with a swanlike neck. How foolish she was. He might lose all respect for her—or pity her. Or laugh it off. It was a risk. But she had vowed to be honest with any man she was close with. When Paul returned, she would face the music. She doubted she'd be hearing "You Are My Sunshine."

FIFTY

—— // ——

"*Ni chi le ma?*" Driver Tung asked her again the next morning as they left to see SOS Booker.

"Well, thanks. And you?" When Rosie told her the greeting really meant *Have you eaten?* Julia felt a pain in her heart for the suffering Chinese people. She was proud Detachment 202 fed its staff well. Many, she was sure, took much of it home.

She knew little about Tung, his family, how he'd ended up at OSS. The only man at HQ who wore an ironed white shirt every day, he was a calm presence with large ears like the Buddha…as Paul had taught her. *Paul.*

On their way to the airbase, she mulled over her message to Donovan about Thieves Row and the possible transceiver in Tai Li's bomb shelter. His succinct reply: *Keep digging. 109.*

Tung turned onto the access road that paralleled the runway. As they passed a C-46 being unloaded onto a line of trucks, she wondered if Betty's printing press had made it. The trucks proceeded down the field to Services of Supply, where the guys were logging and offloading their supplies or transferring them into other vehicles for redelivery.

SOS Booker was not there. As local supply chief, he had an angle onto a world far from hers. If anyone could offer insight into the diversions, he was the one. Frustrated, she left a note reminding him of their drinks date. *PS, I'm learning mah-jongg. Not saying I could beat you. Yet.* After three days of silence, she figured he'd flown back over the Hump.

Julia had other concerns. Kunming was communications hub for

China-Burma-India Command, which kept them informed on the reconquest of Burma—where Mountbatten and SEAC were heavily engaged. At the same time, she had to coordinate with OSS and SACO headquarters in the capital, Chungking. While still wary of SACO's boss, Tai Li, she also knew that Sino-American covert units often provided emergency medical care to the local populace. She'd heard of babies being named Miles and America.

She and Rosie barely had time to breathe, let alone revisit Thieves Row. When she did have a moment, she worried about Paul. Some nights she read *Dream of the Red Chamber* till dawn. Better being awake than trapped inside a death camp nightmare.

———

Twelve days after his departure, Paul walked into the Registry, gaunt and unshaven.

"Oh my!" She squeezed him close in sickened relief. "Are you all right? You look…"

"As bad as my news. Thibaut's post is low even on candles." He glanced at Rosie with sympathy. "Our small convoy carried little more than K-rations, some ammo, out-of-date batteries, and a bicycle—for generating power. I have your guy's photo, though." Reshouldering his camera bag, Paul turned to Julia. "I need a good meal. Join me tonight?"

"I'll cancel everything." Ready to show off her chopsticks skills, she started to consider what to wear. Not that any of it would matter after he heard her confession.

"I need to brief Dick and grab a shower. Pick you up at eight."

The evening was unseasonably warm, scented with a burst of jasmine that reminded her of Christmas in Kandy—without the mistletoe. She'd finally settled on a summery dress with a flirty gored skirt, which seemed the perfect choice when she saw Paul glance at her legs. They drove to a lakeside hole-in-the-wall she'd discovered, where the jaunty, pink-cheeked chef was tossing and pulling noodles with abandon. He grinned in recognition; then his birdlike wife showed them to a quiet corner, wiped down the oilcloth, and brought tea.

"Dick told me about the missing maps," she murmured. "Could it be Lu Mei or Ai-ling?"

"Or next-door neighbor Tai Li has a tunnel—or is paying someone off." Paul mimed lifting a drink to his lips. The woman returned with two foamy glasses of warm beer. They toasted.

As Paul downed his, she said, "The day after you left, our airbase was attacked, and I was so afraid for you. How did you get through enemy territory?"

"Headlights off, at night. The fourth morning, we reached Thibaut's camp, where they lit a fire for outdoor showers. Then I began my survey, sketching and photographing the terrain, incorporating the men's observations. I took sightings from the old pagoda—their radio room and Pacific lookout." He gestured for another beer. "While the men were at dinner, Thibaut was briefing me in the guesthouse over scrambled eggs—suddenly everything erupted."

"*Bombs?*" She tore her gaze away as the small woman served bowls of greens, noodles, and little chicken legs. "*Shi-shi.*" Heaping food on his plate, Julia wanted to pinch him to make sure he was real. "But you two were okay?" When he nodded, she asked, "The others?"

"Fine. Only the pagoda was targeted. And the suitcase radio had been stashed in a dried-up well. But their backup radio, improvised out of oil drums and bamboo tubing, was destroyed."

She stared, aghast. "The lookout where you spent all that time."

He grinned. "I guess my time ain't up yet."

"*Ganbei!*" She lifted her beer, and they toasted to long life.

Paul had more to say. "Camp Six was locked down. The next day five vials of poison and thirty thousand large-denomination yuan were discovered in Cook Wang's room. He confessed to being trained at Japanese spy school on Formosa Island—and planted in SACO."

"That's why they didn't blow up the mess—the spy was inside! But he might have used the poison on the men later." She downed a long slug of beer, then ventured her chopsticks into the chicken.

"Frogs' legs," Paul said appreciatively.

She put down her sticks, gazing at him in silence. What a gutsy guy.

Heroic and humble, hardworking. Brilliant. To her, he was larger than life. Paul Child was her guy. And she was his girl. He might not know it yet, but *she* did. And he would. All she needed was to be steady and sure and prepared to wait. But she wouldn't wait any longer to confess about the map.

Abruptly, he looked up, all levity gone. "In the countryside, we saw people living on grass and worms, babies with bloated bellies."

"While American canned goods, uniforms, and who-knows-what-else are being trafficked on Thieves Row," Julia said in quiet fury. "I observed a radio in Tai Li's basement that strongly resembles one of Thibaut's missing transceivers—advanced components hidden inside older RCA table models. My father has a similar-looking one from the thirties—but the sound quality is nowhere as good."

Paul looked up, startled. "Why were you in his basement?"

"Bomb shelter."

He looked even more concerned, but she shrugged. "Yours came closer."

Paul placed his hand over hers. A brief silence fell between them; then he was all business. "Where would Tai get the radio? From whom?"

"And are Americans in on it?" She imagined people eating worms. "I know you can't jump to conclusions. But…"

"I've come to trust your instincts, Julia."

The little heart-shaped blue box seemed to hover in the air between them, a palpable thing supported by everything they had shared. She felt a warm rush of gratitude. "A pal from my Hump flight runs Services of Supply here. He's been away, but I'm hoping we can get a lead."

He fixed her with a direct look. "Or he is the lead. Good connection."

"I can't take credit. It just happened. You're the world traveler, the one who can maneuver even in a war zone. I think you could do anything," she said shyly.

"I don't know about that. After it's over, I'd like to accomplish something."

"Wouldn't we all?" she mused, picking up her sticks.

"In the meantime," he said. "Jack and I need to redraft the missing maps."

"First," she replied sternly. "You need to get some sleep."

"No one's told me that since I was a boy." Paul sighed. "Then I was the one to repeat it to my gadabout mother." He tapped her chopsticks with his. "Good technique."

Lifting them, she selected her most succulent mushroom and placed it in his mouth. Their eyes met. And she smiled. The hand-fed rice ball would come later. And her apology.

FIFTY-ONE

—— // ——

She was antsy all the next morning, waiting for Paul to be free. She wanted him to meet Booker, and together they would pick his brain. As they drove to Services of Supply, the area south of town was cloaked in pea-soup fog, and they inched down the airfield access road to the depot.

"'China is no place for the Timid,'" Paul read as they entered the Quonset hut. Amid the clamor of voices and teletypewriters echoing off the curved corrugated-metal shell, Booker looked up from his logbook and broke into a big smile. "Julia McWilliams. I got your note. How the hell are you?"

"Waiting for that beer. Where have you been?"

"Where haven't I been? But for the grace of Lady Luck, that bomb attack would have hit harder." His grin broadened.

"Meet my friend Paul Child, Visual Display, mapmaker in chief. Sergeant Sam Booker, otherwise known as SOS Booker, a fellow who can organize a card game in the ruins of a crashed C-46 and roast a rabbit in its embers."

"With that setup, I know you want something."

She saw no need to be subtle. "Our friend Thibaut, from the Hump flight…?"

He nodded. "That tall frog with Madame's piano and the gold."

"The very one. He's in a SACO coast-watcher unit so short of batteries they use a bicycle generator to power their radio. His new RCA transceivers haven't been seen since Calcutta." She didn't mention the similar one in Tai Li's basement.

"India." Booker's eyes narrowed. "Plenty of matériel goes sideways there."

"True enough," Paul said. "But Services of Supplies is known to run a tight ship."

"What happens after you receive the goods?" she asked.

Booker pointed at the hangars across the asphalt road. "Stored by category—jeeps, tires, fuel, food, clothing, etcetera." He checked his log. "Let's see. Radios. We had a recent arrival of SCR-300 transistor units, backpack suitable—with batteries. They were trucked north to SACO camps in Kweiyang and Chungking. I've heard battery life is a problem."

"Any other kinds?" Paul pressed him.

"Some larger Emerson and RCA models for fixed locations. Last week, we got a crate of British RAF receivers. And several Morse key units on lightweight wooden bases for field use. Sometimes the goods come in by dribs and drabs, others in an onslaught." An engine crescendoed overhead. "Sounds like another C-46 made it over the Hump."

"Good news for the crew," Julia said. She shared a look with Booker, recalling the dead crew chief, all the human loss transporting war matériel over the Hump.

He bobbed his head and gave her a salute. "That beer, kiddo."

"Lots of stuff to keep track of," she said as Paul steered the jeep back through the fog. "Peggy's father, General Wheeler, used to run SOS for the Burma Road project. Amazing how they even got supplies up there, all those jungle mountains and valleys."

"The construction is nearing the Yunnan border. Soon we'll have truck convoys, not single planes, bringing in the fuel of war."

"I guess we won't have to worry about diversions then." A horse-drawn tonga clip-clopped beside them, carrying a big burlap-wrapped box and a young man in aviator glasses. Julia regarded him with suspicion—for no reason, really, except paranoia.

"Or they'll expand on a larger scale." After Paul passed the tonga, the mist cleared around the canal, clogged with boat traffic.

She winced. "Booker's unit looks pretty organized, yet the black market is operating openly on Thieves Row." She was annoyed they hadn't returned with anything tangible.

His face twisted in disgust. "After the pagoda was destroyed, the SACO guys climbed the hills with binoculars to monitor enemy movements—nothing kept them from reporting at their scheduled hour."

"This is nasty business." Either one of two well-vetted young women had stolen maps critical to Kweiyang's defense, or an unknown person had access to HQ. The main suspect was their neighbor Tai Li, who had also possibly diverted vital field equipment for his own use. Amid such deceit, Julia was determined to clear the air with Paul. Who knew what his reaction might be. He might merely shrug, or even be amused at the drama she'd created in her mind…Julia couldn't bear for this to remain between them any longer.

As she turned to him in the front seat, he said, "We need a palate cleanser. Care to step out of time with me? Say, a few centuries back to the Golden Temple?"

"You have your camera bag?"

"Certainly," he replied. "I had ulterior reasons when we left today."

More photography? Then she saw the glimmer in his eye. Was he flirting, or was this finally something more? She'd have to postpone her mea culpa, again.

———

"They're actually made of bronze and copper," Paul said as they climbed the many, many steps to the gleaming Heavenly Gates. An elderly couple nimbly bypassed them.

The fog had lifted, leaving only its moisture. "While you were gone, I read *Dream of the Red Chamber*. There are so many characters I made a chart."

"I like your style." Paul smiled. "One of them reminds me of you— she has a bubbly personality, big laugh, and is a great beauty."

Julia wasn't crazy about the big laugh, but a *great beauty*? Never *ever* had she thought of herself that way. She wanted to ask if that was really how he saw her, but didn't have the nerve.

Inside the main gate, more steps led up to the ancient Taoist temple—glittering under the lowering sun. They rested on a stone bench under an archway of trees. A large blush-pink camellia was in bloom, and the garden smelled fresh.

"When I was twelve, Mother and I read *A Tale of Two Cities* for her ladies' book group. 'It was the best of times, it was the worst of times.'"

"'It was the spring of hope, it was the winter of despair, we had everything before us, we had nothing before us,'" Paul recited. "In a way, that might describe this war—do you think?"

Daring to meet his eyes, she blurted, "What was she like?" Then turned away, watching a man in a padded coat limp toward the gold-bellied deity with an incense stick.

She felt Paul's acute gaze, but his words were frank. "Older. Stylish, cultured, a woman at home in any literary salon. Beautiful. Not motherly at all. Yet she—Edith—cared for me, took care of me, in a way my mother never could. People wondered what she saw in me."

Julia saw it. He was strong and masculine, a man of great talent and deep feeling, but one who had not been properly nurtured. How perceptive his Edith had been to grasp not only his needs but his potential, his eagerness to embrace the world with all his senses. Paul had been empty, and she'd filled him.

"She was life-affirming. Like you, Julia."

A flush rose from the center of her being. Embarrassed for him to see her intense emotions, she stared at the tendons on his tanned arms, his strong, able hands. She didn't speak, knowing her voice would come out somehow wrong. As she attempted to calm her flaming cheeks, he delved into his camera bag. How kind of him to give her this moment.

"I loved her. But she's gone." He turned to her, pushing back a damp strand of her hair. "You're here. And I'm glad." A gentle fingertip outlined her lips, his face close to hers, his mouth almost brushing hers but not quite.

Then they flowed together, his kiss long and deep and entirely different than the one he'd bestowed on her, and too many others, under the mistletoe last Christmas.

The world disappeared, every fear and concern. She felt feverish, which had nothing to do with the sizzling sun. He didn't kiss her again, but eased her into the shade and held her hot hand, still and steady.

FIFTY-TWO

— // —

The next afternoon, Driver Tung "chaperoned" Julia and Rosie to the open-air market. They bought more mushrooms, then turned up the side lane. A piece of camouflage fabric covering her lank gray hair, the dealer in US Army gear and Spam was folding a wool-lined leather flight jacket. Coca-Cola bottles were on display next to cans of Dinty Moore stew and jars of Skippy peanut butter. As Tung watched from a distance, twisting his long earlobe, the two women strolled between the stalls. They saw no other trader of American goods.

With a friendly smile, Rosie spoke to the stocky woman, who shook her head no. Still smiling, Rosie picked up two packs of Doublemint chewing gum, opened her thick billfold and removed a large-denomination CN. Waving a palm—*Don't bother about the change*—she kept talking as the woman's eyes skittered between the Chinese banknote…the bulging wallet…the passersby.

Heart in her mouth, Julia watched their back-and-forth…the trader shaking her head, Rosie persisting calmly, keeping her wallet in view. The woman began to waver.

Finally, she indicated a crowded merchandise shelf behind her. After a last wary look around, she half turned and, with a flick of her wrist, lifted a dark-blue cloth cover…

A brass dial glimmered, catching the light. The cloth dropped back down.

But Julia knew what she'd seen—a table-model RCA in a vertical walnut cabinet.

Now the bargaining began in earnest, until Rosie presented an offer that made the dealer blink. She cleared her throat and again checked the surroundings. Then, surreptitiously, wrapped the radio in newspaper, scrawled a few characters inside, and exchanged the package for a thick stack of CN notes.

Afraid to look at Rosie, Julia gulped down some air. "Ask if she has silk stockings. And a garter belt."

Without comment, Rosie conveyed her request. The woman reached beneath her counter, extracting two flat packages. "Last ones," Rosie translated, handing over the rest of her cash. "Foreigner sized, too big to sell. Garters are there, too. She wishes you happiness with your man."

Lowering her gaze, Julia slipped her illicit items under the mushrooms. She was ashamed to be patronizing the black market, but gave herself a one-time dispensation.

At the Registry, they unwrapped the newspaper and examined the radio in fine detail, opening the false bottom to reveal the transmitter. Rosie read the woman's note and address. "She has information and wants to meet early tomorrow. For dollars."

That morning Julia had received a cable alerting them of Donovan's arrival in Chungking. By the time he reached Kunming, she hoped to have more conclusive intelligence.

———

At 0700, Paul picked them up by tonga. Under heavy fog, they proceeded south to a shabby neighborhood. The dirt-floored dwelling housed several people who viewed their arrival with suspicion. And fear.

Wearing her headscarf, the dealer hurried them into a dank room with paper windows. Shifting from one foot to the other, she examined their greenbacks, then slipped the payoff in a front pocket. "Next delivery—follow trucks from airbase," she told Rosie. "*Meikuo.* American."

"Follow where?" Julia tried to catch the woman's eye, to no avail.

Blank faced, their source twisted a loose strand of greasy hair.

Julia pressed her. "Chinese partner?"

"Very big," the woman finally whispered to Rosie, then shooed them out.

The air was moist, and Julia smelled rain. "*Very big*. What do you think, Rosie?"

"She was nervous. Going up against powerful people. But I believed her."

"We need to tell Dick." Paul waved down another tonga.

They ducked under its tattered canopy just before the skies opened. As the emaciated horse clopped ahead, they considered the implications of her tip.

They spoke quietly, their words barely audible under the rain. "Arriving goods go straight to the depot to be logged in." Julia looked at Paul. "They're stored or reloaded for delivery elsewhere. We've never paid attention to the *elsewhere*."

He scowled. "There were half a dozen clerks at Services of Supplies. And all those truck drivers."

As she tried to visualize the faces in Booker's unit, they reached Green Lake, metallic and, for the first time, menacing. Clouds hung low over their lane of colonial villas. While passing Tai Li's yellow walls, she wondered about his connection to the "very big" smuggler.

They dashed inside their compound and almost bumped into Betty, her arms loaded with leaflets. "Have you seen Dick?" Julia asked.

"He left earlier for SACO-Kweiyang. He's to assess battle readiness, then brief Donovan and the brass in Chungking."

"Dick will have a lot more to report if we can catch him first." Julia turned to Paul, who mirrored her concern. Their information about a possible high-level American–Chinese smuggling operation was too explosive to transmit by wireless, even encrypted.

His mouth set. "It's dangerous territory, Julia. I'll go."

"My intel," she insisted. "Rosie and Jack can handle things."

"You bet," Rosie said fervently.

Paul seemed rooted in doubt. Male protectiveness.

"If you recall, Miles offered us his Plymouth at the ball game. I'm guessing he's also in Chungking?" Julia glanced at Betty, who nodded. "We'd make better time. And Kweiyang will need your maps."

"Yeah," Paul said a heavy sigh. "Whoever has the originals knows too much about our strategies, arms caches, and intelligence. The brass needs to review their game plan."

Her intelligence mission had again become *ours*. Julia welcomed the journey.

"I will alert Jack and the girls," he said.

"I'll find Driver Tung and wrangle some food for the road." Jittery, she checked her wristwatch—0945. "We should leave now."

FIFTY-THREE

Her canvas shoulder bag stuffed with food and a pullover, Julia was the first one at the carved red gate. A few minutes later, Driver Tung pulled up in Commander Miles's sleek blue Plymouth. He got out, standing spic and span in a starched white shirt. So earnest.

She tried to conceal her dismay when Paul appeared with Mei, their volunteer translator. But better her than Ai-ling! Mei was a hard worker and deserved a little break.

Paul placed his L.L.Bean bag in the trunk, slinging one of the cameras around his neck. "I thought you could relax today, Driver Tung, and I'll take the wheel."

Tung shook his head, snaking his hand upward. "Twenty-Four Turn Road. Dangerous."

"You take over at the steep part," Paul offered.

Tung broke into a rapid exchange with Mei, wearing a blue padded jacket.

"It is his profession to drive," she translated. "But this is a beautiful car and he understands your wish. To save face, he must sit in the front passenger seat—the driver's side in China. No one will know this car has American left-hand steering."

"Fair enough," Paul said, opening the right rear door for Mei. He showed Julia around to the left side, then slid behind the wheel.

Luxuriating in pillowy sea-blue leather, they set off under a clear sky with magical cloud formations—palaces and dragons, elaborate cityscapes and forests, as they imagined. When Julia unleashed an old camp song, "Wheels on the Bus," Paul joined in. Mei alternately sang and translated for Tung, who found it hilarious. All the while, Paul handled the rough, muddy road with ease, a man with one eye, a man who could adapt to anything.

"Change." Suddenly serious, Driver Tung pointed up the steep mountain, stark granite and velvety green veiled in a scrim of mist— the scene right out of a Chinese watercolor.

"Almost seven-hundred-foot climb over less than two miles," Mei explained.

After the men swapped seats, they zigzagged up into the clouds.

"Stop," Paul ordered.

Perched over a vertiginous drop, Julia saw only the cliffs below while he saw a beautiful churning waterfall above. Moving nimbly over the rocks, Paul sought the perfect angle for his photography. Finally satisfied, he climbed back in, whistling softly.

Taking advantage of the pause, she passed around some dumplings and spring rolls.

Then they twisted on. While her belly could take it, her head was whirling. She braced herself until they reached the top, and her jaw unclenched. By the time they regained their equilibrium, the road smoothed into a gentle incline. Tung mimed handing the wheel to Paul.

As he took over, Paul glanced at her. "How about 'Ninety-Nine Bottles of Beer'?"

They launched into a rousing performance, joined by Mei and Tung, who hummed along, enjoying the view. At bottle fifty, he pointed to an old structure on the hill.

"Driver Tung's high school," Mei said.

"You're from here?" Julia asked.

He placed a hand over his heart. "Home."

Down to twenty-eight bottles, they reached the outskirts of Kweiyang. What first appeared to be a sprawling mass in the distance soon became a throng of gaunt, desperate people carrying babies and sacks of rice. Some were wrapped in blankets; their clothes were threadbare, with few coats in sight. Nearby, at the rear of the crowd, a man pushed a cart bearing an old woman—his mother? The man's feet were swaddled in rags. Their voices died in midmeasure.

"Many refugees," Mei said, lowering her head. "Fleeing Ichi-Go."

A young father bearing his toddler daughter on his shoulders caught Julia's eye, pleading.

Mutely, unblinking, she held his look, her heart trapped in her throat as he disappeared in the crush of humanity. She didn't want to see this horror, but at the same time she needed to stare it full in the face, unshielded by their OSS walls. Her separateness appalled her.

Silence fell over them; there was only the engine's smooth rumble. Then Mei continued singing in her thin soprano and Paul in his clear tenor.

"—should happen to fall—" Tung joined in at the refrain. He didn't know the English numbers but was making an effort. Julia summoned her voice, which cracked and fluttered on and off-key. The gaiety was gone, but they had to carry on.

By nine bottles, they had reached a quiet wooded area. Rounding the next bend, she spotted a road sign: *Naval Group China. SACO Camp 10. 2 Km.* "Almost there. Good job at the wheel, both of—"

An explosion of gunfire rocked the Plymouth.

Glass shattered everywhere, everything happening at once.

Paul hit the accelerator as Tung collapsed against the right passenger window. Blood spattered down his neck…the pale-blue leather seat.

Mei lurched back with a cry. More blood.

"*Paul!*" Julia called frantically.

"Get down!" He careened forward.

Huddling against his seatback, she reached for Mei's hand—speckled red, like her own.

Paul swung sharply left; her head slammed against the door handle, her hand ripped from Mei's. Her right cheek stung. Had she been shot? She gingerly patted her face, tender. The tip of her finger found a shard of glass.

As she tried to pull it out, the Plymouth skidded to a stop between two sturdy pines. When she peeked up, Paul was bending over Tung.

"Two in the right temple," he said dully.

Julia whirled toward Mei. Silent…slumped against her door, blood spurting from her throat. Paul passed her Tung's fresh handkerchief and, pushing open Mei's jacket, she applied pressure to the jagged wound— something they teach you in training when you're green and can't believe it's real.

Mei's eyes fluttered open.

"*Hongse.*" She pointed at her chest.

Red. "It's not too bad," Julia lied, pressing harder against Mei's throat. Blood seeped through the handkerchief. Helpless, she glanced at Paul, his face ashen. Then her gaze rested on Tung, so quiet, as if he were dozing. The left side of his collar still spotless white, his hair combed smoothly behind his long Buddha ear.

Mei's eyes were becoming unfocused. Blood gurgled through her lips.

As she took her final breath, Julia bent her head, her wet, trembling hand falling to Mei's chest. Something rustly…Not undergarments, but *paper*.

Awkwardly, she reached inside her blouse, retrieving a thickly folded envelope: Paul's maps for Kweiyang—and Operation Downfall, the US invasion of the South China coast.

She gave Paul the maps, speechless, both of them.

Julia felt numb—*má*, second tone, came crazily to mind. "I thought she meant *red* for blood, but maybe she was confessing. Remember our first dinner with the gang? Rosie told us *hongse* is the Communist color. Do you think Mei planned to pass them in Kweiyang? Somewhere near the SACO camp? That's why she wanted to come?"

"Possible." Paul checked the rearview mirror: No one. Yet.

"Was someone trying to stop her?"

"I doubt Mei was the objective. This Plymouth is known to belong to Commander Miles, the highest-ranking American in China. A country where the steering wheel is on the right."

An assassination attempt. If so, the car remained a target.

"Only a mile or so to camp." Julia dug her nails into her palms to master her shaking. She threw her shoulder bag across her chest, closing their doors quietly while he grabbed his L.L.Bean bag from the trunk.

They ducked around to the passenger side where he had so recently sat. The Plymouth's right front tire was hissing air. They crouched low, assessing the scene. He touched her wounded cheek. His fingers came back dry, his gaze taking in her hand and arm, stained with Mei's blood.

There were no vehicles on the hilly road, no human signs whatsoever, which made the emptiness even more suspect. Nerves on fire, she moved closer to Paul—at the same moment he moved closer to her, his camera swinging against her side. As she gasped, he tugged her back into the woods, a dense growth of pines and tangled foliage.

The searing silence was shattered by a string of foreign words…a male voice…some kind of command?

Japanese? The image of soldiers charging Deepak through the brush spun into a mass of pink…a sprawling oleander shrub. *Poisonous.* She jerked back and yanked Paul with her.

More gunfire rang out.

Then, an American voice. "ID yourselves. Or we'll shoot."

"OSS," Paul shouted. "Here to see Colonel Heppner."

"Step forward," said the American.

Paul took her hand, and they moved, tentatively, onto the road—and into the gun barrels of two young men in khaki and *What the Hell?!** SACO badges.

Julia glared. "Put down your damn weapons. Someone killed our driver and translator—their bodies are in Commander Miles's car! Hidden in the pines two kilometers back."

The American was still gripping his tommy gun. "That your blood?"

Her trousers were streaked with Mei's dried blood. Sharply red in contrast, fresh blood crosshatched both her arms and Paul's. "Some of it."

"Never mind," Paul barked. "Let's get out of here."

Under the men's protection, they hurried to camp. She ached with pity for Tung, here at their behest. And—she couldn't help it—for Mei. The rusty-brown dirt blurred beneath her feet.

Before setting off with his .45 to lead a search, the Chinese soldier,

Corporal Jiao, gave her a clump of broad leaves and his canteen. "Must clean cuts."

"Those pink flowers—oleander—are toxic, you know," she informed Paul as he sat her on a rock and, with a wet leaf, swabbed her cheek.

"No. I didn't," he said, washing her exposed ankles, which trembled at his touch.

Remembering the leech, she glanced at him, but he had that distant, focused look, so she let it go.

While she was cleansing his cuts, Dick arrived and took them to a table under the trees.

Hearing of Mei's betrayal, he went silent.

"She volunteered to join us," Paul said. "I didn't request a translator."

"Mei concealed the maps under her jacket. I don't know why she still had them, so many days later." Julia began to shiver, and Paul scooted closer. "Why she hadn't already passed them."

"Maybe something happened to her contact." Dick's expression darkened. "This was her chance to move the maps up the line in relative safety."

"'Up the line,'" she repeated. "In this camp?"

"We'll look into it," he said grimly. "People criticize Tai Li, but there are spies and infiltrators everywhere. Look what happened in Camp Six—while you were there, Paul."

A hush fell over them as they thought of the cook-spy. There was much to digest. Then Julia reported their purchase of a US military radio on Thieves Row, Tai Li's similar one—and the vendor's advice to follow the next delivery from the airbase. "'Meikuo,' she said."

"American." The furrows in Dick's brow deepened.

"And his high-level, probably Chinese counterpart. Nothing is corroborated yet, but we'll keep on it." Her voice weakened as her shivering continued. Paul hugged her to his side. She longed only to crawl under the covers and sleep till the end of the war.

"We have hot water at the moment, so let's get you to the showers." Then Dick rustled up some clean clothing, apologizing for the lack of female wardrobe.

"It's not the first time I've worn men's trousers. But please find a white shirt for Driver Tung. For his burial." Her voice cracked, her stomach heaved...*His spotless shirt, his blood, his clear singing voice.* Julia turned to Paul. "He had ears like the Buddha." She swallowed. "We have to notify his family. And we need to take care of them. We must." She sent Dick a searching look.

"He has a son," Dick said. "In our service. I'll find a way."

Later, Dick and a Chinese sergeant conducted a joint service for Tung and Mei. Then, grief stricken, Julia and Paul passed out. In her feverish dreams, Lu Mei and Sally Lu blended in and out of each other.

———

At dawn, Dick prepared to leave for Chungking. "There's a wiring problem on their Dodge. As soon as it's fixed, Jiao will drive you back."

They walked him to his jeep, where a man waited at the wheel. Dick slapped the door, got in, and they bounced up the rutted road.

"My former, very Republican beau joined the Navy," she mused. "I wonder how he'd feel being posted in the middle of China under the jurisdiction of a Chinese spymaster."

"Life takes you places."

Breathing the fresh piney air, she and Paul walked into the hills, bound by shock and loss. As they reached a tumbling stream, she touched his arm. "Shh."

On the far shore, a blue-crowned bird—a paradise flycatcher!—with an impossibly long and magnificent orange tail perched on a low branch, cocked his head at her with his midnight eye, and began to sing. As his cousin, perhaps, in Kandy had once sung to her. A tender song that opened her heart and ended with a promise of hope. It was the overture to everything...for a few moments later, Paul had appeared with a splash of mud—a dramatic entrance if she'd ever seen one.

The tears came over her, she was choked with sobs. Paul held her in his solid arms and allowed her to cry. When she had nothing left, he wiped her cheeks with great tenderness. Taking her hand, he led her to a ring of stumps and sat her down.

"Sometimes it hits you," Julia said apologetically.

"How could it not?"

Her nerves felt shattered, but she couldn't let herself fall apart. "I'll get tea."

Paul watched as she returned with two cups and set them on the center stump. His face was a conflict of sun and shadow. "I love seeing you walk, Julie, so filled with purpose. Your glorious legs taking you wherever you want to go."

"Wherever that is." She passed him his tea.

"I'm still waiting, too. But you are a larger person." He saw her stiffen. "I mean to say, your spirit and force of personality. Your ambition will take you far."

It remained hard to admit. "I don't know about that..."

"You are so ambitious you're afraid to admit it."

It felt wrong to be having this conversation, now. She tipped her cup against his. "To the end of this damn war."

After dinner, one of the guys gave them a flask of fire water.

They finally slept. Side by side. On two cots.

FIFTY-FOUR

———— // ————

At least, Paul slept. Julia was restless, her ping-ponging brain agitated by the merest rustle, which might be footsteps, or a hissing snake…an engine backfire might be gunshots. Her ears were on fire, hyperalert.

She tried to calm her breathing, visualizing what it was all about.

Two things she wanted: Peace. And Paul.

Peace, she would have to say, came first.

As to her other desire, she struggled. She had been raised to think the man was the priority, even as she feared being vulnerable and dependent, subject to a husband's moods and fancies. But, while she knew Paul was her guy, she didn't want to end up like her mother, who had begun life with such a fiery spirit. The first woman in her Massachusetts county to obtain a driver's license.

————

One night in the fall of her senior year, Julia had driven some of the gang to the local speakeasy, the top down on her black jalopy, Eulalie. That could have been the evening she danced on the table; in any case, she'd known by then to stop at two.

Last spring, she had finally buckled down and raised her grades. In June, Caro had met her at the train station with Eulalie, the used 1929 Model A roadster that they drove back east at the end of August. Boy, did they have fun! One hot afternoon, en route to visit Chicago relatives, they'd stopped outside Davenport, Iowa, for a refreshing swim in the Mississippi. Just because they could. *This*, Mother had confided in her as they dried and combed each other's hair—and attempted hilariously to style it for dinner—was the kind of freedom she wished for her daughters. Having one's own car helped.

While her friends carried on without her, Julia headed home. Damp from the early rains, the road was twisty and oil-slick. The fine mist on her face sobered her, and she drove at a cautious pace...until her tires shuddered and slipped.

Julia slammed on the brakes. But the car had its own momentum and spun across the road. She came to a dead stop in the opposite lane— facing the vehicles that might, at any moment, come barreling her way.

She turned the ignition and pumped the gas. The engine coughed awake, then quit.

Staring into the darkness, she tried again. This time, Eulalie responded. Cold air slapping her cheeks, she twisted the wheel and proceeded back to Hubbard Hall, luck riding at her side.

———

Lady Luck. Hearing Booker's jaunty tone, Julia awoke on her cot, sweating. Her hands still gripping the wheel. Slowly opening her fingers, she saw Paul snoring quietly on the cot beside her. Near, yet a universe away. She was grateful for his tranquility, but remained distressed about the assassination attempt—or was her dream some kind of premonition of dangers ahead? She closed her eyes, weary, emotionally depleted.

Under dawn's early light, they left Camp Ten in a weather-beaten truck with their rescuer, Corporal Jiao. Flying SACO's *What the Hell?!** pennant, the Dodge lurched around the first curve. The mountain road seemed windier than ever; the ride was jerky, nothing like the Plymouth. And Jiao was not Tung, a professional driver who navigated with smooth prudence. Jiao seemed to enjoy challenging the Twenty-Four Turn Road.

Sitting between the men, she relived the attack. The horror of Tung's murder. And Mei's. Her treachery. Paul looked a thousand years old—maybe he'd experienced his own private terrors in the night. When a sharp turn flung Julia against him, his body was rigid, unyielding—angry, she felt, at the world. He had been fond of Tung, too. And he'd trusted Mei, so her treachery must have hurt all the more.

Shadowed by her memory-dream, she kept a wary eye on oncoming traffic.

After three near misses, they made it through the last of the twenty-four zigzags. Paul expressed no desire to drive.

Julia couldn't stop thinking of Lu Mei's cousin, Sally Lu, loyal head of the OSS Registry in Washington, DC…Sally's proud immigrant parents in Seattle. Their relatives in China, Lu Mei's parents—this staggering tragedy to their entire family. While Sally had given her heart to America, Lu had given hers to Mao Tse-Tung, and betrayed them all.

"I worked with her every day." Paul shook his head in disbelief.

"Her people are tenant farmers. In such a poor country, Mao's talk of land reform must be appealing." She regarded the barren, uncultivated landscape. Who was she, raised in comfort, to criticize Mei's choices? And she was no stranger to deceit.

As they descended Kunming's foothills, a haze spread over the dusty plateau. In the gauzy distance, pagodas, mosques, and winged gateways soared over the drab city. A C-46 cleared the icy western peaks, bound for the airbase.

Then, from the southern horizon, a line of black dots appeared…a long mass…as in massive…seemingly without end.

Julia sat up in her seat, squinting in the distance. "Tanks?!" As Jiao tapped his brakes, she was seized with renewed fear. "*Japanese* tanks? The invasion?"

His expression taut and compressed, Paul shifted forward, trying to get a better angle on the sight. He reached for her hand.

Abruptly, Jiao pulled off the road, his face blazing with joy. "*Burma Road!* Open."

Julia's jaw dropped. She turned to Paul, who whipped his head around, sharing this unbelievable moment…as the long-awaited supply trucks from India drew closer, bearing desperately needed goods to sustain the war effort and the Chinese people.

"I'll be goddamned." Paul threw his arm around her and laughed out loud.

"If that isn't the feat to beat all." She wasn't ready to celebrate, though. Her brain was leading her somewhere, and she tried to keep up. "Our source told us to follow the Hump trucks from the airbase. But in a land convoy, goods might 'fall off' *before* reaching the depot."

"Even an entire truck." Paul tapped his nose. "You up for a little undercover work, Jiao?"

Jiao grinned. "What the hell?" Throwing open the door, he jumped out and removed the SACO pennant. Then put his foot on the gas.

———

He circled the city to a hillock south of the airbase and parked. Their position gave them an overview of the rough road, fairly straight with only a few curves, a few clumps of trees.

"Rice balls." He held out a basket. "I make them last night. You must eat."

Their hasty breakfast of congee, composed mostly of rice water and chopped pickles, had not stuck with her. Ravenous, she struggled to consume no more than her share. Paul gave her his.

"Growing up, I was always hungry," she said reflectively. "I didn't care what I ate."

"You had a full belly, though," Jiao commented. "That tastes good."

Julia was ashamed. "You're right. I have nothing to complain about. Your rice balls are delicious, Jiao. Thank you."

"Thank you for coming to help our country."

Her eyes flashed. "China has been standing up to Japan for over ten years. You were fighting WWII before it even began. We owe you a great debt."

He bowed his head. "With true friends, even water drunk together is sweet enough."

"Only when all contribute their firewood can they build a strong fire," Paul said, quoting another Chinese proverb.

As his shoulder softened against hers, the purple dusk fell.

It was early evening when the first muddy canvas-topped trucks appeared. Maybe she and Paul were wrong, she thought, as the Burma Road convoy rolled forward at a steady pace—with no diversions.

He shrugged. "It's detective work. We just keep going."

Then, as the tail finally came into view, a gap opened between the line of vehicles and the last two trucks…which were riding low, as if heavily weighted.

The gap widened until, just before the road bent east at a group of willows, the two trucks cut swiftly west on an unmarked track.

The hills folded around them, and they disappeared.

The three of them exchanged looks. Then Jiao nodded.

Headlights off, he coasted down to the road, now empty. Peering into the unknown, he shifted into second with a grinding of gears that screeched through Julia's being. But ahead, the trucks' growl remained steady. After a long pause, Jiao proceeded at a calm pace.

At the dusty track, he turned up into the foothills following the rumble of the engines, which carried through the high empty plateau.

FIFTY-FIVE

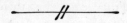

When the engine noises faded, Jiao eased the Dodge truck into a cleft between two jutting boulders. In the hush of a desert evening, they waited another twenty heart-thumping minutes.

Then Paul opened the door, helped Julia out, and placed a rag around the latch before shutting it. They inched along the rock face single file, taking care to avoid the crunch of pebbles or swish of shrubs. If they were discovered, there was no telling what the smugglers would do to protect their illicit enterprise.

After a kilometer or so, maybe almost a mile, they saw several parked vehicles and came to an abrupt stop. Julia squeezed his hand. He squeezed back. *Now what?* They tiptoed forward—then peered into the shadows of an extensive cave complex, illuminated with but a few flickering lanterns.

Although expected, it was a shock to witness the assembly line of well-organized theft—bamboo crates and burlap sacks being unloaded from the trucks, then passed to other men and on to still others who stacked them in the murky interior. The crates had one sound, the sacks another.

In the dim light, it was not possible to make out any stenciled identification marks—was the cargo gold, or arms, or rice? Boots? Batteries? Or all of the above? In the end, though, did it really matter?

Now to survive to report the story. Amid such a vile conspiracy, their lives meant nothing. Paul turned, again leading the way as they slipped back through the darkness in swift silence.

Until a rock burst up at her, and she tried to swallow the "*Ow*" that escaped her lips.

He clapped his palm over her mouth. Too late.

A sharp call echoed from one of the caves. Followed by another. Their calls bouncing off each other, resonating through the clear air.

Surely her own heartbeat would draw their attention. Paul's. He hugged her to him, and they lengthened their breaths, willing their bodies into calm. The echoes pursued them, then gradually faded. The work below resumed its own percussive beat.

Step by laborious step, they made it back to Jiao. And collapsed on the seat. Paul took her clammy hand, fear draining from their bodies.

With a hasty spin of the wheel, Jiao turned north toward Kunming, while she and Paul absorbed the implications of their discovery. Outraged, they debated how to prove the goods had been stolen. And whether or not Services of Supply was involved.

"We need to check Booker's logbooks," she concluded.

"Tomorrow," Paul said. "In the meantime, Jiao, we can't have you driving up Twenty-Four Turn Road tonight. You'll have to bunk in town. So how about we buy you dinner?"

"Okey doke. And I buy *baijiu*."

———

They arrived at SOS the following noon. Booker greeted them from a truck bed, his face dripping with sweat as he and two others ticked off the deliveries.

"We had to see it to believe it," she said. "The Burma Road convoy. Talk about your beneficent Lady Luck."

He grinned modestly. "You'll like this, Julia. The convoy left from our old stomping grounds—Chabua. Eleven days ago. It was slow going, but no injuries or losses."

"They all made it?" she asked guilelessly.

"Every darn one." He wiped his brow. "Say, how about that beer tomorrow?"

Julia faked a smile. "I'm thirsty already."

FIFTY-SIX

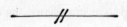

"'Every darn one.'" Her voice quivering with emotion, she repeated Booker's words the next morning to Dick, just in from Chungking. They thought of the Hump pilots who'd risked their lives to deliver the supplies. And the Army drivers risking hairpin turns through treacherous Burmese highlands.

Dick looked from her to Rosie and Paul, his expression a mix of surprise and pleasure. "I'll be damned. The OSS has produced a helluva trio of operatives."

"So we've found the American link," Paul said with a dour look. "What about Booker's Chinese partner?"

"We have to take Julia's findings seriously." Dick rubbed his chin. "Tai Li's radio."

A smile began around Paul's mouth. "The lady is some investigator."

"I know it's still circumstantial…" she began, frustrated.

"Even so, we have the Thieves Market evidence to help soften up the generalissimo," Dick said. "We need him to make an anti-Ichi-Go alliance with either the Reds or Governor Long. Donovan is adept at such discussions. He and the brass are flying in tomorrow to coordinate air defense of Kunming, and contingency plans to blow up Kweiyang's airport, if necessary."

Julia cringed. "It's looking that bad?"

"Between you and me—Army Intelligence advised US embassy staff in Chungking to keep their walking shoes close by. Oh, and Mack says hi."

Her heart gave a little kick, for old time's sake. "What's he up to?"

"He's working on an SOE currency scheme—Operation Remorse." Dick jerked his thumb toward the building in the courtyard's rear. "Self-financing British interests in China, according to Walter Fletcher, that big fellow you've seen around. With the official exchange rate so low, Special Operations Executive is selling pounds on the 'unofficial' market to fund secret ops. I hear they're trying to curry favor with Mao in Yan'an. Just in case."

Julia squinted at him. Although Chiang's financial manipulations were roundly criticized and often subverted, this seemed a peculiar job for the Supremo's aide. After a moment of silence, it clicked in. "So. Mountbatten was Mack's cover for his clandestine work. I—which means, OSS—was his target." She felt Rosie's curious gaze and Paul's loyal one.

"And he was yours," Dick said with a stern look. "Because of your efforts, we closed a major spy ring in SEAC. Remember, things might have been reversed. Mack might have uncovered a leak in Detachment 404. You were both doing your duty." He tapped his desk, his sternness melting. "Then you went on to crack an international smuggling racket. And ferret out a spy in our midst. *Again.*"

Her heart swelled from his praise, then contracted at the image of Lu Mei, so earnest in her pink shirtwaist dress. "Mei was an idealist, like Jane. Many see the Reds as reformers."

"Maybe they are," Rosie said. "After a lifetime of conflict, the Chinese people long only for peace and a full rice bowl."

Julia heard the passion in her voice. "Until the fascist monsters are in the ground, we have to live with our allies. And form stopgap ones when necessary."

"On that note," Dick said. "I'll leave you to prepare for tomorrow."

———

The powers that be assembled in the Map Room around the Kweiyang map, its red pins marking the Ichi-Go threat.

Julia and Paul reported the attack on Miles's Plymouth near SACO/Kweiyang.

Miles, whom Dick had briefed privately in Chungking, looked at Tai Li. "This is not the first assassination attempt against us."

Chiang Kai-shek apologized profusely through his translator and niece, Kung Ai-ling. "In *my* country!" The Generalissimo glowered at Tai Li. "How did you let this happen?"

The security chief bowed his head in shame, making no attempt to defend himself. "The guilty party will be uncovered," Colonel Gong translated.

Julia reported on their black market findings, the US uniforms and canned goods. "Small appliances," she added vaguely, Tai Li's eyes focusing on her all the while.

Chiang Kai-shek apologized again. Staring back at his security chief, he said he was shocked to hear of illegal dealings going on—under the very noses of their American allies.

"I have no doubt General Tai will do his duty," Donovan said. "Colonel Heppner reports the Japanese are positioning their troops to move on Chungking after Kweiyang. There is only one way to stop them. To defend *your* capital, you must make an alliance of necessity."

Chiang Kai-shek exploded as Ai-ling translated in a more moderate tone: "I will not cut a deal with Mao. Or that dirty Yunnan warlord."

Donovan regarded him calmly. "President Roosevelt has pressed me to gain your support for this critical anti-Japanese offense." Everyone knew who was underwriting Chiang's Kuomintang Nationalist Army.

"Nor will I accept Americans telling us what to do in our land," Chiang stated. "*I* am Generalissimo of Free China."

Everyone was steamed. Julia feared the US–Sino alliance might be at risk. But if China fell, a million Nippon troops might pour through Central Asia to support Germany. However, these negotiations were not for her to undertake. She slipped out of the room.

———

In preparation for Donovan's inspection, they were tidying the Registry when the carrottopped Messages clerk, Lewis, raced down from the second floor. Sobbing, he thrust a paper into her hand.

FDR was dead!

Her heart drained through her feet.

Rosie and she fell in each other's arms and wept. They had lost the man who'd led them through the darkest times, whose humor and strength had given them hope. Franklin Delano Roosevelt was irreplaceable. Who would hold them together now? Where could they go from here?

———

A pall hung over the land. It was April, but no one rejoiced that spring. The Chinese shared their sorrow. Posters and banners were hung everywhere, services held at the most remote posts, including Mao's base in Yan'an. FDR's death had left a void that terrified them all. No one even knew the name of his vice president.

In China, white is the color of death. Julia wore her pearls during the ceremony held in their compound, organized by SACO according to American and Chinese traditions. The walls were strung with white streamers, many bearing the president's most famous and popular sayings in both languages. On a side wall, posters listed his achievements. Their united flags were flown at half-mast, and offerings were made to his soul—spirit money, rice, red paper carnations.

The air heavy with incense, the chaplain read in a powerful voice:

> And they shall beat their swords unto plowshares,
> And their spears into pruning-hooks;
> Nations shall not lift up sword against nation,
> Neither shall they learn war any more.

———

Gutted by loss, Julia and Rosie threw themselves into work, handling the flood of condolence messages. Even Pop grudgingly acknowledged how few men could have withstood the pressure of those years. His surprising tip of the hat made Julia proud of her ornery father. She wanted everyone to mourn together.

Given the overwhelming tragedy, both international and personal, she didn't have space inside to think about Booker and his fellow conspirators. It was hard enough opening packets and pouches when almost every one contained tributes and tears.

The Japanese regrouped. According to intel, several of their generals were recalled to Tokyo to discuss a possible new strategy in the absence of strong Western leadership.

Oh yeah? she thought. *We're Americans. We pull together.*

In honor of their late great president, she vowed to resume her black market investigation. They had a war to win. But first, they had to survive the coming battle at Kweiyang.

She had an idea.

FIFTY-SEVEN

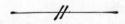

The following Saturday, Julia and Paul drove up West Mountain to Wenquan hot springs, where Governor Long Yun owned a garden hotel near his home base. Their presence would not likely escape the notice of the Yunnan warlord turned elected official, whom Rosie believed to be a reformer with democratic instincts. Perhaps not Chiang Kai-shek's "cup of tea"—but possibly *theirs*.

Paul had agreed with her thinking and booked a two-bedroom cottage screened by bamboo. Inside she noticed a beautiful print of a pair of mandarin ducks, but felt shy pointing it out to him. Prudently, though, she'd packed her silk stockings and garter belt. And a bathing suit. In her outdoorsy life, she'd never been self-conscious before. But now Paul would see how small her breasts really were.

They found a little rocky pool, screened by lush foliage, and immersed their bodies in its clear blue-green waters. Steam swirled around them, like tears. FDR's loss hung heavy and had opened a pathway to grief. Their role in Driver Tung's death still weighed on them, as well, along with Mei's betrayal. During wartime, duty often meant burying one's emotions. In these soothing waters, feelings began to seep free.

Reflections of filmy clouds and lacy white rhododendrons drifted across the pool's surface. "In Washington, my very first mission led to information about a Nazi assassination plot against the president, Churchill, and Stalin in Tehran. My intel saved FDR's life! It seems silly, but after that I felt a special bond with him." She lifted her eyes and stared at the delicate flowers dancing in the breeze. White flowers, the color of death.

Paul regarded her in admiration. "*Silly?* Your heroism helped give him two years—you gave the world two more years of his leadership. Which brought us that much closer to peace."

"You are a good man, Mr. Child." Julia was acutely aware of their palms resting on the granite bench, closely.

"Don't tell anyone. It would spoil my image." He placed his hand on hers. The hot water rippled a moment, then went still.

A long-necked egret perched on the opposite rock, assuming a balletic pose on one leg. *Statuesque*, people sometimes called her, which really meant *big and tall*. But this bird—*she*—was stately...poised and elegant, clothed in the white of clarity and focus. Very alive. The egret seemed to be watching her, inviting Julia to share her pride. She sat up straight.

All her life she had slouched. Finally, in New York, she'd found a man as tall as her, a witty and literary fellow. She thought it was love and spoke the words aloud. He replied only with a kiss—then jilted her. She'd vowed never again to declare herself first. But life changes you.

Paul's gaze was also fixed on the egret—her pure lines, her grace. Julia had learned so much from him. His artist's eye. His mind, so alive and curious. His books and poems and lectures, his belief in her potential. For all his melancholy, he had a big heart, as yearning as hers. His emotion flowed to her, something stirring inside. She felt it, too. Like the bird, she was perched on the edge, waiting to find her moment.

In stillness they sat, bare leg to bare leg. Paul still had a faint tan line from his Kandy shorts. All this skin. She felt transparent.

Julia caught the egret's eye. The bird cocked her head... *What are you waiting for?* Then, as if to lead her onward, she folded her legs and took off like an arrow, a flash of inspiration in the gauzy skies.

"I love you, Paul Child," she whispered, her eyes stinging with tears.

He turned his head, gazing deep into her soul. At least, that was how it felt. *Please don't kiss me and change the subject.*

"What a fortunate coincidence, Julia McWilliams. I love you, too."

He kissed her with a passion and skill that spun from her head memories of every man before him.

As they sat, holding hands in the clear waters, she prepared to apologize about the map.

Paul had other ideas, though. "I have a few more things I want to tell you."

Hand in hand, they returned to their cottage. On the entry table, an envelope was propped against a vase of yellow forsythia. The governor, addressing them as honored guests, had invited them to dinner. In one hour.

With a look that made her woozy, he stepped closer...then murmured, "The first time we make love, we will need much more than an hour."

This was not the moment for confession.

———

In the hotel's private dining room, they enjoyed one-hundred-proof *baijiu* toasts with crunchy spring rolls and tender dumplings. Through his translator, Governor Long Yun paid a tribute to President Roosevelt, declaring FDR had inspired him with a vision of democracy he hoped to bring to the people of Yunnan.

"There will be no democracy," Julia said, emboldened by love and liquor. "Until we defeat the Japanese. We could use your help."

"Tell that to Chiang's Kuomintang forces and Mao's Reds." He stared directly at them during the translation.

"We understand," Paul said. "They are idealogues. But you're a practical man."

"You are right. There is always a way. Often it is merely a matter of details."

"If we come back with agreeable details, would you agree to this alliance?" she dared.

Long Yun laughed and turned to Paul, without waiting for his translator. "Your woman is brave. And direct. Like Yunnan woman."

Paul responded with a wry smile.

Then the warlord-governor turned deadly serious, and his translator's voice trembled. "Yunnan is my province. I know what is going on. I know about the caves where KMT officers—your allies—are hiding your arms. And I know about the caves where others are hiding other things. Including your gold."

While hoping to encounter Long, Julia had not expected this confirmation of all their suspicions. She nudged Paul under the table. With a poker face, he took another sip of rice wine.

Their glasses were refilled, and the dinner service began—several pork, egg, and vegetable dishes, rice, and a platter of wide noodles. "For longevity," their host explained.

A fish steamed in plantain leaves followed, then a whole chicken, surrounded by carved radish roses. "For togetherness and completeness."

"*Ganbei.*" She raised her glass again. "To China. May she know peace."

Always the final dish, the soup was served, gingery, and a little sweet. "Delicious."

"Local specialty," Long Yun said, eyes gleaming. "Hundred-pace viper."

Was he testing them? "I've met a few of those," Julia replied blandly. "Fortunately, I have determination and long legs."

———

Later, as they strolled to their cottage, Paul held her closely to his side. "Oh, you're wearing stockings on those long legs. And garters."

She blushed in the dark. From longing—and shame. Her head was spinning from all those toasts, all that rice wine. All this desire. Suddenly, the egret shone before her, the idea of the bird, but as clear as truth itself. "I didn't lose your Kunming map in the plane crash. I tore it up!"

Paul stopped and turned her toward him with a quizzical look. "Whatever for?"

The shame only grew. "Ai-ling. She's so graceful—and petite. You praised her, profusely, my first day in the Map Room...when I was expecting you to hug me. There I was, tall and graceless. Taking up the whole room, but you still didn't see me." Her words were stumbling over themselves.

As the milky night enclosed them, Paul cocked his head, like the egret had. Then he smiled sadly. "All this time, all we've been through. And you're still worried about Ai-ling."

"I wanted to tell you what I'd done, to be truthful. I was disgusted with these secrets and lies. And I respect you so. I know how hard you work on your maps, how dedicated you are. How much you care! I wanted you to respect me. But I also wanted you to *like* me. I feared putting myself in such a bad light—a violent, hysterical, jealous woman…" Her voice fluttered away.

"My dearest Julia. I do like you, I love you. Remember when we sang 'You Are My Sunshine' driving up to the Buddha caves?" When she nodded, afraid to breathe, he touched her cheek. "*You* are my sunshine, even when I've been your black cloud."

Despite herself, she started to smile, drawing in hope.

"I don't know how you put up with me all this time." Paul frowned. "I do love my work, but it's also an escape into myself—and away from life. You are life. I can always make another map, but I could never find another you." He gripped her hand. "Now, come with me."

Moments after kicking the door shut, Paul planted her on the edge of the bed and began taking off her stockings…one by one. Slowly.

Before he got to her pearls, it began to rain, a rhythmic drumming on the blue tile roof. Soon her heart matched the pounding, as he reached her breastbone with his lips. He didn't seem to mind the size of her breasts and remained there a long time before continuing his slow progression down her body.

When he reached her toes, she pushed him to his back. Every fiber of her being trembling, she kissed the lovely arch of his foot, the hardworking muscles on his calves, the soft skin behind his knees, the faint but precise tan line around his shorts. Her appetite began to grow.

FIFTY-EIGHT

———— // ————

Julia and Paul returned Sunday to their separate abodes. She was relieved to find Betty off with Dick. In the darkness of her room, she relived the weekend, the wonders she had experienced. She knew Paul as a man of competence yet was stunned at his lovemaking skills. She'd seen stars of the outer galaxies. They'd laughed a lot, too. Who knew sex could be so fun! Fortunately, she had always excelled in athletics.

That night, she felt her mother's presence. Her pleased smile. *I promised you the right one would come along. You were wise to be patient.*

Julia ached, missing her. She wished Caro could have known Paul. And he, her. She wished she could attend their wedding. *Julia Child.* It had a ring to it.

But she didn't have a proposal yet. Nor *the* ring.

She understood why Paul was cautious. When he committed, it would be forever. She could almost hear her mother's words: *Perfect husband material.*

———— • ————

Monday afternoon, Dick ordered them to a meeting with Kuomintang Security Chief Tai Li and Commander Miles at 1500.

"Long Yun has offered the Nationalists his support against Japan," Dick told General Tai. "If you do not accept, the twenty oil tankers headed here on the Burma Road will return to India."

Their CO was playing hardball, and even Julia stiffened.

Tai directed his skeptical gaze to Heppner as Gong translated, "What does the Generalissimo have to offer Governor Long?"

"Julia and Paul met with the governor," Dick said. "Julia will convey his request."

She cleared her throat. "Long Yun needs assistance in the form of arms and gold, which he implies are hidden in caves south of town."

"To make such a claim—does he say who is responsible?" Tai Li sat stock still.

"He left that to us." Julia felt all eyes burning into her. "We know the black market exists all over China. But in Kunming, there is an active trade in essential military supplies. Including secure transceivers urgently needed by SACO units in the field." She looked to Miles.

"And?" Miles was almost shaking with fury.

She was shaking for another reason. "I've seen at least one of these radios in town. Two others remain missing." Julia hesitated. Tai Li was key to a political-military relationship central to the final march on Japan. The end of World War II. She stared, dry mouthed, at the general...

Then Tai Li spoke. But Translator Gong appeared to be struck dumb as Tai Li unleashed a storm of words at him.

Regarding the floor, Gong finally uttered his translation, "Are you referring to the RCA Victor radio in my basement? My gift from Colonel Gong?"

"Yes, sir," Julia replied, trying not to look at Paul.

Very big, the black market vendor had told them. Not Tai Li, but one near to him, sheltered by his trust.

"On receiving this 'gift,' I commenced my own investigation," Tai Li said through Gong's feeble voice. "My translator's primary conspirator was an army sergeant in your Services of Supply." All-seeing, indeed, his dark eyes bored into Gong's bowed head.

"Who?" Dick demanded.

"American Sergeant Sam Booker," Gong said without prodding.

"General Tai," Miles said. "You are my trusted friend. I cannot think ill of you. Why did you wait so long to report this?" He turned to Paul. "Bring Kung Ai-ling to translate. Now."

Once Ai-ling appeared, the story flowed. Gong and Tai Li had begun together in police school. Tai Li had needed certainty before confronting his old friend.

"It was Booker's idea," Gong protested, claiming his American mahjongg partner had enticed him with gifts to help smooth the way. "What man would betray the land of his birth?"

Tai Li spoke coldly through Ai-ling. "Then my old friend, you will be proud of your next assignment. You will lead a secret mission to mine the Japanese-held railway line from Hengyang to Kweiyang."

Gong saluted and left.

"What will happen to him?" Julia asked.

"He will be a hero in his death. American justice is more lenient that Chinese. But if Booker were under my command, I'd send him there, too." For an instant, Tai Li looked shattered. "I am a patriot, dedicated to our great land, and it is my honor to never consume alcohol to excess. But on this occasion, I must break my rule. And ask you, my friends, to join me tonight in this sorry undertaking."

———

They had bad hangovers the next day. The following morning, Julia and Paul drove to the airfield, pulling off the access road directly opposite the Services of Supply depot. "Donovan warned me the China theater was riddled with spies," she said, as they watched three trucks being loaded. She still wondered whether Gong had been a double agent. Protected in Tai Li's home, had he used the radio to report—to whom? The Reds? The Japanese? Tai Li's gangster friend in Shanghai? Or had he received reports of over-the-Hump shipments from accomplices in India?

"And all the while, we had our own spy, Lu Mei," Paul said. "Protected in our own home, you might say."

"And Donovan vetted her! I wonder if Chiang or Tai Li used that against him."

"You use what you've got. Especially after their loss of face over Gong." Paul pointed toward SOS.

The trucks turned around, then rumbled forward in tight formation, bearing arms and gold to Long Yun, whose many loyalists would now ally with Chiang's KMT troops in the defense of Kweiyang.

After all, the Fort-Knox-via-Bombay gold had been allocated for payoffs. But it could just as well be seen as a budget line item for defense.

It was money well spent.

Massed outside Kweiyang, the combined force was joined at the last moment by seasoned Communist fighters. In a decisive battle, they stopped the Japanese Imperial Army's advance and, over the next few weeks, would boot the enemy back to the coast.

———

Julia and Paul caught up with Betty and Dick over cocktails at the Servicemen's Club, faded colonial yellow mixed with raucous red, white, and blue. To wall-to-wall grins and tapping toes, Armed Forces Radio served up "GI Jive," by Louis Jordan, King of the Jukebox. Their Hump pilot Lim raised a glass across the room. But never would she share a beer with the perfidious Booker, who had been court-martialed with a sentence of thirty to life at Leavenworth.

"I won a big wager thanks to you two." Betty smiled devilishly.

"What kind?" Julia demanded.

Paul interlaced his fingers through hers. "From whom?"

"Dick thought you might be a confirmed bachelor. But I knew better. Back in Kandy, I saw you cutting Julia's birthday cake. Even while she was dancing with one man—and telling off another. I said to myself, there's a man who is meant to stand by her side. Through thick or thin. So I bet heavily."

Julia was furious. "*Betty.*"

Paul stroked the inside of her wrist. "How much did you win?"

"Not enough to retire on." She winked.

"What about you both?" Paul asked.

Dick cleared his throat. "We have some legalities to deal with."

Betty and Alex had already split, but Julia felt a pang for Dick's wife back home.

"People grow apart during war. And together." Paul cast his gaze her way. "In Washington, my brother dragged me to an astrologer. She predicted a new opportunity would arise, something that would involve a secret mission and lengthy journey to the Far East." He broke into a boyish grin. "It would alter the entire course of my life."

"Paul," she exclaimed. "*You?* Mr. Logical. Didn't you pooh-pooh it?"

"Of course. But soon after, Donovan suggested me for Visual Display with Mountbatten in India. The next day, I revisited the astrologer. She assured me I'd get the job, that it would be a time of adventure and excitement. Despite all obstacles, I would do well in the secret work, make great friends—and 'fall heavily in love in about a year.'"

Betty's eyes popped. "What else?"

"She'd be 'intelligent, dramatic, beautiful—a modern woman.'"

Julia didn't dare ask whom he might have considered before her. Betty was not so reticent. "When did you know Julia was 'The One'?"

Paul considered the question, then turned to her with that calm, detached look. "To be honest, you weren't my type."

She went cold, couldn't breathe.

He gripped her hand, so she couldn't pull away. "Yet whenever I was low, you were there with your high spirits and good heart. You brought me real comfort. Then things changed. To know you is to love you, Julie." Rays of light shone from his eyes.

"You weren't my type, either," she retorted, still in a turmoil of feelings. "I didn't like the way you set yourself apart, so closed and superior. Now I understand it's your protection. But there would have been no 'secret work' without comfortable old me," she said aloofly.

Paul laughed. "You mean daring, undaunted old you."

"You might say I gave you a break."

He flung his arm around her. "You might say I got lucky."

"You might say you both did," Dick said with authority. "And I'd like some credit for matching you on your first joint mission."

Julia saluted him, then looked into each of their dear faces, ending on Paul's...the dearest of all, the man of her life.

"'Of all the gin joints in all the towns in all the world,'" he said. "You walked into mine."

"I *knew* he was Humphrey Bogart." Betty beamed. "Maybe now, someone will take my prognostications seriously." She paused for dramatic effect. "I've heard about a local fortune teller with quite a following. After I meet him, I plan to book the seer for a radio broadcast foretelling a great disaster for Japan."

FIFTY-NINE

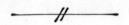

The following week was VE Day. May 8. Victory in Europe. Celebrants swarmed the Champs-Elysées, Trafalgar Square, Times Square, and possibly even Red Square, if Stalin allowed it. Certainly every Main Street in America was going mad with joy.

But the Forgotten War in Asia was still being fought. Under the pitiless oppressors, the peoples of Hong Kong, Singapore, and Shanghai were barely hanging on, while thousands of men and women were held captive in deplorable conditions.

With the Burma Road reopened, Free China was awash in supplies, even if some were still being stockpiled or smuggled to the Reds. Julia only hoped a large portion of rice was getting to the peasants. Leaving a few handfuls to shower on Rosie and Thibaut.

The ginkgo in the courtyard had unfurled its fan-shaped leaves. According to Chinese belief, this ancient tree was the symbol of hope and peace.

But they weren't there yet. The brutal war continued to grind on.

———

In late July, Kunming was hit by the worst flooding in twenty-five years. They traversed the courtyard lake in life rafts. Mosquitoes were rampant. And rats, showing promiscuous appetite. A week later, Donovan arrived. He was on edge, as if tuned to another frequency.

As Julia and Rosie were bailing out the Registry one morning, Lewis burst in with a moist decrypt from Messages. "We attacked Hiroshima," he said. "An atomic bomb."

"I'll get it to the CO." They'd been conducting heavy bombing on Japan since last year. With no urgency, she gathered the latest dispatches and took them to Dick, who was huddled with Donovan.

"What's an atomic bomb?" she asked.

Donovan gave her the coldest look she'd ever received. "The ultimate weapon."

His tone made Julia shiver. Somehow she knew today, August 6, 1945, was a historic date.

"We beat the Germans to it by a hair of history. Following long research at the Manhattan Project—assisted by Dr. Niels Bohr." His raised eyebrow reminded her of her role in the Danish physicist's escape to Sweden.

"Oh my," was all she could say. She still didn't understand, not really. Not yet.

By pure coincidence, the Hiroshima attack took place the day after Betty's "seer" had made his radio pronouncement. Their glee was tempered as more details trickled in the following day. Five square miles of the city had been destroyed by "Little Boy." This was a different order of bomb. Still the Japanese leadership refused to surrender.

Following Donovan's departure for Chungking, the second bomb, "Fat Boy," was dropped over Nagasaki on August 9. The first had been made of uranium, the second, even more devastating, was plutonium. The development of these new bombs had taken place in top secret while American forces were preparing for their amphibious invasion of the Chinese mainland.

The next day, they gathered around an Armed Forces Radio broadcast of President Truman's speech. "The atomic bomb...is the harnessing of the basic power of the universe, the force from which the sun draws its power."

Dick said it had saved tens of thousands, maybe a hundred thousand or more American lives confronting a fight-to-the-death foe on home territory. Hundreds of thousands of Japanese were killed and injured

from the US attack. The people of Japan had paid a horrific price for
their leaders' hubris.

Julia could not rejoice. Heartsick at the desolation, she thought of
the Japanese soldier who had spared her life, only to lose his own. She
also thought of their vile POW camps. Paul's words remained truer than
ever: *This war is an ugly beast.*

———

Out of superstition, their group ate long-life noodles almost every
evening. Jack and Ai-ling—who'd become an item!—had mapped out
Kunming's best restaurants, and they aimed to complete the circuit. Life
felt like it had last Christmas in Kandy, the slow winding down, only
this would be the *real* end. Full stop.

One evening, just the two of them, Julia and Paul went to a tea-
room at the great Lake Dianchi, south of town. From a private screened
pavilion, they viewed the poetic scene, the full moon shimmering over
lotuses and water lilies, the timeless peace. After they ordered, she hand-
fed him a ball of rice dipped in sweet and spicy sauce—not curry, as
she'd imagined on the Bay of Bengal, but close enough. Close enough
to bless the shoulders that had carried her to that moment.

He licked her fingers clean, then asked for seconds. That tongue.
Tingling with sensation, she rolled another rice ball. "In Chinese, *How
are you?* really means, *Have you eaten?* Hunger is a terrible thing." She
dipped the rice again and placed it in his mouth, watching him savor it.

Paul rested his strong hand on her thigh. "My hunger has been
satisfied."

Closing her eyes, Julia covered his hand with hers, awash in memories. Theirs and *hers*. "Some of the people who fed me are gone now.
They taught me food is life. In their honor, I want to grab hold of this
life I was given and taste it all."

"I almost gave up on mine, before…Now it feels full. But I'm also
raring to go."

Go where? "I'll be sorry to leave…" She gestured at the vast lake,
water as far as the eye could see, shining with light, as it had under every

full moon throughout the ages. "I couldn't think of a better person to have experienced this with. All the wonders you've shown me."

"You've done your share—partner. That very *hot* hot springs." He swallowed.

"I admit it, Paul, I choreographed your seduction. How long does a girl have to wait for a guy to make a pass?"

"I probably could have moved a little quicker." He smiled. "Although I must say your patience impressed me, Julie, while I mourned one woman and flirted with others."

"I play a long game, Paul Child."

As he turned to her, a silvery ray of moonlight touched his face. "You have given me your true friendship, Julia McWilliams."

"You've given me the world."

"Soon you will be going back into it."

She didn't like the way he said *you*. Not *we*. They loved each other. Here. Now. But what about *there*? "And you?"

"After we're done in Kunming, the State Department—"

She kissed him on the mouth to silence his words. As to the future, she'd think about it tomorrow.

———

On August 15, 1945, Emperor Hirohito surrendered.

It was her thirty-third birthday! Paul joined them at their hillside compound that evening and presented her a handwritten sonnet that began:

> *How like autumn's warmth is Julia's face,*
> *So filled with nature's bounty, nature's worth,*
> *And how like summer's heat is her embrace*
> *Wherein, at last, she melts my frozen earth...*

His words washed over her, and she wanted to soar. "That's the most beautiful gift I've ever received, Paul. I—I just want to be worthy of you." Seeing his gentle shake of the head, she pressed on. "So I have one more confession." She cleared her throat. "I haven't read your van Gogh book yet. I've been so busy…And I'm sorry, because I've always wanted to be a creative person."

"You *are* a creative person, Julie. And of course you've been busy. We've been fighting this war. Now it's over."

A turmoil of emotions overtook her. Was all this a prelude to goodbye?

As if he were reading her thoughts, he smiled. "And now, toots, the next chapter begins."

"Oh, Paul. I will read that book. I promise!"

"'You have first to experience what you want to express,' van Gogh wrote. Remember what you said about tasting life. You will find your art."

As they stood on the balcony, her heart burst open like a flower. Like the necklaces of firecrackers arcing up into the dazzling skies and down to their plum-laden trees. After almost fifteen years, China was free of Japan.

He touched her collarbone. "Your pearls. They look pink."

Her pearls. Her mother's pearls. She had worried that humidity might be harmful, but by several months into Kandy they'd taken on a new glow that only increased in Kunming. As the fireworks fell around them, radiant with joy, Julia felt her blessings.

Then all her feelings concentrated on a single point at the base of her throat…her pulse, Paul's warm fingers. He pressed his lips there, traveling slowly around her neck. Her knees weakened. He took her hand, led her inside her room, and locked the door. The explosions continued through the night.

———

They were soon given notice to clear their offices.

In Jakarta, Jane was already agitating for freedom. Thibaut had one last mission, to meet OSS asset Ho Chi Minh in Indochina. Then he would join Rosie, Betty, and Dick in Peking, where Paul's maps were guiding POW efforts to rescue her parents. Trixie had found Roy and credited their bronze monkey god Hanuman, who would be accompanying them to Texas for the wedding. General William Donovan joined the prosecution team for the International Military Tribunal at Nuremberg.

Julia was left to close down the Registry, filling boxes upon boxes of classified documents that would be stored away as artifacts of the war to end all wars.

One night, she and Paul enjoyed hand-pulled noodles at the lakeside hole-in-the-wall. "That's its own miracle, isn't it?" she said watching the plump-cheeked chef toss his dough with such flair. "To take flour and water and create some kind of magic."

"There's all kind of creative work in this world, Julie."

They dallied over soup, the final dish of one of their final meals. She dipped her spoon through the swirling egg flowers, watched the broth settle, then dipped it again, wanting to make the moment last forever. The hell that had been World War II had brought love into their lives. But it would never be the same between them. Anything could still happen.

"I seem to recall an invitation to go home over the Burma Road," Paul said, pouring her some hot tea. "I've found a jeep returning empty."

Oh my. The steam rose between them. "That's a long drive."

"I've mapped it."

"I wouldn't mind getting lost with you, Paul." Her toes curled just thinking about it. "Not that I doubt your maps."

"I've located a few hot springs en route. Worth a detour." He smiled mysteriously. "No rush. We have all the time in the world."

"Well, then." She tipped her cup to his. "Let's seize the day."

AUTHOR'S NOTE

I didn't fall in love with Julia Child for her cooking; I fell in love with her spirit and commitment, her hunger for experience. I understood her dreams—become a writer, live in distant lands, hold out for the right mate. I was intrigued by her World War II work in the clandestine services, especially in Asia, a region that shaped us both. There were other connections. I also grew up with Nancy Drew, have a fondness for spy novels, and spent formative years in France.

The Secret War of Julia Child is a work of fiction, an homage to a woman who, like so many of us, struggled to find her own path in life. World War II opened many doors to women, and the strong-willed Julia McWilliams saw her chance. General William Donovan, founder of the Office of Strategic Services, recognized and rewarded her can-do nature, putting her in charge of his top-secret file Registry in Washington, then Southeast Asia. Some of the well-documented political struggles between the American and British allies play a backstory to this narrative. Throughout, I followed the historical record as closely as possible, anchoring Julia's story within the global one.

But there are gaps in history, particularly in the realm of espionage, where so much information is classified. I needed to fill in the spaces, the day-to-day events and emotions that have slipped into the mists of time. I needed to walk in Julia's shoes over terrain that has changed, even disappeared. The Sri Lankan botanist Dushyantha Large and I tromped around Kandy's Royal Botanic Gardens trying to find the exact site of South East Asia Command but, in the end, could only approximate it.

Likewise, we searched vainly for the OSS base in the hills outside town. So it was an absolute joy to stay at Queen's Hotel, which has remained marvelously unchanged!

If you asked me did Julia really read intel about the Nazi death camps, I would say almost definitely. Did she transmit money to the Danish Resistance? I'd say I don't know—but, given her position and proximity to General Donovan, she *could* have. Did she help coordinate the document flow between OSS Detachment 404 and SEAC in Kandy? I'd say yes. Did Donovan ask her to keep her ears open in Mountbatten's HQ? I'd say I don't know—but her boss, a prodigious collector of intel, certainly *could* have. Was she in Bombay during the horrific *SS Stikine* explosion? Yes, but her ship had, in fact, docked five days earlier, and while over one hundred gold bars were flung far and wide by the blast, she escaped injury. Did her plane crash in China? No, but her flight was rocky and hazardous, and too many other Hump planes did go down. Did she tear up Paul's Kunming map in a fit of jealousy? There is no record of it. But amid the tensions and high emotions of war, it might have happened.

During her Asian posting, Julia fell deeply in love with Paul Child, a brilliant, sophisticated man who came to appreciate what he had in her. Besides being a skilled artist, he was a gourmet and a gourmand, and she eagerly joined his explorations of Chinese cuisine, which always remained close to their hearts. Her awakening to the senses must have begun before him, though, in her first encounters with Asia—and all those flavors!

The world opened up to Julia in every way during her time in the OSS. Possessing a very high-security clearance, she had an insider's knowledge of intelligence and sabotage operations around the globe. She also had the determination and sense of adventure to want to do more. To the end of her days, Julia insisted she had only been a file clerk during the war. "She was not a spy, as she would later winkingly insinuate," wrote Alex Prud'homme, Julia's cowriter for *My Life in France*. Or perhaps she was honoring an OSS contract, vowing "to keep forever secret this employment…" In any case, she was an integral part of OSS intrigue.

To deepen my understanding of this era, I immersed myself in hundreds of memoirs and nonfiction accounts of the lives and times of my characters, as well as every relevant novel I could find. A few secondary characters are fictional blends of real ones who could not find their way into this story. Some are entirely fictional, including Jemadar Deepak Binoy, as I wanted to give voice to the vast numbers of heroic Asian participants in World War II. My depiction of his experience in a Japanese POW camp was inspired by Richard Flanagan's powerful work, *The Narrow Road to the Deep North*. I particularly studied the political and military histories of the lands in which Julia served, the battlegrounds of the "Forgotten War" in Asia. I sought, above all, to find her truth, to portray her struggles, achievements, and strength of character in navigating an unknown, often dangerous landscape. To do so required a merging of fact and imagination.

My foundational research was Julia's lively memoir, *My Life in France*, cowritten with Alex Prud'homme, her two remarkable biographies, *Dearie* by Bob Spitz and *Appetite for Life* by Noël Riley Fitch, as well as historian Jennet Conant's fabulous *A Covert Affair*. Two memoirs, *Undercover Girl* by Betty MacDonald and *An Unamerican Lady* by Jane Foster were invaluable. After Dick Heppner's death, Betty wrote *Sisterhood of Spies: Women of the OSS* under her (re)married name, Elizabeth P. McIntosh. I also read *Saints, Sinners, and Scalawags*, Thibaut de Saint Phalle's memoir, and *The Lives of Dillon Ripley* by Roger D. Stone. Prud'homme, Paul Child's great-nephew, and Katie Pratt collected Paul's superb photographs for *France Is a Feast*, which recounts his visit to the Washington astrologer.

My characterizations of General William Donovan and Lord Louis Mountbatten were based closely on documented history. My main references were *Wild Bill Donovan* by Douglas Waller and *Mountbatten, A Biography* by Philip Ziegler. My view of the British leader was also deeply informed by Alex von Tunzelmann's *Indian Summer*.

Through these studies, I gained a new understanding of India and China's unacknowledged contributions to World War II. And a deeper grasp of colonialism. Primary influences were *Forgotten Ally* by

Rana Mitter, *The Raj at War* by Yasmin Khan, and *Forgotten Armies* by Christopher Bayly and Tim Harper. I greatly enjoyed *Two Kinds of Time*, a classic China memoir by Graham Peck, and *The Burma Road* by Donovan Webster.

On the subject of the unusual partnership between Milton Miles and Chiang Kai-shek's security chief, Tai Li, I was fascinated by *A Different Kind of War* by Vice-Admiral Miles, USN, *The Rice Paddy Navy* by Linda Kush, and *SACO, The Rice Paddy Navy* by Roy Stratton. This is an extraordinary piece of American history that deserves to be better known. While historians generally view Chiang's security chief as a very dark figure, I was writing a story about these characters in real time when geopolitical forces necessitated that hard choices be made.

Espionage and political intrigue have been a backdrop in my novels, so it was with interest that I studied the development of OSS and its contemporary spy organizations, focusing on intelligence, propaganda, agent activities, and sabotage ops. Primary sources were *OSS, The Secret History of America's First Central Intelligence Agency* by R. Harris Smith, *The Shadow Warriors* by Bradley F. Smith, *Intelligence and the War Against Japan* by Richard J. Aldrich, *OSS in China* by Maochun Yu, and *The Secret War* by Max Hastings. Leo Marks's *Between Silk and Cyanide* offered a witty and moving peek inside British cryptography and espionage. I "borrowed" cryptologist Herbert Yardley's Chungking mystery, *Crows Are Black Everywhere*, for the China codebook of Julia and Donovan. Their Ceylon codebook was *The Razor's Edge* by author-spy Somerset Maugham.

India is close to my heart. I studied her art history at university, began an export business in Delhi, and have visited often over the years, enjoying her endless marvels and warm, hospitable people. I was honored to see my novel, *The Star of India*, first published there. My husband and I journeyed long ago to Burma when one could move under the radar; how these good people have suffered. The historical Ceylon, now Sri Lanka, is a major setting for the novel, so my daughter and I roamed all over Kandy, getting a feel for the way it was. We explored the island widely, sharing Julia's emotions of wonder seeing the Dambulla

Buddha, the ruins of Polonnaruwa, the great elephant families roaming freely over wide tracts of land. China has been very important in our lives; we've traveled there several times, including twice to Chongqing, where SACO was headquartered, Kunming, and throughout Yunnan Province. As in Kandy, Kunming's modernization has paved over much of the past, so how lucky we were to be shown the traditional town by landscape designer and Asian scholar Timothy Haskins.

After the Chinese Revolution, the spelling of place names was modernized into Mandarin-based pinyin. In this book I used the Romanized versions current in my period, e.g., Chungking instead of Chongqing.

Maps came to figure strongly in my novel. From the beginning, Julia was searching for the map to her future. Along the way, she tested herself, accepting her challenges, learning what she could really do. As she would say in later years, the war made her. It also brought her the man of her life, OSS mapmaker Paul Child.

———

The Secret War of Julia Child is an homage to Julia McWilliams Child, her great spirit and achievements. I must emphasize that it is a work of fiction, a product of creative imagination, based on ten years of deep and wide-ranging research, as well as a lifetime of Asian study and travel. From this treasure trove, I extracted many thought-provoking hints, allusions, and suggestions—like thousands of puzzle pieces—that came to shape my depiction of this formative, yet little-known period of Julia's life, during which she performed her World War II duty in the clandestine services. Nonetheless, I offer my story as one that exists only in the realm of possibility, a personal interpretation inspired by admiration and respect. I hope all my readers will see it that way.

READING GROUP GUIDE

1. We've all heard of Julia Child, the renowned cookbook author and star of *The French Chef*. Did you know she had a past connection to WWII? Does knowing her past change how you think of her now?

2. Julia often makes difficult decisions she believes are for the right reasons, even if she disobeys orders in the process. When is it right to break previously set laws or rules? How do you know when a line should be crossed? Is it different during wartime?

3. The novel talks about both "white" and "black" propaganda, where "white" propaganda is positive toward your side and "black" is negative toward the enemy. Which would you find more effective? Do you think "white" and "black" propaganda are in use today?

4. Julia and her comrades travel to India, living for four weeks on a cramped troop ship under constant threat of enemy attack and, after experiencing an explosion in Bombay Harbor, journeying another week on a dusty train across a vast land mobilizing for war. And then a ferry to an unknown tropical island and a "toy" train up into the rainforest and a mysterious intelligence base. Imagine you were a person who had never flown on an airplane, traveled outside the country, or even, perhaps, your home state. Would you be able to endure such conditions? What kinds of emotional and psychological issues might arise?

5. Consider the differences in travel time between now and the forties. Think about Julia's long sea and land passage compared with that of her boss, General Donovan, who "puddlehops" between the European and Asian fronts on Pan Am Boeing Clippers (on which the first female mechanics were hired to work!). Even with the latest technology, these military seaplanes took about two days to fly from the US East Coast to Lisbon and another two to three more to India and China—with several ports of call en route. How much easier is it for someone to get halfway across the world now? Is there anything we've lost along the way? Have you ever had a harrowing travel experience? Was the trip worth it?

6. Julia thinks about fate, about how she never expected to be where she is, but since she's here now, she's going to keep going. Did you expect to be where you are currently in life, or did you have a more unexpected path? How difficult is it to embrace whatever is thrown at you? Are there times when you should fight back? How do you know?

7. Paul Child and Julia do not get along for the first part of their relationship. How many real-life enemies-to-lovers situations have you known? How important are first (or second) impressions? Have you misjudged people who turned out to be true-blue? Or have you trusted someone who turned out to be trouble?

8. As a woman in the military, Julia is constantly underestimated and demeaned. Have we progressed from Julia's time period? Where might we still improve as a society?

9. While stationed in Kandy, Ceylon, Julia gets dengue fever. Have you ever become ill while traveling? How bad was it? What steps can we take now to try to prevent travel illnesses? How can we have an authentic local experience and still remain careful?

10. During her military service, Julia is forced to suspect even close friends of being spies for the enemy. What would it be like to live in an environment where it is difficult to trust anyone? Where you had to keep deadly important secrets to yourself, lest people die? How would that isolation feel?

11. Julia fully embraces the cultures of India, Ceylon, Burma, and China, enjoying the ambience and the people. How did an open mind enrich her experiences? She had been a meat-and-potatoes girl before her Asian posting. How do you think these new foods and flavors she tastes influenced the rest of her life?

12. How much did you know about WWII in Asia before reading this book? Were you more familiar with the European part of the war, or were you already aware of American involvement in India and China?

13. Julia's late mother, Caro, appears frequently in Julia's thoughts as a source of comfort and encouragement. Do you, or did you, have someone like Caro in your life?

A CONVERSATION WITH THE AUTHOR

Why did you want to write about this part of Julia Child's life when so many people tend to focus on her career as a chef?

It was the idea of this woman whom everyone knows having had an unknown, secret, and surprising life before she came into ours. A light bulb flooded my brain when I learned about her World War II service with America's first intelligence agency—in Asia. I tingled with curiosity about the intrepid young Julia McWilliams who had been so determined to achieve something of worth—and was now, in this critical period of world history, given the opportunity. Rising to head the OSS Registry of secret files in Washington, DC, she yearned for greater challenges in the field. The more I got to know this Julia, the more I was captivated by her enthusiasm and can-do spirit, her appetite for experience. I admired her fortitude and work ethic. I identified with her struggle to find her path in life as I know many of us will. And she was such fun! I adored her. Only recently did I realize that I, too, had first gone to Asia at around age thirty. I, too, had been shaped by my time there, which must have been one reason I felt so connected with her. That, and our mutual "French connection." I knew this was a book I had to write.

Was it difficult to capture Julia's voice? How did you go about doing so?

I immersed myself in everything I could find about her early years, the eldest child in an affluent Pasadena family. Right away, I discovered her spirit of adventure, her energy, and bubbling personality. This was a girl you wanted as your friend! Julia McWilliams was a born leader, outdoorsy, an all-round athlete. And a natural performer, who, from a young age, was creating elaborate theatrical extravaganzas in her home attic. Despite her confidence, she nonetheless suffered from being so tall, never the petite, romantic lead, always the buccaneer; never the girlfriend, always the pal. Along with her height, she'd inherited her fluttery, unpredictable voice from her beloved mother, who promised Julia her time would come; until then, she should relish her freedom and spread her wings at Smith College. I began walking in Julia's shoes, understanding her insecurities yet innate self-belief, her desire to be a "famous woman writer." I sympathized when she drifted through her twenties yet refused to make a safe, socially desirable marriage. She was gutsy.

I read about Paul Child and his complex upbringing. The loss of an eye at age seven, the twin brother who got all the breaks. His refusal to play the victim. A creative being like Julia, he was an artist in many fields, a sailor and teacher, a man of brilliance, at home in Paris. A man who had lost the love of his life.

I learned everything I could about Julia's world, the Office of Strategic Services, her mentor, General "Wild Bill" Donovan. Like her boss, her adventurous friends became their own characters. The Second World War…I needed to set this personal story inside the greater one. Even as I was writing the first drafts, I continued researching…until, finally, I came to have a deep sense of the truth of my narrative. Julia's narrative.

Why did you choose to start the novel in 1943? Why not start at the beginning of Julia's life or at the beginning of WWII?

Julia turned thirty in Washington, with some real-life experience under her belt, both success and failure. At Smith, she played basketball and put on more plays, ever the golden girl. Then came Manhattan, where she did not get a coveted position at *The New Yorker*, nor any of the other prestigious publications she aspired to. Her first job was in advertising, a supposedly creative field that didn't feel creative at all. She fell in love…but was jilted when the guy married his high school sweetheart. Julia returned home to the devastating loss of her mother, then drifted some more…Until, galvanized by Pearl Harbor, she made haste for Washington. This was where she came alive and found her purpose. About nine months later, she has already risen far and fast, gaining the trust of her powerful boss, General William "Wild Bill" Donovan. The story begins with her dramatic decision to follow her duty and possibly risk it all.

How did you go about crafting Julia and Paul's relationship? What sources did you look to for their possible interactions?

Once I came to know each of them deeply, their characters dictated how they would react to the other. In her two amazing biographies, I discovered, in Julia's own words, her antipathy for Paul Child. He was too short, middle-aged, balding, pretentious. Paul dismissed her as not his type, frothy, unsophisticated. Working together, they became grudging friends. I gained more personal insights from Paul's great-nephew who wrote about them both with sensitivity and strong family ties.

How important is it to know Julia's story? What do you want readers to take away from the novel?

Julia Child was a very smart, focused, and competent woman who loved, equally I think, enjoying life and working hard. Her first cookbook had been a huge labor of love. After its (unexpected) success, she sought another outlet for her great energy. Then, just as in WWII, she found a door and walked through it. Julia created *The French Chef*, an effervescent character who made the difficult simple for people…and they took her into their hearts.

After doing so much research into Julia's backstory, do you think you have a better understanding of how and why she became the famous chef everyone knows her to be? How much do you think her dealings in WWII influenced her decisions later in life?

During the long gestation of *The Secret War of Julia Child*, I came to see how formative World War II was for her: the Asian front lines were where she was tested and came to discover her true capabilities and strengths. She had been forged in the fire of war. A survivor and force of nature, Julia McWilliams Child was a creative woman whom I came to love, admire, and deeply respect during my research. All of the inner resources she had developed to serve in and survive that devastating period were waiting to be called upon. Then, with Paul, a feminist before his time, her partner in everything, she stepped onto center stage and became *The French Chef.*

CREDITS

Epigraph text and maps in this work are used by permission and courtesy of the following:

The National Archives for the extensive research that produced the *China-Burma-India Theater* map by an unknown artist, possibly a colleague of Paul Child.

The Office of Air Force History for help in sourcing the *South Asia Theater* map by Fanita Lanier, from *The Army Air Forces in World War II, Volume One*, published in 1983 by the US Printing Office.

Fresh Air with Terry Gross, produced by WHYY in Philadelphia and distributed by NPR, for the extract of Julia Child's interview, broadcast in 1989.

Author Judith L. Pearson for the OSS Special Operations Contract extract I quoted from *The Wolves at the Door*.

Author Lena Andrews for the Katherine Keene epigraph, which she shared from her research for *VALIANT WOMEN, The Extraordinary American Servicewomen Who Helped Win World War II*.

ACKNOWLEDGMENTS

My husband, Everett Chambers, has been at my side since the beginning of my writing life, since the first travel article, the first script...the first novel. His contributions to my work have been profound, and he's never wavered in his support. My gratitude is beyond words.

I am so thankful for Julia McWilliams Child, her courageous life, and the glorious story she gave me. I am but one of the countless people she inspired.

Heartfelt thanks to my agent, Pamela Malpas of Jennifer Lyons Literary, for her staunch belief in this novel. And to Shana Drehs, my wise editor at Sourcebooks Landmark, for seeing its potential and helping me refine it. Her team is the tops! The production and design of a book requires many people, their dedicated effort and patient eyes. I am simply over the moon with the work of Jessica Thelander, Laura Boren, Steph Gafron, Stephanie Rocha, and Erin Fitzsimmons. Also copy editor Rachel Norfleet. Special appreciation to Jeff Miller and Faceout Studio for the stunning cover. Thanks to Cristina Arreola, Anna Venckus, Valerie Pierce, BrocheAroe Fabian, and Monica Palenzuela for their creativity in getting this novel out into the world. And, likewise, to the dynamic sales team, Paula Amendolara, Margaret Coffee, Sean Murray, and Tracy Nelson.

I am so grateful to the brilliant author and inspirational teacher, Nina Schuyler, for her guidance, to Robin Fisher, Amy Holman, Elle Napolitano, John Philipp, and especially Nancy Tingley for inviting me into the Tuesday writing group, during which I wrote many of the best passages of the novel.

Thanks to Heather Lazare for her firm editorial presence when this story was newly born. To John Payne for his sense of structure and pacing. To Carrie Feron for discovering the perfect opening line. To my first book agent, Elizabeth Evans, for believing in me. To my former theatrical agent, Kshitij Kokas, and literary agent, Mita Kapur. Everlasting thanks to my Penguin India editor, Ambar Chatterjee.

I am indebted to my writers' community for giving me a home. It's been a long road, and I am indebted to two authors whom I respect enormously and whose staunch support made all the difference: Kim Faye has been a shining light who buoyed me and carried me forward. Sujata Massey has been a fairy godmother whose generosity I can never forget. I'm so grateful to Susan MacNeal for her insightful critique of my manuscript at an important moment. And the inimitable Rhys Bowen gave me confidence that this was a story people would want to read.

Deep thanks to authors Terry Shames and Susan Shea for mentoring me while I served on the board of Sisters in Crime/NorCal and ultimately became our chapter's president. Sisters in Crime and Mystery Writers of America opened an exciting world to me, including the annual Bouchercon and Left Coast Crime conferences, where I've made lifelong friends.

Thank you to the gifted Lena Andrews for providing my third epigraph, which she generously shared from her research on *Valiant Women: The Extraordinary American Servicewomen Who Helped Win World War II*. I was determined to have some period maps in the book and through my search gained a true appreciation for the US National Archives and especially archivist Jared Chamberlin for his kind assistance in locating a special *China-Burma-India Theater* map. Thanks to the Air Force History Museum and Melissa Lahue for helping source my favorite *South Asia Theater* map by the talented artist Fanita Lanier, who designed *The Army Air Forces History in World War II* seven-volume series. She is one of the countless (mostly unsung) women who, like Julia, received the opportunity to serve and blossom during the war.

So much of myself is in this novel, so much arising from my lifelong

Asia ties. I wish I could thank every kind person I met on the road, each of whom helped convince me that we're all more alike than different. Starting with the person who first got me to India—and if you see this, Shirley Lamb, please holler! I owe special thanks to two other citizens of the world, Timothy Hansken in Kunming, China, and Dushyantha Large in Kandy, Sri Lanka. I'm grateful to Indrajit Obeyesekere of San Francisco for sharing his rich knowledge of Sri Lanka and introducing me to his brilliant parents. A sincere thank-you to Professor Gananath Obeyesekere and Professor Ranjini Obeyesekere for their gracious hospitality, the superb Sinhalese meal she served us…and our excursion to see the sublime reclining Buddha and frescoes of Degaldoruwa in the driving tropical rain.

I named two characters for school friends Caryl and Cheryl, who gave me a place when I was in need. Thank you to my parents for this life, especially to my mother for taking me to the library, faithfully, every two weeks and to my father for all those Broadway show tunes I can still belt out. Thank you to my brothers, Mark Friedman and Paul Friedman, for their big hearts. To Alicia Fodor, my stepdaughter, for sharing her father. To all my extended and blended family and the connections that link us. To my old friend Lili Lim for our forever bond. To my sweet Daisy, now snoring away in doggie heaven, for her companionship during many long hours at the computer.

Well, I could go on and on. Aren't I lucky!

Profound gratitude to precious daughter Lili for the joy she brings to our lives, her unique way of seeing the world, and all she's taught me. And again and always to my dearest husband, Everett.

ABOUT THE AUTHOR

Diana R. Chambers was born with a book in one hand and a passport in the other. She studied Asian art history at university, worked at a Paris translation agency, then began an export business in India. She is an experienced scriptwriter and has followed her stories around the world. She lives in Northern California and Aix-en-Provence, France, with her fellow-traveler husband, artist daughter, and feral cat, Marco Polo. DianaRChambers .com. Insta: @dianarc1